Broken STRINGS

PAMELA O'ROURKE

Cover Design: Y'all. That Graphic.

Editing & Proofreading: Mackenzie Letson

Formatting: CPR Editing

Content Warning

This book contains the following:

- Drug usage
- Dubious consenting drug usage
- Attempted physical assault
- Mention of past cancer diagnosis
- Gun violence
- Explicit sexual content
- Profanities

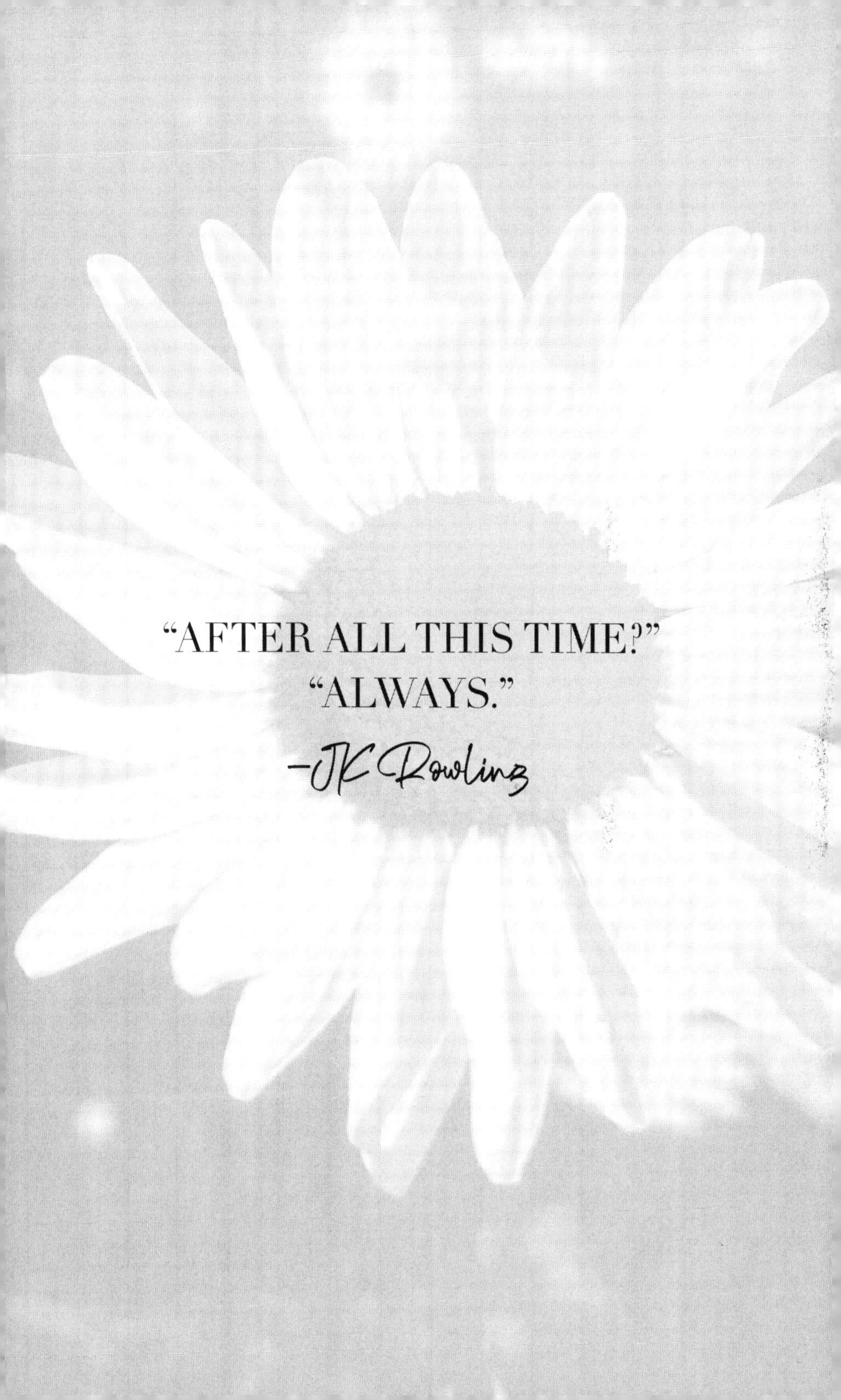

"AFTER ALL THIS TIME?"
"ALWAYS."
-JK Rowling

For Adi.

OUR FRIENDSHIP IS ONE OF THE MOST BEAUTIFUL PARTS OF MY LIFE.

I LOVE YOU.

Playlist

- "Brother" – Kodaline (*The Brotherhood* theme)
- "Something To Someone" – Dermot Kennedy
- "Flaws" – Calum Scott
- "I'll Be Waiting" – Cian Ducrot
- "The Half" - Ruben
- "Locksmith" – Sadie Jean
- "Signal Fire" – Snow Patrol
- "Ghost Town" – Benson Boone
- "Monsters" – Camylio
- "I Tried" – Camylio
- "Perfect For Me" – Justin Timberlake
- "Nothing Else Matters" – Dermot Kennedy
- "Bigger Than" – Justin Jesso
- "Please Forgive Me" – David Gray
- "You Are The Best Thing" – Ray LaMontagne

Prologue

SUMMER
AGED 16

"Come on, Layla. For fuck's sake! There's no need to be like that."

Caden's low chuckle at Archer's antics draws my attention from the grassy meadow around us to his handsome face. The back of his hand brushes off mine as our gazes connect, mirth dancing in his light blue eyes, and my heart skips several beats.

This boy will be the ruination of me.

His smile broadens as though he's heard my thoughts, and I'm helpless to stop my mouth from raising up in an answering grin.

My eyes dart forward to find Archer and Layla still engrossed in whatever argument they're currently embroiled in, and I heave a small sigh of relief.

Placing my forefinger over my lips, I shush him ever so quietly.

Caden rolls his eyes good-naturedly before glancing around quickly, and before I know what he's about, he's closed the gap between us to press a butterfly kiss to my mouth.

With eyes blown wide, I all but jump back, aware that if anyone suspects something untoward between us, it could spell disaster.

I've been a ward of Sutton North—Caden and Archer's father and my own father's childhood best friend—since my parents died in a car accident when I was eight years old.

Falling in love with Caden North happened long before I could do anything to stop it. It's like our souls were fated to be one long before either of us came into being.

I move; he moves, bound by an invisible string. My only wish is to be old enough so we can tell everyone how we truly feel instead of keeping everything behind closed doors, under lock and key, as though our love is a dirty little secret.

"Love you."

He mouths the words silently, intensity flaring within those baby blues, making them darken slightly. I press my lips together as my nostrils flare when I inhale deeply, trying and failing to stifle the butterflies that burst to life within my stomach.

"Ditto, *idiot*."

My response results in a loud, attention-grabbing bellow of laughter—signature Caden all the way—stilling the footsteps of the arguing couple walking not ten feet ahead of us.

Layla, my troubled best friend, and Archer, Caden's identical twin, turn to face us as though in synchronicity, the mismatched looks on their faces making the boy beside me laugh even harder, much to his brother's annoyance.

Archer slides his gaze to mine, his similar blue eyes darkening and narrowing slightly. My brow creases in confusion, but in half a heartbeat, he's smiling once more, making me think I imagined the change in his demeanour.

"What are you two up to that's so funny?"

Caden closes the gap and playfully shoves his brother further along the path. "None of your business, asshat. The more pressing question is, what's got Layla's knickers in a knot?"

Archer smirks when Layla crosses her arms over her chest, looking from one brother to the other before reaching out and grabbing my arm, linking it with hers. A scowl mars her stunning features as she tosses her waist-length black hair over her free shoulder.

"Come on, Summer. I fancy a swim without these two wankers souring my mood even further."

I shake my head, allowing her to pull me along as we widen our strides to put as much distance as possible between the North brothers and us.

When they're out of hearing distance, I whisper, "What's going on with you two, Lay?"

"Nothing."

The single word is spat with enough venom that I don't try to push her any further. Her body is bristling with such rage, and it unsettles me despite being best friends with this girl for close to a decade now.

Layla's dad, Cole Gardiner, was the lead vocalist for Jupiter's Fallen, Sutton's band back in the eighties. Cole, from all accounts, had spiralled into drug addiction, eventually overdosing when we were only twelve.

Her mother was there, but not. Present, but wholly vacant, and so Layla became like a sister to me, sharing my room at the North house almost every night—when she wasn't with Archer, obviously.

We continue in awkward silence until we reach the thicket

of trees bracketing the river that runs parallel to the back of the North family home.

By the time we've picked our way through the underbrush, the boys have reached us, and a look passes between Layla and Archer that sends a shiver up my spine.

Don't be stupid, I tell myself. But I can't quite shake the feeling that something is off.

Archer's face may be almost identical to Caden's, but his eyes hold none of Caden's unfettered love for life. None of his easy-to-love nature.

I'm torn from my train of thought when we exit into an open meadow vibrant with wildflowers as far as the eye can see and the clear waters of the ambling river just ahead.

"Last one in cleans up after dinner."

Caden's shout is followed by a mad dash as the four of us scramble to strip down to a mixture of underwear and swimming clothes.

Sutton is cooking today. He is possibly the sweetest man I've ever met, not dissimilar to Caden in terms of their personalities, but night and day when it comes to their looks. He's an exceptionally gifted drummer and an all-around amazing dad, but when he cooks, he manages to burn the bottom out of every single pot or pan in the house.

None of us fancy cleaning that.

Layla is first, having ripped her top off and unzipped the long maxi skirt she'd borrowed from me to allow it to fall to the grass under her feet. She takes off at a sprint in tiny black underwear that was most *assuredly* worn to be seen.

Caden is next, chasing after her with a grin that puts a matching one on my own mouth. He swats her bottom as he passes her, eliciting a shriek from my best friend followed by a howl of displeasure at being bested, and my smile grows even wider.

"He's fucking her, you know."

Archer's breath ghosts across the shell of my ear, even as my stomach dips uncomfortably at his words. Rather than rising to his taunts, knowing that's what he wants, I continue to unbutton my knee-length bubble gum pink dress.

"He likes it when we take turns." His voice drops. "I like it too."

Dropping it to the ground at his feet, I turn around and hold his eyes, my fake words making my stomach churn. "That's good for you guys."

His eyes narrow minutely. "That's hardly jealousy I hear, is it, Summer?"

I snort. "No way." I shove his shoulder playfully. "I'm busy with school. You know that." Shrugging in what I hope is a nonchalant fashion, I grin. "I wouldn't have time for any extracurriculars. And besides, I'm sure one dick will be plenty for me when the time comes."

Facing back in the direction of the river, I jog forward, catching sight of Caden, fully immersed in the cool water and splashing a laughing Layla.

I've gotten no more than ten feet when Archer catches up and slings his arm over my bare shoulder. He presses a kiss to my temple and sighs heavily.

"Well, I have to say, Summer. That really makes me feel a whole lot better."

We fall into step beside one another as I try to keep my heart from beating clear out of my chest.

"Why is that, Arch?" My voice sounds hollow even to my ears, knowing that the blowback, if our secret gets out, will be life-shattering for all involved.

He stops and looks down at me. Not by much, as I'm tall for a girl, but even so, his eyes pin me with domination and an emotion I can't quite grasp.

It's similar to anger, but deeper. More tightly constrained, almost like he's baited a trap that I've walked right into, and it throws me utterly off-kilter.

"Because we share, *little deer*."

He chuckles darkly, and in that microsecond, when he alludes to Caden's nickname for me—the nickname used only between us and behind closed doors—I *know* that he knows about us.

"And if my brother were keeping you to himself when I'm sharing my pussy with him…well, let's just say, things could turn *very* nasty between us."

One

SUMMER
FOUR YEARS AGO

"Anna, I have more to be doing than reading some trash magazine—"

"Summer, you don't need to go in—"

Cutting my roommate off with the sharp tongue I've honed in my years in New York, I press. "No, Anna. I *do*. I need to do this. Okay? I need to distract my mind. I *need* the money."

Silence is my answer for a long beat.

"Now, I really have to go. I've got another shift, and I can't miss this one too."

The woman, who has been so much more than a friend, maybe even more than a freaking mother to me since I came to the U.S. eleven years ago, holds her tongue, and for that, I love her even more.

"I'm going to hang up now. We won't talk about this again.

And when I get home, we're going to carry on as normal. I'll see you over breakfast in the morning."

She doesn't get a chance to speak again before I've already ended the call.

I'm in no fit state to talk about every blow this week has wrought upon me, but this final one feels like a real kick in the fucking teeth.

CADEN NORTH MARRIES LONG-TIME LOVE IN PRIVATE CEREMONY

His long-time love. That kills me.

That was meant to be *me*.

I suck air in through my nostrils as I pound along the pavement, my destination now within sight, and despite it all, I feel a wave of relief pour over me.

I can let it all out. Just another two hundred yards.

The street around me in Tribeca is bustling. The nightlife is teaming, and none more so than the glitzy glitterati exiting their town cars to the flashes of the waiting paps outside the doors of Rogue, Manhattan's premier club for the high echelons of high society.

I'm scheduled for an eight-hour shift starting at 10 p.m., and I can't wait to disappear into my work persona.

Slipping to my left, away from the flashing cameras, I walk down a narrow alley hidden by shadows, eventually reaching my destination and knocking thrice.

Griffith, my favourite security guy, opens the door with a pout on his face that would rival Anna's from earlier.

"I heard—"

"No, Griff. Not today."

His face falls. "I only wanted to make sure you're okay…"

He trails off, his huge frame only indicative of the gentle giant that we all see daily.

"I know, my sweet friend." I cup his heavily bearded chin in my palm and find his eyes to assure him I'm *fine,* but I falter, allowing him to see too much and altogether not enough.

No one knows, and no one will ever know, the full extent of my feelings. The pent-up, gut-wrenching pain that resides within me day after day. How I struggle to see the *fairness* in this world when it feels as though I've been dealt a shitty hand when compared to others.

I swallow my bitterness and put on a smile.

I'm good at that.

"Griff, I appreciate you. And thank you, but can I just get to work?"

His lips quirk up on one side, his eyes sad as they find mine once more. "Course, Jolie."

I smile appreciatively, recognising he's used my work name.

He steers me back towards the dressing rooms, passing several of my colleagues who spend time on the main floor on the way, all nodding soberly in my direction.

How did they find out about him? Do they know how bad things are?

Ducking inside the final room we reach, I slam the door closed, unable to keep up this ruse in the face of such sincerity. If Vaughn, the owner of Rogue, rears his head, I'm done for. He'll see straight through me.

Falling to the ground on my knees, I look around the area, my eyes landing on my favourite wig.

Hot pink.

It'll go nicely with the silver costume.

And despite my clarity of thought, I don't move. Instead, I

give myself another heartbeat to wallow. Another moment that feels like millennia to swallow my regret, to absorb the decisions of my past and know the choices of my present are what make me the person I *need* to be for the people I care about.

I've done what I need to do to get here. I wouldn't change my path even if I could.

And the fact that Caden North married my old best friend, Layla, today doesn't even make a blip on my radar.

I chose to leave. I *had* to leave. It wasn't safe there. I wasn't wanted there.

And I can never go back, so what difference does it make if he's married her after all this time?

He wasn't made to be mine, no matter what we told one another.

"You're the air I need to breathe, Bam."

Shaking my head, I pull myself together, forcing Caden North, the past and everything that goes with my old life firmly out of my mind. I have altogether far too many pressing matters to deal with. I don't need these stupid feelings right now.

Rising to stand, I root out the silver miniskirt and crop top and begin to dress. It's a fan favourite. The tips will help to no end.

Focus on that, Summer. Focus on the end goal. You've got this.

And I will myself to focus on making it through and doing the best I can with what I have, just like I have done since the day I left the North mansion fifteen years ago.

CADEN

"Your wife's blood panel came back, Mr North. You'll be pleased to know everything is exactly as it should be."

My bloodshot eyes narrow when I pucker my brows in utter confusion. Shaking my head in disbelief, I rub my palms across my fuck-knows-how-many-days'-old scruff that covers my face.

"So what the fuck happened on Isla De La Cruz? She collapsed…I—I don't understand."

The tremor in my tone irritates the shit out of me, and I cross my arms, feigning impatience in an attempt to cover my reaction.

Dr Roberts, one of the best OBGYNs in the States, tilts her head to one side, an almost pitying look in her diamond-shaped hazel eyes.

"Mr North…if I may be so forward, I would suggest talking to your wife because, *medically* speaking, there's nothing wrong. Her physical health is impeccable. Your child is perfectly fine; you have no concerns there, I *assure* you. However…"

She trails off and glances down at her navy Crocs, her forehead wrinkling in thought.

Her movement allows me to glimpse Layla in the private suite beyond, where she appears to be arguing with Noah, the manager of my band, Misdirection.

When Layla had collapsed at our wedding in Isla De La Cruz, the private island in the Bahamas that I'd bought her as a wedding gift, Noah had jumped into the medivac that brought us to Miami. He'd not left my side, nor Layla's, and had somehow managed to keep the entire thing from the eyes of the media.

No small feat when your client is the lead singer of the biggest band to hit the music scene since Jupiter's Fallen.

Dr Roberts raises her eyes to mine once more. The pity from before is more prominent, making me swallow roughly. My gut twists in anticipation, and it's not the good kind like before a performance.

"Mr North, my duty is to my patients. What they may or

may not say must be kept in the strictest of confidence, you understand?"

She nods as though speaking to a child, and the cogs in my brain finally begin to turn.

"Please speak with your wife. I—I believe you will gain clarity from the experience."

As she walks away, she stops to place her palm on my shoulder, patting it twice in a comforting manner before continuing on her way.

Without hesitating a single second, I stride down the corridor and into Layla's room, hearing the tail end of their conversation.

"...and you fucking know it, Noah. There was no need for him—"

"Sorry to break up this little shindig, *wife*. Noah, if you'll excuse us. My father will, no doubt, want an update."

My manager, one of my father's oldest friends and owner of the internationally acclaimed record label, Spellman Sounds—the label that made my father's band the household name it is today—faces me, his cheeks mottled red in anger.

"Why did you have to play that fucking song, you *stupid* boy? What could have possibly been going through your mind!"

I step further into the room, closing the door behind me with a *click* before crossing the distance to Layla, completely ignoring Spellman's outrage.

"I put up with *more* than my fair share of shit from you, Layla. And I do it with a fucking smile on my face."

Dropping my gaze, I drag a hand through my dishevelled blonde hair and blow out a breath, striving to rein in a temper that I rarely lose. I'm hanging by a thread right now.

"Caden."

My eyes find Layla's, her sugary sweet, over-the-top dramatics grating on my last nerve when she speaks again.

"Ask yourself one question, *husband*. Just one. Have you, or have you not, known *precisely* who I am long before today—or are you that much of a fucking idiot that you can't see exactly what's under your nose all of these years?"

Her words hang between us, igniting a fire in the pit of my stomach.

"You wanted this baby. You wanted to get married and ride into the sunset, to live happily ever after. Did I want a wedding? This kid? I'd never have gone along with it if it weren't for—"

Noah cuts her off, stepping forward with a large quelling palm outstretched.

"Layla, that's *enough*."

Silence cloaks the room until it invades my lungs, and I can't breathe without asking the question on the tip of my tongue.

"Was the whole thing on the island an act?"

My wife of three days—or could it be four at this point, who the fuck knows—meets my gaze, triumph flashing in her glacial blue depths as she tilts her chin upwards in defiance.

"You brought *her* to *our* wedding, Caden. To *our* day. How would you expect me to retaliate?"

I grind my teeth, my jaw hurting from the force. "As you'll recall, 'Nothing Else Matters' was *your* song for Archer, too, was it not? What difference does it make if I want to acknowledge both of them on a day they should have been a part of?"

On the day I should have married her *had life not been so fucking cruel.*

My thoughts must show on my face because Layla's hand darts out and slaps me clear across the cheek before I see it coming.

The sound reverberates around the room, and the familiar nausea I've lived with these last eleven years bubbles in the depths of my stomach.

Screwing my eyes shut tight, I step back, edging towards the door. "Noah, have someone bring a car around. I'm going to check into a hotel. I'll expect hourly updates on my child."

His voice follows me down the corridor, but the words don't register. It's just static between my ears. I'm barely holding myself together when I climb onto the empty elevator, grateful for the solitude.

Once the car starts moving, I hit the emergency stop button, throw my head back, and holler my pent-up frustration to the heavens.

With some of the anger drained from my weary body, I slump back against the wall and slide to the floor to rest my head on my knees. The tears begin to fall, and soon my whole body shakes with the force of my long-suppressed emotions.

Summer St James.

The one person I loved more than anything—*still* love, more than anything. The person I should have been with instead of trying to save Layla from herself. The one who left me with more questions than answers at the darkest time of my worthless life.

If I could have chased her to the ends of the earth, I would have gladly done so. On my fucking knees, if that's what it took.

Fuck you, Archer. You left a huge mess behind you, man. Gracias, *asshole.*

And right there, in the middle of the elevator, I let my mind drift back to the last day that things made sense. The day before everything went to shit.

"Come on, wanker. Let's get this party started."

Archer turns wide blue eyes towards me as he emerges from the river. "I've got a pussy that needs a good hammering, and you, my darling brother, are in my damn way."

My brother pins me with a dark look, and I roll my eyes good-naturedly. "Where did Mum find you, you absolute animal!"

I snort with unconcealed laughter as Arch smirks when he comes up alongside me, pushing me further away. "Clearly, brother, I'm the black sheep because I am exactly nothing like the rest of the North flock."

"You're a fucking idiot, Archer." I sprint forward, eager to close the distance between Summer and me, but in usual Archer style, he runs faster, closing the gap before I can reach both girls.

"Who wants to play Spin the Bottle?"

Layla brandishes the now-empty bottle of vodka we'd stolen from her mum's not-so-secret stash.

As we come closer, my gaze slides to Summer's big doe eyes, blown even wider by Layla's suggestion.

"How about Truth or Dare instead, Lay?"

Archer sidles up alongside Layla, and I nod enthusiastically, grateful for his alternative suggestion.

"Yeah! Now that's something I can get behind."

Layla smirks at Archer like the cat who's got the cream. "Okay then. Girls first. Caden—"

Her eyes flit from my brother to me. "Put your money where your mouth is. Truth or dare?"

I shrug like it doesn't faze me.

"Dare, Lay."

Bringing her forefinger up to her chin, she taps it several times while mulling over her options until, eventually, a smile lights up her face.

"Okay, Mr Hotshot. I dare you to take this*."*

Reaching into the pocket of her discarded maxi skirt, she pulls out a small bag containing a couple of blue pills. She takes one out, tossing the bag to the side, and places the pill on her tongue before hooking her forefinger to beckon me closer.

Shit.

Sheer force of will stops me from looking at Summer as I edge closer to Layla, but when I attempt to pluck the pill from her outstretched tongue with my fingers, she stops me, shaking her head.

"I think she means no hands, man."

Layla winks at me, that little blue pill sitting atop her outstretched tongue.

Fuck this shit.

I shoot my brother a droll look that makes him chuckle deep in his chest, then quickly lean forward to suck the proffered pill from Layla's tongue, darting back to my previous position twice as fast. I don't look at Summer once, but I can feel her hurt hanging between us.

Washing the pill down with a swig from a second half-empty bottle of vodka, I pin my brother with a disdainful look.

"Truth or dare, asshole?"

He smiles slowly, his jaw ticking ever so slightly. "Truth."

I narrow my eyes further. He always picks Dare.

That's unusual.

It takes me a hot minute to think of a question, but when I do, it's perfect.

"What's the real *reason you told everyone it was* me *who fucked Ms D'Onofrio in Year 12 when it was* you?*"*

He's quick to repeat the same line he's always fed me, though it's become less palatable as time has passed.

"Cade, man…someone needed to increase your 'cool' factor. We have a reputation to uphold on dad's behalf. The sons of Sutton North—"

I cut him off abruptly. Suddenly pissed as hell that he'd continue to lie his way out of it again. "No, that's not it, man. Stop bullshitting me."

My eyes flit to Summer's, remembering the day I told her the truth.

Reliving the day, she'd told me that I don't need to live up to anyone else's expectations of me—and I'd finally believed it.

"You fucked Mrs D'Onofrio, told her that you were me, *and then proceeded to tell the entire student body. For fuck's sake, I can't even come clean to my best friends without looking like a fucking idiot, Archer. I can't tell anyone the truth—"*

It's his turn to cut me off when he sits forward suddenly. "Aww, poor little favourite child, hmm? Has a rock star rep and his big brother to thank for it—and he's still complaining."

I grit my jaw and repeat my initial question. "Why did you say I fucked her, Arch? Answer the damn question."

He stares at me, a pleased-as-punch smile front and centre on his face, and I barely curb the desire to knock it clear off with my fist. Eventually, he speaks, and his answer is as cryptic as ever.

"Because, dear brother, you're far too perfect."

His eyes move past me to Summer as though that answer should please me. It doesn't, but I let it go, knowing I won't get anything further from him on the topic.

"Truth or dare, little deer."

I follow his line of vision just as Summer lifts her chin and arches a sleek brow. Her tone is confident, her inner warrior on display, and fuck if it's not the ultimate turn-on.

"Dare, Archer."

Without missing a beat, Archer leans forward. "I dare you to kiss Layla."

I can see her swallow roughly, her nostrils flaring with ill-concealed irritation before she rises to stand. Once she reaches Layla, she extends her hand to help Layla up, but before she can press their mouths together, Archer calls out.

"With tongues. Sixty seconds. Go."

My teeth almost chip inside my mouth with how much I'm grinding my molars in vexation. My shit-stirring wanker of a twin.

We'll be sharing words as soon as I'm able because the world is beginning to go just *a little tits up, and I have a sneaking suspicion it was the blue pill that has done the damage.*

And in record fucking time, clearly.

I blink in rapid succession as Summer rolls her eyes at my brother's fuckery. Layla shrugs and then giggles at her boyfriend's request before Summer presses her lips against her friend's.

"Tongues, ladies. Or it doesn't count! And trust me, *you don't want to forfeit…"*

Summer huffs in irritation, but even so, her tongue slides out to tease Layla's lips open. Layla wraps her arms around Summer's taller frame and pulls my girl's head down to meet her searching mouth so that she can deepen the kiss.

"Fuck, yes. Today got a whole lot more interesting. Wouldn't you say, Cade?"

Two

SUMMER
PRESENT DAY

"I've just dropped Ophelia to the sitter, much to her disgust. That daughter of mine is a damn demon child, I swear."

Anna Devon, the woman who's taken me under her expansive wings since I first walked into her diner in Brooklyn fifteen years ago, enters my apartment like a steamroller. Her love-hate relationship with her twelve-year-old daughter never fails to make me smile.

"Now, what do you need me to do, love?"

Oh, this woman. She kills me with her kindness.

"Calm down, Anna. I'm already packed. I've got everything I need. And this time, I won't be going anywhere until I've seen him."

Goosebumps scatter across every inch of my body at the

thought of seeing the man who still haunts my dreams after all this time.

Caden North.

Of course, I see him on billboards or magazines, but the idea of seeing him again, in the flesh…

"If you don't stop chewing that lip, it'll fall off!"

Realising I'm worrying my bottom lip between my teeth, an unfortunate habit of mine when I'm deep in thought, I quickly stop and spin about to finish checking that my handbag has everything I need.

"I've left a list of numbers on the fridge. There's a guy coming to fix my shower on Wednesday. His number is at the top, but he has a key, and the super knows to let him in."

When I face Anna, she nods sharply, allowing me to retain control.

"Could you please water my plants too? They're in the tub in the main bathroom."

Another nod.

"Also, if Jesse calls—"

"Summer." My old friend speaks sharply, cutting me off lest I spiral again. Once this week was more than enough.

My stomach lurches when I remember the reason for my spiral, yet simultaneously my purpose behind this trip is renewed.

I straighten my spine, finding Anna's eyes spearing me intently.

"Do you need a ride?"

I blow out a shallow breath. "Stop wasting your money on a sitter and go pick your kid up, lady. I've called an Uber."

My phone chimes at that precise moment, alerting me to the driver's arrival.

We both laugh softly before she opens her arms, allowing me to step into her calming, motherly embrace. One final piece of comfort before I leave for waters unknown.

"You know you need to do this." Her mouth rests by my ear, her words soothing my soul, even as tears prick my eyelids. "You have no alternative, love."

The trip to JFK takes almost an hour, thanks to traffic, but as I've allotted more time than required, I still have plenty of time to nurse a coffee in the departures lounge.

Time alone isn't something I generally have these days, and I soak up the luxury in its entirety.

When I'd arrived in the U.S., I'd initially gotten a job working for Annalise at Anna's Place as I'd known, even at sixteen, that the money I'd been left after my parents' deaths wouldn't last as long as I would need it to.

My long-seated dreams of attending medical school were put on indefinite hold. Life in the city that never sleeps, where one can also disappear as though they never existed thanks to some phoney documents I'd been given, was expensive even when I was doing it on the cheap.

My inheritance was blown through quickly, leading to my twice-weekly shifts at Rogue.

Hardly the stuff of dreams, but we do what we have to in order to make a life for ourselves. Period.

So finding peace in my hectic life is something I cherish. Except, solitude often leads to wandering thoughts.

Thoughts that always veer in the inevitable direction of *that day* and what we could have done differently. How one choice can affect your whole life.

Archer's smirk makes me narrow my eyes as I step back from Layla.

"You're a good kisser, Summer. Where'd you learn that thing you did with your tongue?"

I can feel my cheeks flush under their joint stare. My eyes find Caden's, except he's no help. He just winks inanely.

My brows draw together, and I tilt my head to the side as I take him in properly. He doesn't look all too good.

Flipping the three of them the bird, I settle back to my seat atop my now-dirty pink dress to toy nervously with the locket resting on my chest.

"Layla. Truth or dare?"

"Truth, bitch." She blows me a kiss, making my cheeks pinken even further as both she and Archer laugh uproariously. Caden blinks several times before reacting with a loud laugh that doesn't sound like his own.

His eyes meet mine. I notice they're glassy—his pupils blown so wide I can't see any blue—before his gaze shifts to the rainbow of wildflowers beneath us.

"Have you ever slept with Caden?"

"Obviously. A couple of times now."

Layla's face is devoid of untruth, her eyes blinking owlishly—innocently—as she glances around our group. Archer shrugs and nods knowingly while Caden stares at the ground.

He swore he was a virgin the night of my birthday.

Meaning he's been with her—in the biblical sense—since we slept together.

My stomach churns nauseatingly at the cold, hard fact, growing even worse when Layla speaks. "You know the boys share, babes. It's just how they are, no harm, no foul. Okay?"

I swallow once, then twice, before dragging my eyes upwards to meet hers and eventually Archer's.

Nodding in assent, I stare at the empty vodka bottle lying atop a sea of coloured flowers, willing everyone and everything to fade into the background so that I may feel how I need to feel without the eyes of anyone else upon me.

"Caden Albus—"

Archer snorts. "It's not Albus, Lay."

"Whatever! It's a stupid middle name." She flips Archer the bird and tries again.

"Caden Atticus *North."*

Archer shakes his head, keeping his laughter silent as I sit there in my reverie, only half paying attention.

Layla's voice makes Caden's head shoot up from where he's been intensely examining the wildflowers beneath him. "Yes?"

"Truth or dare, Mr Hotshot?"

Caden's singular-word answer sounds slurred, and his eyes won't focus when he eventually meets my accusatory gaze.

"Dare."

"I dare you…" Layla trails off, searching for dramatic effect but only finding irritation from me, less than nothing from Caden and even less from Archer. "I dare you to swim to the mill and back. In under five minutes."

Caden glances around, looking entirely put out by her request.

"My legs are tired—"

"Four minutes, fifty-nine. Fifty-eight. Fifty-seven…"

Despite his blown pupils, Caden drags himself to stand and tears off his sneakers, tossing them to the wilds before taking off at a pelt.

"Go on. You can do it, little bro."

Archer's voice rings out behind me as Layla moves off in the same direction as Cade.

Suddenly, it feels like the sun has disappeared behind clouds. My skin ripples with awareness.

With distrust—something I've never felt before in the vicinity of anyone in my found family. And I long for Caden's return.

Instead, he's just dived from the bank into the cool waters of the river, striking out for the mill half a mile downstream. Layla is right at the top of the bank, shouting for him to move his ass, when I feel Archer's hand snake around my wrist.

A voice rings out over the intercom, and I physically jump out of my reverie, spilling my now-cold coffee over the side of my cup onto my shaking hand.

"American Airlines flight 6929 non-stop to London Heathrow is now boarding at Gate 22."

I push all thoughts of that day from my mind. All the memories that are best left in the past. For now, at least.

Because all too soon, it'll be time to relive them in vivid detail.

CADEN

"Daaaaaaaad."

I smirk at my reflection in the mirror as my daughter, Bella, howls for my attention from somewhere in the house.

I call out in response, "Just one second, Bug." Then I continue putting the last touches on my excessively accurate Joker costume.

It's my little girl's fourth birthday today, and in a style all her own, Bella has insisted on a superhero themed party. So, of course, the boys and I would bring our old costumes out of retirement.

I chuckle to myself in remembrance as I finish brushing the green hair dye through my chin-length blonde locks.

My sister Cassidy really nailed it the day she gave us DC characters' nicknames, naming the boy's Batman and Robin, respectively, and yours truly, the inimitable Joker.

I'm excited for my boys to get here. My best friends, Henry DeMarco, CEO of DeMarco Holdings, the international entertainment giant, and Nathaniel Hawthorne, author and cradle-snatcher—that one is a bit of an inside joke after he fell in love with Henry's nineteen-year-old sister, Mila, earlier this year—our relationship is more that of a family than mere friends.

I snort loudly at my cradle-snatcher thoughts, filing that insult away for future usage as I place the brush back on the countertop and give myself a once-over.

Henry had best rock up here as Batman and Nate as Robin—even though I know he hates playing the sidekick—or I'm going to blow a motherfucking gasket.

This little nod to our youth only works if we all do it.

I nod to my reflection and decide that today *will* be an amazing day, repeating the mantra over and over before I stride from the bathroom, through the master bedroom, and down the hall in search of my Bug, humming a tune mindlessly as I go.

It doesn't take long to track her down.

"I don't want to, Rena. Can we go swimming first?"

I stand outside the door as she argues with her nanny, Serena.

"Tomorrow we'll go swimming, Bella, okay?"

Bella's sigh of displeasure goes unacknowledged as Serena ploughs on. "Come on now, sweetie. Please let me get you dressed. Your dad will be here any second. Don't you want to show him your costume and—"

I grin silently, knowing well that this is a pointless battle.

Pushing the door open with one finger, I stand in the doorway as two sets of eyes land on me.

"Why. So. *Serious?*"

I tilt my head to one side and keep the classic Joker deadpan on my face until Bug launches herself at me, wrapping her little arms around my legs.

"You look so cool, Dad."

She twists her head up to look at me, her eyes dancing with delight. "Can I do that?"

My lips twitch, and I nod before looking up at Serena. "Thank you for getting my little madam ready, Serena."

She inclines her head demurely. "It was my pleasure, Mr North. Will you be needing anything else?"

Shaking my head, I step out of her way. "Enjoy your parents' wedding anniversary today."

Nodding her assent, Serena slips from the room, closing the door with a soft *snick* as she leaves.

"Come on then, Harley Quinn. Let's colour those pigtails, so there's no mistaking that you're my number one partner in crime."

"It's great to have you here, DeMarco. After the drama this year…well, some normalcy was top of the list."

Henry nods, his green eyes standing out even more than usual in contrast to the black face paint around his eyes underneath his Batman half-mask.

We've almost reached the front door, having walked from my newly built recording studio. Henry has agreed to paint a mural in there, and I'm chomping at the bit to see what he comes up with, but with a new baby and his duties at DeMarco Holdings, I'm not sure when he'll manage to find the time.

The man missed his calling. He may be a genius in the boardroom, according to his half-brother Alex, but his creativity with a paintbrush is unparalleled in my eyes.

The painting he gifted me when I married Layla is hanging front and centre in the huge double vaulted foyer at the house. The one of Summer and me with Archer and Layla as kids.

I don't know if I leave it there as a reminder or as a torture device. Perhaps it's both.

"Did Nate say what time he'd be here?"

My lip twitches, and I try to stop myself, but fuck it. I simply can't.

"He's probably a bit busy, snatching cradles…"

Henry stops dead, pinning me with a look. "*Don't*, North."

I glance away, lips rising on both sides now, with a wholly irrepressible smile. "I make no promises, brother."

"Well, that's one. You get one free shot. Next time, I'll kick your fucking ass."

We move off again in companionable silence despite my fuckwittery until Henry speaks about ten feet from the open front door.

"Any word from Layla?"

I expected to feel something—anything—when someone eventually brought up my newly divorced ex-wife, so I'm surprised when I only feel numb.

"Nah, man. I know she's still in rehab, thanks to Fletcher's updates."

My divorce solicitor, Fletcher Knowles, is well paid to ensure I know Layla's each and every move.

Just in case. I lost whatever trust I had left in her earlier this year. The day I came home to find my wife partaking in a drug-fuelled orgy with my Bella Bug upstairs, alone after Layla fired all the staff. The whole thing happened whilst I was Stateside doing some Misdirection promo, and even now, we have no idea exactly what Bella witnessed.

The memory still gives me nightmares.

"The last we spoke was the day I served her the papers. She didn't want to see Bug, didn't even ask if she was okay after… well, everything, for fuck's sake. What kind of mother—"

I stop, unable to meet Henry's eyes, and swallow roughly before continuing.

"I'm an idiot for being so wilfully blind, man. I just wanted to save her, you know? Arch would have wanted that. He would have wanted her taken care of. Happy. He would have wanted me to give her the life *he* would have given her. Instead, I've just made everything worse…"

Silence cloaks us until Henry whispers, "At least she gave you Bella, brother. Without all the pain, she'd never have existed. You need to remember that when you begin to doubt the path your life has taken."

Fuck, DeMarco. Liv's softened you right up.

Despite my sarcastic mind, I nod stiffly. My collar is suddenly too tight, my eyes stinging with the force of holding back a river of emotion that has no place here.

My best friend rests his heavily gloved hands on my shoulders, forcing me to look at him. He's a couple of inches taller than my six-foot-one, made more obvious by the OTT boots he's donned for the occasion.

"Cade. You said it before. You gave Layla as much as you could give—"

I cut him off. Self-recrimination is heavy in my tone. "I never gave her my heart."

He doesn't miss a beat. "Because Summer still holds it. That's not on you, bro. We can't help who we fall in love with. And you can't make yourself fall out of love either—trust me, when I thought Peaches was with Alex, those two years of trying to force-feed myself a bullshit lie…it was torture, plain and simple."

I blink heavily, once, then twice, before I nod and inhale deeply through my nostrils as Henry continues.

"All I'm saying, man, is to cut yourself some slack. Summer isn't here. She hasn't been for a long time…"

He trails off, and my stomach swoops uncomfortably in acknowledgement.

She never came back, either. Was it all a lie? Is she dead? Surely my heart would know…

"It's time to truly leave the past in the past, brother. Forget that letter she left, forget everything it said. You were in a bad place after Archer's passing, okay? Forgive yourself for not being able to be who she needed then."

I press my lips together in a semblance of a smile, but fail miserably. The Joker face paint doesn't help.

"Get back out there, man. Find your happily ever after. You're a fucking rock god, for crying out loud. You could have any woman you want."

Just not the one I need.

"Now, come on. Let's celebrate this little Bug's big day."

Henry strides ahead of me, his broad back filling out his ridiculously accurate costume perfectly.

I catch up to him, swallowing down the words that were on the tip of my tongue, but the moment's passed, so I keep them to myself once more as I reach the door at the same time as my companion.

"You *absolute* wanker!"

Henry's indignation fills the foyer where Mila, dressed as Wonder Woman, and Henry's wife Liv—or Peaches, as he calls her—dressed as Catwoman, stand side-by-side.

Striking the most absurd pose, dressed as Superman ala Henry Cavill style instead of Robin circa Chris O'Donnell, is none other than our third Musketeer, Nate.

I shoot the fucker a dark look. "You broke with tradition, man. Not cool, *so* not cool!"

Henry and I descend on the traitorous bollocks who's just grinning broadly, utterly at odds with his usual stoic, stick-up-his-ass demeanour.

I glance in the direction of his happiness, Mila DeMarco, to find her engrossed in conversation with her sister-in-law, and the moment is diffused for me. Just like that.

Witnessing the bond that our found family shares, despite all our ups and downs, it just makes me grateful for what I have. For the life that I've been given.

Once more, I'm reminded that Archer isn't here to live the life he should have, so I need to make sure I live the best version I can for both of us.

Henry launches into a tirade about the importance of tradition while I glance around the space, ensuring no small ears can hear the filth that comes out of his mouth.

My mouth is no less unclean. However, when kids are present, I'm positively angelic.

Liv's voice calls out softly over Henry's escalation. "Oh, come on, you two. Nate can't be expected to play Robin now. He's the leading man in his *own* movie, after all."

She nudges a blushing Mila.

I take the opening. "True."

And before anyone else can chime in, I turn to face Henry. "Besides, DeMarco, you don't get to be greedy. Bash is your own mini-Robin now."

The man preens like the cat who got the cream, and I simply can't help myself.

Here comes strike two.

"Time to let Superman and Wonder Woman here ride off into the sunset. We're all aware at this point of how much they like to ride—"

Henry moves to slap me across the back of the head, but obviously, as I'm baiting him, I'm ready and waiting to jump out of his reach.

My laughter sounds loudly through the foyer when I take off in the direction of the kitchen, Henry hot on my heels, and I laugh even harder at the thought of how fucking stupid we must look.

Some things never get old.

Three

SUMMER

Touching down in Heathrow is somewhat of a mind-fuck. I've not set foot on British soil since I was sixteen years old.

I rapidly collect my bag and march with intent through arrivals, set on grabbing the first cab I see.

The queue for cabs is stupidly long, so I stride further down the path, raising my arm while arching my back to push my ample chest forward. I quickly flash a bright smile at the first oncoming cab I see.

He slams on the brakes, and I laugh softly to myself.

Men on both sides of the Atlantic are so fucking predictable.

The driver helps with my suitcase, and as I slide across the back seat, I give him my destination to the hard-won address in Cambridge. It wasn't easy to come by, but my tips from Rogue certainly helped.

There's not much money can't buy.

"Mind if I turn on the radio, miss?"

I shake my head at his question and slip my cell from my handbag, powering it on to shoot Anna a quick message.

ME

I've arrived safely. On the way to Cambridge RN.

The dots dance immediately as she types her response.

ANNA

Everything is good here. Ophelia said hi, and Jesse called.

And sure enough, my cell vibrates with another message.

JESSE

Just found out I finish up in nine days. Wanna do a movie next week?

I swallow despite having a dry mouth and type back a quick affirmative before silencing my cell and letting my head fall back against the seat, eyes squeezed shut lest the tears start to fall.

Eyes on the prize, Summer. Eyes on the fucking prize.

CADEN

"I still can't believe that other piece of shit came as Super-fucking-man."

Henry, having shucked his Batman mask, scrubs his hands down his face, smudging the black face paint around his eyes. "If you make one more jibe about my sister and her *unmentionable* life—"

I cut him off, throwing a wink at a smirking Liv. "Her *sex* life? Is that it, DeMarco?"

He throws up his hands in exasperation. "I'm out of here, North. You're a prick and a half." Slapping me playfully on both cheeks, he then pinches them with a grin. "Tell Bella we'll see her next week for that sleepover."

I nod, my grin widening as I shove his hands away. "She'll love it. She thinks Bash is her own personal doll."

When Bella had blown out her candles earlier, she'd wished for a sibling. My heart sank, but Liv, always quick thinking, jumped forward and asked if Bella would like to be her helper with their baby son, Sebastian.

Bella can't pronounce his full name, so he's been Bash since he was born last spring.

"She's a great help, and he settles easier when she's around." Liv's voice is quiet, but even so, the sound rouses the sleeping infant in her arms.

Henry is quick to scoop his son into his arms, pressing him softly against his chest, and Bash calms immediately.

Liv narrows her eyes as Henry smugly side-eyes her. "Show-off."

Henry tips his chin in farewell, lest he waken his overtired son, and the trio make their way toward the front door, the final stragglers to leave the party.

I loosen my tie and shrug out of the deep purple Joker jacket I've been wearing all day, tossing it across the back of one of the chairs at the breakfast bar.

"Mr North?"

At the sound of my name, I turn to find Serena standing just inside the kitchen door.

"Bella is in bed, but she's asking for you to sing to her…"

She trails off sheepishly. We both know this is a usual occurrence from Bug. I've never denied her. And I *never* will.

"That's no problem, Serena. You can finish up for the evening. We'll see you in the morning."

She smiles softly, tucking her blonde hair behind her ear. "Of course. I won't be far if she needs me. Goodnight, Mr North."

My heart swells in my chest, hearing the genuine love and concern in Serena's voice, only to crumble to pieces when I think of how her mother, Layla, *should* be like that. But she isn't, and it kills me that I refused to see it for so many years.

The knife twists deeper when I admit to myself that she was right that day in the hospital in Miami. I saw her toxic behaviour long before we ever got together, but stupidly, and out of blind loyalty to my brother, thought I could fix her. That I could bring her back to the girl he'd known.

The girl he'd loved.

My mind unwillingly wanders back as I slowly meander up the stairs towards Bella's attic bedroom. Searching the depths of my memories in an effort to find where everything had gone so spectacularly wrong, I finally light upon a long-buried memory best forgotten.

And, even as I tell myself that blatant lie, my heart skips a beat as images soar through my head.

"Will you tell the boys?"

I tighten my arm around Summer's bare, slender shoulder at the trepidation in her delicate voice. "Not a hope. This is between me and you, Bambi."

Pressing a kiss to her forehead, I can feel her smile against my bare chest.

"Good." She's silent for a long beat, but her shoulders tense up.

"What's the matter?"

As she turns her face up to mine, her big doe eyes pin me with their intensity. "They'll know. Your poker face sucks."

My lip twitches. "Fine. I'll continue to let them believe I lost my virginity with Ms D'Onofrio. She'd love a bit of young cock in her snatch."

She swats at me, and I pull her even closer, her bare pussy pressed firmly against my thigh.

"You are the pits, Cade."

"And you love me all the same."

Her brow puckers slightly, her gaze deepening passionately. "I do."

I bend forward, taking her mouth with mine, giving her every square inch of myself in a long kiss. When I pull back, her eyes are glistening with barely restrained tears.

"Was…was it okay for you, Cade?"

My mouth turns up in a shit-eating grin. "It was amazing. You were amazing, Bam. Happy birthday."

A hesitant smile plays across her perfect face, joy shining from the depths of her expressive brown eyes.

We're so absorbed in drinking in this moment, in cementing it to memory, that neither of us hears the room door creak open.

"Jesus Christ! The boring-ass twin finally popped his fucking cherry."

Summer dives under the sheets, only giving my prick brother, Archer, a flash of white-blonde hair before she's hidden entirely from his view.

"What the fuck, Arch? There's a white sock on the handle!"

He barks a laugh. "That only counts when it's my white sock on the door, brother dearest. When I'm with Layla."

I narrow my eyes at my mirror-image twin. "Get out, fucker."

He scoffs. "You know the rule, Cade. The twins share.*"*

He trails off, holding my eyes pointedly. "Everything, *brother." Smirking smugly, he steps closer. "Come on, then. Spill the beans, man. Who's under there?"*

At the speed of lightning, he thrusts his hand forward, grasping the cover in his fist and tugging roughly. I can feel Summer cling to my bare leg, curling further into herself, and I snap.

Archer may be my identical twin, my best friend, and half of who I am, but Summer is my heart. She's my soulmate. I can feel it in my bones.

I've always known it, from the very first day we met.

Lunging forward, uncaring of my state of undress, I throw myself at a laughing Archer, slamming him back against our bedroom door–and despite the sheer size of our house, the walls themselves vibrate with my anger.

Even so, Archer has a point.

We do *share everything.*

But Summer is mine.

"Seems like getting your cock wet has made you grow a pair of balls too, little *brother."*

Leaning closer, I hold his gaze with eyes that are surely spitting flames and grit from between my clenched jaw. "Get. Out."

My twin quirks a light brow. "Fine. Have it your way, prick."

He shrugs me off roughly, twisting the doorknob as he makes to leave, not without stealing a glance over my shoulder before he does.

"I'll join the dots eventually." Archer winks as he slips out the door, shooting me a perfect white grin. "And when I do…"

The door clicks shut, leaving his parting words hanging between us.

Wanker.

I quickly locate the key above the architrave of the door and turn back to the bed, finding Summer still balled up underneath the covers. Relief floods my body with the realisation that her identity remains secret. For now.

But we need to keep it that way. We can't be this careless again.

Climbing back in beside her, I gather her close once more, brushing her pale hair back from her furrowed brow repeatedly. Soothingly.

After what feels like a long time, the tension drains from her shoulders, and her eyelids flutter closed.

And rather than joining her in restful slumber, I spend the following hours mapping the well-known, much-adored contours of her perfect face as a plan begins to form in my mind.

I'm slammed back to the here and now when I reach Bella's bedroom door, a smile lighting up my face when I hear her singing that song from *Trolls World Tour* she's so obsessed with.

Her voice and her bare innocence remind me of my own childhood. Of Summer, God fucking help me.

She'd never have left under her own will, idiot. She could be long dead.

My stomach drops at the acknowledgement, knowing it's probably not a stretch, and still needing to shove it from my mind as quickly as possible. The desire to live in ignorance is too great to think otherwise.

I'm about to push open the door to Bug's room when my phone buzzes in my pocket, drawing my attention. I pull it out, unlock the screen, and my whole life changes in the blink of an eye.

Larry Simmons, the P.I. who I hired when I was a seventeen-year-old with a mission, has been retired for many years. But the ex-cop often claimed that his search for Summer was the one regret he had in his career.

I'd paid a small fortune chasing leads that got me nowhere, each dead end secretly breaking my already shredded heart. For close to a decade.

Until, eventually, I'd come to the conclusion that she didn't want to be found–or that she *couldn't* be found. And I'd told Larry to call it quits, locking things down with Layla once and for all.

After all, Lay had been the last link to my brother. To Summer. To the life I wanted. The life my parents had that I needed to emulate.

Happily married. House full of kids. Growing old together.

Living the fucking dream...

And even while everything from the last fifteen years plays through my mind, my eyes focus on the image on my phone from Larry.

Because right there–right there in blissfully excruciating technicolour–is my heart. My soulmate.

Summer St James.

It looks as though she's grabbing a taxi outside an airport. In the U.K., considering the car registration plates on display.

She's dressed in black leggings and a grey woolly jumper. Her hair is still the same white blonde, her skin shimmering like translucent silk. Those doe eyes that continue to hold my heart are as big and expressive as the last day we spoke, almost fifteen years ago.

And without any indication, my knees buckle from beneath me, and I fall to the floor outside my daughter's room as Bug continues to sing "Perfect for You." My stomach roils, and my heart palpitates in a synchronicity that, as an artist, would make me laugh.

Instead, my head goes fuzzy, and I think I'll black out until a voice comes over the household intercom from the security tower at the entrance to our home. The one that the guards only use in an emergency.

"Mr North? There's a lady here who's adamant she sees you now—"

There's a slight kerfuffle, and a female voice comes over the line. It's tinged with an American twang but unmistakable all the same.

"Cade? Can we talk?"

Four

SUMMER

There's silence on the other end of the intercom. My eyes flit from the first guard to the second and back again. "Caden?"

His name comes out in a whisper, so I clear my throat and try again. "Caden, are you there?"

"Bring her to the house, Ford."

His hypnotic voice sounds from the intercom, and then there's static.

"Miss, if you'll come with me…"

A man behind me with cropped black hair, covered in tattoos, with a smile that surely would make even a nun's panties melt clean off, gestures towards a door to the side of the room.

"Umm, sorry. I need to pay my cabbie first."

The man—Ford, I'm guessing—glances at his colleague. "Holden, would you mind…?"

Holden drops the intercom mic, nods sharply, and marches in the direction of my cab.

"Now, miss. This way. Holden will take care of your cab fare."

Ford straightens himself to his full, considerable height—I reckon maybe six-three or four to my own, not insubstantial five-six—and, once again, gestures to the rear door.

Upon exiting, he strides past me and opens the rear passenger door of a sleek black Volvo before rounding the back to slip into the driver's seat.

I follow mutely, realising shortly after that I've left my bag in the trunk of the cab. I voice my concerns, and Ford waves me off. "Holden will take care of it, miss."

It's only then that his accent registers with me. Definitely Texan. There's been enough visiting Rogue over the years that I'd recognise the distinct accent clear as day.

He moves away at speed, heading in the direction of the main house. In the direction of Caden.

I take a minute to analyse my fingernails, realisation dawning with every inch closer I get.

After all this time.

My stomach churns nauseatingly, fretting stupidly that he'll find I don't live up to the memory he has of my teen self. I've aged gracefully, yet still. There's padding where there once was none. There are wrinkles where once he kissed my smooth, unblemished skin.

There are scars, both mental and physical, that he knows nothing about.

I'm beginning to spiral when I raise my eyes to find Ford's fixed on me.

"You haven't changed one iota, miss."

My forehead crinkles. "I—I…have we met?"

He smiles, flashing perfect white teeth. "No, ma'am."

His stronger accent makes me grin. "Okay then, I'll bite. How do you know me? Because *clearly*, I don't know you."

His smile dims, his dark eyes too, and something like sadness flashes across his features.

"I've known Mr North—Caden—for a long ass time, if you'll pardon my language. I'm fortunate enough to call that man my friend, and as such, I've been to his house—as a guest, mind you. I've seen the image of his childhood sweetheart. The one that hangs right inside the door. With his brother and his ex-wife alongside. And *you*, lady, are the image of that girl."

I suck in a harsh breath. "His childhood love was Layla. Everyone knows that."

Even now, blatantly caught, I perpetuate the lie Uncle Noah managed to spin to the press. To help cover my disappearance. My sense of loyalty won't leave me, even in desperate times like these.

"To hear Cade tell it, there's a whole other story, ma'am." And without taking a breath, he continues. "We're here."

Ford pulls to a slow halt, shutting off the engine and sliding from the vehicle, leaving me alone for a moment to gather my splintering thoughts.

Now is not *the time to fall to shit, Summer. Get it to-fucking-gether.*

I glance behind the car, finding Ford speaking into a walkie-talkie that he's pulled from somewhere, nodding as though the person on the receiving end can see him. Once he's finished, he opens the door, standing back to allow me to exit.

"If it's not too forward, ma'am…"

His words stop me, the sincerity in his tone tugging at my heartstrings. I nod helplessly.

"You could be Miss Bella's mother. He'd surely wish you were.

The similarities are uncanny."

My stomach roils, threatening to expel the aeroplane food I was not able to consume as I nod, in what I pray is a grateful manner.

Ford rounds the car, slides into the driver's seat, and pulls away down the tarmacked driveway with ease, unknowing of how unsettled I am following that interaction.

He never forgot me.

I put one foot in front of the other by sheer force of will.

He has a picture of me in his foyer.

When my knees wobble, I'm entirely sure I can't go any further, so I stop, gasping for breath as though I've just run a marathon.

His daughter looks like me.

Fuck, if that last one doesn't make my gut clench in agony as images of everything we could have shared—if not for that fateful day—fly through my mind at the speed of lightning.

My palms are clammy as I stand my ground, knowing I've come this far for a reason, and in remembering that, I straighten my spine with renewed purpose, ready to face the past.

Archer's hand holds my wrist firmly in his grasp, and I will myself to remain calm. To hold my shit together.

"Archer, what the fuck, man?"

I go on the offensive, but it's useless. He twists my wrist harshly, making me cry out.

"Ouch, you're hurting *me."*

Layla turns back from Caden for a moment, and I swear she sees what's happening, but turns back to the river, continuing to shout at Caden to move his ass.

"You see, little deer. I'm well aware that Caden has been…let's say, dipping his ink into the familial well…"

He trails off, and my suspicions are confirmed. He really does know.

"And it's past time to share that with me."

Before he has finished speaking, I tug my wrist from his grasp to take off at a run, but it's like he was waiting for me to do exactly that because he reaches to grasp my long platinum hair.

"Get back here, Summer."

His voice, so like my lover's, yet utterly different, echoes through my brain as I take off at a pelt, heading straight for Layla and reaching her in the space of three frantic breaths.

"Lay—"

She cuts my exclamation off with a scream, pointing frantically in the direction of the mill. "Archer! You need to help him. It's worked too quickly."

My eyes move downriver, and my whole world shifts on its axis right as Archer joins our group.

"He'll be fine."

My eyes meet Layla's worried ones before we both look back towards Caden, who's clearly struggling to stay afloat.

"What did you give him, Layla?"

My tone is brimming with recrimination, and my best friend has the grace to blush under my insinuation.

"Nothing bad, Summer. Nothing he hasn't taken before, for fuck's sake. I just—I didn't think—I didn't know—"

Palming her with a quelling hand, I shift on the balls of my feet, facing Archer as though the incident between us didn't just occur. My only thought is to ensure Cade's safety.

"You're the only one here who can keep him afloat, Arch. I—I'm not strong enough."

I'm a good swimmer, but Caden has almost a hundred pounds on me.

I'd never get him to shore by myself.

Archer sidles forward, his eyes narrowed and nostrils flaring. "What's in it for me, little deer?"

My train of thought is halted when the front door of the house opens to reveal…

Fuck, my knees almost buckle underneath me. My heart rate picks up, and tears prick my eyes.

It's him.

I choke on a sob.

After all this time.

Swallowing down my thoughts, emotions, and unrealistic dream of a picture-perfect reunion, I take a shaky step forward as he descends the steps outside his front door.

My mouth turns to cardboard when I take in the sculpted perfection of his idyllic body, clothed only by a towel that covers him from his hips to his knees. Water is dripping down his sinewy form, his hair longer than I remember and hugging his chin as he comes closer.

I'm unable to move. My legs have seized under the weight of the emotions toiling through my body, so I stand there numbly, allowing him to close the gap between us.

He stops not three feet away, coming to an abrupt halt as his deep blue, utterly unforgettable eyes engulf me like a tsunami. He consumes me now, precisely as he did then, and I'm utterly helpless to stop it. And nor do I desire to.

Our gazes hold as if there's not been fifteen years and an ocean of distance between us. As though the ghosts of the past are not haunting our present. We stare into one another's souls until time becomes inconsequential, and I'd be all too willing to live in this moment forever.

He moves first, shattering the stillness to close the gap between us and, in a singular, fluid motion that shocks me to my core, sinks to his knees at my trembling feet to wrap his arms around my waist.

I swallow roughly past the lump in my throat when he rests his cheek against my stomach as his arms lock more tightly around me.

My own arms hang uselessly at my sides until, like a magnet, I'm compelled to bring my hands up to rest them atop his head, brushing a couple of errant strands back over his forehead.

"I'm sorry."

His words bring a frown to my face. "Caden, I—"

Without removing his arms, Caden twists his head upwards so that his chin rests around my naval. "Summer…please just let me say this. I—I *need* to say the words."

The earnestness in the depths of those much-loved blue eyes—eyes I can never say no to—compels me to nod, allowing him to continue.

"When you left, you took my whole entire heart with you. Until…until Bella was born, I was a shell of a man. I let everyone else dictate how my life was lived."

Tears threaten my bottom lashes, knowing I'm utterly undeserving of his love, but greedily soaking it up for however long I can bask in it because I know once I've said my piece, he'll curse the day he met me.

"When I read your letter—"

"My *letter*? I didn't leave—" I scrunch up my face in confusion, but Caden shakes his head, rising to stand and taking my face in his hands.

"I know I went off the rails after Archer died, and I'm sorry I wasn't the man you needed me to be back then."

His eyes rove across every plane of my face, ensnaring me in their depths, and I feel helpless in the thrall of this man—because *then* he was a boy, but *now* he's all man.

"But I am *now*."

"Cade, we need to—"

"*Please,* let me finish." He waits for my assent before continuing. "I've made some piss-poor decisions in my life. I've done things I regret, things that I can't undo, but, Summer…my biggest regret is losing you because in all the years since, I've *never* stopped loving you. The heart you carried with you wouldn't allow me to quit."

My brain feels foggy, my mouth like mush, and my soul vibrates to once again be in the periphery of its mate. I *know* I'm on the precipice of something life altering.

"I loved you then. I love you still."

It's time to sink or swim, Summer.

My hesitance must show on my face because Cade drops his hands and steps back, giving me room to breathe but instead, my whole entire being misses his proximity. I'm hard-pressed to stand my ground when all I want is to wrap myself up in this man.

"I don't know your reasons for leaving—your letter didn't exactly go into detail—but I understand the time was wrong for us then. Your reasons for coming back now are your own. I'll not pressure you to disclose that…until you're ready."

Goosebumps scatter across every inch of my body at the fervour in his deep blue gaze.

"Give me a week. One week to get to know each other again. Leave the past in the past and pretend we have all the time in the world. A week to prove I am the person you need me to be…"

I'm here for one reason and one reason alone. I *know* a good person would tell him that right out of the gate, but I can't seem to get the words out.

And when his next words leave his beautiful bee-stung lips, I know I'm a goner. What harm is one final lie at this point?

I'm going straight to hell anyway; I may as well taste his love one last time before the gates to Heaven are firmly slammed in my lying face.

"A week to fall back in love with me, Bam. What do you say?"

Five

CADEN

When I'd told Ford to bring Summer to the house, my mind ran the gamut of emotions. Shock, horror, surprise, delight, frustration, pain, finally landing on the only one that mattered.

Love.

After spending years asking myself *why* she'd left, *where* she'd gone, and *how* she could do such a thing, I realised at that moment that none of it mattered. Time had not dimmed my love for her.

In fact, time had amplified it.

The knowledge that she was back, within reach, sent a thrill like no other through my body.

Ford gave me an extra couple of minutes to shower the hair dye from my hair and scrub the paint from my face, but I'd not even given myself the extra thirty seconds it would have taken to dry my body. I'd needed to see her in the flesh, and once I did, I knew I was done for.

She could say or do anything, and I'd forgive everything simply to keep her in my life. Because with her here, now, I'm *this close* to having everything I could possibly want.

All the reasons why don't matter. Once I've earned back her love, we can address that. Once she loves me again, she'll never leave. I'll prove it to her.

I remember having a conversation with Dad shortly after she left when he told me words that never left me.

"Son, love is not what you say. It's what you do."

And I would *do* everything in my power to show her exactly how much she means to me. How much she's *always* meant to me.

Having nodded ever so slightly at my request to spend the week, Summer followed me into the house, stopping dead in her tracks upon catching sight of the huge picture in the middle of the foyer.

"Oh my God." Her voice is scratchy from disuse, and I hear the thinly veiled emotions. "Who painted it?"

"Henry." I grin widely when her surprise-filled eyes meet mine.

"As in, Henry *DeMarco*?" She continues, plainly taken aback when I nod. "Wow! He's really good."

I give her another minute to appreciate the image as a plethora of reactions plays across her beautiful features.

She's not changed one iota. Her skin is still like alabaster, smooth and glowing. Her platinum hair sits on her shoulders, shorter than I remember, but it suits her perfectly. Huge doe eyes I've missed looking into dominate her entire face, fringed by heavy black lashes. Her lips are pink, the bottom one just slightly larger than the top, made for kissing.

Her body is the body of a woman now. She is more rounded

and curvy in areas that were yet to fill out when we'd last been together, and the thought of holding her close outside, of being flush with those delectable curves, was making my dick harden at speed beneath my short white towel.

"Er…Bambi, I need to, umm…I'll be right back."

I take off towards the staircase before things get awkward, shouting over my shoulder for Maggie, my housekeeper, to come and make Summer a cup of tea.

"Hello, dearie. I'm Maggie…"

I hear Maggie making her introductions just as I crest the top of the stairs, my towel now tented thanks to my stupid dick.

The fucker has trouble rising on a regular day—something no one other than Layla is aware of—but, of course, today would be the day he'd act up.

I march into my room with a shit-eating grin front and centre on my face.

In the years since Summer's disappearance, I'd been uninterested in sex. It hadn't seemed anything out of the ordinary, as all I wanted to get off was her memory and all I needed was my hand.

It wasn't until I'd made the decision to try to move on that my issues came to light.

Psychological erectile dysfunction, or that's what the therapist called it.

But I knew it was because my heart and my dick are connected. One can't work without the other.

"She makes me feel like a horny teenager." My announcement is for no one, but my grin widens even further at the thought.

Now I just need to make her fall in love with me all over again.

Having re-dressed myself in some worn navy joggers and an old as fuck Jupiter's Fallen 1989 World Tour t-shirt, I zip into Bug's room to find she's moved from the TV to her bed.

She's been cleaned of all her Harley Quinn get-up, instead wearing her favourite Ironman pyjamas. Her mop of blonde curls has been tamed into a single braid down her back, as is her usual bedtime request of Serena—she hates waking up in a tangle of hair.

"Daddy! You took *forever.*"

She sits forward on her bed—book forgotten and tossed to one side—to pin me with a stare as she crosses her little arms over her chest. I stifle a grin at her attempt to intimidate me because I damn well love how fierce she is.

I hope you never lose that ferocity, Bug.

"I'm so sorry I took so long. Washing that Joker out of my hair was tough going."

The corner of her bow-lips twitches for a split second before she gets a rein on her emotions. "Well, I think I deserve *two* songs after waiting so long…"

She holds two fingers up as though flipping me the bird, even though I know she's only displaying the number of songs she wants, and the intense determination on her face almost cracks me up.

"Okay then, Bug. You've got it. Two songs. Which ones?"

Straightening herself up, my little girl smiles brightly in anticipation of this part of her nightly routine. "The sunshine song, please."

Smiling, I climb onto her bed and gather my baby girl close to my chest. Dropping a kiss to the top of her head, I begin to sing, "You Are My Sunshine," and before I've hit the second chorus, she's softly snoring in the safety of my embrace.

Taking another couple of moments to ready myself to go back downstairs, I inhale my daughter's comforting scent to bolster my now flagging confidence.

"A week to fall back in love with me, Bam."

I swallow harshly, suddenly doubtful of my abilities and my willingness to overlook the last fifteen years, but I push it down, deep down, and tell myself I can have this one week before inviting reality back into the mix.

Because I'm not stupid. I know that eventually, we'll have to discuss everything, but I'm hoping that by the time we do, I'll have won her heart back so that she'll stick around, regardless of what made her leave before.

Easing myself out from underneath my sleeping Bug, I slide the covers over her prone form and tuck her favourite plush toy, Huddles Bunny, a gift from Uncle Nate, under her arm. I press a soft kiss to her brow, and she mumbles something about "too many princesses" before snuggling closer to Huddles.

As I back out of her room, I dim the light but don't turn it off, aware that my girl hates sleeping alone in the dark.

I head for the stairs, only to hear Serena behind me.

"Mr North?"

"Yes, Serena. Is everything okay?"

She nods once. "Well, umm…I was hoping that I might be able to begin work a little later tomorrow morning. My sister needs me—"

I hold up my palm and smile. "Of course. How about you take a couple of days, Serena? We'll see you back here on Monday."

Her kind face lights up with a smile. "That would be such a help, Mr North. Thank you!"

I wave her away and move off in the direction of the stairs once again. "Not at all. You've not had time off in months now.

You're overdue this break."

"Don't forget the monitor for Bella's room, Mr North. You'll need to take it overnight."

Taking the stairs two at a time, I grab the room monitor for Bug's bedroom that Serena usually takes overnight. Our nanny smiles in acknowledgement when I flick it on and drop it into my pocket before entering the kitchen.

"And that's how you make the perfect sponge mix."

Summer and Maggie have their backs to the door I've just entered through, so I take a moment to observe them with my shoulder propped against the door.

"I've never used room temperature ingredients, Maggie. I'm pretty sure you're pulling my leg with that one."

I can hear the teasing mirth in Summer's American-twinged tone, which brings a smile to my lips.

"Just you wait and see, dearie."

"You bake?"

My words clearly shock her. Summer spins around and drops an egg to the marble floor at her feet with a loud *crack* that sounds throughout the silence of the kitchen.

"I'll go and finish the laundry—"

Without glancing at Maggie, I cut her off. "You can finish up for the evening, Maggie. Thank you for all your help today for Bug's birthday."

Maggie scoots out past me while Summer finds some napkins to clean up the egg. As she crouches over the mess, I move further into the kitchen to grab the mop, and Summer's soft words carry to my ears.

"I didn't know it was your daughter's birthday today. The internet says she doesn't turn four till next week..."

Having located the mop, I prop it against the countertop and duck down to help Summer clean up the gooey mess.

"Yeah…well, that would have been Noah's doing. Bella came early, and the tabloids at the time were rife with speculation about the dates of conception. About whether Layla and I were together or if she was with someone else…Noah reckoned an early arrival would feed the press, you know?"

Layla. The elephant in the room.

Summer's hands are still as I speak, and her eyes lift to meet mine. "Yes, that does sound like Uncle Noah."

I snort, having not heard him referred to as such in a long ass time. It had taken her months to lose the habit of referring to my dad as her uncle when she'd moved in with us. Her father, Peter, alongside my old man, Noah and Cole Gardiner, Layla's waste-of-space dad, had been best friends their whole lives, but the uncle references were entirely a Summer thing. My parents had called Noah, Cole, and Peter family, hence why Layla had all but grown up in our home alongside us, but Mum and Dad hadn't felt the need to push formalities.

"Uncle Noah…fuck, yeah. I forgot you always called him that. He'll be thrilled to see you back."

She smiles widely, some unknown emotion flittering across her features. "He'll be thrilled, alright."

SUMMER

"So, what exactly do you plan on doing this week, Caden?"

The man in question had mixed some drinks, and we're now sat around a firepit staring out over the Cambridge countryside on a starlit night.

The entire patio area is lit by strings of Christmas lights—or fairy lights, as I grew up calling them in the UK—and the whole place looks utterly fantastical. Exactly like something out of a dream.

He raises his glass and quirks a singular brow. "Wouldn't you like to know!"

I'm helpless to stop a broad smile from spreading across my face, a flirtation I learned from the performers at Rogue coming to the fore. "You talk a big talk, North." I wink, and my smile widens. "But can you walk the walk?"

"With ease, Bambi. Just you wait."

When Caden had mentioned Layla earlier, I'd felt compelled to ask about her, but something in his eyes—a hauntedness—made me keep my mouth shut. Her version of events had never wound up making sense, and as I'd already left with plenty of reasons to stay away, I'd never discovered *why*.

But now is clearly not the time. I promised him a week, after all.

"So, this is your place, hmm?"

His lips rise in an easy smile, displaying his perfect white teeth. "It sure is. Mine and Bella Bugs."

I shake my head, a smile playing on my lips as I mischievously poke the bear. "You and those damn nicknames, Caden North."

My smile hurts when Caden throws his head back and laughs, the sight doing something to my insides. This carefree side of him is the one I loved the most.

The one you love *the most, you big liar.*

My inner thoughts dim my smile slightly as Caden drops his head forward, still chuckling lightly. "Oh, Bam. I've only ever given out two nicknames, both beginning with B and both for the people I love most in the world."

The honesty in his eyes and the transparency in his voice sober me, allowing words to escape my lips that I'd sworn not to speak of.

"So, why Layla?"

His face loses its mirth, and I curse my tongue for stealing the joy of the moment.

"If it couldn't be you, then it had to be her, Summer. I—I was the reason Archer died. I was the reason she was left alone. I was the reason *you* left—"

I cut him off, once again saying more than I mean to. "*You* weren't the reason I left, Caden."

His forehead puckers in confusion, and I glance at the empty glass resting in my palm.

Did he put Veritaserum in this bad boy, or what?

My eyes return to Cade's, knowing he's silently waiting on further clarification, and I rapidly flick through my options—not wanting to say too much but likewise aware that I can't say too little.

"You weren't the *entire* reason I left..."

I swallow roughly, my throat suddenly parched, and Caden rises to grab me a refill.

"Thank you." He pours the clear fluid into the glass until it's about halfway full, holding my eyes the entire time with an intensity I feel in the tips of my toes.

He tops himself up and deposits the crystal decanter on the side table to his right before taking a seat beside me instead of returning to his previous place opposite me.

"You remember that...that day when..."

When I don't elaborate, he nods, knowing I'm talking about the day Archer died. I clear my throat before continuing.

"When we were playing Truth or Dare, I found out you'd slept with Layla and—"

"What?"

Caden's dark blue eyes have darkened to almost black pools as his one-word question is spat from between his lips.

"When I asked Layla to tell me if she'd ever slept with you… she said she had. You were right there, Caden. You didn't deny it."

He stares at me with fury emanating from his usually placid features. "I don't remember that, Summer. I don't recall that question. Or her answer."

I hold up a quelling palm. "Caden, it was the first time I had caught you in a lie. It wasn't the last—"

"Bullshit, Bambi. I don't fucking lie. It's a dirty habit and one I'm not prone to."

Still, I can't let it go. Not after fifteen years of having that confirmation from my old friend's lips play on my mind daily. "I know what I heard. You'll not convince me otherwise."

My tone escalates as I begin to doubt my own memories, and the idea of that makes me really damn angry, but before I can say any more, Caden catches my hand and pulls me to rise.

"Summer St James, so help me, because you are driving me insane."

I open my mouth to speak, but he places his forefinger atop my lips, stopping me.

"Now listen to me. I have loved you since I was eight years old. You were my first kiss. The *only* woman I *made love* to. Hell, I stayed celibate for a fucking decade after you straight-up vanished! I travelled to every corner of the damn globe for ten long years after you left, searching for your face among the crowds. Praying to a god I don't believe in that you were around the next corner—willing myself to believe you were out there, somewhere, just waiting to be found. That you hadn't just disappeared like a thief in the night, taking my heart with you—"

I inhale sharply through my nose and attempt to step back, but Caden's free hand snakes around the nape of my neck, holding me firmly in place.

"No, Bam. If I've had to live with the pain, then the least you can do is *hear* it, okay?"

My eyes well with tears as I give him the barest hint of a nod.

"Earlier, when I said that I let other people guide my life, I meant it. Up until the age of twenty-six, I was so preoccupied with finding you that I had no other goals in life. I travelled extensively, Layla in tow, if for no other reason than to keep her safe from her-fucking-self. I hired a P.I., but he never found a trace…I thought you were dead…"

A tear slips down my cheek as a matching one slides from his own pain-filled orbs.

"Noah said I needed to get my shit together. To move on from you because *clearly* you just didn't want to be found, so he signed me to Spellman Sounds and went on to form Misdirection…but being a singer was Archer's dream, not mine…"

He trails off as hesitancy plays across his wounded features. When he speaks again, his words are a bare whisper.

"*You* were my dream. A life with you, that's *all* I wanted."

My vision is blurry with unshed tears, yet, even so, this man's *pain* is plainly visible, and my soul cries out for having denied him of his dream.

"I'd struggled for years trying to help Layla. She spiralled really bad after you left. She was never the same after Archer…so Noah encouraged me to help her. To try to find happiness together, as we both lost the ones we truly loved. I thought a *baby*…"

He trails off before stepping forward to hold my cheeks in his large palms.

"*Clearly*, I was wrong. She was already far too broken—beyond anyone's reach. I did the best I could to manage her…issues." He huffs a dark laugh.

"I don't know how many sex parties she forced me into attending with her. Not that I partook. I couldn't. I'm…I struggle to…umm, perform…like that."

My cheeks flush bright pink when his gaze flicks to the side, clearly embarrassed at what he's disclosed. My heart breaks all over again for everything we've lost—and my stomach churns with the knowledge that by the time this week is over, my reason for coming back will only add to his burden.

As well as locking his heart from me forever.

Six

SUMMER

"What's in it for me, little deer?"

Archer's voice is menacingly low, and I glance towards my friend, praying this is all a sick joke, but Layla's face speaks volumes.

"Summer, just let him fuck you, and we can be done with this shit. Christ almighty, it's just sex."

She rolls her eyes and looks back out onto the river as my mouth falls open in disbelief. "Oh my God, Layla."

She shrugs in utter nonchalance, not like Caden is currently drowning because of the dare she gave him.

"Tick. Tock."

Archer's drawl at my shoulder sends a shiver of disgust through my whole body, and I whirl around to face him. I'm about to tell him to shove his assistance up his ass when my eyes land on a floundering Caden once more.

Layla's words ring through my mind.

"It's just sex."

In exchange for saving my lover's life, I'd pay just about any price.

With my stomach roiling, I nod sharply once, but that's not enough for Archer.

"I need your words."

Swallowing my nausea, I manage to choke out my assent. "Okay, please just save him."

Both his hands shoot out to land on my neck, squeezing tight enough to leave marks. "Let's seal the deal with a kiss, little deer."

My body shoots forward, sweat dotting my brow and making my pyjamas stick to my clammy skin.

I shove all thoughts of my nightmare from my head as I swing my legs over the side of the bed and slide my flip-flops onto my feet. Standing, I inhale and exhale several times to slow my racing pulse before padding to the window to look out at the beautiful English countryside.

It can't be much past dawn.

Following our patio conversation last night, Caden had given me a choice of sleeping in the main house or allowing me my privacy by giving me the bedroom above his new recording studio a stone's throw away.

I'd opted for the latter, knowing that forced proximity would inevitably lead to some bad decisions.

The studio bedroom is more luxurious and at least twice the size of my first apartment in New York.

With that on my mind, I grab my cell and shoot a quick text to Anna.

ME

Just checking in. I'll be in the UK for the next week if you need me xo

Knowing that Anna and Ophelia are most surely asleep, considering the time difference, I plug in my cell to charge while I make a quick breakfast of poached eggs and toast with the help of the surprisingly well-stocked pantry.

I'm about to finish my last bite when my cell chimes from where I've left it on the bedside table.

I make short work of tidying up after myself before I check the message.

ANNA

I take it the reunion went better than expected. How did he take the news?

My gut tightens at the reminder that I'm keeping secrets that don't have the *potential* to destroy me—they *will* shatter everything I hold dear.

ME

I'm staying the week.

I hit send and then spend the next thirty seconds watching those three dots flicker on the screen.

ANNA

You didn't do it, did you?

ME

I will. I'm waiting for my opening.

Placing the cell face down on the bedside table, as though the sight of it offends me, I quickly get dressed into black jogging shorts and a white vest, pulling my hair back off my face in a high pony.

I'm tying the laces of my trainers when my phone chimes again, but I leave it and head out to jog off my nervous anxiety.

The morning air is crisp and cool, but the sun's rays hold the promise of a beautiful day ahead.

Glancing around, I decide that the best course of action is to jog by the long and winding driveway to the guard's station and back, seeing as I'm unfamiliar with the rest of Caden's property.

So, having warmed up sufficiently, I set off at a gentle pace, soaking in the peace surrounding me. I make it to the guard station in under ten minutes to receive a nod of acknowledgement from two new faces inside before turning back the way I came.

I'm a hairsbreadth from the recording studio when I hear a shout, and I stop suddenly, straining to hear where it's coming from.

"Help!"

The long cry is ear-piercing, and I can just about discern that it came from the direction of the main house.

My feet fly across the distance before my brain has the chance to catch up when I hear it again.

"Help."

Rounding the side of the house, I spot the firepit where Caden had unburdened his truth last night. It's not until I look beyond the seating area that I spot an outdoor pool that I failed to notice the evening before.

My heart leaps beneath my breastbone when I spy someone flailing around in the water. Breaking into a sprint, I round the firepit and vault over the seat at the far side, landing on tiles that are slick with water.

I take a split second to locate the person, only for my adrenaline to spike when I make out a blonde head of hair, and the person is way too small to be Caden.

Bella.

I move forward just as her eyes find mine. She opens her mouth to scream again, only to inhale pool water. Her panicked eyes roll back in her head as coughs wrack her body while an icy fear grapples with my heart.

Without hesitation, I rush across the slippery tiles, falling several times but heedless of the pain in my own body. My focus is on getting to the child.

When I reach the edge of the pool, I push off from the tiles to dive below the surface of the rippling water. My eyes sting from the chlorine when I open them to locate Bella, and my stomach bottoms out when I see her small prone body not ten feet from me.

I swiftly reach for her and push to the surface, cresting the water with a force that almost knocks the air from my lungs. Kicking to the edge with one arm firmly around Bella, I set her onto the tiles and holler as loudly as my lungs can manage.

"Help us. Someone, *please*!"

That's all I have time to yell before I check her vitals. Her pulse is slow, but it's present. I take a moment to shake her, distantly remembering I need to do that first, but there's no response.

Without waiting another second, I begin CPR, trying to remember what the hospital had taught me back in New York.

I open her airway by placing my left hand on her forehead and two fingers of my right hand underneath her chin. Leaning forward, I place my ear over her lips to listen for breathing.

There's a buzzing in my ears that I strive to dim, and my heart seizes when I realise that she's not breathing.

At that, I raise her tiny pyjama top—noting distantly that it's Ironman, my own favourite—clasp my hands with my elbows and fingers locked before beginning chest compressions.

I've counted to twelve, and my inner prayers are answered when Bella begins to cough. Hacking repeatedly, she eventually manages to dispel the water from her lungs and sags against me.

Drawing my palm back and forth over her soaked blonde head absentmindedly, I continue to whisper unintelligible words of comfort as both of us tremble and quiver on the tiles.

And I can't help but think that everything that has happened to bring me to this moment has been to save his daughter. To *somehow* redeem myself in my own eyes.

Until I remember that what I've done is beyond redemption and my body curls around the small innocent in my arms.

CADEN

"Have you ever slept with Caden?" Summer's voice is shaky, and it tugs at my heart.

"Obviously. A couple of times now." Layla is utterly confident by comparison.

I can feel myself staring at the ground, trying to raise my head to say she's lying, but my muscles don't appear to be working all that well.

"You know the boys share, babes. It's just how they are, no harm, no foul. Okay?"

I continue to stare blankly at the colourful flowers beneath me, my jaw ticking with the force of trying to lift my head, and it's just as Layla speaks that I manage to jerk myself upright.

"Truth or dare, Mr Hotshot?"

Her face is swimming, and I can't quite remember what I wanted to say, so I answer her question as my gaze finds Summer's.

"Dare." My answer even sounds off to my own ears.

"I dare you to swim to the mill and back. In under five minutes."

My eyes meet Layla's as though through a fog.

What the fuck was in that damn pill?

I attempt to plead with her. "My legs are tired—"

But she pops a dark brow, a knowing half-smirk on her face. "Four minutes, fifty-nine. Fifty-eight. Fifty-seven…"

Knowing there's no other way out, I push to stand and try to run, but it feels like a stumble. Even so, I'm at the river in a flash.

Wow, those pills are amazing.

"Go on. You can do it, little bro." I can hear my brother's chant behind me.

"Help us. Someone, *please*!"

A shrill cry pierces through the dream that feels more like a long-buried memory, and I jolt upright in bed, my heart hammering out of my chest when I recognise the owner.

Summer!

Without a second thought, I race down the stairs, through the kitchen and towards the sound around the back of the house. My heart seizes in my chest when my eyes lock on a blonde head down by the pool Layla forced me into installing.

If it had been up to me, I'd never have had any large body of water near this fucking house.

I descend on the motionless figure, only to realise there are two.

Despite every inch of my body crying out to run to them, I stop and sprint back to the house, raising the alarm before racing back towards that damn pool.

My knees buckle as I reach Bella and Summer, curled up

together as though sleeping, both soaked to the bone.

A sob escapes my windpipe, sounding like the keening cry of a lone wolf, and Summer's eyes open wearily. Hers hold mine, the moment sending a jolt down to my very marrow.

"It's okay, Cade. I got to her in time."

I hear a commotion at my back as the help I'd called for begins to arrive, yet all I can do is lay down on the tiles slick from the sprinklers to gather these two girls close to my chest.

Resting my forehead against Summer's, we both look down on Bug's wet blonde head as I inhale her exhalations. While she inhales mine.

As we both take a moment to be grateful for our present—yet again reminding me that the past means shit. Living in the *now* is what matters.

And I'll be fucked if I ever take another single day for granted ever again.

Seven

CADEN

"Your little girl should be just fine, Mr North." Dr Kline gestures behind him to where Bella is sitting in front of her Batcave play set, playing happily. There's not a single sign that she almost drowned only an hour ago.

"I understand you'd like to stay home rather than come in for observation, yes?"

Clearly, Noah has been in touch with the doctor because I never said any such thing—but Noah and his aversion to any scandal, big or small, is most assuredly the reason Dr Kline is making this suggestion.

"I don't mind, either way, doctor. I only want what's best for my daughter."

Dr Kline nods slowly. "Well, I'll leave a list of signs to look out for in case of post-immersion syndrome—"

I scrunch up my forehead, holding up my palm to stop him from continuing. "Post-what?"

He smiles kindly. "When someone has had a water incident such as this, there may be after-effects that can cause complications. I'll leave my understudy, Dr Carver—"

He gestures to the woman checking Summer's vitals over by the window.

"And she'll monitor Bella for the next eight hours, after which time she'll touch base with me. Then I can decide whether we need to complete some further monitoring in a hospital setting or if Bella is out of the woods. Okay?"

As he finishes speaking, Dr Carver concludes her observation of Summer, and the two women walk closer to us.

"Miss St James is in perfect health other than some bruises and a mild concussion from hitting her head when she fell on the wet tiles."

My eyes meet Summer's, and before I know what I'm doing, my hand reaches for hers, closing gently around her small fist. She shoots me a small smile that sets my pulse racing.

Fuck, I would walk through fire for her.

Bella had taken a handful of minutes that had felt more like days to rally before the emergency services arrived on the scene. But when she *did*, her eyes latched hungrily onto Summer, who had kept back, obviously fearful of upsetting Bug further with the presence of a stranger.

"You saved me."

Bug's innocent eyes widen as they fixate on Summer, who's standing at my back.

I twist my head, reaching out to automatically pull her closer. "She did, Bug."

Bella's mouth lifts in a broad smile, and she holds out a trembling hand for Summer. The gesture makes my throat muscles constrict as I fight to swallow the ball of emotion suddenly lodged in there.

"I've never met a real-life superhero!"

"Oh, Bella." Summer chuckles softly, stepping forward to gently grasp Bug's finger. "I'm not a superhero. I'm just Summer, an old friend of your dad's."

Bella shakes her head, her gaze firmly on Summer with little to no heed to her other surroundings. "No, you're not. You're my *Summer-hero."*

"I commend you, Miss St James." Dr Kline's words catch my attention. "It's a miracle you made it into that pool, let alone back out with a child in tow. A blow to the head like you sustained should have rendered you unconscious."

Summer's cheeks pinken, and she blinks prettily whilst chewing on her bottom lip.

"When I grow up, I want to be like you."

No one notices Bella's approach until she's right beside Summer, her big blue eyes filled to brimming with unfettered hero worship. My chest suddenly feels too small to contain my heart.

Summer eases her hand from mine to crouch down to Bella's height and smiles brightly. "You're already a mini boss. What you say goes." And she finishes it with a wink that makes my little Bug laugh merrily.

"If I'm the boss..."

Bella trails off, glancing around at the four adults fully fixated on her. She straightens up and lifts her chin, showing that determination I love so much.

"If *I'm* the boss, then I get to pick what we play."

Everyone smiles, but none so much as me, as Bella leads Summer and Dr Carver towards her toys.

"I'll leave you that list, Mr North. And I'll be in regular contact with Dr Carver throughout the day."

I nod, motioning towards the door. "Thank you for everything. I'll show you out, Dr Kline."

We spend the day doing whatever little Miss Bug wanted, which included a superhero tea party, followed by a fashion show of her favourite superheroes—her final, and best costume was when she strode into her bedroom wearing Summer's semi-soaked trainers and announced Summer as her favourite hero of all-time—before we'd bid Dr Carver farewell.

Dr Kline was sure, based on his understudy's feedback and his years of experience, that we were out of the woods. Although I was content to go along with his opinion, I still wouldn't be leaving my little girl's side for the rest of the day.

"How's about we get some dinner, Bella?"

Summer's pure and wholly welcome voice rings out through the playroom, where we've been holed up for almost an hour following Dr Carver's departure.

I raise my head from the beanbag I'm lolling on to fix my gaze on my Bug and my Bam, finding them sitting lotus-style opposite one another. At least fifty play figurines ranging from Hulk to Doctor Strange to a vintage He-Man that my dad found in our attic are propped up all around them in various poses and pairings.

Bella is dressed in her Ironman costume, but Summer is donning the mask, and the whole scenario is beyond hilarious, yet somehow all I feel is fulfilled. As though I dreamed a dream, and somehow it came to life.

A sense of utter foreboding fills my body from the top of my head to the tips of my toes, and I rise to stand in one fluid movement, quick to shake off the feeling.

I flick my gaze to the heavens, silently flipping the bird to the universe.

I can have my cake and eat it, too.

Stretching my arms over my head, I arch my back as Summer slides the mask from her face, allowing her eyes to drop down my body. She catches herself and blushes as her eyes shoot back up to my smirking ones.

"Yeah, let's grab something to eat, Bug. I'm famished."

As though emphasising my point, my stomach grumbles loudly, making the three of us laugh, and we slowly amble downstairs to the kitchen.

Maggie, having finished up for the day, has left a lasagne big enough to feed a small army alongside a fridge full of an assortment of salads.

I turn to grab some plates, only to feel my phone vibrate in my back pocket. Pulling it out, I'm unsurprised to find it's none other than my micro-managing manager.

NOAH

Glad to hear Bug is okay, Caden. I'll send her a get-well gift when I get back to the UK.

I smile at his signature generosity as I pocket my phone, only to pull it back out again immediately when it buzzes with another text.

NOAH

Don't forget the Misdirection gig on Friday for Katherine's House.

I'd forgotten that gig was this week. And Noah is Stateside and otherwise occupied, so tracking down my fellow bandmates will fall to yours truly.

Misdirection performs an annual concert for Olivia DeMarco's non-profit Katherine's House, a charity based in London that helps rehabilitate the lives of London's homeless. This would mark year three, and the proceeds went a long way towards allowing Liv to expand to new premises.

My forehead puckers as I ponder on the time wasted with Summer, when I only have six days left until I make a split-second decision to bring her along.

Bella too.

The Alexandra Palace is a smaller venue than we'd normally perform at, cramming in around ten thousand. I nod to myself in satisfaction as my mouth lifts in a shit-eating grin, proud as punch with my idea.

Glancing up, I find Summer washing Bella's hands at the sink while the two of them giggle softly over a shared joke.

This is the life I wanted. Peaceful. Simple. Happy.

"Come on, you," Summer calls over her shoulder, beckoning me closer. "Your hands need a scrubbing too!"

I cross the kitchen, dropping a kiss atop my daughter's head as she stands on her step stool beside Summer. Sliding my arms around either side of Summer as she washes her own hands, I can feel her body tense at my proximity.

Bella shoots a smile up at me, almost in encouragement, as she rinses her soapy hands, and I'm suddenly filled with a sense of rightness. Like I've spent my life striving to get to this moment, and the realisation is a balm to my long-wandering soul.

"I think you missed a spot, Bam." My lips linger by her ear, and I swear I can almost *feel* her relax back against my chest.

I squirt some more handwash into her outstretched hands as Bella hops down and reaches for a hand towel from the island behind us.

Instead of letting Summer wash her own hands, I interlink our fingers and work the liquid into a lather. The action is way more sensual than it should be, and I force myself to step around her, dropping her hands, when I feel my dick begin to awaken in acknowledgement.

"Your skin is softer than I remember."

The words have left my mouth before I can stop them. She turns towards me, her shoulder against my bicep, as she looks up from underneath her long black lashes. "You got taller."

I press my lips together in a half-assed attempt at stifling my grin. "You're even more beautiful than the last day I saw you."

It's her turn to stifle a smile, and her eyes light up with a playfulness I've missed fiercely. "You've got a lot more muscle these days. You never struck me as the gym bunny type?"

My grin becomes a full-blown, Cheshire-Cat-ain't-got-nothing-on-me smile, and a half-second later, a mirror image graces her perfect features.

"I'm the UK's answer to Dwayne Johnson, Bam."

Her laugh tinkles through the kitchen as she closes her eyes and throws her head back, allowing her mirth to overtake her entire body.

And my heart falls a little bit further, if such a thing were even possible.

SUMMER

Dinner was a torturous affair–if blissfully perfect can be considered torturous.

Today, despite having started out horrendously, has been one of the most relaxed days I've had in forever. Bella is the sweetest soul—her father incarnate.

And it took me precisely a nanosecond to fall madly in love with her.

Despite telling my wayward heart that we couldn't allow ourselves to get too close, it was already too late. She burrowed into my heart as though she'd always been there, right alongside her father.

She took up residence in a space I didn't realise was empty but instantly realised was meant to be filled with her light.

"Can we watch a movie before bed, Dad?" Bella is bouncing on the balls of her feet at the foot of her bed, where I've taken a seat.

Caden closes the bedroom door behind him and side-eyes his daughter playfully. "Depends on the movie, Bug."

A smile lights up her little face. "You know the one…"

She trails off, glancing at me with a slight blush. I smile back encouragingly, only for my heart to melt when she climbs up onto my lap and settles against me.

Caden flashes his perfect teeth, making my melted heart flutter, before switching on the wall-mounted television and hitting a button on the remote control.

"I'm not pressing the play button until you've had your bath, Bug."

Bella instantly stiffens in my arms. "I don't like to, Dad. I'm not smelly."

Her father chuckles. "You know the rule. Now, come on and let Summer have some time without her new shadow."

"Please, Dad." Bella tenses even further. "Can Summer stay with me? She's my Summer-hero."

Dear heart, you're fucked.

"Of course, I'll stay, Bella. Now…let's get you all washed up, shall we?"

I stand, placing her on the ground and catching her hand to lead her to the ensuite bathroom. "Now, Dad will sort out your shower, and I'll grab your pyjamas. Okay?"

Bella turns to look up at me, her small face scrunched up in anxiety, and I know she's thinking about the water from this morning. The shower might be too much right now, but I know a little something about facing your fears.

The sooner you do it, the better.

I crouch down so that I'm at eye level with her, and I can feel Caden's intense gaze upon both of us.

"Bella, I know water might be something you're afraid of after what happened today, but you know what?"

Her voice wavers. "What?"

I smile encouragingly. "When you're afraid of something, the best way to not be afraid anymore is to be *brave*. Okay?"

She worries her bottom lip between her teeth, and my stomach flips at the gesture that is so reminiscent of my own bad habit.

"Okay, Summer."

"Come on, then." I stand, take her hand in mine, and walk her into the bathroom. "So, when I turn on the shower, and the water starts to flow, you need to tell the water that it doesn't scare you. Like this."

I reach into the huge shower, twist the handle, and the water drenches the oversized white Misdirection t-shirt Caden gave me to replace my vest earlier this morning.

Bella giggles when I jump back from the spray, and I answer her with a smile. "Now, are you ready? On the count of three, we shout, 'you don't scare me.'"

She nods, her smile so utterly contagious that my own grows impossibly brighter.

"One, two, three…you don't scare me!"

Her voice whispers alongside my own, so I squeeze her little hand gently. "One more time, let's be super loud. Show that water who's boss. Okay, Curly-Sue?"

I wiggle my eyebrows and blow my eyes wide, making her laugh loudly.

"One, two, three…*you don't scare me!*"

Bella is much firmer this time, taking things even further and diving head-first underneath the spray, fully clothed.

"You don't scare me. You don't scare me. Nah, nah, nah, poo, poo!"

She spins under the spray, twisting this way and that, arms in the air and face turned up to meet her fear until she stills, turning towards me.

"Come on in, Summer. Don't be afraid."

I smirk as I step forward, helpless to say no in the face of such honest-to-goodness innocence.

Once I'm underneath the spray, we both dance around, laughing like lunatics and repeating our little mantra until we are soaked through. Bella plonks her butt on the marble floor of the shower and declares. "I'm too tired to wash."

I grin, grabbing her shampoo from the shelf before kneeling beside her. "Turn around then, and I'll do it." She smiles like the cat who got the cream—a smile identical to her father's, making me remember his presence in the room.

I squirt a blob of the strawberry-scented gel into my palms as I turn my gaze outward to find Caden sat on the floor, legs crossed at the ankles, and looking entirely too pleased with himself.

Swallowing past the sudden appearance of a lump in my throat, I fight the urge to gnaw on my bottom lip as I begin to shampoo Bella's curly locks.

Happiness is fleeting, idiot. Enjoy it while you can because we don't know what tomorrow brings.

And even though I believe this with my whole entire self, considering the life I've lived, somehow, I can't reconcile the fact that *this* is temporary.

Because it *is*. As surely as the sun rises. As surely as it sets, this is not in my future. No matter how much I wish it were otherwise.

Having managed to wash Bella, Caden had taken her from the shower, his eyes only flitting to my breasts twice—which wasn't altogether bad, considering his t-shirt was moulded to my body and left precisely fuck all to the imagination.

He'd left a towel, some unopened boxer shorts, and a vest top alongside a huge soft robe that felt like I'd wrapped myself up in a cloud when I'd donned it over the vest and briefs.

It would have been just as easy to nip out to the studio to grab my own clothes from my luggage, but truthfully, I didn't want to leave our bubble.

And I think he felt the same, considering he didn't mention asking anyone to bring my things to the main house.

Or maybe that's just wishful thinking.

I brush my wet hair out after towel drying it as best I can before taking a long moment to stare at my reflection, reminding myself that my reason for being here is greater than any amount of guilt I feel for stealing some moments of happiness.

Turning my back on my judgement, I stiffen my spine, purpose renewed, and step out of the ensuite.

When I enter the bedroom, Cade has just finished drying Bella's hair, and she's sat at her dressing table, lining up her hairbrushes and hair accessories whilst chatting to her Ironman figurine, who's propped up at her elbow.

Cade looks at me, eyes raking up and down my body with barely concealed desire, and I fight the thrill that fills my stomach. I'd forgotten how he made me feel—or I'd allowed time to diminish the memory—but Christ, it feels amazing to know this man clearly wants me.

Especially after the revelation he made last night.

My cheeks heat at the memory, and I move across the room rather than hold his gaze.

He holds Bella's hairdryer up in question, but I shake my head and pull my wet hair up into a messy bun even though it's far too short to stay atop my head.

"Thank you for the clean clothes."

He waves me away and finishes tidying up Bella's hair dryer, depositing it in a drawer on her dresser before turning towards me again.

"What you did in the bathroom—for Bella…thank you."

I shoot him an almost shy smile. "Of course. She's a really special kid, Cade. You should be so proud."

Pain flashes across his features, and I can't help creasing my forehead in confusion, wondering why my words have caused hurt. He sees the question in my eyes, glancing down at a busy

Bella, still chattering to her Ironman.

His whispered words barely carry across the space. "I've had nothing to do with how special she is, Bambi. She's a truly wonderful human being, and entirely on her own merit."

Looking up at me, he then moves to close the space between us. His action spurs my feet to move so that we meet halfway. "While I was Stateside doing Misdirection PR earlier this year, I left Bug here with her three nannies, a houseful of staff and Layla…."

His voice breaks, and then he trails off as his eyes drift to the floor. I reach between us, catching both of his hands and cupping them in mine.

He continues when I squeeze his ice-cold fingers comfortingly. "Layla had been clean for months. She was happy—or as close to happy as I'd seen since…."

I rub my thumbs back and forth across the back of his hands soothingly, my silence allowing him to continue with a husky tone.

"Everything was good until Serena, one of the nannies, contacted me, saying that Layla had fired the entire staff—herself included—and there appeared to be a free-for-all taking place on the property. I was frantic. The trip home was the longest time of my damn life."

He inhales raggedly before finally meeting my eyes with tear-filled ones of his own. The pain in those deep blue depths makes my heart hurt.

"No less than forty people, male and female, were *here* in our home. Not an item of clothing was to be found, as bodies were being railed left and right."

We both swallow, and his nostrils flare. "*She* was running the show—high as a kite, of course—claiming to have ensured that Bug was locked in here and hadn't seen anything."

Oh. My. God.

I am not a violent person, not by a long shot, but hearing Caden's story—knowing Layla had placed Bella in harm's way—it makes me want to physically *hurt* her.

We stand in silence for the longest time, the sounds of Bella playing with her superheroes quietly soothing the two of us.

I reach one hand up between us, palming his stubbled cheek and tracing his tear tracks with my thumb. "She's special because she has such an amazing father—and don't you ever doubt that, even for a moment."

He watches me openly, questions clearly playing across his handsome face, and there's a part of me that thinks, *'This is it. Time's up,'* but he holds his tongue. Instead, he reaches up to grip my wrist, gently turning my hand over to press a lingering kiss to my knuckles while holding my eyes with his.

"Movie time!" Bella breaks the spell when she bounds over to the bed and jumps on, patting on either side of her for Caden and me to sit.

I shoot questioning eyes at Caden, ensuring that he wants me to stay. After the trauma of the day, I'm sure he'd like some time with his girl, as much as it would pain me to leave.

"Movie time is right." He narrows his eyes at me and mouths the words *"sit down,"* making me press my lips together in an effort to stifle my grin. Even so, I do as he said and take a seat to Bella's left, propping pillows and plush toys at our backs while Caden preps the movie.

With everything ready, he presses play and sits on Bella's right as the opening scene of *Trolls: World Tour* plays on the screen.

"Do you like Poppy and Branch, Summer?"

Bella's small face is upturned, her eyes hopeful, and I nod enthusiastically. "Oh, I *love* Poppy and Branch. But you know…

the sparkly one who farts glitter is the best!"

My smile is so wide it hurts my face when Bella kicks her legs in the air, howling with laughter. My eyes find and hold Caden's over the top of her head, and some of my happiness dims in the face of the hope held in his gaze.

Steal the rest of today. Tomorrow, Summer. You need to tell him tomorrow.

And with that resolution made, I vow to enjoy the rest of the evening for what it is.

Another glimpse of the life that could have been ours.

Eight

CADEN

I wake to the biggest morning wood of my fucking life.

I'd be happy about it, considering my…issues…except I'm on my back, in my kid's bed, staring at the half-exposed curve of Summer's left tit. Clearly, at some point in the night, she'd discarded the heavy robe, leaving her exposed in a vest belonging to me and much too big for her smaller frame.

The sight is glorious. My predicament is less so.

Rolling my eyes, I turn to my side and gently ease myself out of the bed, adjusting my horn as I go. Glancing behind me, I can see both girls are still out for the count, which is only a good thing because the grey lounge pants I'm wearing leave sweet fuck all to the imagination in my current state.

I tiptoe from the room and make a quick detour to the bathroom, where I relieve myself and get rid of my morning breath.

She won't fall for you if she smells that, man.

I'm almost finished when I remember that I left my phone on Bella's nightstand.

Shit!

I'll need to make calls to organise a last-minute rehearsal at Alexandra Palace later today before the concert tomorrow. Quickly making my way back, I stop dead on the threshold of Bella's door.

Summer is standing just outside the door of the ensuite, wearing only my boxer shorts and the far too-revealing vest. One shoulder strap has slid down her arm, exposing her rapidly rising and falling chest with the toothbrush I'd given her last night caught in her fist.

She looks like a deer caught in the headlights and slowly begins to step back into the ensuite so that there's only one thing I can do.

Only one thing I simply *must* do.

I lock the bedroom door—still wary after yesterday morning's incident—to allow my rapid strides to close the distance between us. I edge us into the ensuite, ensuring the door is open a crack to listen for Bella.

My gaze clashes with hers, and she retreats until her back meets the glass door of the shower, and the toothbrush tumbles to the floor. I fist the hem of her vest, tugging her against me to slam my mouth down on hers.

A moan sweeter than a melody escapes from her hammering chest as she opens her mouth to me, her tongue duelling with mine with a hunger that rivals my own. Her breasts press firmly against my bare chest, her taut nipples poking through the thin vest to scrape across my skin and turn me on even fucking more if that were possible.

My hands wrap around her body, one palm holding her firmly

at the nape of her neck, making sure she's not about to disappear on me again while my other one massages the rounded globe of her sweet as fuck ass. I grip her cheek tighter, pulling her body up against mine, and she moans again when she feels my rock-hard shaft pressing against her lower abdomen.

I tear my mouth from hers and fist her hair, tugging firmly until she arches her neck, exposing the delicate column of her throat to my hungry mouth.

Grazing my teeth across her soft skin elicits a shudder that runs all the way through her body and into mine, swelling my cock almost painfully. I grind my hardness against her as she moans into my ear.

"I want you."

The words send a steady stream of precum straight to the top of my dick, and I flatten my tongue, running it up and then back down the side of her neck. I nibble my way across her collarbone, tugging her hair harder. She whimpers half in pain, half in pleasure as I make her arch even more for me.

Her tits thrust forward, with the strap having fallen far enough to expose one dusky pink nipple.

Exactly what I was after.

I drop to my knees to take the hard bud between my teeth and tug aggressively, with years of pent-up longing and more than a little sexual frustration. She cries out softly.

"Yes. *More*. Caden, oh my God."

I swirl my tongue around the bud, teasing mercilessly, building the anticipation between us until she's writhing against me. Then I close my mouth and suck hard.

She almost lifts off the floor, and I smirk against her nipple, nipping the tip again as she squirms in blissful agony.

I ease my hold on her hair, allowing her eyes to capture mine as I move to her right breast, tugging the other strap down with ease, exposing her creamy flesh to my ravenous gaze.

"I've dreamed about this, Bam. A million and one times." I flick her right nipple with my pointed tongue back and forth relentlessly.

"I've dreamed of all the ways I could make you come. On my hands…my tongue…my fucking cock."

My newly freed hand drops down her body to run my index finger along the damp seam of the boxers she's wearing.

"Of all the ways I'd fill each hole of your tight body with every single drop of my cum. With everything I have in me."

Her glassy eyes flare with unmistakable desire.

"I've dreamed of all the ways I'd devour your sweet body. Starting with these *perfect fucking tits*. I'd suck them—"

I close my mouth over one, doing just that.

"I'd lick them—"

Then I flatten my tongue, slowly tracing the areola before moving to the other and flicking the stiff peak.

She throws her head back against the glass, crying out louder this time, and my index finger circles her plainly swollen clit as she rocks her hips into my hand.

"I'd bite them—"

And I do. I graze my teeth over both nipples, then groan as I push the boxers to one side, finding her pussy soaked and just as swollen as I'd thought.

"And then, when you're all hot for me…" I pause as her hooded gaze seeks mine. "I'd fuck these perfect tits until they're dripping with my cum. Until I made them *mine*."

Arousal coats my fingers as I tease her slick lips relentlessly, and I move back up her body to speak against her panting mouth. "Because you *are* mine."

My mouth covers hers once again as I sink two thick fingers inside her tight channel, swallowing her cry of pleasure with a low growl.

"Because I made this perfect pussy mine a long fucking time ago, Bam."

I pump my fingers fast as my thumb circles her clit, working her with a rhythm I remember she likes. But it's when I add a third finger to stretch her wide open that her cunt grips me like a vice, and Summer rips her mouth from mine.

"I'm coming—oh *shit*!" Thrusting my tongue inside her mouth, I swallow her mewls of pleasure as her juices coat my fingers.

Her hands dig into my shoulders, and her whole body tenses while she rides the wave of her orgasm until she shudders against me, gasping for air against my plundering mouth.

Our mouths move lazily against one another while our gazes lock and hold.

I can *feel* the love between us in this moment, and I *know* without a shadow of a doubt that this woman is still in love with me. The knowledge sends my soul soaring as euphoria races through my body.

She loves me.

"Dad?"

We both pull back, eyes blowing wide open at the sound of Bella stirring in the bedroom.

"Hold on—" I stop, clear my throat, and try to calm my racing heart before trying again. "I'm just washing up, Bug. Be right out."

I breathe an internal sigh of relief when I hear her begin to play with Ironman and his mates.

Dropping a kiss on Summer's kiss-swollen lips, I smirk with a wink as I gently withdraw my fingers from her pulsing core. I tug the boxers back into place and pet along the outside of the seam. She jolts slightly, and I'm unable to stop myself from whispering across her trembling lips.

"My perfect pussy, Bam. She's such a *good girl.*" Then I bring my glistening fingers to my mouth, slipping them inside one after the other, sucking her essence from each dripping digit.

Ring finger.

Middle finger.

"Fuck, you taste even sweeter than I remember."

She sucks in a breath as I offer her my index finger before she slowly leans forward, closing her mouth around her own arousal and humming her sound of approval.

"Still tastes like mine, Bam."

I pull my finger from her mouth. She lets it go with a pop, and I slide it between my own smirking lips before shooting her a cheeky-as-fuck grin, followed by a cheekier wink.

Her eyes flutter shut as she slumps back against the shower door, her breasts heaving under the force of her climax and the emotions running riot between us. I take a moment to pull the straps back up on her vest, setting her to rights as she takes me in through hooded eyes.

"You can't go out there looking like *that*."

She slowly raises a single brow, eyes flicking down pointedly. Her voice is a whisper, plainly not wanting to draw attention to her presence, and I glance down my body, wryly noting my rock-solid cock sending me a cheeky wink of his own.

Sorry, fucker. This wasn't about you.

Despite the delight of being able to attain a non-medically induced boner, I can't wait here until he decides to call it a day. Thinking quickly, I yank my lounge pants off, letting them pool on the floor.

I edge around a wide-eyed Summer and flick on the cold water. "Only one thing for it, Bam. A cold shower."

My leaky cock isn't long about shrinking when I step underneath the frigid water, and not thirty seconds later, I'm leaving Summer in the ensuite to attend to my daughter, still tasting her sweetness on my taste buds.

SUMMER

When Cade leaves the bathroom, I stand in shocked silence for another several minutes before managing to shakily turn on the shower and step under the water.

My mind is racing with all sorts of thoughts, but I'm unable to focus on a single one.

That orgasm just about blew my damn mind. Years of battery-operated boyfriends just can't measure up to intimacy with the person you—

No, don't you dare even think it. You can't *love him. This is temporary. And it's a lie.*

Once I've washed away all my thoughts, I climb out of the shower and find fresh, clean clothes—all Caden-sized—on Bella's bed. I quickly dress in the navy lounge pants and red t-shirt he's provided before slipping from the room and following the sounds of activity.

I enter the kitchen to find Maggie cooking up a storm. She greets me with a smile and a steaming cup of coffee that smells too good to be true.

"Good morning, dearie. Mr North is on the patio with Miss Bella. I'll bring your breakfast right out."

The sun is beaming down, and it's a stunning August day.

Happiness fills my entire body when my eyes land on Caden and Bella, my heart filling to capacity. Bella spots me first and races along the patio to throw her little arms around my legs.

"My Summer-hero!"

I press my lips together, trying and failing to stifle my grin.

"Good morning, Curly-Sue. Did you sleep well?"

She nods effusively as she takes my hand and pulls me in the direction of her watching father. I raise my head to find his eyes on me, and my body glows under his heated gaze.

"Good morning, Summer. You look…refreshed."

Flashing his pearly white teeth, he arches an insinuating brow, and I can feel my cheeks heat, which only makes him chuckle.

As I'm taking my seat beside Bella, she turns to me. "Did Dad tell you the news?"

I smile and shake my head. "What news, Curly-Sue?"

"Oh, Summer. It's the *best*. We're going to a Palace."

Caden snorts opposite us. "What Bug *means* is we're going to the *Alexandra Palace*."

My eyebrows crease in puzzlement. "For what?"

"There's a Misdirection charity gig there tomorrow evening, and I'd love to bring you both. Bella's never been to a show—you either, I'd imagine—"

"I've seen you perform several times."

The words have left my mouth before they've even registered, and I wish more than anything that I could take them back when pain flashes across his handsome face.

"Oh, really? Where was that?"

I can hear the hurt in his attempt at indifference.

Idiot, Summer!

"Almost every time you played Madison Square Garden."

He smiles sadly, huffing out a borderline bitter laugh. "You were in New York?"

Shiiiiiit!

I nod once and thank my lucky stars when Maggie appears with breakfast, helping to shift the focus from me onto Bella's grumbly tummy. Even so, I can feel Caden's sadness rolling off of him in waves. I despise being the cause of it, and so I change my plans.

Tomorrow. I'll come clean tomorrow. After the concert.

Nine

CADEN

I spend most of my morning on the phone, organising a setlist that should have been finalised weeks ago while also trying to get my fellow group members to hotfoot it back to London from wherever they're fucking about on the planet.

We're on a break right now, so my four other bandmates are off doing whatever they do when we're not recording or touring.

The quickest and easiest to track down is Beau Maxwell, our drummer. The guy is built like the damn Hulk with a grimace to match, but he's a big softie. He spends his downtime with his elderly parents and wheelchair-bound older sister up in Newcastle.

BEAU

I'll be in London for rehearsal this evening. 6 p.m?

I shoot him back a quick thumbs-up emoji, grateful to have one ticked off the list.

An hour later sees me finding and enlisting Tobias Wolfe, our bassist, and Danny Sheffield, our keyboardist. I'm cursing Jake Milano, our lead guitarist, who has clearly disappeared off the face of the damn planet when Henry calls.

"Hey, brother. Just touching base about the show tomorrow. Liv said her organisers haven't heard a thing from your end and—"

"Henry." My unusually stern tone cuts my best friend off sharply. "I am in the midst of sorting it, okay? I've been a *little* busy."

He snorts. "Doing what? Sitting on your thumb?"

His laugh dies in his throat when I whisper. "Summer's back."

Silence reigns supreme on the line as that soaks in for a minute, and when it does, he hits me with a bazillion questions, none of which I have the answer to because I've been so focused on wanting to keep her in my life, that I know nothing about what's happened in the time we've been apart.

It seems to be a running theme with the women in my life.

Layla goes off the deep end, fucking anything with a pulse and numbing her demons with drugs and whatever else she can get her hands on. And what do I do?

I pretend everything is fine and dandy.

Summer returns after fifteen years of radio silence and a million and one bad choices between us, and what do I do?

Same.

Fucking.

Thing.

I put a stop to my spiralling thoughts and focus on the fact that we have a week. The fact that I *know* she still has feelings for me—and I can use that to my advantage.

If I need to orgasm her into submission, I'm up for that fucking job.

"Did she say why she left, North?"

I expel the heavy breath that I didn't realise I had been holding. "No, Henry. And you know what? I don't need to know right now, okay?"

"I didn't mean—"

"I know you didn't," I cut him off gently. "I don't know what to say, man. I had all these fucking questions in my head for *fifteen years*...I never thought I'd get the chance to ask her any of them."

I close my eyes, squeezing the lids shut tight as I pinch the bridge of my nose. "But Christ, brother. When I saw her standing there in my driveway, looking as though no time had passed between us...I *knew* I didn't need answers. I just need *her*. However she'll have me..."

The silence stretches out between us for a long beat.

"Never mind, man. Maybe I'm being a fucking idiot—"

"The one that got away *didn't* get away. This is your fucking chance. Take it with both hands. You deserve to be happy, Cade."

There's a knock on the door of my office, and Bug bounds in with Summer sticking her head tentatively around the corner until I wave her in.

"Anyway, Henry. I've got to—"

"Can I say hi?" Bella slides onto my lap and slips the phone from my hand. "Hi, Uncle Henry. Can I have my sleepover tonight, *please*?"

I'm about to object when I realise there are only a few other people I would trust to watch Bella overnight–and perhaps, some child-free time would go a long way towards making Summer admit there's still something between us.

Thirty seconds later, the entire evening is planned out.

We'll drop Bella to the DeMarco Holdings penthouse that Henry and Liv use when they need to stay in the city before I take Summer with me to the rehearsal at Alexandra Palace.

A couple of sneaky emails later, the balls are in motion for an evening she'll never forget.

SUMMER

When Caden told me to pack for two nights in the city, I was more than a little concerned, as I'd packed the bare minimum for the trip to the UK as a whole.

I make my way back to my temporary lodgings at the recording studio while Caden is getting cases together for himself and Bella. Mulling over what the hell I'm going to pack out of my sparse case, my jaw hits the floor when I climb the stairs above the studio and enter the wide-open space.

There are rails upon rails of all manner of clothing, shoes, and accessories. My eyes rake along each rail that I pass as I touch a multitude of different fabrics and colours before eventually filling with tears when they land upon a handwritten note:

I wasn't sure what you preferred, so I had a friend deliver a little bit of everything.

You always looked edible in green.

I brush the tears away with the back of my left hand as guilt invades my gut, making it twist and churn with anxiety.

I don't deserve this.

The feeling is further compounded when I finally pick up my

phone for the first time since yesterday morning.

ANNA

You're setting yourself up for disappointment, Summer.

Nausea swirls in the pit of my stomach, knowing she's right. I should have come clean the moment he stepped out of his front door, but I'm in too deep now.

And, even as I know all of this, there's a small voice inside of me telling me to take this happiness while I can. To be selfish for once.

He's going to hate you regardless. Might as well soak in the last of his love…

My self-deprecation is put on hold when I hear voices in the studio beneath me. Female voices that move through the studio and up the stairwell, coming closer.

Two women enter the space. One with curly black hair, the other with flame red hair, both bickering like an old married couple.

"He *said* to be here twenty damn minutes ago, Josie!"

The black-haired woman shakes her short curls. "And I said he called last minute, so he'll get what he gets, Nola. He's lucky I even answered—"

She stops short when her bright blue eyes land on me, blowing wide in the process.

The flame-haired beauty—Nola, I'm assuming—turns a smirking face to her companion. "Twenty minutes, I said. Look who was right, *as usual*."

Josie recovers in a nanosecond, striding forward with her palm extended. "Hey, Blondie, I'm Josie." She indicates her companion with her thumb. "This is Stupid. She's *clearly* with me."

Nola rolls her eyes, and I try my hardest not to laugh at their banter, barely muffling a snort.

"We are here to make sure you have the most wonderful evening with our very own Caden." Josie wiggles her eyebrows, and without meaning to, some of the mirth falls from my face.

Both women pick up on it, and Nola rushes forward. "Oh no, no, no. It's not how she made it sound. Caden is our *friend*. Our best friend is married to his best friend, Henry."

Josie nods voraciously. "He's lovely and all, but he doesn't have the right…equipment for us. Right, Nola?"

And the penny drops.

I exhale a breath I didn't realise I was holding as both girls giggle at my assumptions. "Sorry, Josie." I nod at the woman in question before turning my contrite eyes to Nola. "I apologise for making assumptions."

Both women nod and smile widely, but I continue. "Also, regardless of my reaction just now, there's nothing between Caden and me."

Nola's eyes widen impossibly as she nods. "Of…of *course*, Summer. We would never think—"

Josie cuts her off, sending me a face filled with disbelief. "*Giiiiiiiirl*, you can lie to yourself *all* you like. The man is hook, line, and sinker for you. The picture in his foyer tells everyone who enters his home *exactly* where his heart is at."

I inhale sharply, both appreciating this woman's honesty while hating it at the same time.

"So, do me a favour while we're here at his request, yeah?"

Powerless to do otherwise, I nod, tugging my bottom lip between my teeth to chew mercilessly.

"Don't fill me with shit. I can see your feelings on your face, plain as fucking day. And, if I can, then you can be sure *he* sees them too."

Two hours and a million outfits later, I'm packed for a night in the city. Having bid Nola and Josie farewell, I take a second to admire the make-up that Josie insisted I wear.

Usually, the only time I wear make-up is when I'm at Rogue, and that's vastly removed from the understated elegance staring back at me right now. It's all neutral browns and beiges that suit my skin tone to perfection. She finished the look with a glossy pink lip that I simply love.

After much debate between the two girls, I'd settled on a forest green maxi dress that has tiny pearl buttons down the front and the most gorgeous cap sleeves.

They tried and failed to get me into heels as I'd discovered a pair of exquisitely detailed flat sandals that laced up my calves, and there was no talking me out of wearing them. They are, quite simply, the nicest footwear I've ever worn.

I grab the matching bejewelled handbag, toss my phone inside and heft my overnight bag down the stairs, only to meet Ford, the guard from the day of my arrival, entering the recording studio.

"Allow me, ma'am." His Texan drawl brings a smile to my face. "Caden asked me to help you with that."

He indicates the bag, which I gratefully pass into his waiting hands, smiling wider. "Thank you, Ford."

"Caden left with Miss Bella almost an hour ago."

My shoulders slump at the news, and my smile dissipates. "Why was that, do you know?" We walk slowly in the direction of a waiting black town car.

Ford chuckles; the sound is a rumble in his broad chest. "Miss Bella wanted to be at the penthouse before it was time for little Sebastian's bedtime."

My disappointment turns to amusement. "Sounds like Bella."

"Precisely, ma'am. And Cade can never say no. He threw some shit into a case and lit out after telling me where to drop you off."

I turn to him, meet his gaze, and smile slightly. "Ford? Please, call me Summer."

We reach the car, and Ford opens the trunk to gently deposit my heavy bag as though it weighs less than a feather. Then he rounds the car, sliding his arm in front of me to tug open the door, and winks like he's in on something I have no idea about.

"So, let's get going, Miss Summer."

CADEN

Having dropped a highly amped Bug to Henry and Liv at the DeMarco penthouse, I'd quickly raced to the Alexandra Palace, where the boys—Jake Milano among them as I'd eventually tracked the fucker down—were ready and waiting to have a quick run-through the setlist.

I kept it relatively similar to our recent gigs before this current break, but added in a change or two that raised more than one or two eyebrows.

"Are you *sure*?"

"Are you *serious*?"

"You're a soppy cunt." That last one from Jake earned him a solid slap around the back of the head.

"And you're an asshole, Milano." I smirk good-naturedly. The banter between us feels even better than usual.

We cram a handful of songs into the next hour before my phone chimes with a text message.

FORD

Pina Colada?

I snort a laugh, remembering how I'd told him we needed to come up with safe words in the event that we ever had an incident like Layla's breakdown.

ME

I take that to mean the eagle has landed?

He shoots back a thumbs-up.

"Right, fuckers. Time to call it a day. I've got better plans for my evening."

"A date with your hand and a bottle of lube, eh, North?"

"Shut that hole in your face, Milano. You've caused me enough strife today."

The man in question chuckles darkly. "Well, I can't say I'm not a fan of a week-long binge at Valentine's. That place is *especially* dear to me."

Beau claps Jake on the back as Danny and Wolfe roll their eyes at Jake's signature dicking around. "A week at an exclusive sex club, Jake? *A week*? Your dick must be chaffed to the fucking bone."

Jake grabs the buttons on his jeans, popping them open. "I'll show you little Jakie is as irresistibly beautiful as always. Here, take a look—"

"Caden?"

Everyone freezes on the stage at the sound of my name, spoken ever so softly, and five heads turn in almost perfect synchronicity in the direction of the voice.

There, wearing a full-length green dress, her hair in slight waves down to her shoulders, and looking utterly too exquisite to be real, is the woman who has held my heart since I was eight years old. Her eyes are all for me, and as though they've been previously instructed, the four boys melt away, departing the stage in almost silence.

Her feet move closer, shifting the skirt of her dress to display a toned leg with each step she takes until, finally, she's within touching distance.

I don't waste one more second.

I close the gap between us, pulling her flush against me, and she releases a soft sigh before I claim her mouth with mine.

What begins as a timid touching of lips soon devolves into devouring one another with a voracity I didn't know I was capable of. It's addicting and humbling, and I never want to go another day without experiencing how this woman makes me feel.

Tonight needs to be perfect.

I break our kiss, cupping her jaw in my palms and stroke my thumbs across her soft, slightly flushed cheeks. "I missed you."

Her blush deepens as she tugs her plump bottom lip between her teeth before letting it pop free to smile almost shyly. "I missed you, too."

I fold my arms around her and tug her in against my chest as she encircles my waist with her arms, squeezing tight while I bury my face in her hair. Inhaling deeply, I feel myself fall into an almost blissful state as her comforting, inimitable scent embraces my senses.

"I have a surprise for you, Bam."

Ten

SUMMER

"We're *almost* there."

My smile is front and centre at the sound of Caden's voice. My fingers are intertwined with his as he tugs me across the unsteady ground.

"You said that ten minutes ago."

I can't keep my happiness from my voice, and he chuckles. "Well, this time I mean it, Bam."

Having whispered in my ear that he had a surprise for me, Caden had flourished a blindfold from his back pocket. He'd quickly spun me around, placing the material over my eyes before grasping my hand in his much larger one.

"Come with me." He urged me forward, and I went trustingly, because if there's one thing I've realised in the last couple of days, it's that despite telling myself otherwise over the years, I still trust this man more than anyone on this planet.

And I internally kick myself for ever allowing myself to believe the worst. To believe what I now know were lies, or at the very least, half-truths.

My trust appears to be paying off as my flat sandals step onto a firm surface. We've not long disembarked from what felt like a golf cart, having driven slowly for maybe five minutes.

Coming to a gentle stop, Caden squeezes my hand softly. "We're here. Don't move, okay?"

He lets go of my hand, and I hear him move around the area, his footsteps almost as loud as my joyful heartbeat.

Suddenly, I feel him at my back, unknotting the material behind my head. "Three…two…*one*."

At his last word, the blindfold falls away, unveiling my somewhat blurred surroundings.

I blink rapidly, allowing the world to come into focus around me, and when it does, my stomach swoops as goosebumps travel the length and breadth of my body.

We're on a small dock overlooking a lake that's been lit by no less than a thousand Christmas lights hanging from the nearby trees. There's a blanket with two dozen cushions of varying shapes and sizes, all in assorted pink hues. And to one side, there is a bottle of what appears to be champagne chilling in a cooler alongside two glasses.

Caden wraps his arms around my waist, tugging me back against his toned body as he rests his chin on my shoulder.

"Do you like it?"

I suck in a breath, trying to rein in my galloping emotions lest I fall to pieces. Another inhalation dissipates the frog in my throat, though I still don't trust myself to speak. Instead, I nod, my vision once again blurring, but this time it's the moisture in my eyes that's the issue.

This man with a heart of gold, who clearly wants to give me the world, deserves so much more than what I'm doing to him.

It's with that guilt gnawing at me that I turn in his embrace, grasping his face between my palms to hold his eyes intently.

"Caden, I don't deserve this. I need to be honest with you now, okay?"

His brow furrows, and he blinks solemnly before nodding, allowing me to continue.

"It goes back to…to…to *then*."

Archer emerges from the river, dragging an unconscious Caden as Layla and I watch on in horror. Dropping his twin to the ground with a thud, Archer kneels beside him, checking his airways before commencing CPR.

I rush forward, dropping to my knees to seal my mouth over Cade's while pinching his nose as I blow air into his lungs at Archer's instruction.

Time seems to stop until suddenly Caden begins coughing, and Archer turns him onto his side to allow his brother to expel the river water from his battered lungs. The coughs wrack his body and seem to go on for an age.

"Layla!"

When Archer barks her name, Layla comes closer. "Run to the house and call an ambulance. Tell Noah there's no need to call our parents. Cade will be fine."

Layla loiters there, staring at Archer with confusion running riot in her icy blue gaze. "But, Arch—"

"I said fucking go*!"*

At his bellow, Layla rolls her eyes before turning and heading back in the direction of the house.

"I'll go with her."

Archer turns to face me. "You've got a promise to keep, little deer."

I can feel my eyes blow wide with incredulity at the insinuation in his tone. "What, now? Can't I just make sure—"

"I upheld my part of the bargain. Now it's your turn."

Archer speaks the words with such ease and with an utter lack of emotion that my blood turns to ice in my veins. "Archer, I will uphold my end. Later. Once I know your brother will be okay."

"Has he fucked your ass yet? Layla hates when I take her ass."

I inhale sharply, but he lays an unconscious Caden back on the grassy riverbank and continues as though he's not heard me. "I think you'll like it. You've got fire in your belly. Layla's ice cold inside…"

"Archer, I agreed to—"

His eyes snap to mine, and his impassive demeanour shatters as he snarls. "I don't care what you agreed to. I'm taking something he loves, and he'll never get it back."

I blink rapidly. "I don't understand. You can't just take me away from him. We're in love, Archer. We're going to get married when we're old enough."

I tilt my chin defiantly at that last bold statement, feeling the truth of it in my very bones. But Archer cocks his head to the side, his eyes dropping down the length of my body before slowly returning to my face.

"Oh, little deer. Don't you see? I have you exactly where I want you. The game of Truth or Dare. The GHB that Layla gave our Cade here means he'll be out for quite a while—he probably won't even remember what happened today."

His eyes flash with delight while my breaths come in short bursts. My mind is whirring to catch up to everything he's laid out before me.

"Daring him to swim so that you'd beg me to save him…" He laughs, his smile similar but oh-so different from his twin. "You both *played right into my hands. And now you're here, alone, and ripe for the taking. The same way Caden here took everything from me. Oh–I know we share. Our mother made sure of it from an early age. But Caden here is the golden child. He pisses sunshine and farts excellence—the boy can do no wrong."*

He snorts darkly before rising to stand, and my knees almost buckle when a bolt of fear roots me to the spot.

"It's all because he was so sick when we were little. Almost died from blood poisoning…pity he hadn't."

I shake my head in bewilderment. "Caden almost died?"

Archer presses his lips together in a semblance of a smile that looks more like a grimace. "Yup, he sure did. Stole all their attention and then stole all their love, leaving me in the fucking cold. If it hadn't been for Layla…she's the only person who ever loved me—or as close to love as her parents ever taught her."

He steps forward, one foot then the other, and his grimace turns into something else entirely. His eyes take on an almost manically gleeful look that scares me to the core.

"But you*, little deer, are the one thing my brother loves more than anything or anyone else. A blind man could see that he thinks you hung the fucking moon, as well as all the stars in the damn sky. So, when I fuck you—when I steal that pussy he thinks is his—that love will be tainted. He'll* never *love you the same way he did, and I'll have ruined his life the same way he's ruined mine."*

I swallow roughly as he comes even closer. "Please, Archer. You don't have to do this. I will sleep with you willingly…I'll explain to Caden—"

He barks a laugh. "That's where you're wrong. I'm going to fucking ruin *you. I'm going to hurt you so bad that you won't be able to stand his touch or the touch of any man. It's the only way to make sure he can never have what he wants."*

My hand moves of its own volition, flying out to strike him harshly across his smirking face, and as his head snaps to one side, I spin on my heel to run. But he's too fast.

He reaches out, grasping my long hair in his fist, jerking me back, and my scream pierces the air around us.

"Not so fast, little deer. The fun is just getting started."

His words at the top of my spine are the impetus that my adrenaline needs to fight back. I pull my head forward just enough that I can throw it back with force. The back of my skull connects with his face, and I see stars from the impact.

Archer reels backwards. "You fucking bitch. *I think you broke my damn nose!"*

I stagger forward, shaking my head and blinking repeatedly to dispel the dizziness that threatens to consume me. My feet find purchase on the flower-covered meadow beneath me, and each step I take is easier than the last until, after what feels like an age, the earth has steadied.

Glancing back, I can see Archer is holding blood-soaked hands to his face, but despite his wounded state, his eyes scream violence and unhinged hatred. As he lets his hands fall away, a huge gash across his brow, with another across the bridge of his nose, is revealed.

"You're fucking dead now, little deer. I'll kill you for that."

And the look on his face makes me believe every word, so I turn and run as fast as my shaking legs can carry me. My heart is in my ears, but even louder is the sound of his feet on the long grass, closing the gap between us. He's almost upon me when I veer sharply to the right, heading closer to the river, desperate to put the water between us.

He's bigger and stronger, but I'm the better swimmer.

I make it to the water's edge and dive in, kicking as though my life depends on it.

Because it does.

The splash behind me tells me he's followed me in, but between the swift slowing current and my superior ability, I put the much-needed space between us, reaching the Mill in under two minutes.

"Give up, little deer."

Archer's shout behind me makes me kick my legs even faster, and soon, I've rounded the bend in the river just beyond the Mill. When I'm out of sight, I edge towards the riverbank and pull myself out before ducking into the nearby foliage.

Holding my breath, I lay amongst the overgrown grass and brambles, thorns ripping through my delicate skin, but I don't make a sound. If he finds me, I have no doubt in my mind that he's mad enough and clearly troubled enough to do more than just physical harm to me.

Less than a minute later, I hear him swim by, humming the song he'd penned for Layla at the beginning of the summer. I don't let out my breath until I'm sure he's out of sight, and then I flop over onto my back, exhaling a sob as my adrenaline crashes with a bang.

Tears track down my face, pooling in my ears as I stare at the beautiful blue sky above me. My heart pounds so hard beneath my breastbone I fear it might just explode as I grip my locket in my fist, praying for it to help centre me.

I focus on inhaling and then exhaling.

Slowly.

Evenly.

And before I know it, my eyes flicker shut as I fall into a deep, trance-like sleep.

Eleven

CADEN

"When I came around, I trudged back upriver through the daisy meadow opposite the old Mill and into the field of wildflowers. You were there, surrounded by emergency responders. Layla and Noah too, but Archer…"

I swallow roughly, finding the lump in my throat impossible to swallow around.

"He was nowhere to be seen until…until he was found not too far from where I'd hidden. I would have saved him if I hadn't zoned out—I swear to you, Caden…I swear…"

Summer drops her hands from my face, tearing her tear-filled eyes from mine. She tries to step backwards, but I hold fast to her upper arms.

"Caden, please. Let me go."

She refuses to meet my eyes, so I gently shake her, making her look up. When she does, the pain in her expression forces the air from my body in the space of a heartbeat.

"Summer, just wait—"

"No!" Her cry fills the night around us, echoing across the lake and beyond. "Don't you *see*? It was my fault he was in that river. I hit his head. He was disoriented, and he drowned as a result. It was *my* fault. I *killed* your brother."

Her breath catches on a sob, and that opens the floodgates so that all I can do is gather her in my embrace, waiting until she's ready to hear what I have to say.

To say her story has floored me doesn't even come close. The idea that Archer, the brother I have spent half my damn life hero-worshipping, had not only concocted but *enacted* a plot so vile, it makes my skin crawl.

He *drugged* me.

I almost fucking *drowned*.

He *attacked* Summer…

A shudder ripples through my body when I think of how she must have felt. How she's lived with this for so long, alone and so far from those who love her.

Anger follows rapidly on the heels of my distress. Anger that Archer had gotten what he wanted. He'd taken her from me; the life that we should have lived together had been stolen out from under us.

I want to scream and shout. I want to drag him back from the beyond to ask him what the fuck he was playing at. The fact that I'll never get the answers I so desperately need frustrates me even further as I seethe over his most brutal betrayal.

Once Summer's soft cries have eased, and I've reined in my own heightened emotions, I bring us further onto the dock towards the cushioned space.

"Let's sit, Bambi."

She allows me to ease her to the ground, where I settle in at her back, holding her close against my chest. Her breathing has calmed slightly, though she's trembling like a leaf.

"Summer…I'm sorry that all of this happened to you. I—I'm sorry you've had to live under such guilt for *so* fucking long. But I need you to hear me when I say this, okay?"

She nods as she turns her face to rest her forehead against my cheek, her gentle breath ghosting across my neck.

"It's *not* your fault my brother is dead. It was a tragic accident. There's no room for blame here."

"You don't blame me? I—I don't understand, Caden…."

As she trails off, I feel a tremor run the length and breadth of her body, and I pull her impossibly closer, needing more than anything to take this pain from her. To kick my brother's fucking ass for doing this. To rail against time itself until it allows me to somehow reclaim the fifteen years that we've lost as a result of that wretched day.

"It wasn't your fault. Trust me."

Silence envelops us for a long beat until her breath ghosts across my jaw when she whispers, "*There's more.*"

My stomach dips at her barely audible words, but before I can answer, there's a whistle through the sky on the far side of the lake, followed by a long bang.

We both jump, spinning our heads around just in time to see the first flash of colour explode in the night sky. Red, followed by yellow, then green. The entire night is lit up around us in a haze of fireworks, just as I'd planned, and I remember my reason for bringing her here tonight.

Summer gasps as a hesitant smile plays around the edges of her mouth. "Wow! It's like Independence Day back home."

And that's when it hits me. We've been given a second fucking chance. That's exactly what this is.

"Maybe that's what today is here, Bam. Maybe today is the day we shake off the shackles of our past and focus on our future, yeah?"

She turns to face me, fresh tears glistening in her eyes. "There's so much more you need to know, Cade. The reason I came back..."

I cut her off when I physically hoist her from between my legs to spin her around to straddle my lap.

"I love you, Summer St James. I have loved you almost my whole damn life, and I'll love you until the day I die, of that I'm absolutely certain…I don't care about what took you away from me or what you've done while you've been gone. You're here *now*, and there's only one thing that matters to me…"

I trail off, reaching up to cup her cheek in my palm while my enraptured gaze holds hers captive.

"Do you love me?"

SUMMER

My breath catches on a sound somewhere between a sob and a gasp.

This conversation is *not* going the way I had anticipated. In the slightest. In all the years since I'd moved to the States, I had known beyond a doubt that if I'd ever come clean to a member of the North family, they would call the authorities.

Hadn't I been told as much?

I glance around, half expecting to see blue lights flashing and instead find the twinkling lights dancing across the sparkling lake. The fireworks have ceased, but that fact hadn't even registered in the mess jumbling around inside my head.

Caden's eyes hold mine; the intensity in his deep blue gaze—the pure love that ripples from his every pore, cleansing me with his honest goodness—astonishes me.

"Cade…I don't deserve you. I don't deserve to call you my beloved—or to be called yours. You don't understand—"

He cuts me off, sitting forward at the speed of light so that our chests are flush.

"Answer the damn question, Bam." He bends closer until his lips brush off mine.

"Do."

He presses a kiss to the corner of my mouth.

"You."

He snakes his tongue out to draw it slowly across the seam of my lips as butterflies stir to life in my stomach.

"Love."

Sliding his hands up along either side of my body, his palms fit around the nape of my neck, tugging me forward to take my mouth with his. I part my lips without hesitation, and his tongue caresses mine once, then twice, before he pulls back to rest his forehead against mine.

"Me?"

The answer shines from my face—I can't hide it. I don't want to hide it any longer.

"I do, Caden North. I love you so much. I never stopped loving—"

He slams his mouth back down on mine as a deep-seated groan is torn from his chest. It reverberates through me, stirring a myriad of feelings to life within me. Feelings I've only ever felt for this man, long before I knew what they were.

I kiss him back with everything I have inside of me, both

grateful that we're one big step closer towards there being nothing hidden between us and anxious that once he hears the rest of the tale—and precisely *why* I'm here—he may want nothing further to do with me.

We kiss for hours, or perhaps it's minutes. Time is insignificant as I take what he so freely gives to me, pushing everything else out of my head and deciding that, for the first time in fifteen fucking years, I'm going to have something solely for myself.

I'm the one who deepens the kiss, crushing my body against his as I shift up along his jean-clad legs to press myself against the swelling hardness beneath me.

His groan of desire sends a shock of arousal straight to my core, and I thrust my hips harder, seeking friction.

He rips his mouth from mine, panting heavily against my stubble-swollen lips. "Unless you want me to fuck your pretty pussy right here and right now, I'd stop if I were you."

One side of my mouth twists upwards as I rock against him once more. "I already told you, Cade. You talk a big talk, but I don't think you can walk—oof!"

Even faster than before, he's hoisted me up to spin us around so that I'm underneath him. He's somehow managed to flip my long skirts up, exposing my pink satin panties beneath, and his palms grip my hips so tightly I know he'll leave marks behind.

I suck in a breath when he grinds his pelvis forward so that his hard cock hits all the right places.

He smirks down at me. "Told you, Bam. *With ease…*" he trails off, leaning forward to take my mouth once again with his. Tongues undulate against one another as our fully clothed bodies find a similar rhythm as our mouths.

He kisses me into a frenzy, and I strain against his delicious weight poised over me, needing to be closer. My nails dig into the hard contours of his upper back, tugging him impossibly closer, and he rocks his hips harder against my heated centre.

I break the kiss to throw my head back in abandon as Cade continues the torturous rhythm while nipping and sucking the exposed skin on my neck. His attentions drive me deliriously higher, and his grip on my hips slides around to give the cheeks of my ass a rough squeeze.

My moans fill the air around us as he drives us higher and higher until I can barely stand it.

I grasp his face between my hands, pinning him with a look of desperate desire and longing that will never be sated. "I need you. I need you *now*, Cade."

His nostrils flare as his jaw tics. "I—I want it to be special, Bam. When we finally come together again after *so* long. I want to make it special for you."

My heart palpitates inside my chest as I let my love shine from within. "Oh, Cade. Don't you see? It's *always* been special between us. Every kiss, every touch…every moment…I remember and cherish every single one. *Where* has never mattered, Caden North–it only mattered that it was you. And me."

I press a chaste kiss to his mouth, and then whisper across his lips, "*Together*."

His eyes flicker back and forth between mine before he bends to kiss me softly, his eyes still intent on mine. The love in his eyes sets my soul on fire, and I'm blown away to think I've been without this—without *feeling* like this—for the last fifteen years.

I break the kiss, pressing my forehead against his. "Love me, Caden. It's been so long since I felt your love. I forgot I could feel like this."

"Like what, Bambi?" His question is a whisper ghosting across my kiss-slick mouth.

"Like your touch brings me to life in a way I'd thought long dead."

His brow creases slightly, and he sits up, tugging me with him so that he can look me straight in the eye. "I know the media spin a certain…narrative, Summer. I—I want you to know I went along to those sex parties; I lived the life expected of the lead singer of one of the biggest bands on the planet. But it's all spun to *look* a particular way…"

He trails off, glancing to the side, so I palm his cheeks, pulling his gaze back to mine.

"Cade, I don't care what happened since I left. You lived your life. Your decisions have no bearing on us here and now. You don't need to explain—"

"There's only been one other since you." His words tumble out of his mouth like he couldn't get them out quickly enough, and I draw my brows together in confusion.

"Do you mean…" I trail off, struggling to find the words. "There's only been…your wife?"

"*Ex*-wife. And yes, that's precisely what I'm saying. A handful of times, if that, and all thanks to a little pill that helped my…lack of a boner."

My eyes have blown wide open, my jaw almost hitting the dock as I take in the man before me. His honesty, his trust in me… but the killer is the shame I see lurking beneath the surface.

"I don't see *any* lack of a boner here, Cade."

His lips quirk upwards. "This week is the first time in fifteen years that I haven't needed to medically induce a hard-on, Summer. Do you know what that does to me?" He tugs me forward to press a kiss to my forehead and another to my nose before whispering across my lips. "Do you know how that makes me *feel*?"

I dart my tongue out, encouraging him to open his mouth to me, and although I'm the one to instigate the kiss, he's the one to take it to the next level. His silken tongue caresses mine gently with just the right amount of pressure, and it takes next to no time before I'm losing the run of myself again.

He pulls back, peppering my face with butterfly kisses as he whispers between kisses. "Summer, you are it for me."

He kisses my nose. "You always have been. Your soul understands mine."

He kisses one cheek, then the other. "When I'm with you, the world feels right. It's the *only* time it feels right."

He kisses my jaw, nipping slightly to send a shiver through my body. "I'm done being less because you make me so much *more*."

Pulling back, he locks his gaze with mine. His deep blue eyes are almost black in their intensity, and my heart rate kicks up a notch before he speaks.

"But you need to understand me, Bam…when I drive this cock..."

He stops to palm his blatant hardness through his black jeans.

"Into this tight little pussy..."

His eyes move down, and he makes me jump when he reaches between us with his free hand to lightly slap the obvious wet patch on my pink panties.

"Then you belong to me." He shifts his gaze back up to meet mine. The level of possession in his face does something to my insides, and when he speaks again, something inside of me snaps.

"When I re-claim your body, you're mine. *Forever*."

Twelve

CADEN

Summer's face is a kaleidoscope of emotions as I lay everything on the line.

She needs to know exactly how much I'm *in* this. Not only that she's the sole owner of my heart, but by re-claiming her body, I'm taking possession of her damn soul.

She's always been mine. As I've always been hers.

And I send up a silent vow to the heavens that nothing will separate us ever again.

Ever.

Reaching up to unbutton the first…second…third button on her dress, the swell of her tits comes into view and my dick pulses uncomfortably against the confines of my jeans. She shifts one arm, followed by the other, to allow the dress to fall from her shoulders, pooling at her waist as she bares herself to my hungry gaze.

She pops the front clasp on the blush pink bra she's wearing, shrugging out of the straps and dropping it to the dock. Her nipples immediately harden like little bullets in the cool night air, her pale skin pebbling with goosebumps as my eyes greedily soak in each and every centimetre of the perfection exposed to me.

Desire is swimming in her big brown eyes as I unbutton the first two buttons of my shirt, reaching behind me to tug it over my head. Once my chest is exposed to her fervent stare, she rises to her knees, her dress hugging her waist where she's not loosened the fastenings.

Her gaze caresses my flesh as she takes in the changes the years have wrought on my body.

"These are so beautiful."

She brushes her fingertips across my chest and along my toned bicep, where a full-sleeve tattoo resides. My skin tingles everywhere she touches me, and my eyes roll back in my head under an intimacy that I've never forgotten, but have sorely missed.

The intimacy of being one with the person you love.

"I got my first on my eighteenth birthday."

I can hear the sarcastic laughter in her voice. "Surprise, surprise, Mr Impatient."

Opening my eyes, I watch her as she touches every part of my exposed chest and arms. Her fingers feather across my skin, alternating with her lips when she bends forward to drop closed-mouth kisses across my chest. I wait until her hands slide down along my forearms to hold my own. Then, raising our joined hands between us, I slip my left hand out of hers to show her.

"This was my first."

Her eyes focus on the side of my left ring finger where, just below the knuckle, I have an inked miniature silhouette of Bambi, the Disney doe-eyed deer behind her nickname. She raises glistening eyes to mine.

"You've been with me every day, Summer. *Every. Single. Day.*"

"Oh my God, Caden."

Her visible pain claws at my heart, and I opt for sarcasm to soften the blow I've unintentionally delivered. "I was teased mercilessly for years; I'll have you know, Bam. My ego took quite a blow—"

My words are cut off when she launches herself into my arms to wrap herself around my waist, pressing our naked chests together. Our mouths fuse, and my heart swooshes to life, pounding with such force it hurts.

Palming her cheeks, I tilt her head to deepen our kiss. Our tongues undulate slowly and in a way that sets my entire body aflame. My need to feel her coming on my cock, as she did earlier on my hand, consumes me, dictating my every move.

As we kiss, Summer's delicate hands come between us to frantically tug at the opening of my jeans. She makes short work of unzipping me before sliding her palm inside my underwear and along my hard length.

I groan raggedly into her mouth, the friction of her palm almost my undoing. I'm well aware that she makes me feel like a horny teenager, so I quickly toe off my trainers, kicking them to one side. I'm so focused on her that I don't give a flying shit when I register a splash somewhere in the distance.

Instead, I hook my thumbs into the waistband of both my jeans and my boxers to peel everything down my legs before kicking them to one side as well.

When I move to unfasten the remaining buttons of her dress, Summer stills my searching hands when she drops to her knees, looking up at me with wholly innocent big brown eyes that are simultaneously alive with deviancy.

Without saying a word, her hand reaches out to encircle my cock. Her other hand cups my heavy balls, sending a bolt of lust straight through me. She draws her hand slowly up and down my length before darting her tongue out to swirl the tip inside her hot mouth.

She glides her mouth down my cock, almost to the base, taking me so deep I feel like I'm going to blow here and now. Working her way back to the tip, she paints her tongue in a figure-eight motion before repeating the action, slowly down into her throat and back up.

Her eyes are on me the entire time, and I'm edging closer and closer with no restraint at all as I watch her watch me through hooded eyes.

"This will finish too quick if you keep that shit up, Bam."

She smiles around my cock, taking me even deeper, as though up for the challenge. I reach out and caress her jaw as I growl, "Have it your way then."

Sliding my dick in and out between her plump lips several more times, I begin to pump my hips forward. My hands tangle in her wavy hair of their own volition when she hollows her cheeks and sucks hard.

As my head falls back, I hiss out a breath through my clenched teeth, sliding my cock as far as it can go before she gags around my length. My eyes find hers, and I hold her in place for a long beat before allowing her to retreat, her saliva shining on my dick in the twinkling lights.

After another minute, I pull my hips away altogether, and she moans in frustration, her hands reaching for my retreating thighs. "Oh, please fuck my mouth. Come in my mouth, Cade."

I almost nut on the spot, but hold it together by a thread. "Not a damn hope, Bam."

Bending forward, I reach beneath her, grasping a perfect ass cheek in each palm to lift her from the blankets as she shrieks in delight.

"Cade!"

My laugh is a rumble through my chest as I lay her onto her back, kneel between her silky thighs, and fist the material of her pink panties roughly. "How about you fuck my mouth instead?"

And at that, I stretch the material until the seams rip. Summer's gasp makes my cock pulse almost violently as I toss her ruined panties to the side, letting my eyes feast on the bare pink pussy before me.

Her lips are soaked with her arousal, and her clit is just begging to be touched as it pulses under my intent gaze.

"*Shit,* you're so beautiful it hurts."

My words are reverent as I place my forefinger along the seam of her slit, gathering her honeyed essence and swirling it around the hard bundle of nerves. She whimpers softly, the sound making my hard-on almost painful.

I move backwards, giving myself space to lie on my stomach, pressing my cock into the blankets beneath us before settling myself before Summer's thighs. Without waiting another moment, I drop my mouth onto her sex, eating her like a man possessed.

A groan erupts from my chest as she drops back, arching her chest forward and feeding me more of her pleasure. I take my time, licking and sucking her engorged clit before using my thumbs to part her lips, entering her slick channel with my tongue. Spearing it in and out, I tongue fuck her until she's thrashing against me, holding my hair firmly in place as she rides my mouth.

Her glorious abandon is one of the most beautiful sights I've ever witnessed.

And when I pinch her clit between my thumb and forefinger, her arousal coats my tongue as she cries her pleasure to the twinkling darkness surrounding us.

SUMMER

I feel Caden move up my body as I descend from my pinnacle. The world seems disjointed, and my body is trembling from the force of my orgasm when he slides his tongue into my mouth.

Despite the orgasm I'm still recovering from, my body flickers to life again at the taste of myself on his lips. He grips my hips tightly, bringing my ass down against his knees as he leans over me. My pussy is still throbbing my release when he notches his hardness against my core.

"You're the air I need to breathe."

Immediately, I'm transported back to our first time, when he'd said the same words, and my throat constricts, making speech impossible.

He remembered.

"And now that you're in my world again, I can finally fill my entire body with you."

He pushes himself inside ever so slowly, clenching his teeth as my eyes fall shut.

"Like I'm going to fill *your* whole body with all of me." Gritting his words, he circles his hips, opening me up, and I gasp at the incredible sensation of his thick cock working its way inside me.

"Fuck, you're *tight*."

He works me slowly, his dick stroking every vibrant nerve ending inside my slick pussy.

"And even after all this time, Bam…" He strokes his thumb

across my wanting clit, lifting me higher. "You still feel like *mine.*"

And suddenly, out of nowhere, another orgasm bears down on me.

"Oh fuck, Cade. I'm coming. You're making me come."

My hips rise to meet his, seeking his welcome intrusion as he grips both my hips tight, thrusting forward to seat himself fully and deeply as I convulse around him.

"That's it, baby, *yes*. Give it to me. Come all over my fucking cock."

His hips move at a piston pace to wring every last drop of my orgasm from my ravaged body. I wrap my legs around his waist, locking them at his ass, where I hook my ankles together, holding him tight against me. Deep inside me.

"Oh Christ, your pussy is dripping. Do you feel that? Do you feel how wet you are for me?"

His eyes hold mine when one of his hands leaves its place on my hip to pinch one of my nipples between his thumb and index finger. "Do you have another one in you, Bam?"

Without waiting for an answer, he slides the hand from my breast around my side, cupping my shoulder to bring me up, level with him. I gasp when his length hits even deeper inside of me.

Cade smirks as he closes the distance between our mouths. "Oh yeah, you're good to go again, aren't you?"

I nod as his lips brush across mine, snaking my tongue out to lick his plump lips. He slams our mouths together when he grips the nape of my neck, holding me steady as he shatters me with a kiss I feel in my bones.

As he takes my mouth and makes it his own, he fucks up into me, slowly at first, but gaining momentum as the kiss goes on. I press myself down onto him, harder and harder, until the sound of our skin slapping and our bodies coming together echoes through the night around us.

Fisting my hair, Cade rips himself away to hold our faces apart. His mouth is slightly open, his breathing coming in short bursts with a sheen of sweat across his brow, trickling down the side of his face.

My eyes roam across his passion-filled features before returning to his deep blue gaze. The raw intensity held there is like nothing I've ever seen before. The *love* in his eyes consumes me.

I am the tinder, and he is the spark. Fire within me builds as unbound love and years of denied passion blaze to life between us.

Slowly, he reaches lower, his eyes never leaving mine, to unerringly find my clit.

His words ghost across my lips on an exhalation. "Come with me, Bambi."

And suddenly, the world is aflame.

Cade groans his release in my ear and the feeling of his hot cum shooting into my pulsing core sends me spiralling straight into another smaller orgasm. My pussy clenches around him, and his still-hard dick continues to twitch inside of me as we both descend from the highest of heights.

His head is resting on my shoulder as I stroke his long locks when a breeze across the lake makes me shiver against him.

"That's it, Bam. Let's get you clothed."

I hug him tighter, reluctant to let this moment pass. "I'm okay, Cade."

He pulls away. His eyes hold mine as a smile slowly grows on his lips.

"Well, I'm cold as fuck. You had the foresight not to get fully naked."

We chuckle for a moment before he begins to fix my dress. I've just slid both arms into the sleeves when movement on the lake catches my eye.

"Hey, what's that?"

Cade follows my line of vision, squinting to make out something floating in the lake a couple of feet away from the dock.

I realise what it is before he does, and before I can help it, my body is shaking with unrestrained laughter.

"What's so funny? What is it?"

It takes another minute before I can compose myself enough to answer him.

"I hope you can drive barefoot because *that* is one of your trainers."

Thirteen

CADEN

My phone rouses me from a deep sleep. A deeper sleep than I've had in the longest time, and it takes a moment to register two things that bring a self-satisfied grin to my face.

First, there's a naked Summer in my bed. And I take immediate advantage of that fact by pressing the second thing against her luscious ass.

"Mmph. Too early."

I chuckle at her morning grumpiness. "Some things never change, Bam."

Pressing a kiss between her shoulder blades, I roll over to the nightstand and grab my offensive phone.

DAD

Your mum and I will be at the Palace today, Cade. Smash it, boy!

I smirk, re-reading my dad's text before my phone chimes with another one.

NOAH

Am I correct in assuming you checked into 45 Park Lane last night?

Rolling my eyes, knowing precisely where this is going, I shoot my scandal-phobic manager a quick reply.

ME

Yes. And your spies are right. Summer's with me.

I drop my phone face down on the nightstand and roll out of bed, heading straight for the shower.

"Cade?"

Summer's soft voice halts my feet, and I turn back to find her facing me, now on my side of the bed.

"I love you."

Her words strum the chords of my heart more beautifully than any music ever could, and I'm filled with unbridled adoration for the woman before me. I march back across the floor and bend over her to push her backwards, my thumb and index finger gripping her chin.

"Loving you is as effortless as breathing, Bam. I could never stop."

I press our lips together as her hands come up to cup my cheeks in her small palms. When I pull away, my phone chimes once again, and I tilt my head to the side, rolling my eyes.

"It's going to be one of those fucking days, isn't it?"

She nods, her eyes lighting up mischievously. "Sure is looking like it."

Her own phone chimes on her nightstand, and a smile quirks

my lips. "Ah, but the universe is ensuring we're in it together."

Dropping her hands from my face, she sits up in the bed, and the sheet falls to expose her tits. I'm entirely unable to stop myself from bending down to peck both pert nipples. "Good morning, girls. May I say, you're looking particularly succulent today?"

Shoving me off with a giggle, Summer shakes her head with a broad grin and reaches for her phone as it chimes a second time. "You are such an idiot sometimes."

I stand and wink down at her, my hair falling forward over my face. "An idiot who will love you forever."

She presses her lips together to try stifling her smile, and my shit-eating grin widens even further as she shoos me away. Her words follow behind me. "I'll be in shortly, *idiot*."

My loud laugh echoes through the bathroom when I toss a wink over my shoulder before closing the door.

After relieving myself, I flick on the shower and quickly check my phone again. I can't stop myself from scowling deeply at the email that pops up.

Sender: Fletcher Knowles
(fletcher.knowles@knowlesfamilylaw.com)

Recipient: Caden North
(caden@north.com)

Caden,
I'll cut to the chase. Layla has checked out of rehab. My sources tell me that she's staying in London at the moment. I will keep you appraised of any further developments, and you shall be the first to know if she attempts to reach out.

Perhaps you may want to consider a restraining

> order in that case. If yes, please let me know immediately so that I can have the paperwork ready to go.
>
> I'm sorry to be the bearer of bad news. I do hope you can enjoy the rest of your day.
>
> Regards,
> Fletcher

My stomach churns at the worst possible timing. The very last thing I want is to spook Summer now that we seem to be getting back on track.

I duck into the shower, tipping my face up so the warm water can cleanse me of my negative thoughts. Long minutes pass before I can push all thoughts of Layla from my mind, and I realise Summer never made good on her word to follow me.

Finishing my ablutions, I reach around the glass door of the shower and grab a towel to wrap around my waist before heading for the bedroom. I crack the door an inch but catch sight of my dripping hair in the mirror, so take a couple of steps back to pluck a smaller towel from the rack.

When I reach for the door handle to enter the bedroom, I stop suddenly when I hear Summer speaking.

She's on the phone.

I move to close the door to give her some privacy when she gasps.

"So what did Ophelia say to him?"

There's silence for a long beat before Summer laughs. "Oh, hell yes! You, my friend, are a genius. What would I do without you and my beautiful goddaughter, hmm?"

She laughs again at whatever the response is before bidding the caller farewell.

I step into the room as she tosses the phone on the bed, her hand flying to her breast in surprise.

"Christ, you scared me. I didn't realise I'd been on the phone as long as I was."

I shrug, grinning. "I grew up with four sisters—and you—so I'm well aware that once a female starts into a conversation on the phone, time ceases to exist."

Laughing, she reaches for a pillow and tosses it in my direction, but it falls short by more than a little bit. She huffs in exaggerated disgust when I deadpan. "Your aim is as bad as ever, I see."

"You're a wanker, Caden North. My aim is just fine. The pillow was a little heavy…"

She trails off, pressing her lips together until they're almost white as she tries and fails miserably to hide her smile.

"Heavy, my foot, Bambi. Now, move your fabulous ass. We have a big day ahead!"

She nibbles her bottom lip between her teeth before pouting. "But I don't want to shower alone."

I shake my head, grinning as I drop my towel to close the distance between us. She squeals when I heft her over my shoulder.

"I suppose I can lift the sponge for you, Bam."

Her bare ass gets a playful swat as I turn and march back towards the shower.

"After all, it might be too *heavy*."

SUMMER

The Great Hall at the Alexandra Palace is bursting at the seams. The atmosphere is electric, and from our viewpoint, Bella and I have the best seats in the house.

Off to the side of the stage, hidden in the wings, we will have a perfect view of Misdirection's performance.

The massive curtains are currently closed as the backstage staff, alongside the event staff, set up everything for the show.

Caden and his bandmates are in hair and make-up backstage, so it's just the two of us. I've missed her in the twenty-four hours since we were last together, and the knowledge that I've fallen head over heels for this little girl rocks me to my marrow.

"There's Dad!"

Bella's delighted cry pulls me from my thoughts, and I raise my head to lock eyes with—

Holy shamoly!

The five band members have clearly finished their prep and are making their way towards us, but *shit*, I only have eyes for Caden *fucking* North.

He's dressed in tight black distressed denim jeans that leave very damn little to the imagination. The material hugs his muscular thighs like it's been sewn onto his body, and all I can think of is peeling it *off* as soon as I possibly can.

Bella jumps from my lap and throws herself at her father, a simple act that makes my heart clench almost painfully in my chest.

His dark grey t-shirt, complete with a plethora of rips and tears, stretches as he embraces her. The leather jacket over the t-shirt is seriously sexy, and his feet are bare, as is his preferred style of performing.

When I'd first read that in an article, I'd laughed so hard, remembering how his mother, Clary, used to go mad at him for constantly losing his shoes when we were growing up. We never had any problem finding *one*. The issue was that he always ensured we'd never find the matching pair.

He'd spent our childhood barefoot more often than not.

I stand to join them, and Cade's gaze meets mine. When he sees my focus, he flashes his white teeth, and I can't fail to mirror him.

I pop a brow pointedly when I feed him his words from this morning. "Some things never change."

"Touché, Bambi. Touché."

"Hey, Bella Baby!"

My smile freezes on my face, and my heart stutters when I hear the voice of the man who took me into his home after my parents had died. The man who had taught me how to swim, an act that ultimately saved my life but cost him a son.

Sensing my train of thought, Caden slides his hand down along my arm, slipping his warm fingers into my fist. He leans closer as they descend on us and whispers softly.

"I've got you, Bam. *I've got you.*"

My vision swims with my almost overwhelming emotions when Cade steps to one side, allowing the two newcomers to move into my line of sight.

Sutton North, the drummer for Jupiter's Fallen and my father's former employer. By his side, as always, stands his wife, Clarisse. My old guardians, who I'd left without a word.

My dad had spoken so fondly of how he'd grown up with Sutton. He'd loved telling stories of their boyhood and enjoyed the time spent in his old friend's company. Despite owning his own driving firm with over two dozen employees, he'd *always* made time to drive Sutton himself when he was in the city.

It was that friendship and trust that had compelled my parents to name the Norths as my wards, never expecting to need to utilise that favour. However, the universe had other plans.

"Summer?"

Clary's feminine lilt finds my ears as her sky-blue eyes—eyes identical to the person I love most—meet mine. Hers are brimming with tears, as are my own, and suddenly one—or both—of us move so that I am enfolded in her warm embrace.

Sobs wrack my entire frame when I feel another pair of arms encircle me from beside Clary.

"You're home, Summer. Welcome home."

Sutton's low voice in my ear makes my knees feel as though they might just go from underneath me if it weren't for Clary's strength keeping me upright. The three of us embrace for an age, and it isn't until the silence surrounding us fills my ears that we draw back.

Every single person—the Misdirection band members, all the backstage crew and volunteer staff from the charity, and every other bystander—has stopped in their tracks. Dozens of eyes are fixed on us, but the only ones I have eyes for are Caden, whose own eyes are glistening with tears, and Bella, who looks slightly confused.

She propels herself forward, wrapping her arms around my legs and squeezing tight. "That's *my* Summer-hero. Get your own, Mimi and Pop!"

Sutton and Caden throw their heads back in a move that looks timed to shout their laughter skyward, and just like that, everyone returns to what they'd been previously doing. The surrounding hustle and bustle soon buzz around us, allowing me to take in these two people I have dearly missed.

"Summer dear, I can't quite believe my eyes." Clary speaks first, her voice hoarse with emotion. I swallow around the lump in my throat as unadulterated affection warms my chest, and I struggle to find an appropriate response, but Caden steps in, ever my saviour.

"You can catch up later, Mum. It's almost time to kick things off, and you two still have to get to your seats."

She shoos her son away. "Oh, pish posh, Caden. We'll sit here by our girls."

However, Sutton, ever the observant one, hooks his hand through the crook of his wife's arm and gently tugs. "Come on, Clare-Bear. We can catch up soon."

His wife looks about to object until her face lights up with a bright smile. "What an excellent idea, Sut." Her eyes shift to her son's. "Family dinner tomorrow afternoon before you go back to Cambridge, and I won't take no for an answer."

She raises a brow pointedly when Cade opens his mouth, an objection clearly on the tip of his tongue. He closes his lips, pressing them together when he catches sight of her expression before nodding quickly. "Of course, Mum. Wouldn't miss it."

The corner of her mouth twitches before she nods and grasps my hands in hers. "See you tomorrow, lovely."

She squeezes my hands, letting go to press a kiss atop Bella's head before allowing a grinning Sutton to lead her in the direction of their seats.

"She still wears the pants, I see."

I side-eye Cade with a wry grin as he rolls his eyes good-naturedly. "Any man worth his salt knows his woman *always* wears the damn pants, Bam."

Fourteen

CADEN

The atmosphere in the Great Hall is electric. All five of us can feel it. The high of performing doesn't get old, but the high of performing for the two people who hold my heart has me soaring to new heights.

I belt out the last couple of lines of our latest hit, "Hollowed Heart," giving it everything I've got.

The applause can only be described as raucous as we jog from the stage to chants for another encore, one which I'm only too delighted to give them on behalf of my beautiful Bug. I can't wait until she hears what's coming up, despite the boys telling me I'm soppy.

Jealous wankers.

"Daddy!" Bella's eyes are wide as she takes me in, trying desperately to tug her ear defenders from her head. She bounds from her seat to jump straight into my waiting arms, and I swing her around, much to her delight.

I pull one side of the headphones back carefully, and she flinches from the onslaught of noise surrounding us from all angles. "You having a good time, Bug?"

She nods up and down profusely, her eyes growing wide as saucers. "It's super loud!" Then she covers her mouth with a little giggle. "Can you sing the sunshine song, please?"

I try to stop the enormous Cheshire Cat grin that threatens at her words from consuming my face, but I'm defeated.

I knew changing the setlist for Bug's first concert was the way to go!

"You got it!" I set her down to pull her small hand into mine and lead her back over to a smiling Summer, but Beau beats me to it, hoisting Bella atop his shoulders.

Her squeals of glee draw the eyes of everyone nearby, with Summer smiling broadly when Bug begins telling Beau all about her new Poppy and Branch obsession.

With my daughter occupied for a moment and in my friend's capable hands, I march straight for Summer, catching her hand to tug her closer to the stage, so we're hidden amongst several huge speakers.

Once we're out of sight, I cup her face in one palm and use my other to grip her jean-clad ass to pull her closer so that our bodies are perfectly aligned. I tilt my head to one side and brush my lips off of hers.

She gasps as I tease her with my lips and tongue until soon, she's panting against me. "Christ, Caden. Just kiss me, for crying out loud."

Instead of answering, I move and slowly glide my tongue inside her mouth as she expels a groan of sheer satisfaction. She sucks my tongue, making my dick stand to attention, despite the fact that we are mere feet from the side of the stage.

Anyone could see us.

The thought turns me on more than I'd have thought. I take both her ass cheeks in my hands and pin her to the tall speaker, encouraging her to wrap her legs around my waist, which she does without further prompt.

Her heat is pressed perfectly against my own hard-on at this height, and I'm unable to stop the slight thrust of my hips. She whimpers into my mouth when I rock ever so slightly against her.

"Cade, stop, Cade."

She pulls back, and her eyes are glassy, pupils blown wide. Her hair is messed up just enough to give her a delicious, *just been fucked* look.

"We can't get carried away here, Caden." She swats at my shoulder before arching a brow and rolling her hips into mine. "Someone might see us."

And that's when it happens.

The speaker opposite us teeters over, falling to the floor with a crash. I sidestep the commotion, only to step onto the stage and into view, Summer still attached around my waist.

The chants of the audience dim almost immediately to be replaced at first by one camera flash, then another, and another. Within seconds, we are blinded as camera flashes from the media outlets on site, followed by a low hum of questions that rapidly turns into a free for all.

Beau, ever the cool-headed one, strides onto the stage, his sheer bulk blocking us from the worst of the bombardment.

"Show's over, folks. Thanks for supporting Katherine's House today. See you next year!"

I edge to the wings, where my parents are waiting with Bella and the rest of Misdirection, and chuckle as I whisper in Summer's ear, "Guess the world knows now."

SUMMER

Having finally made it back to 45 Park Lane in convoy with the rest of Misdirection, we bid the guys farewell.

"Come on, Bug. Lights out time."

Caden hefts a dozing Bella higher onto his broad shoulder, and I move to follow him, only for Jake's voice to call out behind us.

"Could we talk for a minute, Cade?"

We glance back at the same time, finding a worried Jake. Caden's forehead puckers as he glances between me and Jake before I step forward to ease the semi-sleeping bundle from his arms.

"Go. Your friend needs you."

"Are you sure? I can—"

Grasping his shirt collar with the hand I'd been resting on Bella's back, I jerk him closer. "I'm sure, *idiot*." Pressing my lips to his in a short meeting of mouths, I step back and shoo him away. "Now, go. We'll see you later."

Without waiting for a response, I head directly towards the elevator and moments later enter our suite with a sound-asleep blonde fairy snoring softly against my shoulder.

Rather than place her in the spare room of the suite, I deposit her in the middle of the super king-size bed in the master bedroom, only slipping her shoes and socks from her feet before tucking her in beneath the pristine white sheets.

She flips over onto her stomach, one knee bent with her face pressed into the pillows, and my heart rate quickens when it reminds me of times long ago in a smaller bed with a boy who slept the *exact* same way.

The similarities are uncanny.

Leaving my phone, some Chapstick, and a bottle of water on the nightstand, I kick my trainers from my feet and make short work of freshening up before bed. I've just slipped into pyjama shorts and a vest and am climbing beneath the sheets when I hear Caden enter the suite.

"Bam?"

His whisper rings through the silence of the suite, and I call back quietly. "We're in here."

He appears at the door, his frown melting away to allow his eyes to shine intensely when he spots Bella beside me, hogging the middle of the bed.

Moving closer, he deposits his shoes beside mine before peeling off his clothes.

"I'm just going to have a quick shower." He makes a show of sniffing himself, and I snort a laugh when he mouths the words, "I reek."

Still smiling, he moves off to the bathroom, and I grab my phone to ensure it's on silent so I don't wake the cherub beside me.

There are a handful of notifications, including a couple of DMs from friends on Instagram and an email from Lucia in HR at Rogue reminding me that I'd missed a shift, meaning Vaughn neglected to tell her about my trip.

Typical Vaughn.

I swipe everything away, deciding to mail Lucia tomorrow with an apology. The DMs can wait.

I scan through several text messages from Anna, none of which require my immediate attention.

I'm about to drop the phone onto my bed when a text chimes through.

JESSE

Are you in London?

Shit, shit, shit.

I'm mulling over my response when another text flashes up.

JESSE

I know you are. You're all over the internet!

My bottom lip suffers as I weigh up my options. I really wanted to have this conversation face-to-face, so I go the avoidance route.

ME

Don't believe everything you read.

The reply is instantaneous.

JESSE

You're being GROPED by Caden North! What the actual fuck?

I grit my teeth, refusing to rise to the bait.

ME

I will explain all when I get back to New York. It's not how it looks.

The dots bounce for several long minutes until a simple thumbs-up emoji comes through as Caden enters the room. He's dressed in a pair of tight grey Calvin's that should be considered indecent and nothing else. His long hair has obviously been towel dried, and not very well at that, as it drips along his bare torso.

He spots my line of vision and chuckles quietly. "Well, you've put Bug in our bed, Bam, so it's safe to say you cock-blocked yourself tonight."

My face splits in an enormous smile when he climbs beneath the sheets on the far side of Bella, and I respond with the honest truth. "Being like this with you both makes me happy. There's very little I'd change about this moment."

Caden leans across Bella's head to press a closed-mouth, open-heart kiss to my mouth before retreating to his own pillow. "I'd change nothing, Bam. Not a damn thing."

I settle on my own pillow, my smile faltering for a second before I catch it and hold it in place as my heart dips at my half-truth.

There's plenty he'd change if he knew everything.

Having only packed enough to last two days at most, I was surprised to awaken to find Caden must have organised for someone to bring an array of outfits from the racks above the recording studio back in Cambridge to our hotel.

When Bella spots a case of clothes for herself, she dances with delighted exuberance, twirling and spinning as she sings at the top of her lungs.

"She loves that 'Perfect For Me' song from *Trolls*, doesn't she!"

Caden chuckles indulgently. "Oh, you have no idea. She likes when I sing as Branch so that she can *harmonise* as Poppy." He opens his eyes impossibly wider to deadpan behind his hand. "But like the other women in the North family, her musicality *sucks*."

I snort, knowing exactly what he meant. When we were growing up, Caden's older sisters, Bree and Rachel, identical twin sisters five years his senior, along with Alyse and Cassidy, three and one year older, respectively, had tried their best. Singing lessons, a barrage of different musical instrument lessons, recitals at the house, anything and everything Clary could think of.

Nothing had helped their tone-deafness and sheer unmusicality.

But Sutton had put paid to their attempts when he called them a bunch of 'screaming banshees' and ran from the room shouting that the harbingers of death were upon us.

The rest of us laughed so hard. Even Clary hadn't been able to help herself.

My smile is bittersweet at the memory. "She's not *that* bad, Cade."

It's his turn to snort. "She's not far off. Though, in fairness, my many nieces have the same affliction, so she's got company, at least…"

The little lady in question twirls over closer. "Do you like my singing, Summer-hero?"

"I *love* it, Curly. Sing to me again."

Caden kicks his leg out to knock his bare foot off my shin, and the action makes me snort-laugh, though I barely manage to cover it with a cough when Bella side-eyes me.

"Can you be Branch, Dad?" She sidles up to her father, who presses his lips to her forehead, and then nods his head. When she turns to me, she furrows her little brow in thought before a smile lights up her face.

"And you can take a turn being Poppy, Summer-hero!"

Her face is so completely triumphant, and I can't deny her, so I just nod whilst plastering a smile on my face.

"Can I have your phone to record it, please?"

Her indulgent father nods, handing her his device, which she takes and works easily to unlock, opening the camera app with ease. The recording button sounds quietly.

"Okay then. Three, two, one…go!"

Caden starts with Branch's opening, and I'm so caught up listening to his beautifully husky voice that I almost miss Poppy's entry until Bella shakes my leg.

Inhaling deeply, I harmonise quickly with Cade, as we used to so many years ago, and within moments, the world has faded into the background. Our voices fill the room. Eyes fixed firmly on one another. And all too soon, the song is at an end, and Bella's enthusiastic applause resounds around the room.

And as the little whirlwind flies about the room, breaking into her own version of "One More Time," Caden reaches between us to slip a loose strand of hair behind my ear. His eyes hold more depth than any words we could exchange. His eyes hold fifteen years of loneliness, regret, and longing, but more powerful than that, his eyes hold hope.

And that's what saddens and scares me in equal measure, because hope is the most dangerous thing either of us could possess.

Fifteen

CADEN

Ford is more than happy to drive us to my parents' house whilst regaling us with tales of his family back in Texas. It's exactly what's needed to keep Summer adequately distracted as she laughs along with my Bug.

My father has used Holloway Security Detail, or HSD, for as long as I can remember. Ford's dad, Jasper—or Jas, as he goes by—managed all the security for Jupiter's Fallen throughout their career. He'd sent Ford, his twenty-two-year-old son, on a mission to prove his worth, to head up my own security last year, and despite his youth, we'd clicked immediately.

Henry's wife, Liv, says he's got an old head on young shoulders or something like that.

He's finishing up on a story I've heard about a million times about his mother complaining that he needs to settle down. His delivery is dry as fuck, his timing spot on, and it never fails to make his audience crack up every single time.

"And what did your mother say?" Summer's voice is heavily accented with amusement, and she sits forward, waiting for Ford's answer.

The man in question chuckles, catching my eye and then Summer's in the rearview mirror.

"She said that all men can be saved by the love of a good woman, so to make sure to bring my good woman home pronto because I'm getting more rotten by the day."

Summer's laughter fills the car as Bella looks at me with big, sad eyes.

"Aww, Dad. Ford's mum hates him, too."

My heart stops, and I blink stupidly a handful of times. My mouth feels like sandpaper, and when I open it to speak, nothing comes out. Ford's eyes in the rear-view speak volumes.

"Oh, Curly-Sue. Your mum loves you, Bella." Summer gathers Bug in the crook of her arm. "It would be impossible not to! You're the best girl in the whole world."

Bella's lips lift as she snuggles into Summer, turning her big blue eyes up to question, "Do *you* love me, Summer-hero?"

Without missing a beat, Summer drops a kiss on my daughter's upturned nose. "Of course, I love you, Bella. I love you *very* much."

"I love you too."

The easy affection between Bug and Summer is both stomach-churning and heart-warming. To think my girl barely received so much as a hug from her mother but is so openly loving towards Summer blows my mind.

Ford's gaze holds mine in the rearview mirror as we turn onto the lane entering North property. He winks once, nodding in the direction of the girls before returning his eyes to the road and his mouth to the telling of tales from his familial ranch in Texas.

Summer is so caught up in comforting Bella that she doesn't notice where we are until we've pulled into the driveway.

"We're here!" Bella extricates herself from Summer's hold and climbs across the car seats onto Ford's lap. "Come on, come on! I need to show you my treehouse."

With an indulgent chuckle, Ford hoists a tittering Bug into his arms and heads in the direction of the massive playground my parents installed for their abundance of granddaughters.

The mammoth double front doors are thrown open and, almost identical to the day Summer first arrived here, my four sisters spill from within, racing one another to be the first to reach the car.

Bree, the oldest North sibling—by a whopping fourteen minutes that her twin Rachel will mention at any given opportunity—outmanoeuvres the rest, tugging the door open in record time.

"You're here. You're here!"

She reaches inside the car, physically tugging a wide-eyed Summer from the backseat, much to my amusement.

Cassidy, who's a year older than me, arrives next, followed immediately by Rachel, with a very pregnant Alyse finishing the line-up while muttering under her breath, "Fucking animals."

Bree draws Summer into her embrace, with my three other sisters following suit, and I'm wholly unable to stop myself from wrapping my own arms around the five strong, beautiful women I grew up with.

It's Dad's voice that rouses us from our long overdue moment of quiet gratitude.

"Dinner's almost ready, folks. Come on in and wash up."

As he returns the way he'd come, my sisters and I relinquish our hold on a smiling Summer. She looks around our group before tapping her index finger to her lip in playful contemplation. "Who's cooking?"

"Dad."

The girls answer in unison, confusion marring their features, until my hand snakes out to grab Summer's, tugging her along behind me as we race towards the house. There's no doubt in my mind that she's thinking what I'm thinking.

"Last one in cleans up after dinner."

Their retorts are muted as we've already crossed the threshold, and we don't stop until we've breathlessly entered the kitchen, only to find my parents bickering comically by the oven.

"I told you, it said three hours on a low heat after searing, not an hour on the max. It's not the same thing, Sutton. I'm telling you."

Mum is sitting at the kitchen island that is strewn with every dish, pot, and pan they possess with her arms crossed, a look of complete disbelief on her still stunning features.

On the marble countertop, there's a large cooking tray with a positively gigantic slab of beef, or at least I think that's what it's supposed to be. It's hard to tell, considering how blackened the outside is.

"I guarantee you, baby, the inside will be just fine. It's like a delicacy. Barbecue charcoal flavour on the outside and all moist on the inside."

My mum pops a perfect brow at him.

"Come on then, Mr Know-It-All. Carve it, and let's see who's right."

This banter between my parents is so commonplace that I can't help but smile as we watch them interact with their signature teasing.

Placing the back of my hand over my mouth, I lean toward

Cass, who's just entered the room, and murmur, "Fifty quid on Mum being right."

She snorts before deadpanning, "No deal. Mum's always right, which you well know!"

Dad makes a big job out of sharpening his carving knife before adding more mess to the already destroyed kitchen, much to the amusement of everyone watching. Then he carves the meat slowly, a look of triumph on his dark features until bright red blood begins to ooze out onto the countertop.

Cutting his losses, he casually places the carving knife into the overflowing sink before turning to face his audience, an enormous shit-eating grin on his face.

"Who wants pizza?"

Dinner is a usual North family get-together–which is to say, it's fucking manic.

Following Dad's announcement, Mum swept everyone outside to the oversized patio that had been made for just such entertaining. Two large rectangular tables run side by side, one clearly decorated for the next generation of Norths, and the adult table has already been set up with a platter of nibbles and wines.

Mum brandishes the menu for a local pizzeria, and within five minutes, the order has been placed for no less than ten pizzas and a plethora of sides.

When Summer excuses herself to use the bathroom, I'm met with twenty questions from my sisters until Mum comes to the rescue.

"Bugger off, girls. Leave your brother alone. It's rare that he comes to visit me."

"Fine!" Cassidy harrumphs, shooting me a look that tells me she's far from done with her line of questioning. "Come on, Lys. Let's check on the girls."

Alyse narrows her eyes at me, before following Cass.

Two down, two to go. And I have the perfect bait up my sleeve.

"Cass?"

She turns back, shrugging her shoulders. "What?"

"Bella's there with Ford if you'd—"

I'm cut off by the sudden movement of Bree and Rachel jumping to their feet, mumbling something about wanting to see Bella before speeding in the direction of the playground.

Mum chuckles beside me. "You are naughty, Caden Atticus North."

My chest rumbles with barely restrained laughter. "Well, we all know their weakness is checking out my head of security. Even their husbands are aware, so you can't blame me for using their flaw to my advantage…" I trail off and shrug, glancing around in search of Summer.

Mum places a quelling hand on my knee. "She's at the window in the kitchen, helping your father clean up."

I swivel in my seat to see just that. Dad and Summer standing side by side at the sink, laughing at some shared joke. My heart is simultaneously full yet empty at the same time.

All that missed time.

As much as I hate to even think it, I can't help letting the questions as to her whereabouts for the past fifteen years taunt me. And as much as I want to know, there's a part of me—currently, it's the bigger part—that is too afraid to ask.

Too afraid of the answer.

Too afraid that she has demons bigger than mine just waiting to come into the light.

Mum squeezes my leg with the hand still resting there and brings her free hand up to shove my hair back over my forehead.

"Caden. Baby." She exhales a heavy sigh before continuing. "To pretend that you can go back to the way things were before she left…well, baby, it's unhealthy. Not to mention impractical."

"I know why she left, Mum. It's not as…cut and dry as you might think."

She nods slowly, glancing over my shoulder and smiling at whatever Dad and Summer are doing inside the house.

"I'm so happy that she's back. And that you're in a good place. I just can't stop thinking of the decade after she'd vanished, baby. You were vacant. There's no other way to put it. You filled your time with travelling and God knows what. You weren't *you*. I just want to be sure *that* version of you won't make a comeback if she leaves again."

Any chance of a reply is cut off when Dad's voice bellows from behind me.

"Pizza's here!"

I'm altogether not sure which is more full–my stomach, after all that pizza, or my heart, from seeing my heart's desire back where she belongs.

My family welcomed Summer back into the fold with open arms; it was like she'd never left.

After being introduced to my eight nieces and discovering Alyse was due my ninth one in three months' time, Summer sat back in her seat with wide eyes. "Wow! You guys have been *busy*."

The girls laugh good-naturedly, and Alyse speaks up. "I'm having another two at the very least!"

"Rather you than me." Cass, mother of one and done, speaks up. "Girls are hellish. I can't deal with Rhiannon's mood swings." Her eyes blow wide dramatically. "And she's only five years old, for Christ's sake. Her teen years will be merciless, for sure."

Mum chuckles, nodding her head in agreement. "Teenagers, in general, are hard, love."

"But at least when it's a teenage boy, you're only worried about one dick. When it's a teenage girl, you've got to worry about all the other dicks!"

Dad's signature no-shits-given comment sets everyone off again.

Mum sobers first and indelicately opens a can of worms I'd have rather she left closed. "And what about you, Summer? Did you ever want to settle down? Have kids?"

I shoot my meddling mother a dark look as Summer blushes and nibbles furiously on her bottom lip.

"Mum, I think you—"

But Summer cuts me off before I can berate my mum. "Of course, I'd have loved to live that dream, Clary. A husband who adored me. A gaggle of kids to run me ragged. A home to call my very own. However…"

She trails off to clear her throat. Her eyes are serious, her face wistful. And my heart clenches painfully at all we've lost.

Her brow knits together, and she glances around the table to find all eyes on her. Visibly sitting up taller in her seat, she continues. "When something isn't in the cards for you, you learn to be grateful for the life you've been given."

Rising to stand, she pushes her chair back and plucks her handbag from the table. "Now, if you'll excuse me, everyone. I need to use the facilities."

The space is silent except for the sound of the girls eating at the kids' table as we all watch her leave with a stiff spine. Pride flows through me, followed rapidly by anger once she disappears from sight.

Twisting about in my seat, I round on my mother to find her shame-faced, but that doesn't stop me.

"What the *fuck* was that about, Mum? Was it really necessary to get your two cents in?"

I stand, pushing my chair back as I do, and allow my gaze to sweep around the table, taking in the various faces of my family. My sisters are varying emotions, from Rachel's anger to Cassidy's frustration to Alyse, whose face is tear-stained as she mumbles, "Damn hormones."

Our father is sat at the head of the table, sadness marring his beloved features. His big brown eyes are glistening with tears, and he rises to stand with a sustaining palm out.

"Sit, son."

I swallow roughly but do as he bids.

"I'll say this, and I'll say no more on the matter." His eyes scan everyone's faces, taking a moment to rest on each one of us before he continues. "That girl's reasons for living her life are her own. She was entrusted to me—to *us*—and somewhere along the way, I failed her. I failed her parents. I *won't* fail her again."

Mum stands and walks around the table to Dad's side. "Okay, Sutton. You have my word. I'll let sleeping dogs lie."

Dad nods, allowing her to help him back into his seat. His hands are trembling with anger. Perhaps it's frustration or even sadness. Either way, I'm thankful for his words, as I know now that there'll be no more mention of the past.

As we settle down to attempt to resume our family meal, Dad's phone chimes with a text. Then mine vibrates in my ass pocket, and like dominos falling, everyone's phones begin to sound with notifications. We glance from one another around the table, everyone wearing the same worried expression.

No one moves until my phone rings. I pluck it out to find Ford's name.

An ominous feeling fills my chest, knowing he's at the front gate, checking security footage with Dad's head of security, Thomas, from an attempted break-in at one of my parents' country properties last week.

I slide the button across and hear the commotion before I've even uttered a word. Ford's voice is barely audible over the din.

"Cade? Cade, I'm at the front gate. There's been a leak to the media that you're here with Summer. The hounds are at the gate."

I stand, pacing away from my watching family while cursing the fucker who leaked our whereabouts. We'd been fortunate enough to escape 45 Park Lane by using the staff entrance, thereby avoiding the circus outside the front door. "We can just use the entrance on the other side of the property. We can easily avoid them—"

"No, Cade. It's a whole lot worse than that. Layla's here. She's the one who leaked your whereabouts."

Fuck. Fuck. Fuck. How the hell did she *know where we are?*

"What does she want?" It's always been about what she can get, so she'll undoubtedly have a bargaining chip.

Ford's voice is clearer now, and I can only assume he's been able to move further away from the media onslaught. His words make my blood run cold when he speaks again. "She wants inside, or she claims she's got a juicy story about Archer and Summer that the media would love to get their hands on."

Sixteen

SUMMER

Having successfully escaped to the house following Clary's uncharacteristic passive-aggressive questioning, I'd sought out the sanctuary of my old bedroom. I can understand she wants to protect her son, but it still stings.

The fact that they don't know the whole story weighs heavily on me as I push my old door open to find everything is exactly the way I'd left it fifteen years before.

A sob catches in my throat. Both the culmination of defending myself outside and the sorrow I feel at finding my room to be kept in an almost shrine-like state.

My bed is made, and upon taking a seat on the old pink bedspread, I find it's freshly washed, meaning Clary and Sutton upkeep the space in my stead. The lump in my throat is almost too big to swallow past as my eyes rake around the room, finally landing on my old hiding place underneath the dressing table.

I'd found it quite by accident. A loose floorboard near the architrave, where I'd stored all my most valued items.

Before I realise it, I've dropped to my hands and knees to dislodge the board. It takes some nudging, but with a little persistence, it pops off.

There is still a multitude of handwritten notes from Cade and a couple from Layla. A pink and purple woven friendship bracelet she'd made for me when we were ten. The stubs from our first trip to the cinema. A pressed daisy from one of our many afternoons in the meadow talking about the lives we had compared to the lives we dreamed of.

Noise from downstairs hits my ears with force, and I unintentionally jerk upright, only to bash my head off the bottom of the dressing table.

"Christ!"

I ease myself out from underneath the table carefully this time, rising to stand while I rub the throbbing area on the back of my head. When I catch sight of myself in the mirror, I use my free hand to scrub it down along my make-up free face in an attempt to remove all signs of emotion. My red-rimmed eyes and flushed cheeks remind me of my annoyance at dinner, and I use both thumbs to wipe beneath my lower lids, brushing away all signs of my frustrations.

When something isn't in the cards for you, you learn to be grateful for the life you've been given.

Words that I've fed myself more times than I'd care to admit.

Words that drove my resolve to stay away.

Words that eventually strengthened my need to come back.

My phone chimes from the pocket of my maxi skirt, and I tug it out.

VAUGHN

Tut tut, sweetheart. I thought your trip home would see you flying under the radar, not trending on TikTok.

I narrow my eyes at my boss's usual ribbing before shooting him back a middle finger emoji.

Caden's raised voice downstairs draws my attention from my phone.

"What could have *possibly* made you think you'd be *welcome* here?"

Without conscious thought, my feet move from the room and towards the stairs leading to the foyer. Blood rushes in my ears, and my heart threatens to escape the confines of my chest when I stop at the bannister at the end of the hallway.

Gathered on one side of the foyer with their backs to me are Caden, Sutton, and Bree. All three stand tall, Sutton's and Bree's darker heads flanking Caden's blonde one as he bristles with anger, facing my old friend.

"I want to see my daughter, Cade. You can't keep me from my child." Her eyes are narrowed as she tosses her long poker-straight black hair over one shoulder before bracing her feet apart to stand her ground.

Caden's growled response sounds like it's been ripped from his voice box. "Over my dead fucking body, Layla. You need to go through the courts. I know your solicitor told you, so don't try to play dumb."

She opens her mouth to speak, hands flying to her hips in indignation, but Caden cuts her off before she gets a word out. "I'd never keep my daughter from her mother, but you need to prove you can be the mother she deserves."

He takes a faltering step forward, and when he speaks again,

I need to strain to hear his hoarse words. "I'm not blameless, Lay. I'll hold my motherfucking hands up there. I've always loved you. That's never been the problem. I was never *in love* with you, and that's on me. I'd have happily played my part to give our girl the life I had with a caring, loving family…but, *Christ*, after you exposed her to—"

"I never *exposed* her to anything, Caden. I kept her locked in her room. I fed her. Gave her water. She didn't lack for anything—"

"She lacked your *care*, or can you not *see* that?" Caden's words ricochet off the walls, and my eyebrows meet my hairline when his bellow hits me right in the chest.

Layla grimaces, her mouth down-turned, her body emanating pure vitriol. I move back towards the safety of my old room, but her eyes flicker upwards, spotting me, and a look of satisfaction overtakes her face.

She jerks her chin upwards, and the North's turn to follow her line of vision. "And I suppose you think *she* would be a better mother for *our* child, Cade?"

Tears sting my eyes at the animosity in her tone—not for me, but for her own child—and I can feel my nostrils flare as I inhale sharply.

As I blink rapidly in an attempt to repel the tears, my eyes zone in on Caden. He sends me a small comforting half-smile before turning back to his ex-wife. "It's not about who's better, Layla. It's about doing what's best for Bella. It's about keeping her safe. I can't trust you with her anymore. Not—"

Caden stops short when Layla throws her head back, laughing hysterically. While she's distracted, he exchanges a look with first Sutton, who nods. Then he turns to a stony-faced Bree.

"Tell Ford I said 'Tequila Sunrise.'" His sister nods, and then discreetly slips out of the foyer and into the kitchen beyond.

"You think your precious daughter is *safe* with that fucking *killer*?"

This is not how I wanted this to happen. There can be no return from this. Sutton and Clary will know that I am the reason their son is dead, and they *won't* be as understanding as Caden.

Hadn't that been at least *part* of the reason I'd left in the first place?

I'd been told in no uncertain terms that they'd press charges if they knew. Accident or no accident.

"Sutton, you do realise you've invited the woman behind your other son's death into the fold, yes?"

The man in question looks from his son to Layla and back again, confusion predominant on his features before his eyes find mine. I swallow harshly, holding his gaze, willing this man who was like a father to me to feel my regret.

"That's enough, Layla." Caden's voice is firm. Strong enough that it encourages me to pull my gaze from Suttons. To move my feet in his direction, seeking Caden's strength.

His forgiveness.

His love.

"Oh, I get it! She told you what happened, but she put her own spin on it. Is that what she's done?" Her eyes flick to mine. "Nicely played, Summer. Only took you fifteen years to come up with those *lies*."

And something inside of me snaps.

I square my shoulders and steel my spine as I continue descending the stairs with my eyes fixed firmly on my accuser.

"It's not your fault my brother is dead. It was a tragic accident. There's no room for blame here."

Caden's words from the night before the concert ring in my ears, and I believe them more with each step closer I get.

"Lies? Which part is the lie, Layla? The part where you *knowingly* gave Caden GHB, which caused him to almost drown? Or the part where you told me to fuck Archer so that he'd pull Caden from the river?"

Reaching the end of the stairs, I move past Caden and Sutton, embracing the me that has been fifteen years in the making. The me that's strong enough to do what I need to do, regardless of the personal cost.

"I'm not the meek girl I was back then. My emotions aren't so easily played as they were four years ago when I called you in desperation. You can't lie your way out of things this time, Layla."

I quirk a brow as her eyes blow wide at my insinuation, and I can feel the eyes of Caden and Sutton on me, waiting on me to elaborate. Except that *now* is not the time.

"You won't find me as easily manipulated this time, *friend*."

Layla takes a slight step backwards, and I smirk knowingly. "I thought we were friends, Layla. But being back here now has given me a perspective I didn't have then."

I drop my voice to a dramatic stage whisper. "News flash: I know you left Caden a letter on my behalf."

Her face freezes, and that's all the answer I need.

I'd suspected from my first day back, but now I know for sure. She'd been one of the only people I'd trusted the whole truth with, and she'd blatantly stabbed me in the back.

She tries to salvage the situation. "I didn't want him to pine over you, that's all. I wanted to ease the transition to being with me—"

"*You*!" Caden's low growl of disgust resounds through the foyer, and I turn to find his face mottled with barely restrained rage. "*You* left that letter? The one I pored over, cried over—the one that made me think I was a piece of shit for *years*, for no good reason?"

Layla flounders, and a sadistic piece of me rejoices. "Cade, I—I—"

The rest comes out, almost like word vomit. I hadn't meant to share this part, but after visiting my old room upstairs and reminiscing with those ghosts, I couldn't hold it back.

"The final icing on the cake was when she took a pregnancy test and said she didn't know if the baby was yours or Archer's. That…that was the night I left."

CADEN

Many times throughout my life, I've heard people tell me they've been angry enough to see red. I've nodded, smiled, and empathised, but I've never truly understood the meaning.

Until now.

Until I look at my ex-wife's face and see that the last fifteen years have been manipulation after manipulation. My mind flits back to the first night she crawled into my bed, consoling me after pulling the plug on a decade-long search for the woman I loved. We'd slept in each other's arms, and I'd thought that *maybe* despite all her flaws, I could fall in love with the woman she was underneath.

Because she understood my loss. And I understood hers.

Because maybe *together*, we could save each other from a lifetime of crippling loneliness. That I could save her from the nameless, faceless men she invited into her body in an effort to fill the hole in her soul.

That we could connect on a different level because I'd loved the person she'd lost, and she'd loved the person who'd left me.

Before I can march forward to do something I might regret, I feel my father's quelling hand on my shoulder. His quiet words of wisdom in my ear. "Take a deep breath, son. Think of how your actions could affect your little girl."

The wind rapidly goes out of my sails, and I can feel myself visibly deflate as Ford enters through the front door.

He smirks. "Tequila Sunrise."

Before he can deal with the Code Black, the front door is pushed open once more to admit an irate Noah Spellman.

That man can smell trouble, I'd bet my life on it!

"For Christ's sake, Sutton. Can you not control your fucking mutt?"

He turns to face me. His face is almost purple with rage. "What have I told you about media shitshows, Caden? It's going to take weeks before this insanity ceases. She needs to leave. She needs to piss off back to New York right the fuck now!"

Noah's eyes cast about the foyer before landing on Summer. She's standing there, arms folded across her chest, and a distinctly hostile look on her face. "I'm right here, *Uncle Noah*. Nice to see you too!"

The man openly blanches. "Holy shit, you haven't changed one bit."

Summer pops a brow, giving him a pointed look. "Oh, I think you'll find I've changed plenty."

It takes him a minute to salvage his wits, and Summer stares him down the entire time as he stammers. "I—I didn't mean—that's to say…umm—"

Paying him no heed, I stride towards Ford. "Get Layla out of here *now*. Under no circumstances should you allow her within a hundred yards of my daughter. Or me, for that matter. Because I won't be held responsible for what I'll do to her if I so much as glimpse her face unless it's across a courtroom."

I turn as Noah abandons his half-assed attempt of apologising to Summer to approach Layla like she's some fragile creature.

"Come on, Layla. I'll get you back to your hotel."

She allows him to tuck her beneath his sizeable arms, a frown marring her face as she takes in everyone in the foyer. Her gaze lands on Summer and stays there as she is led from the house while a plethora of emotions flashes across her features.

I move to Summer's side, clasping her limp hand in mine and squeezing softly in silent comfort. Layla's eyes move down to our joined hands, and her brow furrows at the sight right as she disappears from view.

Seventeen

CADEN

Once I've confirmed that Layla has left the property and is well on her way back to London, I look about to find Summer, to find only my father. Before I can ask, he answers my unspoken question.

"She headed back into the house a little while ago, son."

I can feel my body relax at the knowledge she's only gone inside. She hasn't disappeared.

My father claps his hand on my shoulder, stilling me when I move to follow her.

"I can keep what Layla said just between you and me, so don't worry on that front. But, son, could you please explain to me what Summer meant about your brother? I…I don't follow…"

He frowns, trailing off, and I heave an internal sigh of despair at having to be the one to tell him the truth of the matter.

Fucking Layla.

"Dad, there's a lot I didn't know about that day that has recently been disclosed to me. Through Summer."

He shakes his head in disbelief. "But Layla was there too. She's the one who got Noah to call the emergency services. She's the one who gave the statement when you were too high to talk—"

"That's just it, Dad." I cut him off gently, grasping his hands between my own. "I wasn't *high*. They—both Layla and Archer—gave me a date rape drug, knowing that it would affect my judgement. My memory. It knocked me out, and Layla went for help, leaving Summer with Archer."

His eyes move back and forth between mine. A heaviness in their depths I've not seen in many, many years. And I have to force myself to continue.

"And he attacked her. He—he said he wanted to take my love because I had stolen your love from him."

Tears fill my father's dark brown eyes. His face crumples, and I draw him into my embrace, holding tight as we both mourn not only the loss of Archer but the heart-breaking reason behind it.

Sibling jealousy, plain and simple, but Archer had covered his resentment with sarcasm and laughter–a trait I'd begun to use after his passing to cover my pain. To hide my grief.

I continue to tell Summer's story in part, leaving out much of Archer's deviousness so as not to tarnish my brother's mantle too much in our father's eyes.

"I can't believe we never saw it, Caden. I can't bear that he thought we loved him less than you or your sisters, for that matter. I don't understand…"

He runs his hands through his chin-length, more salt than pepper hair as he shakes his head. "What will your mother think?"

I freeze on the spot, knowing she can never know. My mum is strong, but losing her son almost broke her. The knowledge that he'd brought about his own death through some twisted scheme to try to ruin my life…

"No. You can't tell Mum. She can't ever know, Dad. She needs to keep Arch on that pedestal. She needs to remember the son she mourned. To tell her the truth now would be an unkindness."

Conflict flitters across his face, and for long minutes, I think he's going to tell me to piss off with my demands until he nods sharply. "You're right, Cade. She can't know."

I nod back in assent. "I'm just going to find Summer—"

"What did she mean about a baby, son?"

My forehead creases as I try to think about what he's referring to. I'd been so fixated on the fact that Layla had been the one to leave the letter I'd read at least once a day, every day, for the last fifteen fucking years that it takes a minute to replay the conversation in my head.

"The final icing on the cake was when she took a pregnancy test and said she didn't know if the baby was yours or Archer's."

Realisation dawns, and hot on its heels is even more grief. "Was she pregnant with Archer's kid?"

We take one another in for a long beat until I see a weariness enter my father's eyes, and I once again tug him closer into my arms so that we can offer the other comfort.

My father doesn't look his age typically, but right now, at this moment, he looks every inch of his seventy-seven years. Older even, and once more, I curse Layla for her fucking timing.

I hold my old man close for a long time until he slaps my back and clears his throat. "They'll be wondering what the fuck we're doing, son. Come on, let's find your mother."

When he slips out of my hold, he pats my cheek roughly, the way he used to do when I was a boy stealing chocolates out of his pockets. A loving gesture that he's not done in years, and I can feel tears sting my eyelids as a lump forms in my throat.

"How's about I find your mum, and you find Summer? I'm thinking she could use a hug right about now."

The lump in my throat swells massively at my father's thoughtfulness, so that all I can do is nod succinctly. He pats my cheek once more before walking in the direction of the kitchen, humming "You Are My Sunshine" under his breath.

I exhale a breath I didn't realise I was holding before slipping up the stairs in search of one Summer St James.

She's nowhere inside the main house, though when I check her old bedroom, I can see she took a trip down memory lane earlier. The hidey-hole underneath her dressing table is open, letters and mementoes scattered across the floor. All of them are familiar to me, as it had been the first place I'd gone to seek answers when she'd left.

I sit for a moment, sifting through pictures of us from age eight to sixteen in all manner of situations.

I stop when I spot a photo from her first Halloween with us, where she'd pleaded with me to be the Ken to her Barbie. I can't stop the grin that consumes my face as I take in how absolutely ridiculous I look in my Malibu Ken Bermuda shorts, sending blatant puppy dog eyes her way. Even then, I was helpless to deny her. Utterly head over heels for her.

I pack all the pictures up and stack them inside the box before picking up some letters, landing on one in particular. As I'm skimming it with a small grin on my face, I chuckle softly as I remember *exactly* what had happened that day.

My Bam,

Meet me in the foyer when everyone has gone to sleep. I have something I need to share with you, and I just can't wait till morning.

Always,
Cade

My grin turns into a full-blown smile as I refold the paper and tuck it back into the box.

I rise to stand, and my smile drops from my face. Having checked everywhere inside, I take a moment to stare out Summer's old bedroom window across the expansive property at the back of my childhood home, and like a bolt from the blue, I realise where she's gone to.

I race down the stairs and spill onto the patio, where my family is in quiet conversation. My mum turns to me with a sympathetic pout. "You okay, love? I heard—"

She stops suddenly when I expel a breath, unable to deal with her inherent empathy right now. Only desirous of one thing at this damn moment in time.

"Can you guys please keep an eye on Bug for a bit? I think Summer has gone for a walk, and I…I—"

"*Go*, Cade." My mother stands and rounds the table until she's in front of me. Her eyes are sad. Her face is drawn. But her voice is firm and filled with support. "Bring her home, my love."

I press a kiss on her cheek and scan the area to spot Bella and her cousin Mia happily playing with some Hot Wheels before catching Dad's eye and nodding in silent understanding.

Before I take off across the patio, I kick my shoes off, chuckling lightly when my mother tuts at my bad habit. Then I take the steps down onto the manicured lawns two at a time and vault over the hedgerow that marks the boundary between the lawns and the landscape beyond.

As I speed through the long grass, a smile overtakes my face when I let my mind drift back to that night. To the night Summer had just turned fifteen. The night we'd had our first kiss.

My heart rate kicked up a notch when I heard the creaky floorboard at the top of the stairs.

Please be Summer!

From my hiding place in the shadows, I can just about make out a white figure descending the final steps, landing on the black-and-white tiled floor with silent bare feet.

"Cade?"

I breathe a sigh of relief at her loud whisper and step forward into the dim light spilling in through the glass door from the full moon in the night sky.

"I'm here, Bam."

Her mouth turns up in a smile that makes my heart beat faster and my palms sweaty. I take a deep breath to calm my latest heart palpitations, though this time, my heart isn't racing because I'm afraid. It's racing because of what I'm about to do.

Something I've wanted to do for the longest time, and tonight I'm going to lay myself bare for her.

"What did you want to show me?" She tucks a pale strand of her almost waist-length platinum blonde hair behind her ear as her big Bambi eyes find me and hold me a willing hostage in their depths.

"It's not something I wanted to show you. It's…" I trail off, suddenly scared.

What if she rejects me? What if I ruin our friendship?

She widens her eyes when I don't continue, then nods encouragingly. "It's okay, Cade. You can tell me anything. You know you're my absolute favourite person in the world."

Her words bolster my flagging confidence and propel me forward so that we are toe to toe.

My breaths are her breaths. We're so close that I can feel the warmth of her body penetrate my cold skin. I peer into her eyes, searching for that big, beautiful soul of hers.

The soul I fell in love with the first day she arrived at my house as Dad's ward. I'd taken one look into her expressive brown eyes and lost my soul to her.

I was hers from that day. I'll be hers until my last day.

She inhales sharply, and it's then I realise I've spoken aloud.

My eyes blow wide, and I open my mouth to take it all back, fearful that I've come on too strong, too fast, but before I can utter a word, she palms my cheeks to tug my mouth down to meet hers.

She presses her lips against mine for the space of a couple of heartbeats before she pulls back. Shock and embarrassment are front and centre on her beautifully flushed face, and I can't help smiling like the cat who got the motherfucking cream.

"I—I'm sorry. I—" She steps backwards, slowly edging towards the stairs, and before I can gather my wits, she's gone, racing for the safety of her bedroom.

I'd stood at the foot of the stairs for more than an hour, running my finger back and forth across my lips, reliving her soft lips pressed to mine no less than a million and one times.

The grandfather clock had chimed, pulling me from my thoughts, and I'd trudged up to bed with a smile on my lips and hope in my heart.

It had taken weeks to get her to even look at me properly again, but I'm nothing if not persistent.

A movement in the distance catches my attention, and I narrow my eyes when I spot her about five hundred yards away, kicking at the wildflowers beneath her bare feet.

Picking up the pace, I quietly approach her as I allow years of repressed feelings to bubble to the surface.

I'm just about done with her running from me when things get hard.

It's time to show her that this is it. We are end game. And she's never running from me again.

Eighteen

SUMMER

Coming here was a mistake. Being back is twisting me up inside. And the guilt is damn near crippling.

You should have just told him why you were here in the first place, idiot!

I kick at the blanket of wildflowers underfoot, mad at the world, but mostly mad at myself. Furious for thinking I could have an ounce of happiness, a handful of halcyon days before returning to the unfairness of my reality.

Emotion clogs my pores, making me feel uncomfortable in my own skin for the first time in a long time.

Coming face to face with Layla. Hearing her unconstrained malevolence, and having her announce my sin before Sutton with such ease, I feel completely exposed.

And on top of everything, the overriding newly acquired knowledge that I was so fucking *stupid* to leave back then. Foolish to believe her lies. Naïve to put my trust in the worst person I could have. Someone who never looked out for anyone but themselves. I see that now.

I should have come back when Layla had sent me a letter to say she'd lost the baby. I should have fought for my future—for *our* future.

For the future we all deserved.

Instead, I'd felt ashamed. Everything was so messed up by that point.

And more than that, I'd felt betrayed that Caden had been sleeping with her in the first place, though now I know that was also another lie.

So many mistakes. And plenty of blame to go around.

But I'm seeing now that despite blaming him for years, Caden is the innocent one in all of this. I'd thought I was righteous. I'd thought I was justified.

And the day he'd married Layla, I'd been vindicated.

But I was so, so wrong. And there's only one way to set things right.

I'll tell him. I'll lay everything out on the table. Tonight.

"Summer!"

My spine stiffens when I hear Caden's voice at my back, and I pick up my pace, not yet ready for the conversation that needs to take place.

I need to pretend for a while longer. Just long enough that I can hold tight to these last few days in the lonely years to come.

He calls out once more, and I duck into the tree line, heading further into the underbrush of the surrounding countryside. I can hear his feet pound the earth behind me, and I break into a run as I shout over my shoulder.

"Leave me alone, Caden."

I break out into a field of daisies that runs parallel to the river, just opposite the old Mill, and I stop dead in my tracks, remembering the last time I'd run towards that same body of water.

My hesitation gives Caden enough time to catch up to me. He grabs my bicep, pulling me around to look at him. We're about a foot apart, both of us panting from exertion. His eyes find mine, locking me in his deep blue gaze, and for the longest time, we stand unmoving.

His thoughts are clearly visible on his face, and the knowledge that I am about to break his heart all over again makes the air around us feel unbearably heavy.

I open my mouth to speak, needing to shatter this illusion before I allow us to fall any deeper—though I know in my heart that it's already too late—but he reaches forward to slap his palm over my mouth. He holds me firmly against his hard body with his free hand wrapping slowly around my throat, and my body surges to life, even while my brain tells me this madness needs to stop.

My hands wrap around his wrists, trying and failing to remove them from my body, all while our eyes are locked firmly on one another.

After allowing me to struggle against his hold for a couple of minutes, Cade increases the pressure of his hold on my neck and leans forward until his lips are brushing the shell of my ear. He chuckles when I shiver visibly in his hold before whispering words that make my heart begin to pound.

"Stop."

He nips my ear, and I make a noise somewhere between a shriek and a moan stifled by his hand over my mouth.

"Running."

Then he soothes my lobe with the flat of his tongue before swirling it around the sensitive skin where my jaw meets my neck. I inhale sharply as my lower stomach clenches in desire. A wave of heat washes between my thighs when he presses his clearly aroused hardness against the flat of my stomach, making me squirm deliciously.

"From *me*."

He sucks my neck and removes his palm from my mouth, allowing me to suck in a gasp before he takes my lips with his.

His tongue slowly dances with mine, sending tiny, potent sparks of heat to every corner of my body. I hum to life beneath his touch, my heart quickening in my chest despite my mind telling me to stop this recklessness. To tell him the whole sorry story. To fall at his feet and beg forgiveness.

But I don't. I can't—or perhaps it's because I'm selfish enough that I *won't*.

Instead, I stop fighting and move my hands from his wrists, allowing them to rest on his muscular chest.

His agonising kisses give me as much pain as they do pleasure, and it's not long before I can't take it any longer. My fevered fingers fly to his belt buckle, undoing it with ease.

His sharp inhalation as he continues to make slow love to my mouth is followed by a growl as his palm tightens almost painfully around my throat. I rip my mouth from his, moving as far back as his grip will allow before grabbing the hem of his t-shirt.

"Take it off. Take it off *now*, Cade."

His nostrils flare as he lets me go to do as I've demanded, going a step further to peel his jeans and underwear down his legs until he's naked before me. His cock juts out, standing tall, and I almost grin when I see the pride for his self-achieved hard-on play across his face.

"Please. Oh please, fuck me now. I need to stop *feeling*. I need it *all* to just stop." I'm unable to disguise my anguish, and it frustrates me even further as I lift the hem of my paisley maxi dress. "Make it all stop, Caden. Make it go away."

He drops to the bed of daisies at my feet with his heated gaze holding me as his willing prisoner. "I don't want to fuck you, Bam. I want to *worship* you."

I choke back a sob as he edges closer on his knees, his face saying more than a thousand words ever could. The depth of his adoration, his utter love, takes centre stage, and I'm helpless before him.

Even on his knees at my feet, this man holds all the power. He owns me. It's as simple and as complicated as that.

He catches the hem of my strapless vest to push it upward, but my hand snakes out to tug it from his grasp, stopping him.

"No." My tone is firm, brooking no argument.

His head tilts to the side questioningly as confusion dances across his beautiful face. "I want to see you, Summer. Please, let me see all of you."

I play with the hem of my vest, wholly conflicted. I'm aware that time has a way of dimming your memories of those you love. However, time has not changed Caden's body. If anything, time has perfected what our teenage years had but hinted at.

Caden's body is 6 feet one inch and 180 pounds of sheer magnificence. There's not an inch to pinch. He's ripped without being overly so. He's lean but well-defined, a sculptor's dream.

I've been covered either by clothes, darkness, or both before now. I've ensured it. My body isn't the same as it used to be. I'm more rounded; my curves are more predominant. I have the body of a woman. A woman who's earned the right to own her flaws, and I'm proud to be who I am now.

But he remembers me from *then*. And there's a part of me that's terrified I won't live up to the memories.

"I don't look like I used to, Cade. Maybe parts of me do, but I'm not…I don't look—"

Moving at the speed of light, Caden rises to stand, grasping my jaw in one palm while sliding his other hand around my waist to pull me up against his body.

"Do you not *feel* what you do to me, Bam? Do you not realise I haven't been able to get my dick up for anyone that's not *you*? That I fell in love with your soul at eight years of fucking age, and souls don't age. They *remember*. They hold tight to the memories of how you felt, of who mattered. I didn't fall in love with your face or your body—even though, *fuck*, both are magnificent."

He drops his forehead to mine, his breath ghosting across my trembling lips as I barely hold it together.

"I fell in love with your soul. I fell in love with your *heart*. Christ, Bam. You should *know* that you alone have always made this heart of mine beat."

A single tear slips from my eye, only for Caden to lean forward to catch it on his tongue.

"Now show me nirvana so that I may worship at your feet, Summer. Give me this so that I can have something of my own because, *Christ*, I gave you all of me so fucking long ago I forget what it's like to be whole."

The absolute honesty in his voice is my undoing.

Gripping the hem of my vest, I raise it higher and higher, exposing more and more flesh until I lift it above my head and drop it to the ground beside us. My bra follows, landing softly on the sea of white and gold surrounding us.

My nipples draw up into tight little buds, jutting out and

simply begging to be touched. A small breeze skates across the flower-strewn meadow, making me shiver despite the heat of the sun overhead.

My eyes slowly drift from the daisies at his feet, up along every inch of his nakedness all the way to his face.

I swallow roughly, overwhelmed at the emotion in his gaze as I reach behind me to work at the zip fastening on my skirt. It falls to the ground when I inch the zip down until I'm bared to his gaze, clad in just a simple pair of plain white panties.

"Christ almighty, Summer. There are no words…"

Caden swallows harshly, his eyes leaving mine to caress every sweep, curve, and dip of my matured figure. He brings his hand up to caress my rounded hip, his index finger brushing across some light stretch marks along the way.

Reverence dances in his eyes as they follow the path of his fingers from my hip, across my stomach, and up my rib cage to cup a heavy breast in his palm.

My eyes flutter shut when he bends his head to take my nipple into the heat of his mouth. His tongue swirls around the erect bud before he nips it sharply between his teeth, making me cry out. The sound resonates through the air around us as my hands fly to his head, gripping his hair tightly to hold him in place.

He takes his time with one breast before moving on to the other. Nip, suck, tug, soothe. His mouth works its magic as I undulate against him.

Letting my breast go with a pop, he grips the nipple between his thumb and finger, pinching roughly while tugging his hair free of my grip. His mouth swoops up to capture my cry of pained pleasure while his hands dip around my ass to hold me flush against his hardness.

His assault almost knocks me off balance when he plunges his tongue inside my mouth, teeth clashing as our tongues duel for dominance.

He snakes his hands around my hips, and his fingers wrap around the thin material at the sides of my panties. The sound of ripping hits my ears, and I feel a rush of arousal pool directly in my core as he tugs the ruined material from my body.

I rip my mouth from his, panting with exertion when I peer into eyes almost black from how wide his pupils are blown.

His jaw tics before he nudges his knee between my legs, forcing me to widen my stance so that his hot palm can cup my bare pussy.

"Mine."

The guttural single word sounds as though he's torn it straight from deep within his chest, and I struggle to hold his eyes as mine threaten to flutter closed in the ecstasy of this moment. One side of his mouth tugs up when he's rewarded with a surge of wetness at my core, and when he sinks a long, thick finger between my folds, I almost come on the spot.

He draws his finger back and forth, letting the heel of his hand brush off my pulsating clit with each pass he makes. My mouth drops open as he continues his torture while watching my every reaction with an intensity I feel in my bones.

Adding another finger escalates the pleasure so that I'm a panting mess being held up by the power of his gaze alone. He increases the speed of his thrusting fingers, adjusts the angle *just* right, and I go off like a firecracker.

He slams his mouth onto mine, drowning the sound of my orgasm with the taste of his love before I feel him remove his drenched fingers from my wetness.

My eyes flutter open when he steps back, and I whimper at his loss.

"One second, Bam." There's amusement in his tone as he grabs my maxi skirt and lays it out on the bed of daisies like a blanket before sinking down onto it.

Crossing his hands behind his head, he smirks up at me devilishly. "Now, be a good girl and come sit on my face."

Nineteen

CADEN

The sun overhead illuminates Summer, shining behind her like a halo. She looks positively ethereal. Every curve, every mark, every flaw, every single piece of her is visually stunning, and it blows my mind that she could ever believe I'd think otherwise.

But her true beauty shines from within, filling my soul with boundless joy.

"Come on, Bam. Don't go all shy on me now."

She purses her lips together and tilts her head to the side. "I'm not *shy*. It's just that orgasm has turned my legs to jelly, and I'm waiting until I can feel them again before I move."

I arch a brow at that. "Well, I'm too impatient to wait."

Sitting forward in a flash, I wrap my hands around her waist and lean back, taking her with me so that she's straddling my chest. Her shriek turns to a groan when I draw the tip of my nose through her shimmering folds.

"Now give me that wet pussy so I can lick her until you scream."

Her nostrils flare as she stares down into my heated gaze. "Christ almighty, Caden. You're killing me with that mouth."

I shoot her a naughty-as-fuck smirk. "Oh, baby, you ain't seen nothing yet."

Ducking my head down, I draw the pointed tip of my tongue along the seam of her slit, and her honeyed arousal fills my mouth. She's absolutely fucking soaked, and the feeling of her silky slick sex gliding along my mouth makes my cock pulse against my stomach.

She parts her legs further, her previous reticence forgotten as she leans backwards. I bring my arms around her trembling thighs to use my thumbs to part her lips before drawing the swollen bundle of nerves into my mouth, sucking softly at first, then increasing the pressure.

Her soft moans fill my ears, and her hips begin to undulate and circle, seeking more as I worship her clit. All the while, my eyes are fixed firmly on her as she plays with a hard nipple, her head thrown back and eyes closed in wild abandon.

She's fucking glorious.

I flatten my tongue and lick long and slow from her slit all the way to her throbbing nub before sucking harshly and retreating, only to repeat the process again. And again.

When I roughly thrust two fingers inside her tight channel, she whimpers as her hands find purchase in my hair, holding me in place.

"Yes, Cade. Just like that. Yes, fuck me harder."

I inhale sharply, those words on her lips doing things to my insides. I thrust a third finger inside, fucking her mercilessly with my hand as I feel her orgasm build inside of her.

Her body begins to falter in its rhythm as she climbs higher, and then I suck her hard clit into my mouth.

She cries out, helpless to fight the climax that ploughs through her. Her hips buck against my face, and my cock leaks a steady stream of precum when her sweetness floods my tongue.

As she descends from the highest of heights, her body trembles under the force of her blissful surrender. When she opens her glassy eyes, they unerringly land on my own similar ones.

Whatever she sees within the depths of my gaze has her scrambling to climb off my chest, to line her hot core up with my weeping dick. She lowers herself onto my length with a low hiss of pleasure as she holds my eyes with an intensity that knocks the breath from my body.

Our joint moans of rapture fill the air when my cock is fully sheathed inside her tightness.

"Oh, shit. You're so damn wet, Bam. You're fucking perfect."

She rocks her hips, then circles them, opening herself up to me, her eyes never once straying from mine.

"You're so *deep*, Cade."

Her palms rest on my chest as she rides my dick like she's been made to do this and only this. Like she's been made to take my cock.

My hands shoot forward, grasping her hips to increase the speed of our bodies.

"That's it, Bambi. Ride me. Ride my fucking cock like you were born to do it."

She trembles, her eyes threatening to fall shut, but managing to keep holding mine. I begin to buck against her when her pussy clamps down on me as a third orgasm builds deep inside of her.

"Yes, fuck yes. Choke my cock with that sweet cunt of yours."

Her channel flexes around my dick as she rides me in earnest. Her hips bucking now, faltering in their rhythm as her climax crests. The sounds of our bodies slapping together, the feel of her wrapped around my cock, the heady scent of her arousal surrounding me.

It's all too much.

"I'm coming. Fuck yes, take it all. Take all of me."

My words spur both of us onwards, climbing closer and closer towards an inferno of our own making until suddenly, we're consumed by the fire.

My balls draw up tight when her cries of pleasure fill my ears. We continue to hold one another's gazes when our bodies ignite, and an orgasm, unlike anything I've ever experienced, ricochets through me. Her eyes flicker but don't close as they pin me in place, and we burn together in the exquisite flames of an earth-shattering climax.

Long moments pass as our bodies return to earth until I've gathered enough energy to push myself forward, pressing my ear against her sweat-slick chest. The galloping cadence of her heart fills my ears, and I'm immediately at ease in her loving embrace.

"I love you, Summer St James." Turning my face, I press a kiss to the curve of her breast right over her heart and whisper softly. "Please don't run from me again. My heart can't take it."

SUMMER

Once we've descended from our joint high, Caden pulls me into the crook of his arm, holding me close against him.

He presses his nose to the top of my head, inhaling deeply as the steady cadence of his heartbeat fills my ears.

"About what Layla said…back at the house…"

He trails off, clearing his throat before kissing my forehead. I twist my neck so that I can make eye contact, silently encouraging him to continue with a small nod.

"What did she mean about being pregnant back then?" His forehead crinkles in confusion. "*Clearly*, there was no baby. I…I don't understand."

Sighing internally, I can feel my own face scrunch up—more in distaste than confusion—before I try to find the right words.

"I don't know a lot, but it was the day of your brother's…the day of…"

I trail off uncertainly before drawing a deep breath in through my nostrils and steeling my spine.

"You had been released from the hospital three days earlier, but you'd stayed in the city with your parents and your sisters. Layla and I had stayed at your parents' house with Uncle Noah, so the first time you saw his room was when you came back…after the funeral."

"I remember." His eyes are glazed over. Agonised. "I got shit-faced on some pills and booze I found in his private stash."

I nod, letting my mind go back.

Caden's soft snore echoes around his brother's room when I peek inside to find him lying face down on Archer's bed. As I draw closer, I see his face is red and mottled with any number of emotions.

I don't dare analyse my thoughts too closely, fearful of what I might discover in the depths of my mind.

Guilt. Betrayal. Suspicion.

That last one has been niggling at me since the afternoon in the meadow. Layla's revelation that she'd been sleeping with both twins had rattled me, and it had only been because of everything that happened since that I'd not found the right moment to ask Cade about it.

Something feels off.

I scrunch up my face, thinking hard about what it is I'm missing, but I'm torn from my thoughts when a red-eyed Layla walks in the door.

Her thin arms are wrapped around her waist. Her long dark hair is hanging limply by her gaunt cheekbones, and my heart clenches in my chest as I cross the room to wrap her in my embrace.

"Oh, Lay."

Her shoulders start to move as silent sobs wrack her small frame.

"I don't know what to do, Summer. I'm in big trouble."

I pull away, frowning in genuine confusion. I'd assumed the tears were for Archer.

My uncertainty must show on my face because Layla drops her hands from around my shoulders, placing them on her almost concave stomach.

"I'm pregnant."

My eyes widen as tears track along her pale cheeks. "Oh my God, Lay. Archer's baby…"

I trail off when her eyes flick to the prone figure on the bed. My stomach sinks, and the world feels unsteady when her gaze darts back to me, containing a wild look I've never seen in her before now. "I don't know whose baby it is, Summer. I don't know who the father is."

Caden presses a kiss to my brow, alerting me to the fact that I'd fallen silent upon disclosing some long-buried secrets.

"Thank you for sharing that with me, Bam. I—I know none of this is easy."

I snuggle closer as a cool breeze snakes across our naked flesh. "It's not easy for either of us, Cade."

Raising my face to his, I pour every ounce of hope into my words. "But maybe now the truth is coming to light, we can make peace with the sins in our past."

CADEN

Having made love one more time, we slowly set each other to rights and walk back to the house hand in hand. With the smell of the summer evening surrounding us, the feel of the sun as it sinks lower on the horizon, the taste of my lover on my tongue, it feels as though the stars have aligned.

As though this moment and everything leading up to it had been fated. Like the time is finally right for us.

The thought puts a shit-eating smile on my face that's wider than the Golden Gate Bridge.

Summer nudges me with her shoulder, and I shift about to face her, my smile growing impossibly when I take in her beautiful bewilderment. "What's got you so happy?"

"You, Bambi. *You* make me happy. Everything about this moment makes me so fucking happy, I could shout it from the rooftops."

But since there are no rooftops here, I do the next best thing. I throw my head back and howl into the evening sky.

"I love this woman! I'm so fucking *happy*."

When I lower my head, she's grinning and shaking her head. "You are one strange cookie, Caden North."

I stop in my tracks, tugging her back using the hand I've been holding so that we are chest to chest. "But I'm *your* strange cookie, right?"

She presses her mouth to mine, softly at first, but with more urgency the longer it goes on, and I'm both pleased and horrified in equal measure to feel my cock stiffen in my pants.

I break the kiss reluctantly, knowing we still have the drive to Cambridge ahead of us, and I want to wish my parents a proper farewell before we set off.

"Come on, Bam. The last one home has to eat a slice of that beef my dad annihilated earlier."

She's off before I can even finish, flying through the long grass of the meadow and clearing the low hedgerow to land softly in my parents; landscaped garden with ease. She spares a moment to glance back, finding me hot on her heels, and squeals in surprise.

"Give up, Bam. You're going to lose."

And as though my words are the impetus she required, her body surges forward, putting another couple of feet between us as we reach the paved patio, now devoid of my family members.

"I win. Happy eating!"

I reach around her waist, tugging her backwards against my chest to growl in her ear. "There's only one thing I want to eat right now."

Dipping my hand lower, I palm her bare pussy through her long skirt, and she swats me away playfully.

"You are the pits, Cade."

I smile broadly, burying my face in the nape of her neck as I remember this playful banter from our teen years.

Inhaling deeply, I give her the same response now as I used to then. "And you love me all the same."

She spins in my embrace, her eyes shining in recognition before she palms my cheeks and presses a soft kiss to my waiting lips. "I do. I truly, *truly* do."

We're still smiling when we walk in the back door, hand in hand once again, to find only my parents sitting around their kitchen table, doing a crossword puzzle together.

"Good evening, you two." Mum glances up first. She stands and then closes the distance to grasp Summer's hands in her own.

"Summer, I—I need to apologise for my inconsiderate comments earlier. I truly meant no harm." Mum's eyes flicker between the three of us before returning to Summer's face. She rubs their joined hands together in a comforting gesture.

"I'm so terribly sorry that I hurt you today, Summer. I only hope that you can forgive me."

My mum's face is the very picture of sorrow, and Summer bends forward, forgoing words to wrap her arms around my mother, squeezing tightly.

"I know you didn't, Clary." They hold one another tight for a couple of beats before both women step back, smiling.

Mum rubs the back of her hand off Summer's soft cheek. "You know we adore you, and seeing you back here with Caden—well, it's like a dream come true for us."

I can feel my face scrunch up in confusion. "A dream come true? That makes fuck all sense, Mum. Surely you don't mean that you wanted your son and your ward to bump uglies—"

"*Caden*!" My name is a high-pitched screech as she whips her blonde head, about to waggle her index finger in my face. "Could you *please* word things with a little more delicacy?"

I roll my eyes and rephrase, stifling a grin as I wind her up even more. "*Fine*, Mum. Did you want your son and your ward going to Pound Town—"

She throws her arms up in exasperation as Summer covers her face with her palms, and Dad tosses me a wink and a chuckle from behind Mum's back.

"How's about rolling in the hay? Knocking boots?"

Rolling her eyes, she shoos me away. "I give up. Come on, Sut. Let's bid our granddaughter farewell."

She stalks into the foyer, heading upstairs towards the playroom she'd installed when Bree had Dawn, the eldest of my nieces, ten years ago. Before she can reach the first step, Ford arrives back through the front door.

She glances back and forth between us and him before pointing upstairs. "I'll get Bella."

Dad kisses her cheek, and there's silence as she ascends the stairs. Once she's disappeared from view, Ford nods towards my father's office, and the three of us move to follow.

"Noah offered to stay with her at her hotel. There was evidence of drug use that she attempted to hide from both of us, but even before that, it was clear that she was on something."

"Do you have eyes on her? I won't have her leaking shit to the media again." I gesture through the window and across the expansive manicured garden that separates my parents' house from the media circus camped on the road outside my tall walls.

Ford nods sharply. "Phones have been tapped. There's a man in her building. Another in a car outside. I've hacked into street cameras in the area and sent the live feed back to the guys in Cambridge. She's not moving without us knowing."

I can feel myself relax somewhat just as my mother steps inside with my daughter in tow.

"Daddy!" Her legs move towards me, but her eyes flicker sideways to find Summer, and she changes direction. "Summer-hero!"

She launches herself and her mass of blonde curls at Summer, wrapping her small frame around her hero. "Hey, my little Curly-Sue. Did you have fun today with Mimi and Pops?"

I catch Mum and Dad exchanging a smiling glance, and my heart grows wings, fluttering in my chest with absolute contentment.

"Come on, girls. Let's get home."

We walk through the house, entering a cavernous garage filled with vintage cars my dad loves to tinker with. Nearest to the electric door is our SUV with black-tinted windows.

Having settled in the backseat, we wave my parents off as we journey across the rear of their property until they are small specks in the distance with their arms wrapped around one another. By the time we've reached the other entrance on the far side of the river, Bella is fast asleep at my left, Huddles Bunny wrapped tight in her arms. And ten minutes later, Summer is fast asleep on my right, her small hand resting on my thigh.

Ford catches my eye in the rearview, his white teeth flashing with a wry grin before he mouths, *"Lucky fucker."*

I'd flip him the bird, except he's right.

My phone chimes, and I pick it up with an easy grin when I spot my group chat with Henry, and Nate is active.

HENRY

Peach wanted me to say thanks for yesterday, Cade. Sorry about the paps!

I shoot back a thumbs-up emoji.

NATE

Mila showed me a viral video of you dry-humping a girl that looks uncannily like Summer St James.

HENRY

Where have you been, Hawthorne?

I can't help myself. It's too easy.

ME

In bed with your sister. Duh!

Nate sends back a facepalm emoji, and I can see the dots blinking as Henry, undoubtedly furious, is manically typing a response.

HENRY

Why do you have to keep that shit up, man? You're owed a punch in the gut for that one.

I chuckle softly lest I wake the sleeping beauties on either side of me.

ME

And yes, Hawthorne. That girl IS Summer. She's back. It's a long ass story. Drinks next week?

Both boys send thumbs-up emojis, to which I respond with a peach in reference to his nickname for Liv, knowing it will really rattle Henry's cage. My thoughts are proved right when he replies with a middle finger.

The trip home takes around ninety minutes, during which time I rest my head on Summer's and drift off alongside her.

"Cade? Caden, wake up."

Ford's voice is tinged with urgency when he rouses me.

I sit up in my seat, stirring Summer, but thankfully not Bella when I move. Taking a second before answering him, I glance out into the darkening night sky to find we've arrived at our destination.

The house is lit up in anticipation of our arrival, light spilling out from within.

"That was quick."

Ford spins in his seat and doesn't mince his words. "We might have a Tequila Sunrise on our hands."

I sit up straighter, piercing him with a stare.

"I got a call about ten minutes ago from Holden. He's on duty tonight. He said someone showed up asking for Miss Summer, but rather than leave them in their Uber outside with the pap-hounds, he had them shown inside."

I scrunch up my face in utter bewilderment. "Why the *fuck* would he do that? This person could be an undercover pap. They could be fucking *anyone*."

Summer sits up, scrubbing her palms down her face before she stretches like a cat against my side. "Oh my *God*. I need to pee *so* bad."

Without warning, she tugs on the handle of the door and slides out onto the tarmac. Her feet move swiftly to cross the space as the front door opens.

"Wait, Bam!"

She stops dead in her tracks, and I finally mobilise to follow after her as the shadow of a man appears in the doorframe.

My heart climbs into my throat, and I call for Ford as this stranger bears down on a stock-still Summer, only to stride right past her. Relief fills me for a split second until my forward momentum propels my jaw right into this stranger's waiting fist.

Stars fill my vision as my ass meets the tarmac beneath me.

"*Jesse*!" Summer's indignant tone reaches my ears, and I blink rapidly to dispel the myriad of stars in my eyes following that complete sucker punch.

Ford, having reached me, stops right at my back and doesn't move a muscle. I reach up to rub my rapidly swelling jaw to find intense deep blue eyes bearing down on me.

Eyes that I'd know anywhere.

Eyes identical to my mother's. To my daughter's. To *mine*. Eyes that, right now, are filled with absolute hatred.

"Keep your fucking hands *off* my mother, asshole!"

Twenty

SUMMER

The scene before me unfolds as though in slow motion.

My fourteen-year-old son can't be here. But he is.

And his eyes, so like his father's and his half-sister's, are spitting deep blue flames in their anger as he marches past me to knock Caden on his ass with a right hook.

This can't be happening. Not like this. Not *now*.

Not after the most blissful evening.

Not after I'd decided to bare my soul tonight and beg his forgiveness for my betrayal.

Not now that I know I *can't* live without him in my life any longer.

My feet feel glued to the tarmacked driveway until Maggie appears in the doorway.

"Mr North? Holden radioed to say he thinks there's a pap drone over the house."

Jesse appears at my side, his face flushed with deep-seated rage, to hook his arm through mine and urge me towards the house. He's tall for his age and strong enough to propel me forward with relative ease.

I glance backwards to find Ford helping Caden from the ground before heading towards the car to undoubtedly grab Bella. Caden's eyes find mine, and my heart sinks when I find them utterly devoid of their usual warmth.

Absent of the love and laughter from earlier, to be replaced by a coldness I've never seen in him before.

When we reach the house, a stiff-spined Caden marches past us, calling over his shoulder. "My office, Summer. Five minutes."

I shift my gaze to the side to find Jesse bristling with rage. "How dare he speak to you like that, Mom. Who the hell does he think he is?"

My stomach roils, knowing now that I've delayed the truth for far too long. Fifteen years too long.

"Come on, baby. I'll get you something to eat."

I move towards the kitchen, glancing around when I hear Ford cross the threshold with a sleeping Bella in his arms. His eyes are filled with judgement, but instead of cowering, I jut my chin out in defiance.

His assessment of the situation steels my spine in anticipation of what's to come.

"What are you doing here, baby? How did you fly on your own?" I set about making my son a sandwich as he slides onto a high stool at the breakfast bar.

"Well, I wasn't going to put up with some British simp manhandling my mother and not do something about it, was I, Mom?" He tilts his blonde head to the side, his big sapphire eyes shining with a mixture of devilment and deviance.

It's a look I know very well, though I've not witnessed it on my child's face before, only his father's.

"But how did you fly here? You're a minor!"

He snorts a laugh. "Yeah, umm…well, Miguel Flores—you know the Connecticut camp leader, right?" I nod, and he continues. "Well, he saw the clip. It's gone viral, in case you weren't aware—"

I cut him off. "I wasn't."

Kill me now.

"Well, Miguel felt all kinds of bad for me. I was really pissed off—"

"Language, Jesse!"

He shrugs sheepishly. "Sorry."

I place a plate with a ham salad sandwich before him, and he takes a bite before continuing to speak around the mouthful.

"So Miguel's wife, Melinda, had business in London and flew with me."

I'll be having words with Miguel—well-intentioned or not!

"And how exactly did you find where Caden lives?"

Jesse smirks devilishly around a mouthful of sandwich, shooting me a cheeky nod that's entirely too like his father's. "Remember when I didn't want you to put that tracker app on my cell?"

Realisation dawns. "And the only way you'd allow me to turn on the tracking was if you could see my location in return!"

His triumphant grin at having used my own app against me sees me stifle a grin.

The little shit!

I roll my eyes before running my palms down either side of his face. "Baby, you should be in big, big trouble for being so reckless."

His big blue eyes widen—the epitome of innocence—making me narrow my eyes in remembrance. "And you're in massive trouble for swearing in that text message, mister!"

He smiles that Cheshire Cat grin of his, and I pull him into my arms. "But right this moment, I'm just so relieved that you're okay."

Maggie enters the kitchen then. "Jesse, dear. I have a room made up for you."

Pulling out of my embrace, my son meets my eyes. "We're staying at Caden North's house? Really?"

I swallow roughly and nod with a tight smile. "Yup."

Well, you're staying. I'll be unceremoniously kicked out, and rightly so.

"Oh my God, Mom." His face flushes bright red. "I thought you were like…a groupie or something. I was defending your…your honour."

He drops his face into his hands. "Oh my God, I *punched* Caden North."

His words are muffled through his palms. "I hit my *idol*."

Turning horrified eyes to mine, he whispers, "All those times I begged you to bring me to Madison Square Gardens, and I said I wanted to be just like him…oh my God, he'll never sign my *Hallowed Heart* album now!"

My heart clenches, knowing that by the time this is said and done, my son will hate me too.

I press a kiss on Jesse's temple. "I'll chat with him on your behalf. Now, eat up, and I'll see you in the morning, baby. Okay?"

My son nods enthusiastically before taking another bite of his sandwich. "May I have a glass of milk, please, Maggie?"

I slip from the kitchen as Maggie launches into a story about how she makes the butter from scratch here, and despite feeling like a lamb headed to the slaughter, I can't help but smile at her ability to distract Caden's house guests with inane chatter.

The walk from the kitchen to Caden's office is short, but even so, it feels interminable. I slowly ease the door open, my eyes locking with Cade's as he pours himself what looks to be at least his second glass of whiskey before closing the door behind me with a soft *snick*.

I've made it less than three feet inside his domain when his voice breaks the silence with a hoarse bark.

"Start at the *fucking* beginning, and leave *nothing* out."

Knocking back the contents of the tumbler, he slams it down on the desk, lifting his head to penetrate me with a stare.

It's part confusion, part anger, and absolute pain. I swallow the lump in my throat before slowly moving to the sideboard to pour myself a hefty measure of the amber liquid.

Downing it in one gulp, I grimace and pour a larger one, then shift around to find Caden's steely gaze hasn't left me.

"It's a long story, but it happened on the day of Archer's burial…." I suck my bottom lip between my teeth, nibbling furiously before raising the glass to my trembling lips to take a large gulp.

Crossing the room, I settle into a high-backed armchair and straighten my spine.

I can do this.

"The day Layla told me she was pregnant…"

"I don't know whose baby it is, Summer. I don't know who the father is."

My mouth drops as my stomach roils.

Caden's going to choose her.

The thought runs around and around inside my head, each repetition like a blow to my palpitating heart. It isn't until Layla speaks again that I realise I've spoken aloud.

"Why would you think that?"

I don't hesitate, knowing without a doubt what he'll do because we are that *connected. "Because he's an honourable person, Lay. He won't let your baby—regardless of who their biological father is—grow up without a dad now that Archer isn't here to take care of you both. You know that."*

Her forehead puckers as she contemplates my words, and then her face lights up.

"Oh my God, you're right. That's exactly what he'll do!" The stark relief on her face is like salt in an open wound, but she carries on, oblivious to my agony.

"I don't mind sharing him with you, Summer. It's not like I love him or anything, you know?"

Swallowing heavily, I nod and force a tight-lipped smile, glancing in Caden's direction as he snores away, blissfully unaware of the turn his future has taken.

Of the turn our *future has taken.*

And despite it all, my mind is still whirring with possibilities. I'd do just about anything to be with him, the boy who makes my heart beat.

Maybe sharing him won't be so bad.

There's a soft knock on the door, and Uncle Noah pokes his head inside. His face falls when he spots Caden. "Poor chap." Then, he glances at Layla and me, motioning to leave. "Come on, girls. Let's leave him to sleep it off."

We follow his tall frame into the silent hall and down the stairs through an empty house, eventually winding up in the kitchen. There's an underlying veil of sadness permeating the air that even makes breathing a chore.

"Everyone is passed out, or drunk, or both. Did you two have dinner?" We shake our heads simultaneously. "I can fix you something if you're hungry."

"I need to phone my mum. She's back from Thailand today, so she won't know about…about Arch." Layla forces a smile that's more like a wince as she ducks out onto the dimly lit patio at the back of the kitchen with her phone in hand.

"Summer?"

Uncle Noah's eyes are on me, expecting an answer, but I can't seem to make my mouth move.

He repeats my name twice more before coming to stand beside me. And when he places his warm, comforting hand on my shoulder, I fall to pieces.

I disclose every sordid detail of the day Archer drowned, my own part included, while Noah stands next to me the entire time, never once interrupting. He just lets me spew the entire sorry tale as I sob my heart out.

"And who else knows of your involvement? Of this crazy scheme? Of Archer's attack?"

"Only Layla."

He nods, glancing towards the patio where Layla is pacing whilst on the call to her mum.

"Okay. If that's everything, Summer, then you can trust me to keep it a secret. Layla is very easily led. I can keep her in line. You don't need to worry. No one need ever know it was anything but a terrible accident."

My watery gaze meets Uncle Noah's eyes, and he smiles softly. "I've got your back. Trust me."

I return his smile, albeit slightly wobbly. "But I'll know."

He waves me off. "Summer, it was a tragic accident. Put it from your mind, at least for now, okay?"

Clapping his hands, as though I didn't just tell him of my involvement in a murder, Uncle Noah announces, "Breakfast for dinner is just what we need."

I frown and sober, tugging at his shirt as he tries to walk away, suddenly remembering what prompted my outburst. "There's something else, Uncle Noah."

His eyes find mine, and he nods a handful of times. Concern is etched on his kind, familiar features.

"Layla is pregnant, and she doesn't know if the baby is Archer's or Caden's…" I trail off, my eyes drifting to the floor. "She was sleeping with both of them."

My heart tenses in my chest as I utter the words that I don't want to acknowledge but can't deny now there's possibly physical proof of their intimacy.

He inhales slowly, holding it for a long beat before blowing it out. "Well, that's a pickle, Summer. That right there is a scandal in the making."

My eyes shoot back up to search his face.

"We'll need to get ahead of this." His eyes drift towards the floor, and I can almost see the cogs of his brain working on figuring a way out of the mess.

"Archer's or Caden's, it doesn't matter. The grandchild of Sutton North needs two parents." His eyes raise to mine just as a frown crosses my face.

I'm not stupid. I know what he's saying, but I need him to say the words.

"I'm afraid, dear girl, you'll need to be removed from the picture entirely."

My mouth falls open, and I round on him, shrugging his hand off my arm.

"I didn't confide everything to you, Uncle Noah, so that you could

send me away. I'm not going anywhere. I—I can't. I love him. He needs *me."*

All signs of kindness drop from his features as unusual selfishness reign supreme on the face of the man I've called family since I was old enough to walk.

"Do you think Caden will want a damn thing to do with you once I tell him the part you played in his brother's murder?*"*

I suck in a horrified breath, nausea swirling in the pit of my stomach as terror constricts my throat. I barely manage to choke out a question. "Uncle Noah, why are you saying that?"

He carries on as though I've not spoken. "How about I make you a little deal, hmm? I'll help you disappear—to a place of your choosing—I'm not a complete monster—and in return for my silence, you'll go quietly."

His eyes hold mine, and the horrifying sincerity in his gaze shocks me to my core. "If you insist on sticking around, I'll tell everyone—Sutton, Clarisse...Caden—"

He smirks at my sharp inhalation before continuing. "I'll tell them you're the reason their son, Caden's twin, *is dead. Do you think any of your loved ones will look at you the same again when they know? When they realise what you are."*

Tears fill my vision, hearing the truth of his words as I drop my gaze to the floor, watching my tears land on the kitchen tiles one by one.

"You're a murderer, Summer. However you want to sugar-coat it. You *are the reason Archer North is dead and buried."*

And then he hammers the final nail into the coffin.

"They'd have no choice but to call the authorities. You'd wind up in prison, and I doubt the inmates would take kindly to a kid killer, my dear girl."

My tears continue to fall, landing silently on the tiles beneath us. My brain is whirring frantically, desperately trying to find a way out of this mess and coming up with nothing. The tears fall faster, and it feels difficult to breathe.

"Do you really think you'd be able to share Caden anyway? It would kill you to stick around here and watch him play house with another girl's kid, Summer. Be smart about this."

He places his hand on my shoulder once more, but this time the gesture isn't even one-tenth as comforting as it was before. "You can have a life away from here. I'll make sure of it."

I raise my tear-streaked face to him as he speaks again. "Trust me."

"I made my decision and packed a small bag. Uncle Noah—"

"Would you *stop* calling him that, for fuck's sake! After the part he's fucking played, you can drop the 'Uncle,' yeah?" His words are a vicious snarl, so far removed from his usual self that I feel myself visibly recoiling in my seat.

I swallow heavily. "*Noah* went to get a car, but I…I *needed* to see you one last time."

The hallway is silent, Archer's room devoid of snoring, so I move on further down the eerily silent hallway towards Caden's bedroom, where I find him staring at a picture in the middle of his bed.

"Caden…I need to go for a while…" I can't meet his glassy eyes. Instead, I keep my stare trained on my feet, but I hear when he moves off the bed and approaches me.

Gripping my jaw in his palm, he lifts my head to brush his lips softly against mine. I snake my tongue out, parting his lips, needing to taste him one final time, and that's all the encouragement he needs.

He slams me back against his dressing table, making me cry out in pain, and in the face of what I'm about to do, I welcome the hurt. My hands scramble to the zipper of his jeans, freeing his hard cock as he hikes my leg up against his hip, giving him access to my leggings-clad core.

Grinding himself against my hand, he breaks our kiss, drops his forehead to mine, and groans in frustration. "Let me feel you, Summer. I need your warmth. I'm so fucking cold inside. I need you so that I can fucking feel*. Something. Anything!"*

I nod against his forehead, needing the same thing, possibly even more than he does.

He palms my ass, lifting me up to deposit me on the dresser behind me, then leans around me to grab his pocketknife. He brings the knife between my legs and cuts the seam of my leggings, the threads unravelling with ease, giving him the access to my warmth that he so desperately needs.

That we both *so desperately crave.*

Tugging my panties to one side, the pocketknife falls to the wooden floor at our feet with a muted clatter, and he drops his forehead onto my neck as he enters me in one sharp thrust.

I cry out, throwing my head back against the wall as tears silently stream down my face.

He drives into me repeatedly, hitting deeper and deeper with each forward movement, and I cling to this moment of precious agony with every atom inside of me.

His movements grow frantic and despite the emotion roiling through my veins, I can feel the stirring of an orgasm coiling in the depths of my stomach.

He lifts his head enough to suck my exposed throat while driving his hardness as deep as he can go, groaning his orgasm into the delicate skin of my neck. I know that I'm on the precipice of something amazing, and when I feel him erupt inside my core, I'm thrown off the edge with no warning.

My body clings tight to his, my channel rippling around his length as I take him impossibly deeper, and all too soon, I'm slammed back to reality.

His bedroom door creaks open unceremoniously. "Cade, are you awake? We need to talk."

Layla strides in the door, taking in the aftermath of our coming together with nonchalance as Cade tucks himself into his pants without looking up, and I lower myself onto the floor.

My reason for leaving is twofold when Layla smirks knowingly before shifting her eyes to Cade, linking her arm through his. "Come on, lover boy. You need to sleep off those pills so we can have a serious conversation."

I slip from the room to the sounds of my best friend settling the boy I love into his bed, glancing back one final time to see her climbing in beside him.

My heart splinters into a million pieces as I run down the stairs, grabbing the single rucksack of items that I had time to pack.

Before I walk out the door, I gently slip my necklace from around my neck. It's the heart locket my father gave to me for my last birthday with my parents. Inside there's a photo of me with Caden on the opposite side.

It feels fitting to leave my locket behind for him, because as I walk out that door for the last time, my chest feels hollow.

Twenty-One

CADEN

I take a deep breath when Summer pauses her tale to take a sip from her tumbler.

My feelings are scattered to the four winds.

My heart is screaming to stop wasting time. There's been enough time lost to fill a fucking ocean liner.

But my head is begging for caution, telling me that something needs to change. That *I* need to change.

I welcomed her back with open arms, willing to overlook everything that went before. Willing to plead ignorance in exchange for her simple presence.

Am I willing to do that again and risk *more* secrets and pain in the long run?

Am I willing to open not only myself to this, but my daughter too?

My *son*?

My stomach drops at that, and I know I can't follow my heart. Not this time. She kept my child—my *son*—from me and from his family for fifteen fucking years.

Meeting her glistening eyes, I steel my heart to her.

I'm shutting her out. Washing my hands of everything that's gone between us these past five days—*Christ*, has it only been five days—because I don't know if I can trust a damn word that comes out of her hypnotic mouth at this point.

"I left and never looked back. Is that what you want to hear, Caden?" Narrowing her eyes, she throws her hands up in exasperation. Or perhaps, in defeat. "I left, and I didn't care. Is that what you need me to say? Because that would be an outright lie."

She rises from the chair in a fluid, graceful movement that makes my heart sing for her, the stupid prick. "I looked back every damn day. I longed for you. Never so much as the day I found out I was pregnant six weeks later…"

Trailing off, she steps closer, begging me with her eyes to understand. "The day I got Layla's letter about losing the baby was the same day I took a test of my own. I'd been sick, though I thought it was homesickness initially. It came back positive. But I was in a dark place, Cade. Noah said that if I came back, the repercussions—"

"I *swear*, that meddling piece of shit is going to get what's coming to him!"

My words are low, but I feel them with everything inside of me. Noah Spellman is going to fucking pay for his interference.

"Now finish your story because I *know* you didn't come back here for me after all this time."

Her eyes flash with hurt before she catches herself, noticeably standing taller, blatantly not taking my wrath lying down.

I'm fuming at myself for not being able to keep the emotion from my voice, so turn my back on her, unwilling to give her even more of myself than I already have. More than she already *owns*.

"*Noah* had set me up with a new identity, an apartment, and the money from the sale of my father's company, but that didn't last long. New York is an expensive place—"

My forehead scrunches up. "Wait, did you say Noah set you up with a new identity?"

She nods, wide-eyed at my fury.

The double-crossing fucker.

All those years, he'd claimed to be helping me to search for her, and he knew precisely where she was. Because *he'd* sent her there.

But why?

I file that question away for further thought when Summer begins to speak again.

"Following the positive pregnancy test, I moved from Manhattan, where Noah had set me up. But I was afraid that he could find me and change his mind. I had nightmares of him sending me to prison. Of giving birth there. Of him taking my child away from me. So, I got an apartment under a different alias and found a job in a diner where the owner took me under her wing."

Realising her tumbler is empty, she crosses the room to the sideboard, holding the decanter up in question. When I nod yes, she leans forward, refilling my own tumbler while leaving her intoxicating scent tauntingly under my nose.

She props her hip against the sideboard, facing me as she sips from her refilled tumbler.

"I questioned contacting you *so* many times over the years until eventually, around the time Jesse turned six, I came to the stark realisation that I'd gone too far beyond the point of no return. It wasn't until around his tenth birthday that I ever even contemplated it again…"

She trails off, her eyes dropping to her glass, and before I can ask what she means, the door of my office slams open.

"Ford, for fuck's sake. Ever heard of knocking—"

My head of security's face is pulled up in a frown, indicating incoming shit that I don't think I have the ability to deal with right now. I hold up a stalling hand, about to tell him as much, but he ploughs on inside regardless.

"Cade, I've just listened to the audio recorded from the phone in your ex-wife's hotel room only fifteen minutes ago."

I pinch the bridge of my nose, my temple throbbing painfully as I inhale deeply. "What trouble is that waste of fucking space creating *now*?"

"It wasn't her on the phone, Cade. It was Noah…"

He trails off, uncertainty heavy in his usually confident voice. I glance up to find his brow knitted. "What, man? Spit it out! I don't have the time nor the inclination for theatrics today."

Stop being an asshole, North.

And even while I'm thinking it, I can't stop myself from tutting impatiently.

Because clearly, I'm an asshole now.

Ford squares his shoulders, drawing himself up to his considerable height. "Noah called an automated voice mailbox. The message he left was cryptic, to say the least."

When I stare deadpan at him, allowing my newfound asshole to shine bright, his jaw tics, but he continues despite my uncharacteristic lack of niceties. "He left in a town car shortly thereafter. Layla rang down to reception for room service and fresh towels, which my man delivered, posing as staff. He's confirmed she's alone and was running a bath."

"And Noah's voice message? What's being done about that?"

"I have our best guy, Eduardo, from Dad's main office in New York running point. He should have access within the next few days."

I nod sharply. "I want to know the second you do, Ford. No more Tequila Sunrise, yeah?"

He inclines his head, his gaze sliding to Summer, who has returned to her seat in the high-backed armchair for a split second before he pivots on his heel to leave us in silence.

I don't mince my words. "And then what? What stopped you from coming back when he was ten, Summer? Why keep him from me for another four *fucking* years, hmm?"

Her eyes are on the swirling liquid inside her tumbler as she swishes it around the glass. I can feel the tension rolling off her body in waves, and the silence between us continues to stretch.

Eventually, I stand and walk over to pluck the glass from her hand. Her eyes slowly climb my body until they come to my face. I arch a brow, feeling my jaw tic before I place the tumbler to my lips and knock the Macallan back in one burning mouthful.

"Why *now*, Summer?" The question is a hoarse rasp as the whiskey sets fire to my throat on its descent to my churning stomach. "Answer the *damn* question. Give me something to go on here. Any-fucking-thing!"

She sucks that pouty bottom lip between her teeth as her brows crease. Her nostrils flare, but she holds my eyes unflinchingly.

"You might want to sit."

I cross my arms over my chest and widen my stance. "I'm perfectly fine where I am."

She sits back in the seat, folding her hands atop her lap before her eyes glaze over, and I just *know* she's reliving whatever it is that drove her back here. Silence abounds for long minutes until her voice whispers through the air so quietly that I need to strain to hear it, even with how close I'm standing.

"When Jesse was ten, I brought him for a wellness check-up. He'd been too tired to participate in his favourite sports, and his appetite was shockingly low."

Goosebumps break out on every inch of my skin when her eyes refocus and shift to mine. "A blood test showed abnormalities. So we went for more tests." She swallows, clears her throat, and raises her voice slightly. "Non-Hodgkin's Lymphoma. Early stages. Entirely treatable."

Every inch of my body is on high alert, unable to even acknowledge what she's just told me.

"It was the same week news of your wedding broke, actually. I—I wasn't in a good place…." she trails off, glancing at her lap where she's wringing her hands, her knuckles white from the exertion.

"I did reach out, I swear…." She raises haunted eyes to mine. "I know *now* that she was lying, but *then*, I had no reason not to believe her."

My forehead creases in sheer confusion, and I'm unable to keep the impatience from my voice when I snap, "You know *who* was lying?"

She swallows, clears her throat, and holds my eyes unwaveringly as she stumbles through her response. "The week of Jesse's first—his first chemotherapy session. I—well, that's to say my boss was able to get your cell number for—for me. I rang…and Layla answered."

Her nostrils flare, and her jaw tics noticeably as she tries to keep a lid on her emotions. "I told her about Jesse. I told her everything."

My stomach churns, threatening to dispel the pizza from earlier.

Layla fucking knew *I had a son for* four *damn years!*

Silent tears track down each of her flushed cheeks as she continues. "She said you guys were *happy*. With a child of your own on the way, which only broke to the media shortly thereafter. She said if I contacted you, it would ruin everything—I had no way of knowing she meant it would ruin everything for *her*, Cade. I swear, I didn't know…."

My emotions are barely hanging by a thread when I pin her with a stare. "What about Jesse?"

Pain flitters across her face, but in a flash, it's replaced with determined resolution as she sets her jaw and continues.

"My boy made—"

"*Our boy*!" I cut her off without even thinking, narrowing my eyes in distaste at how quickly she forgets that I'm his damn father. "Our boy made…Christ, Summer."

I rake my hands through my hair while anger simmers, barely restrained beneath the surface. It's a sensation that's utterly new to me, and I intensely dislike it already.

She holds up her hands, palms facing me in a quelling manner. "My apologies. *Our* boy made a complete recovery. Kicked cancer's ass." She smirks softly, eyes glossing over as she remembers some anecdote or other that I missed being a part of. "He was checked over regularly, and all signs pointed to full remission. Until they didn't."

My lungs feel deprived of oxygen as her gaze falls from mine once more, and I feel more than a little light-headed, but she marches on unyieldingly.

"That was last year. He was slower to respond to the chemo. It was…" She shakes her head, her eyes pained. "It was rough. *But,* he fought hard, and—"

She breaks off and lets out a sound somewhere between a sob and a laugh that makes my heart clench in my chest with the need to pull her into my embrace. The ingrained desire to comfort her in her time of need.

Raising her eyes to mine again, I'm astounded to find tears streaming down her cheeks even while a smile lights up her face. "He's a miracle, Cade. A walking, talking, living, breathing *miracle*."

I can't stop my lips from turning up, and for a beat, we just hold one another's eyes. She's the first one to break away, glancing towards the door when voices in the hall draw our attention.

"I'll show you to your room, Mr Jesse."

There's a boyish laugh that tugs at my fraying emotions. "It's just *Jesse*, okay, Maggie?"

My small smile disappears from my face at the reminder of what she stole from me—from *us*—and I lose all semblance of patience. Reaching out, I grip those hands she's refolded in her lap to tug her roughly to standing.

"Enough, Summer! *Why now*? Spit it out, for fuck's sake."

My voice is louder and more intimidating than I'd meant, but even so, she stands tall, not backing down for a moment.

"He's healthy now. Ten months cancer free."

The pride is evident in her voice, and I can't help but feel proud of both of them, having fought cancer twice.

And won.

"I've spoken to his doctors at length, and they believe the best course of action is to be proactive. Following the high doses of chemo, alongside the fact he's a second cancer survivor, they would recommend doing a bone marrow transplant twelve months into his remission…but I'm not a match."

She stops, letting that sink in. I frown heavily, unfamiliar with almost everything she's said and having way too many questions to address while I'm still fuming mad over her deceit.

"Okay, so I'm guessing you're here to ask if I'll check whether I'm a match or not, right?"

She nods, starting to speak, but I cut her off, "Why not lead with that, Summer? Why spend the week when you knew this was what you really came back for? Why not ask that first day?"

A single tear glides down her cheek, but she answers without hesitation, her voice steady. "Every day since I've been gone has had one singular purpose: to do the best I could for my child. When I had no reason to get up in the morning, he gave me life. I've centred everything I do around him or with him in mind. So this week, while he was away at his annual camp for Childhood Cancer Survivors in Connecticut, I got on a plane with the intention of coming here. Of coming clean and begging for your help."

She pauses, eyes flickering down to her clenched palms.

"But when I saw you again, you awoke feelings that I buried years ago." Her voice breaks, and she raises pleading brown eyes to mine. "You welcomed me with open arms. It was more than I'd ever dared to *dream*. And in that moment, I was helpless to deny myself the chance to feel your love after all this time. Because I *never* stopped loving you, Caden."

She holds my eyes, willing me to feel the sincerity in her words. My heart cries out to take her in my arms and forget the rest. I'm about to do just that when the heavy oak door to my office flies open, slamming off the bookcase housing my favourite Jupiter's Fallen records.

Jesse storms across the threshold, anger vibrating in the air as he fixes his mother with a look that knocks the wind from my sails.

Fuck, he's a mini version of me!

His blonde, longer-than-the-norm hair is messy, falling into his sapphire blue eyes as he rakes a hand through it in annoyance. Every single inch of him is me—except his mouth. That's all his mother's.

My focus is on his lips in wonderment when they begin to move in earnest. "The man you've watched me idolise from afar for *years* is my *dad*! Are you fucking shitting me, Mom?"

Twenty-Two

SUMMER

I tug my duvet higher over my body, shivering despite the heat on this beautiful August morning.

Glancing at my nightstand, I can see my phone, and despite needing to call Anna, or even Vaughn, for a sympathetic ear, it feels too far away just now.

A glass of water sits alongside it, though how it got there, I don't know. My mouth feels and tastes like ass, but even so, the temptation of the cool liquid isn't enough to make me stir from my puddle of self-hate.

After Jesse had stormed into Caden's office, I'd not gotten a word in edgewise. Ford had appeared as though out of nowhere, whispering to follow him.

I'd not been able to move under my son's vitriolic attack until Caden had spoken aloud, quelling my son—our son—with a simple solution.

"Summer, I think it's best if you go back to the recording studio. We all need time to adjust."

Jesse had stood at his side, staring me down until I'd moved to follow Ford.

The trip back here had been made in absolute silence—proof of just how far from grace I'd fallen—and once he'd seen me inside, he turned and walked back to the house without a glance.

I'd pilfered a bottle of rum from Caden's stash and drank the lot until I'd thrown up for hours. After falling asleep, literally with my head *in* the toilet, I'd crawled back to bed and sobbed myself into a fitful sleep.

Thankfully, I didn't drunk dial…

My eyes widen when I realise I did, in fact, drunk text.

Summoning the energy to reach for my phone, I click into my messages and cringe.

ME

Jesse, baby. I love you. There's so much you don't know.

JESSE

I know you're a liar. And a thief. You stole my life from me.

I hate you.

ME

You don't mean that, baby.

JESSE

I do. Go home, Mom. No one wants you here.

I swallow roughly as tears swim in my vision. This is worse than I could have ever imagined. I knew it wouldn't go well, but I can't get the image of his hatred-filled eyes from my mind.

Eyes that were identical in both colour and emotion to his father.

You've lost them both now.

ME

Do you really want me to leave? I will if you say the word. I'd do anything for you, baby.

My heart tremors when I see the dots blaze to life immediately, praying that he only spewed that venom in his anger last night.

JESSE

Go back to New York. You've done enough already.

A whole new wave of sadness washes over me, pulling me into its soothing embrace as a fresh onslaught of sobs wracks my body.

My mind is racing, my heart is breaking, and there's only myself and the stupid decisions I made as a teenager to thank for it.

For the millionth time in my life, I ask myself *why* I trusted Noah Spellman, and I'm reminded, once more, that trusting people leads to regret. I should have known Caden's offer of a week, no questions asked, was too good to be true.

Eventually, my tears dry up. My mind goes quiet. My heart stutters beneath my breastbone, and I reach for my phone again, determined to do the right thing this time.

Determined to give both Caden and Jesse what I stole from them.

Time.

Bags packed, I glance around the studio one last time, scanning for anything I've left behind. Finding none, I heft the bag into my arms and navigate the stairs, spotting my waiting Uber when I exit the side entrance to the studio.

The driver hops out—a friendly looking guy in his early twenties—and takes my luggage from me with a smile.

"I just need to say goodbye to someone inside. Okay?"

"No worries. I've got time." He nods, ducking back into the driver's seat, and I quietly enter the main house, eerily quiet in the morning light.

No signs of Maggie in the kitchen. Ford is nowhere to be found either.

As I crest the top of the staircase, I can hear Bella pottering around her room, singing her favourite Trolls song softly. I can't help but smile when I stop to listen to her sweet voice.

But the smile slowly recedes from my face with the realisation that I'm leaving her behind too. The little girl with the big heart who's made me fall crazy in love with her in a matter of minutes.

Like father, like daughter, clearly.

Forcing my feet to move further along the hall, I arrive at the room Maggie allocated to Jesse. I know it's his because his small green rucksack is outside the door, which he must have abandoned downstairs last night in his distress.

I open the door, surprised to find him asleep on his stomach. He must have fallen back asleep after texting me. Once I've approached the bed, I lower myself to sit alongside him and brush his mused hair back from his forehead.

His eyelids flicker open. "Mom? What are you doing?"

I smile softly, cupping his cheek with my palm. "Oh, baby, I'm doing what I should have done years ago."

His brows draw together in confusion before I continue, my

smile twitching and threatening to fall from my face as tears sting the back of my eyes.

"I'm giving you time together. It won't make up for the time you've lost, and for that, I'm more sorry than you'll ever know."

My breath catches on a sob, and my beautiful boy sits up in the bed, wrapping his arms around me as my shoulders shake with silent tears.

"I'm really hurt, Mom. But I didn't mean it when I said I hate you, okay?"

I manage a watery smile as I pull back to palm his cheeks. "I'm going back home. Take all the time you need, baby. Text me. Call me. Just get to know your father. You both deserve so much more than I've given you."

CADEN

I wake cold, alone, and broken as fuck.

My whole world splintered apart last night. Everything I thought I knew was blown to smithereens in the space of a moment.

I can hear Bug moving about her room through the monitor, and my mouth twitches with a semblance of a smile, knowing that today she'll meet her big brother.

And even though I tell myself not to, I can't stop my mind from wandering to Summer, who's surely waking cold and alone out in the studio.

I reach for the remote control, point it haphazardly in the direction of the television, and watch as the screen flickers to life. But instead of the usual image of Disney Plus filling my vision, I'm met with the live feed from the security cameras in the recording studio.

Ford, having clearly lost all trust in Summer following the spiralling events of last night, had suggested streaming the feed to my bedroom. A suggestion I had taken and run with, but not for reasons he'd thought.

My trust in her has been broken. However, I'm aware that I, too, am at fault here. I welcomed her back, arms wide open and willing to ignore everything else. Had I not declared my love for her that first day, she'd never have had cause to further deceive me.

So the opportunity to allow my eyes to feast on her from afar had proven far too tempting.

Once I'd checked on Bug and seen Jesse to his bedroom—where he'd accepted a hug goodnight, much to my delight—I'd holed up in my lonely bed and watched as Summer drank herself sick.

My heart had broken for her as she face-planted on the bed and fell into a drunken sleep.

I'd left the house to go check on her, telling myself that I didn't want her to be sick in her sleep when really, I just needed to be close to her.

After spending half an hour watching her sleep, I'd turned her onto her side and left a glass of water on the nightstand, knowing beyond a doubt that she'd have need of it sooner than later before I'd slowly ambled back to the house.

I decided to check on the kids once more before attempting to seek my own slumber.

Bella was face down against her mattress with one knee drawn up against her side, snoring softly. I smiled softly, loving that she sleeps in the same position I sleep in, before moving down the hall to Jesse's room.

Peeking inside, my stomach dropped and tears prickled my eyes when I found him in the *exact* same position as his sister. His blonde hair had fallen forward over his forehead, and he looked so completely at peace, so utterly content, that I, once again, felt a rush of bitterness towards his mother.

A flood of such overwhelming resentment followed me to my room and into an erratic sleep interspersed with all manner of crazy dreams.

What a strange feeling to love someone as much as you hate them.

My eyes scan the TV screen for signs of movement, immediately spotting the rumpled sheets of her bed and the untouched glass of water on the nightstand.

I flick from one camera to the next, my heart rate kicking up a notch with each empty screen until I exit the live feed and access the recorded video files from earlier.

"Fuck!"

The expletive bursts from my mouth when the screen finds what it is I'm looking for.

Summer, dressed in blue jeans and a white hoodie with her hair scraped back off of her drawn, pale face, carried her small luggage bag down the stairs and exited the studio while we all slept.

I throw back the covers and run from the room, heading straight for the recording studio, praying that I'm mistaken. That what I've just seen is some big joke.

She hasn't just run from me again, *has she?*

I run directly into Ford when I throw open my front door, the look on his face stopping me in my tracks.

"What do you want, Ford? It's too early for drama, yeah?"

His eyes hold mine, and the wind goes out of my sails at the seriousness on his face.

"Do you want the Tequila Sunrise, the Tequila Sunrise, or the Tequila Sunrise first?"

I blow out a breath and scrub my palms up and down my face. "I'm just going to check the studio first, and then—"

He cuts me off. "That's the Tequila Sunrise."

"Don't say it. *Don't* fucking say it."

He purses his lips together for a beat before exhaling heavily. "She's gone, Cade. She spoke with Jesse in his room for a moment before an Uber brought her to London Heathrow."

His words, while not unexpected, drive all the air from my lungs, and I feel light-headed in the face of her desertion once again. My words—my plea—from yesterday echoes through my cavernous mind.

"Please don't run from me again. My heart can't take it."

I blink rapidly several times to dispel the black spots dancing in front of my vision. It takes a moment before I can see clearly. Ford is brandishing a sealed envelope bearing my name in cursive.

"She left this with the kid for you."

I reach out and snatch it from his hand, stuffing it into my back pocket before striding barefoot in the direction of my office, snarling over my shoulder. "I fucking *hate* Tequila Sunrise."

Hearing his feet on the tiles, I slip into the office, frowning deeply when I spot my now empty decanter of Macallan. I grit my jaw, needing to take the edge off before the next round of bad news, though I struggle to think of what could be worse than Summer doing the one thing I'd begged her not to.

Ford closes the door behind him quietly, scowling when he spots the empty decanter in my fist. Rather than berate me, he just grits his jaw till it tics and waits patiently for my nod to throw more shit my way.

"Spit it out, if you must."

"My guy, Eduardo, was in an accident last night. Car accident. I've been informed that he's in a medical coma while he recuperates, but..."

He trails off, and I curse silently. "That means he's out of commission and can't hack the voicemail box Noah left the message on."

Ford nods. "I have assigned it to another hacker. He's not as good as Eduardo, but he'll do it. It just might take a little longer than anticipated."

I heave a sigh as I nod. "Of course. I understand. Do we have eyes on Noah?"

"Yes. He's at Spellman Sounds HQ in London. Has been since he left Layla's hotel yesterday."

"Okay. Keep eyes on him." I place the decanter back on the sideboard and move to the desk, where I drop heavily into the seat. I raise my eyes to find Ford hasn't left yet.

"Yes?" I pop a brow questioningly.

He looks uncomfortable for the first time in as long as I've known him. Ford may be only twenty-two years of age, but he's got the quiet confidence of a man who's seen twice that number of years. Seeing him falter like this is disturbing me.

"There's more."

"Do I really need to know?"

He frowns, then hesitantly replies. "It's Layla, Cade."

I inhale deeply, feeling the incessant throb start in my temples that always hits me at the mere mention of her name.

"What's she done now?"

He swallows heavily. "One of my men posed as a hotel staff member this morning, delivering breakfast to her suite. He knocked more times than he remembers, but there was no answer. There had been no guests to or from her rooms last night. No phone calls either. But he...he felt that something was *off*."

Ford stops, blowing a breath out through his nose. "He let himself inside, but there was no sign of Layla to be found. Until he checked the bathroom..."

My eyes fall shut, knowing exactly what's about to come out of his mouth.

"She was in the tub, track marks on her arm and a syringe on the floor by her hand. She overdosed, Cade...Layla's dead."

Twenty-Three

SUMMER
THREE DAYS LATER

"Are you sure you don't need me to stay on, Anna?"

My beautiful friend spins on her heel and fixes me with a stern look before waggling her index finger in my direction. "I *swear*! So help me God, if you don't get the hell out of here, Summer, I will slap you silly."

I hold up my hands in defeat. "Okay, okay. Sheesh, woman. I'm gone for less than a freaking week, and you've replaced me—"

I'm cut off by Anna's twelve-going-on-twenty-year-old daughter, Ophelia, jumping into the conversation. "Yeah, she's replaced you alright, Aunt Summer. With *child labour*."

She mops her brow theatrically, blowing her dark hair out of her face.

"Not cool, Mom. You realise I could report you for working me to the bone!"

Her mother snorts, shooing her away. "You're the one who said you wanted to be treated like an adult. Time to put your money where your mouth is, my love."

Ophelia rolls her eyes, wandering back in the direction of her misplaced tray. "Whatever helps you sleep at night, slave driver."

Anna makes a face behind her daughter, making us both grin quietly.

"Seriously, Summer. Take a couple of days. Today's shift was probably too soon to be back anyway."

I shake my head and chuckle darkly. "I need to stay busy, Anna. I need to keep myself occupied. I've even signed up for extra shifts at Rogue."

My old friend slowly nods her head, but keeps her obvious thoughts to herself. "Okay, love. You know I'll never stop you from doing what you feel you've got to do."

I force a smile before hugging her goodbye and stepping out onto the Brooklyn pavement. I'm back at my apartment in less than ninety seconds.

My phone chimes with a text as I cross the threshold. I yank it from the pocket of my black work pants like a junkie in need of a fix. My heart smiles when I check the sender, only to plummet to my feet when I read the text.

JESSE

Caden said I wasn't to tell you, but we buried Bella's mom today.

My knees feel weak, my head fuzzy, and I stumble toward the frayed old couch we inherited from the previous owners to sit heavily on my ass.

Layla is dead?

I've not seen any reports on the TV or in the news. I'm equal parts shocked at the news and amazed that it's clearly remained a well-kept secret until I remember that, of course, Noah Spellman would be running point. Keeping the rumour mill at bay.

Maintaining a scandal-free client list, as he always has done.

I type a quick text back.

ME

Oh, baby. Is she doing okay? What about your father?

My immediate instinct is to order an Uber to JFK and hotfoot it back to Cambridge as fast as I can. My feet twitch with the need to move, but I fight it with everything I have inside of me.

I promised them time. They need time.

Without me. As much as that tears me apart.

My phone chimes with another message. My heart soars upon seeing the sender.

CADEN

We buried Layla this morning. I thought you deserved to know.

I bite down on my bottom lip in an effort to stop the emotion that flows through my body.

To the point. Almost clinical. As though he's informing a stranger.

I guess you know where you stand now, and you've only got yourself to blame.

My forehead puckers as the realisation strikes. I don't only have myself to blame. Noah Spellman forced me out of the UK. He stole the life that was mine.

And he's going to fucking pay.

Having changed out of my work gear from *Anna's Place,* I slip into a jogger set and grab the subway, heading uptown to Tribeca. When I'd realised Anna meant to pussy-foot around me, I'd organised for extra shifts, needing to keep my hands moving and my mind on something other than feeling sorry for myself.

Arriving at Rogue a good forty minutes before my shift, I slide in past a grinning Griffith. "Evening, Jolie!"

I smile brightly at this great big teddy bear of a man. "Missed you too, Griff."

Instead of heading to the changing area, I head right and upstairs, arriving outside Vaughn's office on silent feet. I'm about to twist the handle without knocking when I hear low grunts followed by a high-pitched cry.

I roll my eyes and lean against the opposite wall, waiting on him to finish.

There's giggling, followed by rustling, and without warning, the door flies open. Vaughn spots me, smirking at my unimpressed pout.

"Thanks for that, Mandy—"

"It's *Brandi.*"

He shrugs indifferently. "To-may-to. To-mah-to."

Her indignant gasp sees me hiding a smirk behind my fist as she storms from the room in her tassels and little else.

Vaughn's laughing eyes land on mine, and I shake my head, even as I can't hide my twitching lips. "You're *disgusting.*"

I move past him into his office, which damn well reeks of sex. It's never bothered me before, but now it just makes me crave the intimacy of being with my lover.

Focus, Summer!

Vaughn closes the door behind me, strides around his desk, and pours us both two fingers of Cognac. I accept the tumbler gratefully, downing it in one gulp.

As I gently deposit the glass on his massive teak desk, he raises a silent, surprised eyebrow before sipping from his own.

I don't preamble. "I need help."

His brow edges higher. "Haven't I been telling you that for years, sweetheart?"

I narrow my eyes and gesture for a refill. "I'm serious. I need one of your I.T. guys—the *specialised* ones—to look into someone for me."

"Who?"

Taking my refilled tumbler, I sip slowly, holding his dark eyes, letting the question hang between us. I trust Vaughn. Implicitly.

Somewhere along the way, my boss, Vaughn Burton, has become a friend of mine. He's rude, crass, and downright mean oftentimes, but he has a heart bigger than Texas, even though he hides it from almost everyone.

Maybe it's our shared heritage—both Londoners with no family to speak of—or maybe it's because *sometimes* the universe brings what you need into your life right when you need it.

When I'd been struggling to make ends meet, Vaughn had happened upon *Anna's Place*. It was well past midnight, and I had a toddler trying to sleep in the booth next to him.

I'd not told Anna things were as bad as all that.

I couldn't tell her that I'd resorted to overnighting in her booths with Jesse because we'd been evicted. I couldn't bear to see her pity. Or to experience my shame in vivid reality.

To expose just how *terrible* of a mother I felt I was in not being able to provide a basic necessity for my child.

But Vaughn had taken one look at me, at Jesse, and for some reason, he'd decided to take a chance on us.

Somehow, he'd sensed that my pride was at stake and that I

didn't trust easily, so he'd left that night, returning the following day with news of a cheap apartment nearby. Conveniently housing two rooms and fully furnished by the previous inhabitants.

In exchange for the money to pay two months upfront and a month's deposit, he'd had a proposition for me.

Work at his exclusive patrons-only club, Rogue, in whatever capacity he needed me. I'd agreed almost immediately, sensing a kindred soul of some sort despite my trust issues.

He explained that Rogue housed three sections: *Rapture, Risqué,* and *Ravish.*

It had begun as cleaning after hours, which fitted in with my daytime shifts at Anna's. Bar work in *Rapture,* the first tier of membership, was next. The tips were exorbitant, to say the least.

One night, we were talking in his office before my shift in *Rapture* when a performer from *Risqué* called in with the stomach flu. It was the same week I'd had reached out to Layla and been turned away. And Jesse's treatment was expensive.

Too expensive.

I'd pleaded with Vaughn, and after I'd threatened to find similar work elsewhere, he'd reluctantly allowed me to fill her slot.

"Are you sure *you want to go through with this, sweetheart?"*

Vaughn's concerned orbs hold mine as I shrug out of the satin dressing gown he'd left out for me when I'd changed into my 'performance' outfit.

It wasn't an outfit so much as a nod towards underwear. A sheer black eyelet lace bra with slightly darker lace covering my nipples alongside a matching sheer lace thong and garter belt, finished with a pair of elegant black Louboutins.

Vaughn's eyes drop down my body when I pass him the dressing gown, unmistakable desire flaring in his chocolate eyes.

"Eyes up here, soldier!"

His brow lifts lazily, and he slowly drags his gaze up along my body, making me squirm uncomfortably. When he finally meets my eyes, the desire is gone, and he smirks knowingly. "If me *looking makes you uncomfortable, sweetheart, then it's time to call it a day."*

I narrow my eyes, refusing to fall for his sly tactics. Placing my fists on my hips, I stare him down. "I'm not *a charity case, Vaughn Burton. I can provide for* my *son. Now scoot. You're giving me the ick."*

Vaughn sighs softly, fixing my masquerade mask perfectly to the contours of my face before he steps back. Reluctance is clear in his posture, but he shrugs it off in that signature devil-may-care way he has about him. "For what it's worth, Jesse has one hell of a mum in his corner."

I inhale through my nose, keeping my emotions at bay, as I sidestep him to walk further inside the private rooms, finding the designated room for Jolie. *Upon pushing the door open, I stifle my gasp of surprise to find two masked men sitting side-by-side.*

"Good evening, Jolie."

I nod demurely. My heart is beating so harshly against my breastbone that I think I might just pass out before this evening is through.

"Turn around and place your palms on the back of the seat."

Barely stopping my eyebrows from flying to my hairline, I do as they bid, placing my hands on the back of a high-back chair with wobbly legs.

The music is loud in my ears as I await further instruction. These private rooms are known for certain proclivities, *though I don't think Vaughn would place me anywhere dangerous. Even so, the skin on the back of my neck is raised.*

There's movement at my back, though I can't see what. I shift my head slightly to the side to find both men with their dicks out, wanking one another off as they stare from behind their masks at the barely covered globes of my ass.

My face flushes as my mouth drops open. One of them catches my eye, winking before dipping his head to take his companion's cock into his mouth.

Shifting my head back so that I can't see them anymore, I focus my eyes on the wall, block my ears to the intimate sounds of their coupling and count.

One Mississippi. Two Mississippi. Three…

I make it all the way to two hundred forty-seven when I feel a hand pat my black lace panties, making me jolt upright.

"You've been amazing, Jolie. I'll make sure to tell Vaughn just how perfect that pussy was."

I keep my eyes on the wall, making a non-committal grunt as the men leave the room. Once I know I'm alone, I fall to the floor, hugging my knees to my chest, and I remain like that until Vaughn pushes the door open.

He drops the satin gown over my trembling shoulders. "Come on, sweetheart. Let's get you home."

I raise teary eyes to his kind ones. "I don't know…I don't—"

He crouches down beside me, pinching my chin between his thumb and index finger. "They weren't even interested in you, sweetheart. Only as being their beard, you get what I'm saying? I would never put you in danger."

At first, I'd been horrified I'd allowed myself to do—or not do—what I'd just done. But that first night alone paid for all the bills we'd accumulated since Jesse had been diagnosed.

Five *thousand* dollars. For standing there and keeping myself to myself.

And to afford my kid's excessive hospital bills, I would do just about anything, which was the truly scary realisation.

I agreed to repeat visits in *Risqué* with the two mystery men—men in loveless political marriages who had fallen in love with one another, despite the obstacles—every couple of weeks until I'd paid all the debt from Jesse's treatment. We'd even had enough money to take a trip to Florida, where we drove through the Keys for ten glorious days.

And I've no doubt that Vaughn was behind it. Ensuring I was involved in a setting with as little discomfort as possible. That I was in no way involved intimately. That I didn't have to *perform*.

He'd found a way to give me the money to pay for my kid's cancer treatment without making me feel like a charity case. And for that, he'll always have my friendship and my gratitude.

So while I do trust him, I need a moment to be sure I'm doing the right thing. If I go down this path, there's no coming back. I need to be sure I can live with the repercussions.

My hesitation makes him narrow his eyes. "Come on, sweetheart. If you need someone looked into, you know I'm your man. For the low, low price of a blowie, I'll—"

"*Vaughn*!"

He chuckles at my shriek. "Spit it the fuck out then. You're killing me here."

Fuck it.

"Noah Spellman."

He sits back in his chair, scratching his messy dark hair. "As in the owner of Spellman Sounds, *Noah Spellman*?"

I nod, and he scrunches up his face in apparent distaste. "That man is as clean as a whistle, sweetheart. You'll find sweet fuck all in a search."

Pinning him with a dark look, I lean forward until my stomach hits his desk, willing him to understand just how much I need this. "Everyone has skeletons, Vaughn. Some are just more adept at burying theirs down deep."

He exhales heavily, tipping his head in assent. "Fine. I'll have a guy dig into him." He pierces me with a stare. "How deep are we talking now, sweetheart?"

I answer without hesitation. "Back to before he was who he is now."

"Okay, but this shit will take time. You'll have to be patient."

I smirk sadistically. "I'm well versed in patience, Vaughn. I can wait forever, so long as it means he gets what's owed."

Vaughn whistles before standing and offering me an arm, which I take. "I've never seen this side of you. Have to say, sweetheart…" He shoots me a devilish wink. "It makes my cock twitch in my fucking pants."

I roll my eyes and bump his hip with mine.

Incorrigible man.

"I see right through you, Vaughn Burton. You can take my word for it that someday, you'll meet your match and when that day comes…" I trail off, and he looks down with mirth on his face.

"And when that day comes, *what*?"

I swallow my smirk to deadpan. "And when that day comes, I'll be right here when you fuck it all up."

His guffaw echoes through the busy changing area where employees are scrambling to change, either before or after their shifts, and all eyes land on us when everyone stops dead in their tracks.

"Get back to work, ladies."

His words make everyone kick it up a notch, and he leans

down to whisper in my ear, "Spoiler alert, sweetheart. All men fuck up. It's an ingrained character flaw."

He unlinks our arms, patting my shoulder almost awkwardly before he turns to go back upstairs, calling over his shoulder, "I'll text if my guy finds anything."

Feeling as though I've done something productive with my day, I move off to the bartenders' changing room, chatting with some girls along the way.

As I've known most of the girls for years, it takes an age to get where I'm going. All of them are full of questions about my London trip. About how Jesse is. One girl who goes by the performance name, Fantasy, but is really called Lucille, even asks me if Caden North's dick is as big as his on-stage ego, much to the delight of everyone listening in.

A new performer I don't recognise sidles up alongside me, asking if I've seen Vaughn's latest cocktail menus. She introduces herself as Kellie, and we spend about twenty minutes looking at the new recipes.

"I used to work at Angel's downtown, and they had a very similar selection, Summer. I'm new here, and my shifts are still a little on the slow side, so I'd be *more* than happy to help you learn how to mix these."

I smile brightly at the younger girl. "I would love that!"

"Great." Her mouth matches mine as her name is called from the far side of the room. "I better go. My shift starts soon."

Smiling at her friendliness, I try to focus on getting through the shift and how happy I'll be *when* Vaughn digs up all of Noah Spellman's skeletons.

Twenty-Four

CADEN
TWO DAYS LATER

Bug waves out the back window of my mother's SUV. Huddles Bunny is snuggled up by her smiling face until they drive out of sight, and even then, I continue to wave.

I've never been so grateful to send my daughter away. Grateful and utterly fucking miserable.

Mum decided yesterday that she needed to take Bella on an impromptu week-long trip to Disneyland in California.

"She's a baby, Cade. She has no clue what's just happened. Let me spoil her. I need to spoil my grandbaby."

And I'd been helpless to say no.

Especially since it had come after witnessing her and Dad meeting their only grandson for the first time.

"Son, we're here."

Dad's voice calls through my foyer and into the kitchen where I'm sat in my funeral best, waiting to bury the mother of my daughter.

"I'm in here." They quickly follow my voice, their sad eyes landing on Bella playing quietly on the floor with the copious toys that Noah had sent her the day after Layla was found.

I rise and quickly embrace my mum, who moves off to pour herself a coffee, and then Dad. As I step from his embrace, Jesse enters from the patio door.

"Did you want me to keep Bug occupied today?"

I smile at his casual use of my nickname for his sister as my mother turns to greet the newcomer. Her face freezes, and the coffee cup falls from her hand, smashing to bits on the tiles at her feet.

Dad follows her line of vision, clutching at his breastbone when he spots my miniature in the doorway.

"Mum. Dad. Meet Jesse" My voice breaks when I see realisation light up their faces, followed by an outpouring of love. "My son."

Neither of them waits for another second before they move around the kitchen island that separates them from their grandson, and together they wrap him in their joint embrace. Mum's sobs fill the kitchen as silent tears stream down my father's face.

The lump in my throat makes breathing difficult as I find my son's smiling eyes. He wraps his arms around his grandparents, holding tight, and I file the image away into my memory to be treasured for always.

Knowing that I'm likely to give her just about anything, having seen her and Dad dote upon Jesse over the last two days,

I'd agreed to the Disney trip without hesitation.

Life's too fucking short.

Bella had spent the entire five days since Summer's abrupt departure unmindful of her mother's passing, instead asking where her Summer-hero was.

And rather than fill me with joy as it once had, every question from my little girl's mouth made my heart harden even further towards the mother of my son.

Serena had called to let us know her sister had taken a turn, and she would need a couple more days, meaning we didn't even have Bug's usual routine back in place to distract her from the incessant questions about Summer.

The one bright spot in the midst of her confusion had been meeting her big brother.

His easy grace, so similar to his mother's, had Bella instantly gravitating towards him to fill the space her Summer-hero had left behind.

And he'd been quick to take up the mantle of protector, after passing the superhero tea party test with flying colours.

Mum had been quick to follow up their Disney trip with the idea of regrouping at Dad's ranch, North Star, in Texas afterwards. It's right next to Ford's parents' place, Circle H, which is how we got to know the Holloway family in the first place.

It's not a bad idea, seeing as I'm due to make final changes to the vocals on Misdirection's latest album, and the studio that Dad built there is second-to-fucking-none.

My mother. The master manipulator.

The thought puts a half-smile on my face as Jesse appears at my side.

How I'd have handled these past days without this boy beside me, I don't know.

My son is filled with a quiet strength I've only ever experienced at the hands of one other person. His mother.

The fact that he's a well-reared boy with thought for others and an inherent kindness built into his soul makes the wasted years somehow seem less so. As though his mother—because I can't think of her as anything closer to my heart, in case I hop a plane and beg on my knees for her to come back to me—had spent those years moulding him into the most perfect version of our love.

"Have you heard from Mom?"

I turn my head to the side, finding him facing forward. His face gives nothing away.

"I texted her two days ago to tell her Layla died. I can't tell her anything else because we haven't released the news to the media, kid."

He nods slowly, not meeting my eyes. "Oh. Okay."

A frown crosses my face as he stares into the distance. "Have *you* spoken to her?"

His face lightens considerably, and my chest clenches in envy. "Yup. We talk daily."

I grunt before spinning on my heel, making a beeline for the recording studio.

It's been aired out since she left. Should be safe now.

I need to strum some chords. Hit some motherfucking drums. I need to do *something*.

"Mind if I watch, Caden?"

I grit my teeth at his use of my first name, but force a nod.

It's like he's doing it to punish me. For not claiming him sooner? For letting his mother leave? For getting his mother pregnant and not remembering the damn act?

Fuck.

Her revelation of us being together before she'd left had broken me. I had *no* recollection. None at all. It *had* to be that time. The dates line up perfectly, plus from Summer's recollection, I'm relatively sure I didn't wrap it up.

How had she lived? What was his delivery like? Had she been able to afford proper medical care? A decent apartment?

I had a million and one questions, and like a fool, I'd let her leave. I'd not given chase. I should have stopped her. Or made her come back.

I should have done *something*. Instead of staying here, festering in emotions I can't put a name on.

It's no wonder my son thinks I'm unworthy of the title of his father.

My phone beeps with a text message, and I swipe to read as we reach the building.

FORD

The automated message server was a bust.
Led back to his driving service.

ME

Keep. Looking.

I barely stop the expletive on the tip of my tongue as I jam the offensive device into my back pocket with a scowl.

Flicking on the lights as I enter, I head straight for the only instrument I know is set up and tuned to my liking.

My acoustic guitar.

I strum some chords, sensing more than seeing Jesse settle himself on the oversized plush couch opposite me. Once I've found my stride, I play the opening of "Nothing Else Matters," cursing myself for picking a song that only reminds me of her.

Rather than sing the lyrics, I just play, focusing on the familiar beat until a voice resonates off the vaulted ceiling, piercing my soul and almost making me drop my damn guitar.

My head shoots up, and I continue strumming to find Jesse has moved closer. He's a little over a metre away, eyes closed, forehead creased and softly singing along.

His voice catches me off guard. It's deeper than it should be, considering his age, and pitch perfect. He opens his eyes to find me staring. A flush graces his face, and he stops suddenly.

I set my guitar down gently beside me. "That's quite a gift, kid. Your voice is beautiful."

His flush deepens, reminding me of his mother. "Mom always said I got it from my dad."

My chest constricts at his words, and I rub the spot over my heart before indicating that he should sit by me.

"Did your mom tell you much about me?" I try to keep the hopeful tone from my voice, but I don't think I succeed.

"Well…" he trails off, looking away for a beat before his eyes shoot back to mine. "She said it was safer for me if I didn't know who you were."

He chews his lip in a gesture so reminiscent of his mother's that I can feel my heart fracture further inside my chest.

"I guess she had her reasons." His tone is so low; I think he's mostly speaking to himself.

"But, she was actually really honest about everything, now that I think back. I'm surprised I didn't put two and two together before now." When he grins at me, I can't help but mirror his beautiful smile.

"She said that you guys were soulmates but that the time just wasn't right."

I rub my chest again.

Damn, that stings.

"She told me stories. Loads of them." His big blue eyes light up when he's talking, and I sit by him, just soaking up his contagious exuberance as he relays tale after tale of our misspent youth.

Of days together that even I'd forgotten over time.

"She said she couldn't look at you for like two weeks after she kissed you." He laughs as he finishes the story of our first kiss. "She always liked that one best. She used to repeat it every time I had a chemo session because it made both of us smile. She's such a nerd."

The reminder of his ill health sees me gritting my teeth. "I've touched base with your doctors in New York. They've sent your medical records to the best of the best. We'll get you a donor with plenty of time to spare."

His doctors had indicated that they believed in waiting until Jesse was in full health and twelve months cancer free before doing the transplant, and the haematologist that Dr Kline recommended to us had agreed.

Unknown to Jesse, I'd already had the HLA test to check my compatibility. Bella and my parents too. It had just been a quick cheek swab and blood test.

"Mom said I have a rare blood type, so getting a match won't be easy."

His pragmatism makes him sound years older than fourteen, and I nudge him with my shoulder, preferring his carefree exuberance of before. "Don't worry, Jess. There's a whole extended family just waiting to be tested. I *guarantee* someone will be a perfect match."

Following a morning in the studio, I side-eye Jesse as we head back to the house. "Fancy a road trip?"

He nods enthusiastically, and within thirty minutes, we're on the road to London. The boys are having lunch at Mila and Nate's apartment, and when they'd initially invited me, I'd declined.

Now, it seems like the perfect opportunity for them to meet my son. And I can't help smirking when Ford pulls up alongside the curb as I anticipate their reactions.

"I'll call when we're ready, yeah?"

Ford nods before pulling back out into traffic. Parking in the city is a bitch.

"So let me get this straight. Henry is the CEO guy, right?"

"Correct. And Nate is the writer who's dating Henry's sister, Mila."

He nods, then pins me with a questioning look. "Did he write anything good?"

"Nah. Absolute crap, Jess."

Jesse purses his lips together and looks at the floor as he tries to hide his smile. It's not long before we're pressing the buzzer to gain access to the penthouse floor.

"Hello?" Mila's voice calls down the line. It's filled with laughter and a little breathless.

"It's Cade. Can I come up?"

"It's your funeral, Joker."

I shake my head at her reference to my sister's nickname as the elevator doors open to admit us.

"Why did she call you that?"

I snort and roll my eyes as I step on. "When you meet your Aunt Cass, she'll definitely tell you *all* about it."

The doors close once Jesse has stepped on, and as the car moves, he begins to shuffle and fidget.

"Nervous?"

He meets my eyes, his mouth twisted in a semblance of a half smile, and he nods slowly. "Yeah. Mom said your friends are more like your family. She had loads of stories about them too."

I place my hand on his shoulder, squeezing lightly in reassurance. "They're going to love you."

He inhales deeply through his nose and blows it out of his mouth just as the elevator doors open with a chime.

We step off into an empty apartment. There is a mountain of dirty dishes piled on the table and evidence of Mila and Nate's Italian cooking all over the messy kitchen.

"Hello?"

My call is met with laughter, and Nate's voice sounds out from down the hall leading to the bedrooms. "We're in here."

The door to the second bedroom is open wide, and when we arrive at the threshold, I can't stop a massive grin from splitting my face in half.

Liv and Mila are sat side by side on the spare bed, laughing uproariously at Henry and Nate, who are kneeling on the floor, trying to change little Bash's nappy. A nappy that looks absolutely toxic if the smell is anything to go by.

"You need to hold his legs, Henry."

"He won't stay still, for Christ's sake." Bash flips over onto his belly, kicking and smiling as some of the foul-smelling contents of his nappy leak out the side. Nate cringes and edges closer to his girlfriend.

"Christ, Peach. A little help here!" Henry looks at his wife with frantic eyes, and Mila and Nate dissolve into floods of laughter.

Liv inclines her head, holding her husband's eyes and speaking slowly, as though to an infant, much to his consternation. "I believe you said—and this is verbatim—'I'm a pro at this shit. Hold my beer, Peach.'"

He shakes his head in clear desperation. "I'm not a pro. You are. You're a damn queen, baby!"

Liv stands, plucks her wriggling son from the floor, somehow managing to keep all poop contained and heads in the direction of the bathroom. "And don't you forget it."

Three sets of eyes turn towards us when Jesse chuckles lightly, and as though in slow motion, all three mouths drop open.

I throw my arm across Jesse's shoulder, tugging him in against my side. His face mirrors my smiling one as I puff out my chest. "Meet my son, Jesse."

Twenty-Five

SUMMER

I'd never realised how lonely New York would be without my son.

After being glued to his side, pretty much for everything other than work or school, for his entire life, I've found myself at a loss when it comes to having free time.

I've tried to take extra shifts with Anna, but to no avail.

I've taken a trip out to Coney Island. It was a dumb idea. The boardwalk was not only congested, but the sights, sounds, and smells all reminded me of my boy.

And I was overcome with the insane idea that I'd love nothing further than to take Bella on all the rides. I had no doubt that her fearlessness would make her the best ride buddy.

My arms cried out to hold both the son of my body and the daughter of my heart, despite having no right to feel that way.

And on top of all these rampant feelings, my brain was still ticking away with ideas of how to get a bone marrow transplant should we not find a match within the North family.

I've been fixated on unearthing a donor since the doctors had first noted their recommendation almost six months earlier. The only time I've been able to shut off that side of my brain has been while I've been working, or with Caden.

And therein lies the other issue.

Having spent five blissful days close to my siren song, my entire being itches with the need to be close to him once more. I'd thought that since I'd deprived myself of his proximity for fifteen years, I'd be able to return to that state. However, the more time we are apart, the heavier my heart aches.

I miss the three of them with a bone-aching hunger.

Keeping busy is the only thing for it, and since Anna won't have me at the diner, and everywhere else reminds me of Jesse, I find myself gravitating towards Rogue more and more.

Kellie is as good as her word, teaching me her mixology skills with relish. We even go for lunch one afternoon, and I feel happy at the beginning of a newfound friendship.

It's one thing I've struggled with over the years. After trusting Noah, I'd been very slow to trust anyone else.

Anna had taken years to win me around. Vaughn too.

Kellie seemed to burrow in under my skin in a matter of days. And it felt nice to open myself up to a new friend, not to mention the fact that spending time with her was a welcome distraction from the myriad of thoughts inside my head.

Until Vaughn sends me a cryptic message.

VAUGHN

Come upstairs. Tell no one where you're going.

I drop my phone into my pocket and turn to Kellie. "I'll be

right back."

She smiles brightly, continuing to apply her make-up.

When I slip into Vaughn's office, I find him at his desk, a scowl front and centre.

I gingerly take a seat. "What's up?"

"Your new friend, that's what's up."

My forehead creases in confusion. "What does that mean?"

"Kellie recognised you as being the woman with Caden North in all those stupid viral videos."

A sheen of sweat breaks out across my forehead. "Oh my *God*."

"She's gone to the media, told them she knows the mystery woman and her whereabouts."

I feel like my world has just spun on its head. Tears prick my eyes at my naivety in thinking I could ever trust *anyone*.

"And worst of all, my media contact told me that she said she has photos and video footage of you backstage here, which are ruinous to both you and my business."

CADEN

Once the gang has recovered, and little Bash has been changed into a new outfit and a fresh nappy, we gather in the living room. Mila makes short work of passing out enough Italian food to feed a small army.

As we're finishing, Jesse's phone begins to ring. His face flushes, and he can't meet my eyes when he tugs it from his pocket. "I need to take this."

"You can use the spare room for some privacy, Jesse." Mila nods kindly, and Jesse slips from his seat beside me. His voice echoes through the hallway before he closes the door. "Hey,

Mom!"

I exhale heavily, waiting for the inevitable onslaught, only to glance around the table to find four pairs of sad eyes trained upon me.

"What?"

They glance at one another, exchanging silent questions. Henry is the first one to speak. "You okay, brother?"

"I'm fine." I pick up my glass of water to soothe my suddenly parched throat.

"Where is she?"

I force my lips downward as I shrug indifferently. "I haven't asked. Gone back to the States, presumably."

"He's a wonderful boy." That's Liv.

I meet her kind blue eyes, and she continues.

"He's very like you. Not just in looks, but in his actions."

"Yeah!" Henry chimes in. "They have the exact same laugh, the same sense of humour. It's uncanny."

"I think he's like his mother." The words have left my mouth before I can help myself.

Four faces stare at me askance, so I'm obligated to continue. "He's kind. Caring. Thoughtful. Selfless…"

I trail off at the last, my forehead crumpling as tears prick my eyes.

"Sounds like his mother *and* his father have a lot in common, in that case."

I raise confused eyes to Mila as she smiles softly.

"It's okay for the heart to want what it wants, regardless of the apparent rights and wrongs of it, Cade. Life isn't ever black and white."

Nate presses a kiss to her temple, and I can feel my brows draw together in bewilderment, but before I can question what she means, movement down the hallway indicates Jesse's return.

"Mom wants to speak to you, Caden."

I stiffen at his insistence on using my first name, but plaster a smile on my face as I stand, plucking the phone from my son's outstretched hand.

"I'll be right back."

Jesse takes his seat at the table with my found family, as my long strides take me in the direction of the roof garden outside. I can hear when they engulf him with tales of our youth, and the thought that they've taken him to their hearts so quickly puts a smile on my weary face.

Once I've closed the glass door behind me, I hold the phone to my ear.

"Yes?"

Summer doesn't preamble. "I'm so terribly sorry for Bella's loss."

I make a noncommittal grunt, unsure how to answer. I still don't know how I feel about Layla's death.

"Umm…also…I know that you've had Jesse's medical records transferred to the UK. I…I was hoping you'd keep me in the loop. Umm…please?"

"Like you kept me in the loop?"

There's a long silence while I berate myself for my newfound asshole status.

"I deserve that." She huffs a dark laugh, her voice dropping to a whisper. "I deserve worse."

"Once I know details, you'll know, yeah?" My words are clipped, and she murmurs her assent.

"For what it's worth, I'm sorry, Cade."

"For what part, Summer?" My words are a snarl that sounds foreign even to my own ears, yet I can't help the emotions bubbling inside of me from spewing over. "For keeping my son from me? For not coming to me when he got cancer the first time? The *second* fucking time? For making me *hope* that we could find our way back to one another, despite every obstacle? For making my daughter fall in love with you?"

I break off, breathing heavily as though I've just run a marathon. "Or perhaps you're only sorry now because your lies caught up to you. Is that it, hmm?"

Silence ensues. It's long and tense. My temple throbs painfully.

"I *hate* what you've done to us, Summer."

My words are a bare whisper, and her sharp intake of breath pierces my heart.

"Are you ready or what, sweetheart?"

A male voice on the other end of the line breaks the silence between us.

"I need to go, Cade. I—I agree with everything you've said. I know I've hurt you beyond all hope of redemption, and for that, I am more sorry than you can ever know, but I do hope that we can at least stay on the same page…for our son."

Her understanding in the face of my uncharacteristic contempt irks me even more than the strange fucker who's with her.

"I'll text you."

I hang up without another word and turn to go back inside, only to find Jesse in the doorway, sad eyes fixed on his phone in my hand.

"Do you hate my mom?"

He raises eyes identical to my own to my weary gaze. For a moment, I contemplate saying yes, that I do hate her.

But I don't want to lie to my kid.

Partly because I'm not a liar, but mostly because I *don't* hate her. God fucking help me. The rational part of me knows that she did the best she could with what she had.

"When something isn't in the cards for you, you learn to be grateful for the life you've been given."

Her words from last Saturday—fuck, was it only last Saturday—resound in my ears as I close the space between us.

"No, Jess. I don't hate your mother. I could never hate her. For one thing, she gave me *you.*" I tug him roughly into my embrace when I see his bottom lip begin to tremble.

He wraps his arms around my waist, tucking his face against my chest as I press a kiss atop his messy blonde hair.

"I hate what has happened to us. To *all* of us. But I don't hate her."

And that's the worst part.

If I could hate her, I might be able to quit loving her.

"Come on, kid." I ruffle his hair playfully while plastering a smile on my face. After fifteen years of practice, I'm a damn pro. "Let's see what these guys have for dessert."

Twenty-Six

CADEN

Following an evening of Tiramisu and Twister—Mila had dug it out, claiming it was for Jesse, only to kick everyone's asses with some Matrix-style flexibility—Henry and I ring down for our respective drivers.

Liv packs up Bash whilst Mila and Nate monopolise my son in a conversation about some new Netflix series that I have zero interest in.

"What self-respecting man watches that shit?" Henry's face is scrunched up in pure distaste. "Hawthorne is such a fucking pussy."

I snort, agreeing with Henry's statement, but instead of verbalising that, I take the opportunity to irritate him.

"I agree. He really does love fucking that pussy."

I watch his nostrils flare out of the corner of my vision, pressing my lips together so hard it hurts.

He bumps me with his shoulder forcefully enough that I stumble, and the laugh I was attempting to withhold rings out across the apartment. All eyes land on us, and I shrug like I've no idea what's just happened.

"You make it too damn easy, brother."

He rolls his eyes as everyone returns to what they were doing. "Jesse's a great kid, Cade."

I sober immediately, nodding my agreement. "It just stings that I missed out on so much of his childhood, you know?"

Henry's brows draw together in a deep frown as he turns to face me. "Do you remember what you said to me? That day on the phone when you told me she'd come back?"

I frown in thought, immediately knowing what he's referencing. My own words replay in my mind.

"I knew I didn't need answers. I just need her. However she'll have me."

I don't realise I've spoken them aloud until Henry questions me.

"Do you still feel the same way?"

Scrubbing my palms across the stubble on my cheeks, I blow out a heavy breath but opt for my signature satire. "Einstein said the definition of insanity is doing the same thing over and over and expecting different results."

"Ah, Cade. Have you missed the memo?"

I look at my best friend dubiously, and he continues, the beginning of a smile lightening his green eyes.

"All women drive men insane." He leans closer to stage-whisper, whether conspiratorially or theatrically, I'm unsure. "Insanity is worth it when it's the *right* woman who's driving you there."

I see Liv wave Henry over in her peripheral vision before Jesse sidles up alongside us. Henry straightens and begins to move off, clapping Jesse on the shoulder in a loving gesture.

"And, North?"

"Yeah?"

"Sometimes you've got to take a leap of faith and trust that the universe knows what it's doing, brother. Just because the time's never been right before doesn't mean it's never going to be right." He winks. "Keep doing your thing, yeah?"

He sends Jesse a warm smile as I mull over his uncharacteristically deep words.

"It's been crazy and wonderful to meet you, Jesse. Welcome to the family."

Henry walks over to his waiting wife, pressing a kiss to her brow before plucking his son from her hold.

Who the fuck are you, and what happened to Henry DeMarco?

My face must be a picture as I hear my phone chime with a text from Ford, alerting me to his arrival.

"Come on, kid. Let's blow this popsicle stand!"

I sling my arm over Jesse's shoulder, tugging him in against my side playfully as we step onto the elevator.

"You are way more cringe than I'd thought you would be, Dad."

Did he just say…

A frog appears in my throat, taking up residence for the entire trip to the ground floor. Jesse stands at my side the entire time, his arm wrapped around my waist as I hold him close to me.

When the elevator opens, he steps out of my hold and is halfway across the lobby before I can move after him.

The biggest, most shit-eating smile I've ever smiled splits my face clean in half as I jog after my boy, catching up to him before he reaches Ford's waiting vehicle.

He shoots me a shit-eating smile of his own when he spots mine. "But I have to admit, I like your cringe better than Mom's."

I open the door, ushering Jesse inside first while I chuckle at his statement and then follow after him.

"Evening, Ford."

Ford tips his head in that strong silent way of his before pulling out into London city traffic. "Heading back home, Cade?"

I nod once as I buckle in, spinning slightly in my seat to face Jesse.

"You're going to have to elaborate on that one, kid. Just how cringe *is* your mom?"

His face shines with adoration at the mention of his mother, and I can see as clear as day that she never had a thing to worry about when it came to telling our son the truth of his parentage. He's a mama's boy through and through.

Being one myself, I can easily spot the signs.

"Okay, so the most recent one I can think of was when I aced my Geometry test last month. She picked me up early from school just as Mr Wiseman was passing out the grades, and when she saw mine…" he trails off to eye roll dramatically. "She *danced* out the door, down the hallway, and into the street singing 'Ain't No Mountain High Enough'!"

I can't stop myself from smiling. I can clearly see the memory in my mind's eye despite not being present to witness it.

It's such a typical Summer thing to do.

"She took cringe to a whole new level when she used her cell phone as her mic and held it out for me to sing the harmony!"

I can't stop myself from sniggering at that. She's long been a sucker for a duet.

"Come on, tell me more."

Jesse's face lights up, and I feel lighter in myself than I have all week.

"Well, I remember when I used to beg her to take me to your Misdirection concerts, she would wear all the fan merch. She'd belt out the lyrics louder than anyone standing near us. I remember one time she *cried* and…" he trails off, as though realising the reason why.

His face falls, and I can feel mine mirroring his.

"I get it now. Why she cried." He turns in his seat, facing forward once more to slide his phone from his pocket. "I made fun of her for crying, but she was crying because she missed you. And I *made her* take me."

He opens his text messages, and I can see him start a new one for Summer. I pat his knee, squeezing gently before facing forward myself.

My head and my heart were already in complete conflict, but that right there—that had the scales tipping in favour of my heart.

Yeah, I'd thought she'd left me. But she'd only been able to watch from afar, fearful of reaching out for any number of reasons, and when she *had*, she'd been turned away.

I can only imagine how difficult it would be to watch the person you love seemingly make a life without you while you watched on, helpless to change things. The fact she'd brought Jesse to my concerts and had willingly put herself through that turmoil…

No! Stop that, dumb heart.

I close my eyes and take a deep breath while I forcibly shove all thoughts of Summer St James from my damn mind. When I recentre myself, I grab my own phone and type out an email to my old P.I. Larry.

Sender: Caden North
(caden@north.com)

Recipient: Larry Simmons (simmons.larry.@outlook.com)

Larry,
Thank you for your recent update on the elusive Miss St James.

I wanted to touch base with you regarding some questions I have about your investigation into finding her over the years.

It has come to my attention that our mutual friend, Noah Spellman, had a hand in sending her away. Obviously, this is very much a he-said/she-said situation, and I'm hoping you can be my tiebreaker.

Can you confirm that Mr Spellman had nothing to do with Miss St James's disappearance?

I'm aware this puts you in a predicament. However, you can be assured of my discretion in this matter.

As always, thank you for your help.

Regards,
Caden North

I hit send, and a reply pops up instantaneously as my phone beeps an alert.

Swiping the screen, I tap on the email and quickly skim the contents.

Sender: Larry Simmons
(simmons.larry.@outlook.com)

Recipient: Caden North
(caden@north.com)

I am currently out of the office and will reply upon my return.

Best,
Larry

My forehead creases.

Shit!

Just as I'm about to lock my screen, a text message pops up in my notifications. I tap it with my thumb, and my whole body thrums with nervous energy as I slowly turn towards Jesse.

"Kid?"

He raises a questioning gaze to mine, and I can barely get the words out.

"They've found a donor!"

SUMMER

Since returning to New York, I've been circumspect.

I've kept my head down, gone about my business, and avoided the media.

Until now.

"Are you ready or what, sweetheart?"

Vaughn enters his office briskly, impatience emanating from

his immaculately dressed body. I shoot him a quelling look, to which he responds with an eye roll.

"I need to go, Cade. I—I agree with everything you've said. I know I've hurt you beyond all hope of redemption, and for that, I am more sorry than you can ever know, but I do hope that we can at least stay on the same page…for our son."

Caden is silent for a heartbeat until he speaks curtly. "I'll text you." Then he hangs up immediately.

I heave a sigh and look up into Vaughn's frowning face. "That the pretty boy?"

My nod of acknowledgement sees my boss standing and rounding the desk between us to rest against it. "Does he know the issues you're having with these motherfucking paps?"

"No. And I want to keep it that way. He has enough on his plate right now, okay? So, I need you to help me out." My voice is firm, and Vaughn has known me long enough now to know when I won't be swayed.

Cade has more than enough to deal with. I can handle some idiot news hounds.

"I've fired Kellie and had my lawyer slap a gag order on her big fucking trap too."

I feel some of the tension drain from my shoulders at that.

Vaughn had stepped in and was in the process of, at least, *trying* to prevent the story from being more than a rumour amongst the hounds.

Once it comes to light that I work here, all bets are off. For everyone involved. Vaughn included.

It's the exact reason he makes *all* employees sign airtight contracts—and the reason Kellie will be prosecuted for violating hers. Or perhaps Vaughn will hold it over her to ensure her silence.

The fact that I've always worked at Rogue under an alias, worn my trusty wigs and painted my face to be almost unrecognisable would all be moot. My anonymity went out the window when that video from the Alexandra Palace went viral.

My connection with Cade thrust me into a spotlight I have *no* interest in. I have long sought to keep to myself, but now that choice seems to have been taken from me.

"I won't let them run any of it, sweetheart. I've got connections in the media. If I can't nix the story, I'll spin it. *Trust me*!"

"I trust you, Vaughn. More than almost anyone. I know you'll keep your word."

His dark eyes hold mine, his brow knitting together as he nods. "I've got your back."

"Thank you."

He waves me off, sliding a file out of his desk drawer and dropping it onto the desk between us. I pick it up and begin to flip through notes, records, and pictures of Noah Spellman.

"This is what my guy has dug up so far. Nothing you wouldn't already know."

There's credit history, bank balances, and various phone accounts, but there's absolutely nothing out of the ordinary.

"How far back did he go?"

"Far enough to find that Noah was the result of an affair. His mother refused to tell anyone who his father was, so that's something I've had my guy dig further into."

I nod my head in agreement, looking back at the files. I stop to look at a picture of Noah, Layla, and Caden at some kind of black-tie event.

Vaughn leans over the counter and presses a finger over Layla's face.

"Now, *she* could be someone worth looking into."

"Why?"

"Because while it appears that there's a lot of information about her available online, it's all very generic. You said she was involved in drugging Caden. She was the only other witness to that day. And she lied to you about their supposedly happy marriage when you told her about Jesse. Unfortunately, she's pushing daisies—"

"*Vaughn*!"

"Just because someone's died doesn't make them a fucking martyr, sweetheart. I call it as I see it. It's a pity we didn't get any answers before she kicked the bucket. From what you've told me, for some reason, she remained very close to Spellman. If anyone knew his secrets, it would have been her."

Ignoring his usual crassness, I drop the file onto his desk with a frown. "I think you could be onto something, Vaughn."

He nods succinctly. "I'll get my guy on it."

As I blow out a deep exhalation, my stomach rumbles loudly. My eyes fly up to meet my friend's laughter-filled ones.

"Oh my God, excuse me!"

"When's the last time you've eaten?" He pins me with a less-than-impressed look.

I blink several times, and my eyes blow wide when I realise I've not eaten yet today.

"Umm, maybe yesterday?"

He huffs dramatically as he stands and holds out his hand. "Come on, sweetheart. Let's grab a sandwich. I could use some air."

Twenty-Seven

SUMMER

Having spent some time wandering around the busy streets, we hit Vaughn's favourite deli, Luciano's.

"You are freaking obsessed with this place."

My boss shrugs. "They make the best meatballs, okay?"

"Meatballs are disgusting."

Vaughn hits me with a deadpan. "The fact that you'd say that to me makes me doubt whether we can be friends, Miss St James."

I shake my head, getting into the queue as Vaughn steps inside behind me.

Once we've filled our order with an overly chatty Adamo Luciano, we slowly meander towards Rogue several blocks over in companionable silence.

As the building comes into view two blocks down, now lit up by streetlamps and tastefully done uplighting, I can see that it's already gearing up to be a busy night.

"Why don't you take the night off?"

Vaughn's suggestion catches me off guard, but I playfully bump his hip with mine. "Have you forgotten already? I need the distraction."

"Anna still not giving you any more shifts?"

I shake my head. "She says it's best if I take time to let everything sink in." I shrug. "Or something along those lines. I know she means well, but for now, I need to stay active. Keep my mind from running wild, you know?"

"True. But if you fancy heading home after we meet with my media contact, just say the word."

I glance up, smiling softly at him. "You're too good to me, you know that?"

Throwing his arm over my shoulder, he tugs me in tight against his side as he chuckles. "I know. I'm positively angelic."

He bats his eyelids exaggeratedly, making me laugh out loud.

"Now come on. Move your ass so we can get these eaten before he arrives."

We duck down a side alley about half a block from the actual building and slide past Griffith at the hidden staff-only entrance. I reach into the deli bag in Vaughn's hand, slipping out a turkey on rye sub with low-fat mayo.

Griffith smiles as I press the wrapped sandwich into his hands. "Someone's got to watch that cholesterol, Griff."

Vaughn turns slightly as we climb the stairs to his office. "As if he wasn't already head over damn heels for you, then you go and feed him!"

I shrug with a grin. "I'm watching out for my friend. I'd do the same for you."

He grimaces. "I'd rather pull every one of my leg hairs out with tweezers than eat that shit, sweetheart."

Having reached his office, he opens the door, about to launch into detail about why turkey on rye is disgusting when he stops short.

"Alex!"

I stop behind Vaughn just as his mysterious media contact, Alex, turns to face us.

The first thing that pops into my mind is how he effortlessly exudes sheer charisma.

His suit is black and impeccably tailored to his tall, deceptively muscular frame. An immaculate white shirt is opened down to his collarbone, giving him a carefree look. His brown hair is styled back off of his tanned face, and striking amber eyes light up when he smiles at our arrival.

It's got to be the most contagious smile I've ever seen because I'm powerless to stop an answering one from appearing on my own face.

"About damn time, V."

Vaughn turns to usher me inside ahead of him, and his guest's face freezes when he sees me. "You didn't say this mess was personal, Vaughn. You *know* I can't be involved with any of Henry's business."

"This is nothing to do with your brother, Alex. Summer needs help making a story disappear—"

"A story involving Caden North, by chance?"

Vaughn glances at me before we round on the newcomer with questioning eyes.

"You're Caden's Summer. I'd recognise you in a heartbeat."

"How did you—" I stop, changing my question when I realise he's likely seen the portrait in Caden's foyer. "How do you know Caden?"

Alex quirks a brow devilishly, allowing a small smile to tug at his lips. "I'm the middle DeMarco sibling. Henry's my uptight older brother. If you've met him, I'm sure he made an impression. You'll likely recall the massive stick he's got lodged deep inside his ass."

I can't stop the snort that escapes me, even as Vaughn laughs aloud. "An accurate description, by all means."

They chuckle together while Vaughn sets about plating up our sandwiches.

"Fancy some of mine? You look like you came straight from work."

Vaughn moves to rip his meatball marinara sub in half, but Alex grimaces and raises a hand, stopping him.

"How can you put that shit in your body? Gross! I'll grab a turkey on rye on my way home."

I press my lips together as tight as I can as Vaughn's lip curls in revolt. Tearing my sub down the middle, I hold out half in offering. "I'll never finish it all."

Alex nods his thanks before plucking the sub from my outstretched hand and taking a large bite. "I'm famished." He speaks around the mouthful as a lock of his hair falls forward across his forehead, making him look much more boyish than moments before. "Today was a long ass day, and I have another meeting across town in a couple of hours, so it's not over yet."

Vaughn hands him a tumbler of whiskey and offers one to me, which I decline before he settles back into his chair to eat his own sub.

Alex, having swallowed his first bite and washed it down with a healthy swig of the amber liquid that is uncannily similar to his own unique eyes, turns to face me. "I've done everything I can. Called in a *lot* of favours. My name carries weight here, especially in the industry."

DeMarco Holdings is an entertainment giant known worldwide and owning more than its fair share of media outlets. I feel a thrill of hope starting to build in the pit of my stomach as Alex continues.

"I've been able to kill it. *For now*. That's not to say your involvement at Rogue won't leak in the future. I very strongly believe something like this *will* happen again, Summer."

"Surely, once enough time has elapsed, I'll become a blip on their radar. I'll go back to being nobody. They'll leave me alone, and my working here won't matter to anyone, right?"

Alex doesn't pull any punches. "It's unlikely."

My shoulders slump, but he continues. "You've been linked to arguably the most sought-after newly divorced singer on the planet. Not only linked, Summer, but have you actually *seen* the footage?"

I shake my head. "I haven't been able to bring myself to watch it."

"It's clear to see that the man worships you. He looks at you as though you hung the moon. A great number of the comments online mention that. And therein lies your next issue."

I turn confused eyes to Vaughn, finding him as perplexed as I am.

Alex shakes his head and expels a breath before injecting a healthy dash of patience into his tone. "Misdirection, in general, has a serious fan base, but Caden, in *particular*, has attracted some true…how shall I put it? Some true *gems*. Many of his female fans would send death threats to Layla regularly. A woman spotted asking him for an autograph on Broadway was hospitalised hours after pictures of their innocent chat appeared online."

Alex stops for a moment when he takes in my astonished face. "Oh my *God*!"

He nods slowly. "That story never saw the light of day, thankfully for Misdirection. For now, I'm concerned that if news of your association with Rogue leaks, it may question your loyalty to Caden. That was Layla's downfall. Their on-again, off-again status, alongside rumours of her indiscretions, made it very hard for his fanbase to take her to their hearts. Now, while everything is *technically* above board here, rumours abound about secret *performances* and illegal *auctions* in back rooms."

He winks dramatically at Vaughn, making my friend roll his eyes right back into his head. "Shut up, you idiot."

Alex grins, then sobers before I can ask what he meant about auctions. Having never been privy to the *Ravish* side of Vaughn's business, I have a lot of questions, but Alex goes on. "I just want you to be aware that you, being linked to any part of this establishment, could see the true crazies out in their droves. I would *strongly* recommend getting ahead of this."

My hope ebbs as despair takes flight, and I fall back in my seat, dropping my nibbled-on sub onto the wrapping on my lap as a frown crosses my face. "I don't mean to sound obtuse, Alex, but *how* would I do that exactly?"

He holds my gaze unflinchingly, and I instantly see the resemblance to his older brother.

"Come up with a plan to either get ahead of it by way of staging something for the media or find a way to bury your days here. Either way, I would talk to Caden. Or at the very least, his people. I know his manager is fucking allergic to any kind of media storm—he's the one who put the kibosh on the Broadway incident, obviously. Even though you two didn't do him any favours at the Alexandra Palace recently, I reckon he'd be more than capable to downgrade this potential mess. The man owns half the media around the damn globe and has the remainder in his back pocket."

I can feel myself shaking my head, but the words won't come out.

"We won't be involving Noah Spellman, Alex." Vaughn's voice is firm, and I shoot him a thankful look. Alex glances between us, heaving a heavy sigh before biting another chunk off his sub.

"Well…" Alex trails off in apparent thought, chewing his sub quietly as he mulls over my options. "If it were me, I'd distract the masses with a bullshit story. Spin the truth to suit the narrative, ensuring that the club and you, Summer, come out crystal clean."

I chew my bottom lip, nodding along with him. "Your plan definitely has merit, Alex. Thank you."

He tips his chin, his eyes finding mine again. "For what it's worth, I genuinely think going straight to Caden is a must here. He'll appreciate your honesty in the long run, even if it pisses him off in the present. Think damage control, Summer."

I know he's right. I know I need to tell Caden about working here before the news leaks, but I also think this could well be the straw that broke the camel's back.

I'm the mother of his son and nothing more. I know where I stand now, even as it pains me to admit it, but I don't *want* to tell him this. I don't want to risk him removing me from Jesse's life.

But what alternative do you have?

"Thanks for thoroughly raining on our parade, motherfucker."

Vaughn, having finished his marinara in record time, scrunches up the wrapping, shoots it at the wastepaper bin like a basketball, and levels me with a look.

"Time to decide, sweetheart. Are you getting ahead of the narrative?" At my obvious confliction, his forehead furrows in empathy. "This may not count for much, but I think you should do as Alex suggested. Talk to North. Let him do what he will. At least he'll have the truth."

A text message chimes on my phone, and I slip it from my pocket, needing a moment to digest what my options are, despite *knowing* I only have one option.

To tell him I've been working here for years. Paying bills with the money I've earned here, fair and square.

But then it opens a whole new can of worms when he'll inevitably question whether I worked in *Risqué*.

His words from our conversation earlier echo in my mind.

"Or perhaps you're only sorry now because your lies caught up to you."

I don't want to lie. I want to re-earn his trust.

I *need* to.

And there, I have my answer.

We need to talk.

Just when you thought you couldn't fall further from his grace.

As I unlock my phone, I verbalise my thoughts to the waiting men. "I'm going to tell him. I need to be honest and let the chips fall where they may. He *deserves* my honesty."

My phone finally loads the text that appears to have been sent hours earlier, and my heart rate kicks up a notch.

CADEN

I'm his match, Bam. I'm his motherfucking match!!!

I'll FaceTime tomorrow so we can discuss the next steps.

Twenty-Eight

CADEN

I tug Jesse closer while I shoot a message to Summer, letting her know the most wonderful news ever. There's a pleased as fucking punch smile front and centre on my joy-filled face, and I don't think anything could bring me down right now.

Ford's eyes meet mine in the rearview, his face a carbon copy of mine, and it makes me smile even wider in response.

"I can't believe you're my match. I just can't believe it!"

I pocket my phone while centred on the disbelief in my son's tone, and I vaguely note that we've arrived home. My eyes drift to the cling-on paps, hungry for a candid. Desperate for something to feed off of.

Fucking vultures.

The absolute *worst* part of this lifestyle. Seeing them is a constant reminder that this is not the life I dreamed of.

My newfound contempt for my manager—and my father's

oldest friend—swells in my throat as nausea swirls in my stomach. The desire to find something to make him pay for his interference in my affairs is almost overwhelming.

"Looks like your father arrived while we were away, Cade."

Ford's words draw my attention away from my thoughts as my eyes continue to watch the handful of camping paps lingering outside my gates to the waiting car in my driveway.

It's strange that Dad didn't text or call, and I find myself wondering how long he's been here.

Once we enter the house, a smile blooms on Jesse's face when he hears Dad's deep voice singing softly in the kitchen. We follow the sound, a smile of my own appearing when we find him elbow-deep in a butter churn alongside Maggie.

"You've missed some there, Mr Sutton."

Jesse side-eyes me, and we snort simultaneously, drawing their attention.

A shit-eating grin lights up my old man's face. "I've made butter!"

The sheer joy in his voice matches the delight on his features, and I chuckle as my heart tightens in my chest at his boyish earnestness.

Fuck, I love this man.

"I'll take over shaping it. You go and have some tea with your boys." Maggie forcibly removes two large wooden paddles from my father's unwilling hands before nudging him in the direction of the patio with her hip.

"Go on now. I'll be out in a minute."

Having no other option, Dad exits the kitchen with slumped shoulders, but they don't stay that way for long as Jesse runs after him and launches into relaying his news.

"The doctor's found a match."

Dad's smile reappears as I catch up when they settle onto the benches by the firepit. "I already know! I've been calling the lab every hour since the samples were sent." He scrunches up his face as if this should come as a surprise to us.

"I have...what's it the kids say these days? I've got *no chill* when it comes to family, Cade. *Family* is the most important thing—"

Jesse lunges forward from his seat opposite Dad and me, throwing his arms around both of our necks to embrace us in a three-way hug. My eyes meet Dad's glistening ones behind my boy's head.

He sends me a watery smile before shutting his eyes and just absorbing the emotion involved in this unexpected and thoroughly longed-for hug.

"I wish Mom were here." His words are a whisper against my neck, and I force my body to remain loose instead of stiffening up as I automatically start to do.

"I know things aren't good between you guys right now, but I *know* she loves you." Jesse leans back slightly, finding my eyes. "She spoke about you every day. Brought me to all your concerts, even though it must have really hurt her. I feel I know you because of the picture she painted of her life before me. She let me *see* you through her eyes so that I could *love* you too, even before I'd met you. I know that counts for *something*."

My eyes sting at the heart in his words. At how easily he tells me he loves me.

"I've missed out on fourteen years of your life, kid. I could have missed out on knowing you entirely had you not needed this transplant." I keep my tone even and lean closer to rest my forehead against his. "I can't just snap my fingers and move past that, Jess."

"You can love her back, though, right?"

The hopeful hesitation in his sweet voice almost breaks my heart.

I close my eyes, and when I open them again, I hold his gaze, giving him nothing but sincerity. "There's no denying I love your mother, kid. She's the love of my damn life, but right now, I think it's best if we focus on *you*. On getting this transplant and your recovery done and dusted, yeah?"

He swallows roughly with a puckered brow, then bites his bottom lip just like his mother. The familiar, much-loved tick is a swift kick to the nuts.

"I've never seen her as happy, you know."

My stomach dips, but I need to ask the question. "When?"

"In the footage with you. When you were at the concert. The viral stuff."

He's silent for a beat. My heart stills in my chest, awaiting the next blow.

"You haven't watched it, though. I know you haven't." He pulls back enough to meet my eyes. "If you had watched it, you'd have seen how much she loves you. *I* saw it every day growing up."

He pulls out of my and Dad's embrace, stepping backwards to sit on his own bench opposite me. His eyes are as intense as I've ever witnessed, and it's a look I know well by way of my own reflection.

It's the look of a man on a mission.

"Did you even *read* her letter?" The accusation in his tone is another blow to my already battered chest.

"What letter?" I'm genuinely confused until he speaks again.

"The envelope she left with me before she went back to New York."

It finally clicks when I distantly recall Ford handing me a letter the day Summer had fled, but I'd been so preoccupied with news of Layla's death and dealing with events since that I'd put it out of my head entirely.

Suddenly, my feet are itchy with the desire to find and read her parting words, but I make myself sit still under my child's apparent disdain.

"I have it in my office, kid." I find myself almost squirming when he turns up the accusation in his gaze. "I have yet to open it."

Jesse's eyes narrow and turn steely. There's a part of me that really doesn't like it, but the bigger part of my heart rejoices at him championing his mother. Of retaining a loyalty to the person who's loved him more than anyone else.

The thought passes through my head unbidden, chipping away at the ice I've tried to erect around my heart.

"Why don't you go and read it, son?" My Dad's voice breaks through my thoughts. "I've got a present inside the house for Jesse, and when you come back down, we'll have some of that tea Maggie mentioned."

And in the true innocence reserved for childhood alone, Jesse's scowl is replaced with a bright smile for his grandfather. "A present for me! Really?"

"Come on." Dad stands, his dark eyes twinkling merrily with some secret or other. "It's this way."

He leads Jesse off through the kitchen and out into the foyer beyond. Once they've disappeared, I quickly follow after, moving towards my office and shutting the door firmly behind me.

I turn the key for good measure, pour myself two fingers of whiskey and settle into my chair behind the desk

The letter is locked inside the top drawer. I'd dropped it there when I'd rediscovered it in my back pocket as I'd begun damage control involved in having Layla's body removed from her hotel without alerting the media. I fish the plain white envelope out and sit, staring at it in my left hand with the tumbler of whiskey trembling in my right.

Long minutes pass, and my stomach dips and swoops as I mull over what could possibly be inside. Now that the moment is here, I'm not altogether sure that I want to know what she's left me with.

I knock back the whiskey with a wince, place the tumbler on my desk, and rip the envelope open without further thought. My fingers don't work very well as I try to unfold the two sheets of paper inside, but I manage it after what feels like a long time and start to read.

Caden,

The last time I went away, I left my heart—literally and figuratively—in your keeping. This time, I do the same except double fold. I don't doubt that you will take care of our son as carefully as you have treasured my heart all these years.

This is the letter I should have left for you back then had I not been scared and stupid.

Oh, Caden, where do I start?

I suppose the beginning is usually best…

Well, I've loved you since I arrived at your parent's house at eight years of age. I remember that my knees were muddy from falling at my parent's graveside when I refused to leave them. My snotty nose was running like a tap from crying the entire way from London. My heart was broken, and I'd never felt more alone.

But it just took one face to recentre me. To light up my dark world after surviving such devastation. I took one look into your big blue eyes, and I saw your heart.

It was good, pure, and it called to mine like a siren song, singing me home.

You and I were as inevitable as the changing of day to night. However, some houses are made of cards and are simply not built to last.

Despite that, I will never regret a moment of our childhood love because it gave us Jesse.

Our boy is your miniature. He's kind and gentle. A deep thinker with an easy smile and a heart bigger than the state of Texas. He can be stubborn, but he loves fiercely with a loyalty that's all you.

These precious few days have been more than I could have ever dreamt of. Thank you for reminding me what butterflies feel like. Thank you for allowing me to come back home. For giving me a chance to feel your love one final time so that I can treasure it always.

If you can find it in your heart, please don't keep me from Jesse.

I understand that you need to form a relationship with him. I strongly encourage you two to spend as much time as possible together, and I won't put any strings on your time with him.

Just...please, I beg you. Don't cut me out of his life.

You won't need to deal with me directly unless absolutely necessary. I won't make things harder than they need to be. You have my solemn vow.

And when you allow yourself to move past the love of your youth and are able to love again, just know that I would never use Jesse as leverage to try to continue being a part of your life. I will return to watching from afar, wishing you all the happiness in the world.

Please believe that the love of your life is out there waiting for you to seize it with both hands. You just need to let it in, Cade. You need to allow your whole heart to fall in love again so that you can have the life you dreamed of.

Build a happy home on strong foundations. No more houses of cards.

Have as many kids as your heart desires. Fill that damn house to bursting! There's no denying that you make absolutely breathtaking children.

Find a woman who loves you, whom you love back just as much, and make her your wife. A lover untainted by the sins of the past and memories of a life half-lived. A wife whose presence doesn't remind you of everything you've lost.

Live that life, Cade.

Be happy. I'll be happy for you, and that's always been enough for me.

Twenty-Nine

CADEN

My throat is clogged, my eyes are burning, and my chest feels unbearably tight when I finish reading.

She's gone. It's really over.

The knowledge that she's clearly telling me to move on makes my stomach churn as beads of sweat erupt across my forehead.

I'm going to throw up.

I grab the wastepaper basket, physically heaving into the damn thing while internally berating myself for being a fucking idiot.

I love her.

I'll *always* love her. My chest is an empty cage since she left, my kids the only reason to function, but the light in my soul has dulled painfully in the interim.

Yes, we have some issues to work through, but the only way we can find a way forward is *together*.

I drop the basket onto the table and rise to stand as I go in search of Jesse and Dad. My mind is made up. Nothing will sway it now.

They're back out on the patio, both looking at my phone with Dad's favourite Fender guitar resting across Jesse's lap. My brows crease in question until I hear my own voice carry through the air. I'm singing "Perfect for You," and I smile, wondering how they found a recording. I don't have to wonder for long because Summer's voice suddenly fills the air, harmonising easily with my deeper tone.

Goosebumps break out across every part of my body. This feels like the universe is telling me that I'm making the right call.

I drop down beside Jesse, startling him before he grins easily. "She's an amazing singer, right?"

Nodding my agreement, I drop my arm over his shoulder. "How's about we go and surprise her in New York before we meet Mimi and Bug at North Star next week?"

At my suggestion, Jesse's eyes blow wide in his beautiful face. "Really?" I nod, and he jumps up. "I can't wait to hug her, Dad. I'm going to pack. Right. *Now*!"

He takes off in the direction of his room before I can even tell him I'm not too sure when we'll leave. I need to get my head on straight before I lay it all on the line.

All I know is, I'm not ready to let go. I don't think I'll ever be ready to let go, and the thought of being without her, of having to watch her from afar while she moves on with someone else…I can't imagine how much it hurt to watch me with Layla for all those years. Even though it wasn't any kind of real marriage, or even a real relationship, to be honest, Summer wasn't to know that.

And judging from the phone conversation she'd had with Layla when Jesse had been initially diagnosed, she'd believed that I'd been in love with my wife.

The pain of seeing and not touching. Of wanting and not having. I can't do it.

I'm not normally a selfish man, but right here and now, I'm making the decision to be selfish when it comes to her because I *burn* for her. I can no longer live without her. It's a visceral need inside of me, and being with her in recent weeks has only stoked the fire.

I've kept it to a manageable level, but the images her letter evoked within me has made the flames soar into life.

Dad smiles easily, his eyes lit from within as though he can hear my thoughts. "I think this is the right move, Cade. There's been more than enough pain—"

My phone beeps with a notification, followed by another and another. Nausea swirls in my stomach, knowing that when this shit happens, it's never good.

Dad sees my face fall and moves to slide the phone from its place on the bench between us, but I get there first.

There are several messages, all from different people. There's one from Noah, several in my group chat with the boys, and a handful of emails. I swipe them all to one side, intent on the final one.

I don't recognise the number, so I almost delete it, but something makes me click into it and onto the shared link inside without thinking.

It's a link to a website called *Hawt Goss*, something I've never heard of before, but it appears to be based in the States. There's a headline that, at first, makes no sense, but upon reading it several times, my stomach roils.

Spots blur my vision, and my hands begin to shake as I slowly scroll through the article that's interspersed with pictures of *my*

Summer. With a tall, dark-haired prick.

He has his *hands* on her. On the body that is supposed to be *mine*.

His eyes are fixed on her, and she's laughing at something he's said as though she doesn't have a care in the world.

She meant for me to move on. Her letter damn well said to.

And clearly, that's what she's doing here. The thought that we're over leaves a sour taste in my fucking soul.

I'm not having this. We need to talk.

SUMMER

He's his match.

Our son has a donor.

Oh. My. God!

I gasp as tears fill my eyes, dropping my phone when my hands tremble with a mixture of nervous excitement. Before I realise what's happening, I've dissolved into floods of tears.

Tears of disbelief and shock.

Tears of happiness and wonder.

Tears of weariness and relief.

We have a match!

My sobs carry through the space as Vaughn rounds the desk, taking me into his arms. Alex leans forward, plucking my phone from the ground at my feet.

At any other time, his absolute disregard for privacy would make me laugh.

He reads the text aloud, and Vaughn palms my cheeks as his own eyes fill with tears of joy. "Oh, Summer." His voice hitches. "I—I haven't got the words, sweetheart."

"He's a match, Vaughn." I choke the words out between gasps. "I *knew* he would be. Even if he hates me for all time, it's worth it. *He's* the *match*!"

I distantly hear my cell chime again, but think nothing of it as I continue to allow all of my pent-up emotions out against my friend's broad chest.

"Umm…guys?"

Alex's voice is hesitant behind me until he clears his throat and speaks more firmly.

"Summer? There's another text here. It's from someone called Anna."

I disentangle myself from Vaughn and practically snatch my cell from Alex's hands, pleasantries forgotten in my haste.

ANNA

Hawt Goss posted photos of you and Vaughn Burton on what looks very much like a date. They were shared several hours ago, and the headline isn't good, love.

"Son of a *bitch*!"

Vaughn's whispered words are filled with barely tampered rage as I quickly type in the website for *Hawt Goss*, the New York equivalent of TMZ but far more ruthless.

FAST-MOVING MANEATER ALERT: NORTH'S MYSTERY LOVER MOVES ON WITH VAUGHN BURTON, NEW YORK'S MOST RECLUSIVE BILLIONAIRE.

The pictures are from earlier, on our way to the damn deli. We're deep in conversation, but the way they've spun it makes it look far from the innocent walk along the street that it was. There's an image of Vaughn's hand on my lower back as he steers me inside Luciano's that seems particularly damning, but I *know* it's because of the angle the photo was taken from.

I close my eyes, blow out a breath, and look up to find both men's eyes trained on me.

Alex speaks first. "Silver lining. You can use this as your smokescreen for your name being associated with Rogue."

Vaughn shoots his friend a withering look, and Alex shrugs. "Why are you looking at me like that, V? I'm trying to make lemonade from these motherfucking lemons you keep throwing my way!"

"And *how*, may I ask, would this make lemonade, DeMarco? It's bitter, through and through."

"*This* is how you spin it, Burton. Twist the narrative. Give them what they want, and keep the real story under lock and key. She's your girlfriend, hence the association with Rogue. Paint a friends-to-lovers story. The media will *devour* it."

"But Caden…" My voice cracks as I trail off. My only concern is for how he'll take this bullshit. He'll think I ran from him to be with another man. He'll think *everything* was a lie between us.

Ignoring Alex, Vaughn turns to me. "I don't mind what way you want to play this, sweetheart. Just say the word. I told you already. I've got your back."

Vaughn's words rouse me from the trance I've been sitting in these last couple of minutes, and I jump into action. "I need to speak to Caden. I need him to know there's no truth in this article. I know he hates me right now, but he needs to know I will never keep anything from him ever again. I need—I need…"

I trail off as I dial Caden's cell number, standing to pace frantically, but there's nothing. No dial tone. No connection.

It might be off, so I try Jesse's, and it rings once before going straight to voicemail.

Swearing aloud, I hang up and try Caden again, but to no avail.

Following ten long minutes of trying both father and son, I dial Jesse one final time as Vaughn and Alex converse in low tones on the opposite side of the office, shooting concerned glances in my direction every couple of minutes.

When I hear the beep, I leave a message for my son, keeping the urgency in my voice to a minimum.

"Call me when you get this, baby. I really need to speak with your father. I love you so much. *So much.*"

Vaughn's cell rings just as I hang up mine for the final time. He answers it swiftly, responding with single-word answers to whoever is on the other end.

With each second that passes, his expression darkens further. His brows draw together. His lips purse into a straight line. His jaw clenches and tics.

His face is thunderous when he finally disconnects the call.

"There's been a break-in at your apartment, Summer." I gasp in shock, my knees feeling weak as Alex helps me stumble into my chair. "My friend, Garth, is an NYPD officer, and he's over there now. Says the whole place is destroyed, but they've got the culprits in custody."

"Really! Already?"

"Misdirection superfans, Summer." The severity in his tone, mixed with the concern in his eyes, sends a shiver up my spine.

"Had you been there, I have *no* doubt they were out for blood. Garth said they were…there's no elegant way to put this, sweetheart. He said they were fucking insane, and needless to say, you're not leaving this building tonight."

Thirty

CADEN

I'd immediately gotten in touch with Henry. My oldest friend had been more than generous in having one of his company jets readied, knowing that chartering one would have taken more time than I was willing to wait.

Jesse nods off about an hour into the journey while Ford makes small talk with the pilot and flight attendant.

"Fancy entertaining the old man, son?"

I shift my gaze from watching my sleeping son to my father waving an unopened pack of cards in my direction. Smiling in response, I lean forward and tug the blanket higher on Jesse's body before moving across the aisle to sit opposite Dad.

"Poker?"

He nods at my question, opening the packet quickly and shuffling with a speed that belies his age.

"Let's keep it interesting, though. My favourite Fender for

your Ducati."

I huff darkly. "That's hardly a fair trade."

"Are you afraid you'll lose, mister rock star almighty?" He winks mischievously, devilment flashing brightly in his loving brown eyes. "Do we have a deal or what?"

Shrugging, I give him my hand. "Fine, but it's your funeral."

He deals both of us two cards in silence, and despite my eyes being fixed firmly on the cards, I can feel his gaze on me.

"Go on then. Spit it out." I lift my head suddenly, meeting his concern-filled eyes just before they dart away guiltily.

"You know my feelings, Cade. I wear my heart on my sleeve, son. A trait you've inherited, clearly. It's not a bad thing."

He deals the Flop before pressing his mouth closed to hide a grin.

"You need to work on your poker face."

He doesn't miss a beat, deadpanning from behind his cards.

"You need to work on your forgiveness."

I ignore his dig as I weigh up my options. A pair of twos in my hand with the Jack and Ace of Hearts alongside another two, giving me three-of-a-kind.

Keeping a straight face, I check. "I'm working on how I do things, Dad. It's called maturity and learning from my mistakes."

He checks, then pulls the Turn. Another fucking two.

What are the odds?

I check as my father focuses his eyes on me. "How's about we make this a little more interesting?"

I narrow my eyes sceptically. "What do you have in mind?"

His familiar brown eyes dance with mischief as he quirks a bushy brow. "Winner's choice."

He laughs at my bewildered expression before elaborating. "The loser owes the winner one. Can be anything the winner demands, no questions asked. Full disclosure."

I glance at my four-of-a-kind, knowing the odds are *not* in his favour, then back at my father before inclining my head in assent.

"Okay, I'm game. Play the damn River."

The ten of hearts is placed face up on the small table between us.

"Okay, let's see then, old man."

"Ladies first."

I shoot my father a look at screams *bite me*, but lay my cards on the table.

A low whistle sounds between his lips, and he settles back against his seat.

"Four-of-a-damn-kind. Well, fuck me, son. I did *not* see that coming!"

I roll my eyes, moving to scoop up the deck and deal a fresh hand. "As if Mum would have let you near my damn bike anyway."

He shoots out a stalling hand, and I instantly stop what I'm doing. "What?"

"Game's not over until you've seen my hand."

I tilt my head to the side, about to launch into the fact that there's only *one* hand that can beat mine, when my sneaky-ass father drops the King and Queen of Hearts onto the table.

"Royal Flush. Looks like I live to see another day–*and* you owe me one on top of the Ducati, which I look forward to selling so that I can donate the proceeds to Katherine's House."

He sits back and folds his arms with a triumphant look on his face. There's a cheesy-as-fuck grin front and centre on his rightly smug face.

My mouth drops open in disbelief before a chuckle vibrates within my chest.

"What is stopping you from being happy, Cade?"

My laughter dies in my throat. I swallow harshly and frown. "I beg your pardon?"

Dad unfolds his arms, leans forward, and grips my hands in his much older ones. "I'm cashing in on my 'winner's choice' now, son. And I want you to tell me—and be a hundred percent honest too—why have you never allowed yourself to be truly happy since your brother's death?"

I blink a handful of times, trying to gather my thoughts, but I only have one. "I spent so many years believing it was my fault he'd drowned. I tried so *fucking* hard to live the life he would have…but it all felt worthless without her…."

My words trail off as emotion overcomes me. Fifteen years of pent-up feelings come rushing to the surface. Anger, betrayal, disappointment, grief, love, loss, and everything in between.

My father stands, lifting the table between us and sending the deck of cards flying with little care to kneel before me and grasp my face in his palms. "Caden Atticus North. You are the most loving and caring soul I've ever had the fortune to know. A hopeless romantic. You are a man who never asks for anything, but gives his whole self in return. Even to those who are undeserving…"

My brow knits tight, knowing what, or who, he's referring to. "Layla." Her name is a whisper from my lips.

"Being with Layla was vastly different from being with Summer. Yes, you have some issues to work through with Summer, but I have no doubt you *will* work it out. Because when it's the great love of your life, nothing is impossible."

A tear falls from my lashes, and Dad catches it with his thumb, brushing it away as he frowns. I can feel the passion in his words as he wills me to understand.

"Son, it's about time you started living life for *you*. Follow your own dreams. Grab life by the balls. Go for what you want. Quit the fucking band—"

He breaks off when I suck in a surprised breath.

"You think your old man didn't realise your heart's never been in it? What kind of fool do you take me for, hmm? When I formed Jupiter's Fallen with Cole Gardiner, we lived and breathed the music. The lifestyle. The parties. The women. We lived it up, whether we were on tour, in the studio, or just down the corner pub on a random Tuesday."

His eyes glaze over slightly when he pauses, and a small smile tugs at the edges of his mouth. "Everything changed for me when I met a little-known lingerie model with an ass you could bounce—"

"Dad!"

He snorts as I shake my head. He drops his hands from my face, instead gripping my hands tightly in my lap. "My wife is still shit hot, son. A blind man could see it. Forgive me for knowing I'm one hell of a lucky man."

I roll my eyes as a hint of a smile lifts my lips.

"My dreams shifted when I fell in love with your mother, Cade. Everything I'd wanted before her meant nothing. Yeah…I still enjoyed the music, but I preferred being home with you guys to spending months abroad or recording. And that's something I recognise in you, son."

My mouth opens to ask what he means, but he just talks over me.

"We're the same in that sense. In knowing when our hearts have met their other halves. *I* met the love of my life when I was in my late thirties after I'd lived the craziest damn life possible. *You* met Summer when you were only eight. You're not supposed to meet your soulmate at that age, but you did, son. You fell in love, only to fall apart, and I've watched you stumble through life without her in the years since. Honestly, I don't know how you've survived being parted from her for as long, so I need to say my bit, and I'll leave it at that, okay? You can keep your Ducati, I only want your happiness."

I nod, afraid if I open my mouth that I'll sob like a goddamn baby.

"Forgiveness takes strength. Acceptance takes bravery. And love takes work, son."

He stops, spearing me right through the gut with the fervour in his eyes.

"It's a miracle that you both found your way back. That you both still share the same love as you did then. It's a miracle—and you're *wasting it*, Cade. Life is too damn short to throw away a split second of it. You have had fifteen *years* stolen from you. Please don't allow your pride to keep you from losing any more. Time is too precious, and it's something we don't *ever* get enough of. Once it's gone, we can never get it back. Spend yours wisely, son, and with the people who make your soul happy."

SUMMER

The office got boring really fast after Vaughn walked Alex down to the main floor. I spent what felt like an age poring over the *Hawt Goss* pictures of me and Vaughn, tearing each and every one of them apart from Caden's point of view.

It doesn't feel nice. I would know because I was the one watching him with Layla from afar for years, and every time I came across a picture, it was like a knife twisting in my gut.

When I don't hear from Jesse or Caden, and their cell phones are still unreachable, I try to take a nap on Vaughn's sofa.

It doesn't work.

I text Anna back. There's no reply for the longest time until I'm in the middle of playing some solitaire at Vaughn's desk. The cards go flying everywhere when I scramble to unlock my phone.

ANNA

I've been by your apartment. I explained to the cops, and they let me grab Jesse's memory box from underneath your bed.

A wave of relief washes over me.

The blanket box Jesse had slept in as an infant had doubled as a place to keep all his milestone treasures. His hospital tag and first swaddle. His first shoes. A lock of baby hair from his first haircut. Photos of everything ranging from birth to present day, and millions of trivial items like the painted handprint from his first day at kindergarten.

The stubs from our tickets to Misdirection and memorabilia that he'd insisted on purchasing were in pride of place right at the top, as Jesse often liked to pull them out and relive their concerts whilst watching the live recordings of those special gigs.

The thought of Anna being able to save something so utterly irreplaceable brings a frog to my throat. I cough, trying to get a handle on my emotions, but it feels as though the events of the day, alongside the fact I can't get through to my son or his father, are about to send me spiralling.

Instead of allowing that, I steel my shoulders and decide to keep my mind busy.

You've not lost your head in a crisis so far. You don't get to start now, silly woman!

An idea pops into my head to ask Vaughn if I can oversee the staff performing in *Risqué* this evening.

I can wear a mask as the performers and guests do. I'll even throw on my favourite pink wig for shits and giggles. I just know that I can't continue to sit here, waiting on one of them to call me back. I'm slowly going insane.

ME

Can I please oversee Risqué tonight? I'm going out of my head up here!

Please?

I see the dots begin to flash immediately.

VAUGHN

Take Griff with you. I'll swing by to check on you soon.

Without wasting a second, I descend the stairs and weave my way through the thronging mass of employees in various stages of undress to swing right into my usual changing area.

My pink wig is nowhere to be seen, and I narrow my eyes, silently cursing the thief before I grab a flame-haired one with bangs. I scan the room, searching for an outfit that might serve, and find a secretary-style pencil skirt with a white shirt. Matching black pumps completes the look.

It's not the usual attire that's required for bar work; however, for overseeing *Risqué,* it's ideal. Vaughn is always kitted out in tailored suits, so I feel like I fit the part.

Once I've slipped into the clothes, I settle the wig into place and grab a black masquerade mask from the plentiful stash.

I've just slipped my phone into an inside pocket on the side of the skirt when there's a knock on the door.

Griff's voice calls from the other side of the door. "Summer—erm, I mean, *Jolie*? The boss said I was to stick with you tonight."

When I glance in the mirror one final time, I decide that my lips need some colour, so I stop to apply a deep crimson matte. I nod to my reflection repeatedly, content with the end result, even as my entire body is on high alert, waiting on my phone to buzz against my hip with a reply from one or either of them.

Keep your shit together, Summer!

When I stand to open the changing room door, I firmly shove all thoughts other than the job ahead of me out of my mind. Distraction is the key right now, or else I'll drive myself mad.

Thirty-One

CADEN

It's ten p.m. local time when Henry's jet touches the tarmacadam at Teterboro, a small airport in New Jersey.

All three of us had grabbed some shuteye, and when I woke my son, he bounced to life in his seat. "Let's go find Mom!"

I chuckle at his exuberance. "*You*, mister, are going directly to the hotel with your grandfather—"

"I prefer Pops, which you *well* know!"

I roll my eyes at my dad's hatred of the title of grandfather. My reaction makes Jesse smile broadly, and despite the anxiety flowing through my veins, I can't help smiling too.

"I'll find your mother and bring her to you, okay?"

Jesse nibbles the side of his bottom lip, and his brows draw closer together as indecision flitters across his face.

"I *promise* to bring her to you as soon as I locate her."

His eyes blow wide, as though my statement has reminded

him of something important. He reaches into his jeans pocket. "I have her location on the tracker app on my cell. Here, look!"

He waves his cell under my nose triumphantly before opening the app and finding the dot indicating his mother's whereabouts. Pinching his thumb and index finger together, he zooms closer until he can read the street names, and he chuckles.

"She's in Tribeca. Most likely with Vaughn."

My face freezes, but I manage to question him through stiff lips. "Vaughn?"

Ford's search had been fruitless. Vaughn Burton was so reclusive that even the media had sweet fuck all on the prick. All that Ford had been able to find was the fact that Burton owned the fabled membership-only club, Rogue. In Tribeca.

"As in, Vaughn Burton?" The question is rung from my vocal cords.

Glancing up from his phone, Jesse meets my wide eyes and nods enthusiastically. "Yup. Vaughn is super fun. He's got season tickets for the Yankees!"

The muscles in my throat stretch uncomfortably as I try to swallow. I clear my throat, but it's little help.

Two black cars pull up alongside us on the tarmac. Dad places a hand on Jesse's shoulder, watching me closely with concerned eyes as I take a few steps backwards in the direction of one of the cars.

"Here." Jesse steps closer and thrusts his phone at my chest. "Take my cell so you can find her. And don't forget your promise, Dad."

I nod numbly while Dad steers Jesse into the second of the waiting town cars before they silently leave the airfield. My son's eyes hold mine for as long as possible before they disappear into the night.

"There's security inside the car with them, Cade. And I've arranged for more at the hotel."

Ford's voice jolts me to awareness. "Christ, man. You should have gone with them!"

I turn to my loyal friend as he quirks a questioning brow. "And if you run into a *Tequila Sunrise*, who's going to have your back?"

Glancing down at Jesse's phone in my hand, I zone in on the tiny dot indicating Summer, and I feel my heart rate tick up several notches.

She's with *Vaughn. At Rogue, by the looks of things. What are you even doing, North?*

Indecision flows through my veins until I remember my promise to my son. To find her and bring her directly to him.

"Come on then, for crying out loud!"

Ramming Jesse's phone into my pocket, I jog to the waiting car to unceremoniously bark an address in Tribeca at my unfortunate driver as Ford slides into the front passenger seat.

He presses his lips together apologetically before shrugging. "Don't mind my asshole friend. He's had one too many cocktails of late. *Tequila Sunrise* is the *worst*!"

His flippancy almost makes me laugh.

Almost.

As the car eats the distance between Teterboro and Tribeca, questions rampage through my brain more quickly than I can register them. Does she miss me as much as I've missed her? Is there a chance for us? Or has she moved on?

How long has she known Vaughn fucking Burton? Clearly, she's known him since before she came back, considering our son knows him too!

Fuck!

I focus on my breathing, trying to keep my inner asshole at bay until I get to the bottom of things.

After about fifteen minutes of effort, I have an epiphany.

I'll just text her and ask her outright!

The idea eases my trepidation, but when I pull out my phone, it won't power on. I swear internally—which is a feat in and of itself at this point—before tossing the worthless device onto the seat beside me. All hope is not lost when I suddenly remember Jesse's phone in my pocket.

Unlocking the screen, I exit the tracker app, find his text messages, and type out my question.

JESSE

Where are you now?

"Would you like me to park right outside, Mr North?"

My driver's voice shifts my attention from the phone in my hand, and I glance up to realise we're already in Tribeca.

The streetlights are bright, and we appear to be on a street heavy with both pedestrians and car traffic. The infamous Rogue is lit up in red on my left, a low and steady beat pumping from within.

"You can park here. We'll be back shortly."

Jesse's phone chimes, drawing my attention.

MOM

I'm at work, baby. Can you have your dad call me as soon as he can?

I grit my teeth, and my nostrils flare as I realise her meaning. If she's at work *here*, does that mean she's a goddamn *performer*? Or worse?

Is *that* how she met Burton?

"Deep breaths, Cade."

Raising my eyes, I find Ford has shifted around in the passenger seat and is watching me with concern.

"I'm *fine*." As I pocket the phone, I force my unusually stern face to soften slightly. "Come on. I need to get this done."

I slide from the car onto the cobblestone street as a group of women in the shortest short skirts imaginable saunter past, whispering between one another as they shoot unconcealed glances in my direction.

Shit!

The main downside of notoriety is the sheer lack of freedom.

"Come on, Cade. Let's get you on inside."

As the women begin to reach for their phones, I allow Ford to lead me to the entryway, where he converses lowly with two burly security guards before jerking his chin to follow him inside. I nod my thanks as we enter, and I'm instantly transported to a different world.

Deep hues of green and blue lighting shift along the walls of a long entry hall. It almost gives the illusion of being under the sea. Once we round the corner at the end of the hall, a scantily clad blonde in a masquerade mask meets us, her eyes roving over both of us as a flicker of a smile crosses her lips.

"*Rapture*, or *Risqué*, gentlemen?"

I open my mouth to speak, but Ford beats me to it. "Neither. I need to see Vaughn Burton."

She narrows her eyes minutely, her lip curling slightly in distaste before tipping her chin over her shoulder. "He's here in *Rapture*. Somewhere over there."

And without further instruction, she turns and weaves her way through the crowd.

Ford turns to me, gripping my biceps with his hands. "I know this isn't what you want to hear, but I need you to stay here. Keep to yourself, and I'll bring him to you, okay?"

He nods once, sharply, and then, without waiting for a response, he, too, disappears through the throng of bodies.

I take a moment to absorb my surroundings as a heavy bass permeates my bones.

The entire club seems to be fully open plan, lit up in varying shades of gold and bronze. It's decadent, but not distastefully so.

Gigantic chandeliers hang from the vaulted ceiling above me, giving the place an elegance I wasn't expecting, considering the rumours surrounding Rogue.

Long gilt bars line both sides of the room, with large booths shrouded in sheer gold drapes interspersed throughout the space.

The drapes surrounding these areas are sheer enough that I can just about make out bodies on the other side of them, but can't quite see enough to know what's going on, which I'm sure is the entire point.

Female servers of all shapes and sizes are behind the bars and dotted throughout the club. All are easily recognisable by the black masquerade masks covering most of their faces.

My inspection of Rogue comes to an abrupt halt when I feel a tap on my shoulder. I turn toward the interruption, finding three women side by side. Two blondes with a brunette in the middle.

One of the blondes pops a brow as she speaks first. "You look hungry, Caden. Come on, I'll buy you dinner."

I glance around, noting several other groups gathering, and heave an internal sigh of annoyance before I plaster a smile on my face. It doesn't reach my eyes, but the women don't give a shit.

"Thanks. I always appreciate my fans, but I'm not—"

The brunette steps forward, placing a finger over my lips. "I'll be your dessert…."

She winks saucily as her friends giggle at her audacity. I take a step back, followed by another. Before I realise what I'm doing,

I veer to the left of the closest bar and duck out through a 'Staff Only' door into a darkened hallway beyond.

I can hear a commotion at my back, and in my rush, I don't allow my eyes to adjust to the darkness around me. I focus entirely on moving further and further away from my pursuers.

There appears to be a mixture of open and closed doors on either side of the hallway.

But, as my eyes adapt to my new surroundings, I can make out that the open doors are actually small alcoves where couples and bystanders are engaging in openly explicit sexual acts.

It's very similar to Valentine's back home, though I've not been there in years. Except this place has a slightly more debauched edge that Valentine's was lacking when I'd last been.

No one pays me any mind as I meander through the labyrinth of corridors, finally coming to a stop outside a black door with gilt edging. The word *Ravish* is lit up in gold neon lights above the frame, and when I push it to enter, I'm met with a loud beep.

I try again and again, eventually realising the beep is coming from a wall-mounted box beside the door. It appears to require a palm print to access.

Shit, shit, shit!

At a loss, I turn back in search of an alternative exit.

I don't have to look far when a flame-haired woman in a secretary-style outfit sashays out of the wall, moving further down the corridor in the opposite direction. I take a closer look and realise it's a hidden door flush with the wall so that, to the naked eye, at least, it's completely invisible.

Upon trying to enter the invisible door, I rush after the redhead, needing to escape this place, but she's disappeared. Her scent lingers in the air, and a surge of desire makes my cock stir in my pants.

That's fucking strange!

I blink several times as though to clear my suddenly foggy brain before I remember Jesse's phone. Once I've unlocked it, I open the tracker app and zoom closer to the dot that's literally right beside me.

My heart rate ticks up a notch as I glance around, searching for a head of platinum hair. The thought trickles through my mind unbidden.

What if she's performing?

I push it from my head and place one foot in front of the other. My footsteps bring me closer and closer to the dot, which is now stationary and even closer than before.

I spin about as I enter an alcove.

She should *be here.*

But she's not. There's a couple of guys fucking against a couch, another watching on with his hands rammed down his pants.

I spin about, but there's nowhere else she could be until I spy a black curtain to the far left. Glancing back at Jesse's phone, I zoom as close as the app will allow me, only to deduce that she *must* be in there.

Marching past the three otherwise occupied fellas, I lift the curtain to be met with another long corridor.

How fucking big is *this place?*

I walk further inside the long dark hallway that leads into another alcove, my heart threatening to break out of my chest as I hear the unmistakable sound of her voice ring out.

"You know I love you, Vaughn."

She trails off, and a deep male voice answers, though I can't hear his words over the sound of my racing pulse.

Inhaling, I stop to find purchase against the wall. I need to be mistaken. I don't want it to be her, even though I'm fully sure that's her voice.

Please don't let it be her.

I don't know where we stand, but I know I can't allow her to be with anyone else.

She's mine.

The thought sends a thrill of possession through me, and I stand taller, stiffening my spine, ready to take what I want.

Ready to take what's mine, fuck the consequences.

I know, here and now, regardless of what's passed between us, that we are meant for one another. I'm only hers. She's only mine. No one can ever come between that.

And the knowledge sets me free to do what needs doing.

I stride on confident feet all the way to the end of the black corridor and into the alcove beyond to find the redhead from before.

Her hair is long and wavy, wrapping around her shapely waist. She's wrapped in the embrace of a very tall, dark-haired man, who presses a kiss atop her head.

"And you know I love you too, Summer."

His declaration is followed by an inimitable laugh, and my breathing stalls as the bottom falls out of my world.

It is *her*.

Summer's distinctive laugh fractures my heart—alongside my already barely restrained temper.

"Get your fucking hands off my girl!"

Thirty-Two

SUMMER

Having ducked out of *Risqué* when I'd felt my hip buzz with Jesse's text, I'd replied and tried Cade's phone several more times. My brows pucker in a deep frown when I get sent straight to his voicemail repeatedly.

My frustration is further compounded when Jesse's phone doesn't even ring. Instead, I just get an incessant *beep beep beep* in my ear.

Griffith's hesitant voice calls out through Vaughn's office. "Summer—erm, I mean, *Jolie*—erm, I'm not feeling too hot…"

My gentle giant flushes bright red to the tips of his toes when I turn to him, and a smile parts my lips. "Do you need to call it a night?"

He nods gingerly before his hand reaches up to massage his dewy temples. He looks pasty, a light sheen of perspiration dusting his forehead. "I don't know what's come over me all of a sudden…"

"You go on home. Get better soon." I step closer, ready to help him get where he needs to go, but he holds up an enormous palm. "Don't come too close. It might be the stomach flu. Or worse. You don't want Mr Jesse to catch that!"

His thoughtfulness brings a lump to my throat, and I smile in farewell as he nods quietly before leaving me to myself.

I slump into Vaughn's desk chair, wondering what to do with myself. Checking the time, I register vaguely that there are many hours left before I'll have Vaughn's company as a much-needed distraction.

Heaving a sigh, I switch on his huge television. I'm opening the Netflix app when there's a knock on the door.

Lucia, Vaughn's HR manager slash PA, pokes her head around the door. "Hey, Summer!"

I offer her a semblance of a smile, sitting forward as she comes closer. "He's in *Rapture* if you're looking for him."

Lucia shakes her head, chuckling quietly. "I was hoping to find you, actually."

"Why?"

"Vaughn is leaving early and asked me if I knew where you were. He's over in *Risqué*, breaking up a quarrel, but I met Griff on his way out. He told me that you were in here."

Standing, I grab my bag, drop a peck on Lucia's cheek, and all but fly out the door, calling my thanks as I jog down the stairs as quickly as my heels will allow.

I slip into *Risqué* after securing my mask to my face via one of the secret staff entryways, sharply turning away from *Ravish* as I've never had access to that part of the building and decide to start my search in the front of the area.

I don't have to look far. Vaughn is slipping between alcoves when I almost bump right into him.

"Woah, there you are!" He grips my upper arms gently, steadying me. "I've decided to call it quits early. You can stay here, or you can—"

"I'm coming with." The words tumble from my mouth as Vaughn smirks at my rush to leave. "This place is great and all, but my head is all over the place tonight."

My friend nods as I shoot him an impish grin.

"I thought as much."

His thoughtfulness warms me. "You know I love you, Vaughn."

"Oh, I know. You owe me a bunch too."

My grin softens into a genuine smile when he pulls me in against his chest. "And you know I love you too, Summer."

I laugh softly as I begin to pull out of his hold, but a voice at my back makes my knees go weak so that all I can do is grip Vaughn's arms uselessly.

"Get your fucking hands off my girl!"

Vaughn's body stiffens, and I force myself to move before these men come to blows. I turn to face Caden, whose face is filled with enmity, his body bristling with rage.

"Caden. It's not what you think. It's not what the article said..."

He steps forward with clenched fists, eyes fixed firmly on Vaughn, who hasn't moved from his place at my back. "I *said*, get your fucking hands *off* my girl! I won't ask a third time, Burton."

Vaughn increases his grip on my shoulders until I reach up and pat his knuckles gently. He glances down at me, questioning me with his eyes.

I give him a small smile of reassurance, convincing him with wide eyes, and he reluctantly moves his hands.

"Vaughn, could you give us a moment? Please?"

My friend's jaw tics as indecision flickers across his face.

"I believe she said you can take a hike, wanker!"

Irritation rolls off of Vaughn in waves as he huffs a sigh, but he nods at me and edges backwards and out of the alcove. "I won't be far, Summer."

Once we're alone, I stride past Cade and into the darkened corridor beyond. My hands easily find the security pad for a private room that I know is not in use. I press my palm atop the scanner, and the door swings open.

I enter first, Cade follows, and I close the door after us with a heavy bang.

Finally, alone, we stare at one another for a long beat.

For several long beats.

His hair is messier than usual, as though he's been running his hands through it in frustration for hours on end.

His eyes are bloodshot, with pupils dilated, giving him an almost feral look.

His chest is rising and falling as rapidly as my own, but neither of us moves. Neither of us speaks. The only sound in the dimly lit room is that of our combined breathing.

Until suddenly, without warning, Caden stalks closer. I step backwards and find my body flush against the wall behind me. His hands snake out, one catching my mask and tossing it to one side. The other grips my wig tight in his fist. He tugs harshly, and the flame hair falls away from my head, floating to the floor beside us.

Our eyes move from the wig at our feet back up to one another's faces.

"I shouldn't be surprised at the lie."

I scrunch up my face in confusion. "What do you—"

He holds up a phone in his hand. It takes me a moment to register that it's Jesse's.

"You said you were at work and needed to talk to me." Spreading his arms out on either side of his body, he smirks unkindly. "So, here I am, Summer. *Talk*!"

I swallow down a retort, unused to this cruelness in his tone, but forcing myself not to rise to his taunts.

"Yes, I do need to talk to you. It's about an article that ran in a gossip column today. I needed to tell you that there's no truth behind it. The truth of my working here can't come to light—"

He slaps his hands onto the wall on either side of my head, boxing me in when he brings his face right down into mine. "So you *do* work here!" The words are hissed through his clenched jaw, and I curse the timing of that damn article. "At least *that* wasn't another lie."

"It's not what you think..."

"*Stop saying that*. If it looks like a duck, walks like a duck, and quacks like a motherfucking duck, then it's not a goddamn chicken now, is it Summer?" He drops closer to hiss across my lips. "What kind of *fool* do you take me for?"

I exhale heavily, my mind whirring with ideas of how I can explain so that he will hear what I'm saying, but I come up with nothing. I've never seen him so enraged.

"I think it's best if we both get some sleep and talk things through with clearer heads in the morning, Caden."

"*Don't. Patronise. Me.*" Each word is enunciated with crystal-clear precision.

He leans forward, running the tip of his nose along my jawbone. I can hear him inhaling deeply before he rests his forehead on my shoulder. "You don't smell like a woman who's been freshly fucked." His tone is light, in complete contrast to his harsh words. "Are you *sure* you're working tonight?"

I suck in a sharp breath at the insinuation in his tone. "I told you—"

"It's not what I think? Yeah, you said that already." He lifts his head, drawing up to his full height to glare down at me. "You can hardly blame me for not believing you this time, Summer. Fool me once…" he trails off, shrugging.

My eyes fill with tears, knowing that I've lost him entirely. His respect. His trust. His love. Nothing I can say will change how he feels, and I feel a fool for having *hoped* otherwise.

Hadn't I told myself back in Cambridge that hope is the most dangerous thing either of us could possess?

You pure-bred idiot, Summer.

"So he's the pimp around here, is he?"

"What?" My voice is high-pitched with utter disbelief.

"Burton. He's your pimp, or is he your lover? Perhaps he's both—"

My hand flies out of its own volition, connecting with his left cheek with a harsh *thwack*. Cade's head snaps to the side from the force behind the blow, and when he twists about to face me once more, his eyes are dark and thunderous.

Still, I don't back down.

"How *dare* you speak to me like that, Caden North! Who do you think you are? You have *no* clue what I have done to survive. You couldn't possibly know how—"

His hand flies from the wall to grip my throat, cutting me off and pinning me in place.

"How *could* I fucking know, Summer? You *left* me. You left when I needed you the most, and you only came back because you had no alternative. You kept our son from me for *fifteen years*, for fuck's sake!"

His eyes hold mine as he exhales his next words. "You *broke* me."

Pain flashes across his face as he stops, clearing his throat. "You broke *us*."

His nostrils flare, and I can feel tears crest my bottom lashes to track slowly down my flushed cheeks. "I had no choice, Cade."

"And then, you run *again* immediately after I'd explicitly asked you not to." His voice hitches, and he blows out a frustrated breath. "Not only *from me*, but into the arms of another man. Or other *men*, judging by where we fucking are right now!"

My throat is dry, my face is wet, and my heart bleeds out behind my breastbone.

So much hurt. So much pain.

I was young, too trusting, and scared out of my head. How can I make him see that I'd never wanted this for us?

I don't realise I've spoken aloud until Cade increases the pressure around my throat as he whispers. "But you did it all the same."

He clenches his jaw so hard I can hear his teeth grind together. Rage fills his every pore; I can feel it with every part of me, and not for the first time, I regret everything that happened that day in the meadow.

The day that shattered so many lives.

"I need to hate you right now for what you've done. For all the lies you've told, for the life that you kept from me. For showing me what we could have, only to run at the first opportunity."

My tears fall more rapidly, and I try to suck in enough air to expand my lungs. Cade lets his hand drop from the wall at the side of my head, and when his other hand falls from its place around my throat, I greedily inhale as he watches me intently.

Without warning, he closes the gap, slamming his lips to mine. Taking my mouth with a bruising passion edged with unrestrained ferocity.

His assault slams my head back against the wall, and I cry out in pain against his mouth, only for him to plunge his tongue past my lips to spar with mine in nothing less than savage desperation.

Tears form behind my closed lids as I take what he offers me. Pleasure masked as pain. Or is it pain masked as pleasure? I don't know.

And I don't care. He needs this.

So, I kiss him back with everything I have inside of me as I realise it's not only Cade who needs this.

I need this.

We need this.

He reaches between us, fisting the material of my shirt at the collar. His eyes spear mine with an intensity that sends a ripple of desire right through my body before he pulls roughly, tearing my shirt in half. Buttons fly in every direction as the fabric renders and falls away, exposing my white lacy bra.

He leans back slightly, taking in the sight before him.

He brings a hand up between us to cup my breast, pushing the lace aside to free a hard nipple begging for his attention. Bending forward, he sucks the bud into his hot mouth, swirling his tongue around and working me into a frenzy.

I moan loudly. "Yes. *Yes*."

As though my encouragement has brought him back to the moment, he jerks back as a frown mars his beautiful face. He shakes his head, slowly at first, but picking up momentum.

"No!" He speaks almost as though to himself.

I palm his cheek, drawing his eyes to mine. Darkness flits across his face, and he clenches his jaw as he narrows his eyes.

"You want to be a whore, Summer? You want to be fucked like a working girl? I'll treat you like one."

Fisting my hair at an awkward angle, he steers me towards

the booth to my right, spinning me around. He yanks the ruined shirt from my body, unclipping my bra at the back to allow that to fall to the ground, too, before he pushes me face down into the scattered cushions.

He works my skirt up my hips, stopping when I'm completely exposed so that he can flick my panties to one side. Running the tip of his finger along my sex, he circles and taunts my clit before dipping inside.

He bows over my hunched form and brings a glistening finger to his lips. Sliding the slick digit past his lips, he narrows his eyes and his mouth ghosts across the shell of my ear. "Doesn't *taste* like you've been working."

"I told you—oh, *fuck*."

My protest is cut off when he roughly plunges two fingers into my wet centre, making my damn toes curl.

"I know what you told me, Bam."

My stomach flips at his casual use of my nickname, only to tighten again when he continues to play me like an instrument with those talented fingers of his.

"And I don't fucking believe you."

I cry out desperately. "No, *no*. You've got it wrong, I swear."

"You're trying to tell me I can trust you, is that it?" He rotates his wrist, adding another finger, and my body vibrates under his touch. "You trying to tell me that we can go back to what we had? What we *could* have been, is that what you're saying?"

My breath comes in short gasps when he picks up the pace, reaching his other hand around the front of my thigh to strum my slick clit mercilessly.

I lift my head from the cushioned booth, my eyes hooded as they find his fixed on me.

"Or are you just another liar, out for herself and her own

pleasure?" He spits the final word, driving his fingers even deeper as he angles them perfectly to stroke the swollen bundle of nerves deep within me.

My eyelids flutter closed as an orgasm barrels through my body, shaking me to my very core. I press my face down against the soft cushions beneath me, grinding back against his magical fingers as I come undone while I scream his name.

"Yesssss. Oh, Caden. *Oh, Cade*!"

He drops to his knees behind me, covering my slick centre with his mouth to enter me harshly with his pointed tongue. His slick digits slide along the curve of my hips, angling me just right as he eats my pussy like a starved man.

His thumb slides higher, dipping precariously close to no-man's-land, and I try to tug out of his hold.

"*No*!" His single-worded command stops me in my tracks.

"I *told* you, Summer. You want to be a working girl? That means you *take*…"

He dips his slick thumb into the crevice of my ass, sliding over the most private part of me.

"What…"

He circles my puckered opening with his thumb, and I jerk while his heavenly mouth abandons my soaked, needy centre. He raises above me as I cry out at the loss.

"I give…"

I turn my head, pressing my cheek against the booth just in time to see him spit onto his fingers. His eyes lift from his actions to spear through me, piercing me with their uncompromising rage.

"You."

He bends closer, holding my eyes with his dilated pupils as he presses an open-mouthed kiss against my left ass cheek. His face dips lower behind me, and I moan as his hot mouth covers my sex.

His fingers glide over my untouched hole, smearing his saliva around it before his thumb dips inside my ass as he eats me with abandon. I can't help crying out as I turn my face into the cushions, screaming my fulfilment to the seat beneath me.

Endless sensation consumes my entire body, and I can do nothing but hold on as another orgasm powers through me, leaving me helpless in its aftermath.

I'm quivering as his thumb leaves me with a pop I feel more than hear. My sex is still vibrating with the aftermath of his attention when I hear his clothes rustle and his zipper slides down. My breath hitches as I come back to earth, and I jolt slightly as he runs the bulbous head of his cock against my slippery folds.

Placing my cheek against the booth, I shift my gaze around to find Cade's eyes fixed firmly on his actions. His jaw tics and he exhales heavily as he continues to coat his hardness with my climax.

"I told you before, Bam." He lines himself up with my slick centre, his eyes rising to meet mine. Pushing forward, he enters me teasingly, only to withdraw suddenly and slap his cock against my raised ass.

"I told you, but you *clearly* didn't listen."

He lines himself up against my folds once more, covering my back with his body, and he leans closer until his breath is hot on the back of my neck.

"I *told* you that when I re-claim your body, you're mine. *Forever*."

And at that, he drives home in one swift movement, seating himself so deeply that I'll never not feel him there.

"Now, hold on..." He nips my ear, and I can feel his cock

pulsate deep inside of me. "I'm about to fuck you as hard as you've fucked me."

Thirty-Three

CADEN

Summer cries out when I thrust my hips forward, seating my dick in her tight pussy. My vision blurs as I begin to move, driving into her with force.

"Oh, fuck. You're so tight. You *definitely* weren't working tonight, Bam."

I reach into my pants pocket, pulling out my wallet to toss it onto the booth beside her.

"You're working now."

She stiffens at my actions, but I continue to thrust into her wet heat without pause.

My blurred field of vision is utterly focused on my cock driving in and out of her soaked channel. My whole being is completely intent on making her *feel* my pain.

I reach around her thigh to press my thumb against her throbbing orgasm-slick bud. She moans when I increase the pressure, and a surge of her arousal coats my hand, making my cock pulse inside her.

"*Yes*. That's it. Your sweet little cunt likes working for it, doesn't she?"

I hold her in place as I continue to fuck harder and harder, my balls hitting off the hand that's playing with her throbbing clit.

The rational part of me knows that *if* she does work here, it's not in any kind of debauched capacity. I *know* that.

But rationality has left the building, and in its place stands only pain and heartbreak. Fifteen years of pent-up longing. An ocean of lies and a mountain of hurt.

My vision blurs to the point that the entire room is one obscure mess.

"I hate—" I pant with exertion as sweat drips from my temples. My chest continues to rise and fall at speed as I fuck her faster and faster.

She tries to rise onto her elbows, but I palm the curve of her spine, pushing her down harshly as I continue to fuck her without hesitation. Without thought. Without remorse.

I grit my jaw as I try to force my traitorous mouth to tell her that I hate her, but the words won't come out.

"I hate—"

She cries out, half in pleasure, half in pain, and I pinch her clit firmly between my thumb and index finger. Her pussy clenches around me as another orgasm bulldozes through her body.

"I love you, Cade. *I love you*."

The sincerity in her voice cleaves open my heaving chest to pierce my wounded heart.

I blink rapidly, trying to clear my blurry sight as Summer begins to descend from her pinnacle. My hips falter when her words register.

I'm dumbfounded to realise I'm crying when a sob catches on an inhalation. My vision finally clears as tears fall down my cheeks, only to blur once more with a fresh onslaught of emotion. Tears fall from my lashes to land on Summer's bare back as I fight to get control of myself.

My breathing is ragged as all the fight drains from my body, and I hunch over to rest my head between Summer's shoulder blades.

"I *hate*…that I can't stop loving you."

My words are a sob against her perspiration-soaked skin, and I can hear her breath catch in her throat.

"I *hate* what happened to us, Bambi."

I inhale raggedly, unable to stifle the sobs that escape my lips. My chest feels tight, like I can't draw a breath. Like I might go into cardiac arrest.

"I hate it *so* fucking much."

Withdrawing from her body, I gently turn her around to gather her against my chest. Her arms wrap around me as silent sobs course through her small frame. I settle on the floor with my back against several dislodged booth cushions before catching her chin between my fingers to bring her tear-stained face up to mine.

My father's words from the jet ring through my mind.

"Life is too damn short to throw away a split second of it. You have had fifteen years *stolen from you. Please don't allow your pride to keep you from losing any more."*

I ghost my lips across her quivering ones, speaking my truth. The only truth that matters.

"I hate a lot of things, Bam. But I could never bring myself to hate you. Ever."

Her breath catches in her throat, and a fresh rush of tears streams down her flushed cheeks.

I rub my thumb across her trembling bottom lip, my eyes tracking the movement. "The article doesn't matter. If you've moved on with Burton, then I can be happy for you. You deserve—"

"I haven't. I wouldn't." She stops me in my tracks as her eyes spear mine, begging me to believe her. "There's only ever been you. I only ever wanted *you*, Cade."

I inhale deeply, filling my lungs with fresh air. And relief. A breath has never been sweeter.

Palming her cheeks, my eyes find and hold hers. Those big doe eyes hold no blame. They're filled with an outpouring of love, and instantly I'm suffused with a deluge of remorse.

"I don't know what..." I exhale shakily, shaking my head in disbelief at my own actions. "I don't know what I was thinking. I—I'm sorry—I—"

She gently places her hands on my cheekbones, holding me still and forcing me to feel the love that ebbs between us.

"You're hurting. You've *been* hurting. For a long damn time, Cade. I get it."

She strokes the pads of her thumbs underneath my bottom lashes, wiping away the fresh flood of emotion that her empathy brings to the surface. I close my eyes, the guilt almost overwhelming me as she continues.

"I don't want you to hurt anymore. There's been enough hurt to last ten lifetimes, Cade..."

"I'm sorry for hurting *you*." I swallow down my self-hatred as I meet her eyes. There's not an ounce of judgement in those chocolaty depths.

"We've *both* hurt one another. Maybe it's time to stop." She rests her forehead against mine, her hands cupping my cheeks comfortingly, and I can feel the tension leaving my body under her touch.

I exhale a silent sigh of relief as she glances away before I continue. "If you work here, then I *know* you have your reasons. I—I—wouldn't hold anything against you…"

She raises her head, her eyes peering into my soul. "I bartend. Mostly." She nibbles her lip, glancing skywards in thought. "And I was a beard for a while—"

I can feel my face freeze when my eyebrows hit my hairline. "A *what*?"

She tries and fails to stifle a smile. "It's a story."

"I'm thinking we have a lot of them to tell. Giving you a week to fall back in love with me may have been great in theory…" I smirk self-deprecatingly. "But when you've got fifteen years' worth of catching up to do, I could have led with a lunch date."

"I thought it was romantic. Very on-brand for you."

She giggles as I press my lips together in a suppressed grin.

Sobering slightly, I reach up and wrap my hands around her wrists. "You did the most amazing job raising our son, Bambi." Her eyes fill with fresh tears. "He's magnificent. And that's entirely you."

She presses a soft kiss to my mouth. "He's always reminded me of you, Cade. His looks, his mannerisms, his musicality–his ability to love with his entire self, freely and with complete abandon."

"Our kind of love isn't easy…but it's a once-in-a-lifetime love." I swallow roughly, clearing my throat. "And I *know* that it's worth working at. That what we have is worth all the hardships because the reward is that much sweeter."

My eyes drink in the rapt expression lighting up her beautiful face as I hesitantly ask the question I need the answer to. "Do you think we can work at it together, Bam?"

Her face splits in a blissful smile, and she nods slowly before pressing another kiss to my upturned lips. "Caden Atticus North, that would make me the happiest woman on the face of this earth."

I lean closer, taking her mouth in a slow, leisurely kiss. A kiss that promises more.

A kiss that promises we have all the time in the world.

I deepen the kiss, and she moans into my mouth as she winds her arms around my neck, tugging me closer. Her bare tits scrape off my shirt, begging for my attention as I register sounds in the hallway.

"Summer? Are you—oh, *shit*!"

I shield Summer's bare chest with my clothed body when Vaughn spills into the room, Ford hot on his heels, slamming into his back when he stops suddenly.

"Ever heard of knocking?" I roll my eyes at the two men before they give us their backs, almost in synchronicity.

"This is *my* club. Knocking is not a requirement for *me*."

Without missing a beat, I reach around Summer to my discarded wallet atop the booth before launching it at their turned backs. It hits Vaughn's back, then falls to the floor with a soft thud.

"Add it to my gold card, and get the fuck out."

Ford bends to retrieve my wallet, tossing it to Vaughn with a smirk. "I'll have what he's having, but make it brunette."

Vaughn strides through the door, calling behind him. "I charge by the half-hour." Once he's crossed the threshold, he turns to us, giving me a once-over with a no-shits-given look on his face as he tugs the door closed. "Though your bill should be substantially less. You strike me as a two-pump chump, pretty boy."

Ford chuckles deeply in his chest as the door swings closed, locking with a *beep*.

Summer drops her head against mine, nibbling her lip. "Oh my God, I'll never be able to look either of them in the face again."

"Who cares about them? I say we show that fucker I'm at *least* a three-pump chump."

Summer's laugh chimes through the room, turning to a low moan as I take her mouth once again, kissing her as though I can't get enough of her.

When I lean back, she whimpers at my abandonment of her mouth. I grasp her around her waist, lifting her onto the booth at her back with ease before sliding my hands along the inside of her thighs.

"Open for me, Bam. I've got some serious apologising to do to my girl."

Her whole body shakes with laughter at my words until I reach the apex of her thighs and gently but firmly press them apart. Her sex is still glistening with her pleasure, and I raise my eyes to her hooded ones as I close the distance.

"Let me kiss you all better."

SUMMER

The car is silent as we head to whatever hotel Caden has booked. He's been quiet since we left the sanctity of the private room in *Risqué*.

Ford had been sitting outside the door with a fresh change of clothes for me and any other personal items Vaughn had rustled up from his office.

There had also been a note atop the clothes that simply said: *"I'll keep looking."*

I knew automatically that he was referring to his digging into

Noah Spellman and Layla Gardiner, and I'd taken a moment to look up towards the hidden camera I knew was blinking in my direction to send a small smile to my dear friend.

A town car had been waiting outside the private staff entrance, which had reminded me to send Vaughn a quick text about Griff's sickness once I was settled inside.

ME

Could you please check on Griffith? He wasn't well earlier.

I get an immediate thumbs-up emoji and drop my cell into my bag as Caden's phone chimes.

"Son of a *bitch*!"

I snuggle closer on the back seat as Ford swivels about. "What now?"

Caden drapes his free arm across my shoulders, shaking his head with a self-deprecatory smirk playing across his kiss-swollen lips. "He billed me. The motherfucker actually *charged* my gold card."

I press my lips together. "How much?"

"Ten dollars."

My eyes blow wide, and I can't stop my laughter from bubbling up my throat to escape my mouth. "Those rooms *start* at $5,000 per half hour. He really must think you're a two-pump chump."

He shakes his head, his smile broadening as Ford laughs to himself in the passenger seat. "Never seen anything like it, Cade. That place was freaky…"

Ford lifts a fiendish brow, and his smile grows enormous. "I think I *like* freaky. Just don't tell my Mama."

We're still laughing when the car pulls up kerbside at the Greenwich Hotel.

My jaw drops, knowing it's a very high-end boutique hotel

close to Rogue. "Fancy schmancy!"

We steamroll through reception, leaving Ford at the bar as we head directly to a suite. I'm assuming Cade stays here regularly, as he seems to know precisely where he's going.

"The Tribeca Penthouse is Dad's favourite."

Upon entry, I can see Sutton all over it. It's unique and totally suits his character.

I exchange a small smile with Cade as I step further inside.

"Mom!"

A blonde whirlwind barrels into me, almost knocking me off my feet, only for Caden to reach out a steadying hand. "Easy, kid. She's breakable."

My eyes search for his over our son's shoulder, and I deadpan with a cynical brow. "I'm stronger than I look. I'm most definitely *not* breakable."

Cade presses his lips together, moving off to embrace Sutton, who's appeared from one of the bedrooms. I bury my nose in my boy's neck, inhaling his comforting, familiar scent as he holds me tightly to him.

"I missed you, Jess."

"I missed you too, Mom. I'm sorry for what I said." His breath hitches, and every part of me can feel the sincerity in his warm embrace. "I didn't mean it."

I squeeze more tightly, and he reciprocates. "I know, baby. We've all said and done things we don't mean. I never meant to hurt anyone, but here we are." I pull back slightly to palm my boy's flushed cheeks.

"If there's one thing I teach you in this life, it's that it's okay not to be perfect. It's okay to make mistakes. The important thing is that we *learn* from them and try to do *better*."

Caden catches my eye, mouthing, *"I love you."*

"You know you're my world, baby." My eyes are firmly on our boy as I choke out the words. "Nothing you can say or do would *ever* make me love you any less than I do right now, at this moment."

He gifts me with a lopsided, watery grin. "I'll get to learn from my mistakes, Mom. It's all going to be okay. Dad's my match."

Tears fill my eyes as disbelief flows through my body.

"I know, my sweet boy. I can't quite believe it."

The anxiety gnawing away in the depths of my stomach is surely nerves and nothing else.

Having spent so long feeling like an axe would drop on my head at any given moment, I push that uneasiness deep down inside, forcing myself to forget all about it, and just be *happy*.

Thirty-Four

SUMMER

The next morning, we leave Tribeca behind, venturing to a small airport in New Jersey.

Caden and Ford converse quietly at the front of the private plane as Sutton, Jesse, and I get settled. I quickly shoot both Anna and Vaughn a text, telling them I'll be out of town for a while. Noting that my battery is definitely on the low side, I put my cell on silent without waiting for their replies.

"The jet is Henry's. He's nice." Jesse sits opposite his grandfather, who's setting up a card game over a small desk. "He told me tonnes of stories of when you guys were kids."

I laugh indulgently as I raise a disbelieving brow. "He hardly had many of me, baby. I kept myself to myself." I narrow my eyes in remembrance of just how quiet I was back then, snorting a laugh. "I suppose that was mostly because I was afraid of my own shadow back then."

Cade moves past us to occupy the seat opposite mine. He reaches forward, grasping my hand with his, and I watch as he brings our joined hands up to press a kiss to my knuckles. "You're fearless now, Bam."

He lifts a brow while smiling softly into my eyes. The brush of his soft lips across the back of my hand sends a wave of goosebumps across every inch of my skin. "You're not afraid of a damn thing!"

I smile almost shyly, glancing away when the love in his eyes gives me butterflies. My eyes land on Jesse, who's watching our interaction intently.

He looks up, meeting my gaze as a beautiful smile lights up his face.

My heart fills almost to bursting, and emotion clogs my throat as I mirror his happiness with a smile of my own.

How is this my life?

Once the jet is in the air, Sutton begins to teach his grandson the fine art of poker. Laughter ensues between both of them for the next couple of hours as Cade holds my hand in comfortable silence.

His gaze flickers between my face and watching the game to his left. He looks completely and utterly relaxed, and I find myself unwinding more and more just by being in his soothing presence.

"Your poker face is worse than your old man's." Sutton's words draw our combined attention when he laughs, and Caden reaches across the aisle to push him playfully.

"Yours isn't much better, *grandad*."

Sutton narrows his eyes at his laughing son, but it's Jesse who answers for him. "He prefers Pops, Dad."

My chest tightens, and my heart takes flight at the everyday normalcy with which our son refers to his father. My nostrils flare as my emotions threaten to get the best of me, and Cade rubs his thumb across the back of my hand, lending me his quiet strength.

Ford walks down the aisle from his position by the cockpit. "The pilot is about to land. There are SUVs on the ground in Austin, but we do have a minor Tequila Sunrise. Somehow, the media got word of your imminent arrival. The airport is swarming with paps."

"Son of a bitch!"

Sutton and Caden's voices ring out together in a combined expletive that makes Jesse's mouth twist upward in a lopsided grin.

The hero worship in his bright blue eyes grows tenfold. "Cool!"

I swat his hand. "Not cool, mister." Swinging my gaze around, I spear first Sutton and then Caden with a stare. "*So* not cool."

I'm met with a mumbled "Sorry!" before Ford speaks. "I've radioed down, advising the SUVs to be on the tarmac as soon as the plane stops. Your luggage will follow, but it's best if you guys make for North Star immediately."

Cade nods slowly before blowing out a heavy breath. "I love the music, but I hate the intrusiveness." He tilts his head to one side, his eyes roving over my features. "I won't miss it. I won't miss any of it."

I tilt my head, confusion plain on my features. "What do you mean?"

He shoots me that shit-eating grin I know so well. The one I love so much. "I'm quitting the industry."

My blown eyes and gasp of shock make his smile impossibly broader.

"I'm going to make that life, Bambi. The one I always dreamed of." He leans closer, taking my head between his hands as love flows freely between us. "The one with me and you, growing old together in a big old house with two dozen grandkids. I'm getting the life we deserve. And I'm not wasting another damn second."

CADEN

When we'd entered onto North Star property, both Summer and Jesse fell silent as they took in their new surroundings.

I take a moment to send Noah a quick text. Like I said back on the jet, I'm not wasting any more time.

Starting right now.

ME

I'll pay whatever it takes. I'm done with the band. I want out.

Locking my screen, satisfied that I'm working towards the life I want, I return my gaze to watch my family's reaction to one of my favourite spots on the planet.

Their eyes grow wide as our driver takes us on a long, winding road through wide open fields, slowly edging closer to the contemporary-style ranch house Mum had insisted was built here.

When the two-storey sprawling house comes into view, Summer gasps audibly, and Jesse plasters his face to the window of the SUV with his mouth hanging open.

"Holy *shit*!"

"Jesse Sutton St James, watch that mouth, mister!"

Jesse rolls his eyes, returning to take in the surrounding view as my dad reaches for Summer's hand from the passenger seat of the SUV. Tears fill his big brown eyes as his hand squeezes hers. "Thank you."

Summer dips her head in acknowledgement, raising her eyes

to meet my dad's. "I named him for the man who treated me like his own."

Emotion hangs heavily in the SUV when the vehicle slowly rolls to a stop outside the doors of the ranch house.

Jesse, utterly oblivious to what's passed between his mother and grandfather, swings open the rear driver's side door and practically bounces onto the driveway. "Do you guys have horses? I *really* want to ride a horse." He spins back to pierce his mother with a pleading look. "Please say you'll let me ride a horse, Mom. Please?"

He holds his hands together in a begging gesture, making my father bark a laugh as he slips from the passenger seat with an agility that men half his age would love to possess.

"Come on, I'll give you the grand tour, and then we'll visit Maisie. She'll like you so long as you bring her an apple for tea."

Dad and Jesse walk just ahead of us, talking animatedly together. Thick as thieves already, and the sight fills my heart.

Summer takes my hand, slipping from the car with an easy smile, and I tuck her hand into the crook of my arm to walk her to the front door of the house.

Dad reaches for the handle as we catch up to him and Jesse, only for the double doors to spring open.

"*Surprise*!"

A small blonde blur sprints across the threshold and launches herself right at her "*Summer-hero*!"

"Curly-Sue!" Summer kneels and wraps her arms around my baby girl, holding her tight against her chest. Jesse drops down behind his mother, his hand resting on Bella's sea of curls.

My little girl's exuberance, and easy acceptance of Summer back into her life, makes my face split clean in half with a cheesy as fuck grin.

Their relationship took flight right from the very first day, but this reunion right here makes me certain—as if I was ever in doubt—that Summer was always meant to be in Bug's life.

Bella looks up, and her smile is nothing short of blinding when she spots her big brother.

"Hey, Bug! How was Disney?"

"It was okay. I wasn't big enough for the fun stuff." She huffs unhappily, and Jesse clucks her under the chin with an exaggerated pout of disappointment. Bella rallies in that way only four-year-olds can as a mischievous smile erupts on her bow lips. "So Mimi said we could come here instead!"

Mum steps out onto the porch as Bella continues. "And *then*, Mimi said we better call in the…call in the…" She pulls out of Summer's embrace to glance back at her grandmother with a questioning look on her pretty little face.

"What did you call all the people, Mimi?"

Mum shakes her head, a hint of a smile playing around the corners of her mouth. "I said it was time to call in the troops, Bella."

Bella laughs, looking back at Summer, then at Jesse, and finally, her eyes land on me. "*Daddy*! Oh, you're never going to believe what fun we're going to have." She closes the distance between us, wrapping her arms around my legs. "*Everyone* is here!"

I look from my daughter's face as all eyes shift to my mum. Her smile is broad and entirely Cheshire-Cat-esque. She winks, grabs hold of Dad's hand, and steers him around to go back inside the house as she calls over her shoulder, "Come on, everyone. You'll see."

We file inside, following my mum just as Ford's SUV pulls up in the driveway. He salutes us with a nod before rounding the vehicle to unload our luggage.

Mum leads us through the house, but before we've reached the back doors, I can hear it. The inimitable sounds of a North family get-together.

As Mum throws open the back doors, my suspicions are confirmed when we're greeted with a loud cheer. My four sisters, their significant others, and all eight of my nieces are in attendance, alongside the Holloways, my bandmates, and a handful of friends from the industry.

Henry and Liv, alongside Nate and Mila, are stood a little further to the back with great big smiles on all four faces.

"Mum?" The incredulity in my voice earns me a smile from my mother, the master manipulator, when she turns back to face me.

"We wanted to introduce Jesse—and Summer, of course—" She stops, smiling softly while placing a motherly hand on Summer's upper arm. "To all our nearest and dearest."

Dad speaks first, throwing his arms around his wife and pressing a kiss to her upturned lips. "You're one of a damn kind, Clare-Bear. I'm the luckiest man alive."

She nudges him slightly with a roguish wink. "And don't you ever forget it."

I'm once again reminded of why my parents' love story is a love story for the ages, and the one I aspire to attain someday, when he presses a kiss to her forehead, whispering, "Never."

Then, turning to the waiting guests, he booms across the patio. "Now, who wants to meet my grandson?"

Jesse is engulfed in a swarm of bodies—mostly female, all family—the moment he exits the house. Similarly, Summer is rapidly stolen from my arms by a chin-wagging Bree, steering her in the direction of her husband, Drew, who's manning the barbecue with a grin on his face and a beer in his free hand.

Ford comes up behind me so silently that I almost jump when he speaks. "My guy in New York called me in the SUV."

Turning around with hope flaring to life in the pit of my stomach, I instantly slump at the beat-down look on his face.

Ford shakes his head sadly. "He's got absolutely nothing on Spellman. I'm sorry, Cade. What do you want to do now?"

I swear softly but shrug, knowing the chips will need to fall where they may at this point. "I've already quit, Ford. I don't have leverage, but I don't care anymore. I want *out*. I'll pay any price."

My friend's face scrunches up, clearly not wanting to give up. "I thought you wanted to make him pay for forcing Summer to leave. For keeping her whereabouts to his-damn-self!"

I exhale heavily, scrubbing my hands down my face. "It's like my father said on the jet. Life is too short. I'm done. I just want to be happy."

I clap my hand on his shoulder, levelling him with a determined stare. "I'm *choosing* to be happy, Ford."

Shaking his head slowly, he blows out a breath. "That asshole is not going to make it easy for you, Cade. I can guarantee you your contract is air-fucking-tight." Ford's brows knit together in concern.

"He can do and say what he wants. I'm done being his goddamn puppet. He took advantage of me at my lowest. Steered me towards a life I had *no* interest in living, and has made a fucking fortune off my damn back."

"Caden?"

I turn at the sound of Bree's voice calling to me, holding up a stalling hand as I call out. "One second."

I turn back to Ford and continue my rant, needing to say the words. "He knew where she was *all this time*. He's a lying bastard, and I'm done playing nice with him. He can do his worst. I'm ready."

The front door slamming earns our joint attention before Ford can respond.

Footsteps across the marble tiles resound with a *click click*, getting closer and closer until the new arrival rounds the corner into the open-plan kitchen and stops dead in his tracks.

My mother breezes into the kitchen, coming to a halt when she spots the newcomer. "Noah, dear! So glad you could make it." She air-kisses his florid cheeks, waving her hands about excitedly. "Come on, I need to introduce you to our Jesse."

My soon-to-be ex-manager smiles saccharinely before nodding gently. "Be out in a sec, Clary."

Mum spins on her heel, pleased as punch with her party organising skills and none the wiser of the wolf in sheep's clothing who she's invited into the fold.

"I'd say it's nice to see you, Cade, but, well…" Noah trails off, depositing his briefcase on the kitchen counter before huffing a dark laugh. "Well, to be honest, you're being a real pain in my goddamn ass lately."

He stops, chuckling to himself exaggeratedly. "I see your shitstorm followed you from London only to gain momentum in Manhattan."

He stops suddenly, holding up his hands in front of his face to clap slowly. "Bravo, Cade. Bra-fucking-vo! I've never quite seen the like before. You'll notice the shit hitting the fan results in a lot more mess when I'm not cleaning it up after you."

"I don't *want* or *need* your help, Noah. I'm—"

Cutting me off, he carries on as though he hasn't heard me in the slightest. "I'd offer my condolences on the passing of your wife—"

I repay the favour and cut him off with a hiss. "*Ex*-wife. And

I'll kindly ask you to keep your damn mouth shut. My daughter is present and doesn't need any further unpleasant memories of her mother."

He shrugs as though he's not got a care in the world before he shucks his jacket and rolls up his shirt sleeves.

"Now, if you'll excuse me, I have a long-lost kid I need to meet."

Thirty-Five

CADEN

"I wanted to punch him right in his smug fucking face." I blow out a breath as I shake out my palms, needing to do something to stop from clenching my fists. The overwhelming desire to strike out at Noah Spellman as he watches me from across the enormous entertainment patio my parents custom-built is at a fever pitch.

Henry steps into my line of vision, blocking Spellman's view of me. "There's a time and a place, man."

There's a warning tone in my friend's voice that matches the severity in his eyes. "I think it was a mistake to show your hand, Cade. I can't lie." His brow crinkles deeply in concern. "Spellman isn't a man to be crossed, and he's not going to let you off the hook easily. You should have spoken to someone first before you told him you wanted to quit."

I shake my head impatiently. "I won't live this way any longer, brother. He's a manipulative piece of shit; I can see that at last. I'm finally going to live my life. The life he *stole* from me."

Exhaling heavily, I can't stop a frown from appearing on my face. "I'll let sleeping dogs lie because, as Dad says, life is too short. But I *refuse* to play by his rules anymore."

"Okay, North. I hear you…please just remember, Spellman is a damn shark. He's shrewd, calculating, and utterly selfish. I wouldn't underestimate how far a man like that would be willing to go to retain control."

I clap my hand on his shoulder, squeezing lightly. "Thank you."

Henry nods, shoving his hands in his pants pockets as he glances about the jam-packed party. "Your mum always knew how to throw a party, didn't she!"

I snort a laugh. "She's really something." When I gesture towards the woman in question, Henry spins about, laughing when he spots her singing softly to his sleeping son as Liv watches on with a dimpled smile on her face.

"She's always had a knack with kids. When I basically moved into your house, she never once made me feel like I wasn't part of the family…" Henry trails off, his eyes glossing over as he remembers something from that dark time of his life.

He physically shakes himself out of his reverie, widening his eyes and pasting a smile on his tanned face. "Your parents were the only example of real, unrestricted, *true* love that I witnessed growing up. Nate, too." His smile reaches his eyes when it grows. "I always wanted that kind of love, and it fucking amazes me every damn day that I found my Peach. That I get to experience the love I'd thought I'd never deserve."

My face mirrors his. "I know what you mean, brother."

Henry's smile becomes a self-satisfied smirk, and he raises a knowing brow. "I see taking that leap of faith and trusting in the universe did you the world of good!"

I throw my head back and laugh. It feels good.

Life is good.

"What are you two whispering about, like a pair of grumpy old men?"

Nate appears at Henry's side, passing both of us a beer before sipping from his own.

Henry side-eyes our friend with a down-turned bottom lip. "Doesn't Metropolis need saving, Mr Kent?"

"Are you *still* harping on about that, Batman?" Nate rolls his eyes, blowing out a breath. "It's a damn costume!"

"That's not the point, Hawthorne."

I press my lips together, glancing around the party in search of Summer, only for my eyes to once again find Noah watching me intently. As I narrow my eyes, Jesse bounds up beside me, brimming with his signature exuberance.

"Ford said he'll take me horse-riding tomorrow if Mom agrees…" he trails off, smiling up into my eyes with beseeching eyes. "Might you talk her round, Dad?"

My mouth turns up in a smile, and I throw my right arm over his shoulders as I steer him in the direction of his mother, who's currently hosting a tea party at the edge of the patio with his little sister.

"Come on. Let's ask her. Together."

A grin splits his face, and he chews on his bottom lip with wide, excited eyes. "She'll definitely say yes if you ask. In the stories she used to tell about you, she always said you talked her into doing things she'd never have done for anyone else."

I ruffle his messy blonde hair as I snort, nodding my head in acknowledgement as we approach our quarry. I lift a brow devilishly, allowing my biggest smile to spread across my face.

Time to dial the charm up to ten!

"Let's see if I can meet with your expectations, kid."

SUMMER

My afternoon passed in a blur of faces and names I would surely never remember, yet happiness surged through me with every single genuine interaction I had.

"I see you're still trending on TikTok."

Beau Maxwell, drummer extraordinaire, sidles up alongside me, a huge smirk on his round face. I narrow my eyes, ready to hit him with a retort, when I hear a voice at my back.

"I see you've finally grown your whiskers."

I choke on my sip of prosecco when Caden appears almost out of nowhere, encircling his corded forearm around my waist to tug me back against his chest.

My entire body relaxes into him, forgetting where we are and who we're with, only caring that it's joined to its other half.

Beau guffaws, shoving Cade playfully before stroking his newly grown beard with a brow raised pointedly. "It makes me look dashing, according to your mother."

Cade presses his lips together to suppress a grin at his friend's taunts as Ford appears to my left. My eyes widen when I see he's sporting a black Stetson and looks nothing like his normal self.

"My parents are heading on home, Cade. I'm going to drive them, if that's okay."

"Course, Ford." Cade waves him off with an easy smile. "Take your time."

Ford rolls his eyes under the brim of his broad hat. "My dad got a new Quarter Horse, and he won't quit until I've seen him. I won't be long."

Bella appears, almost as though out of thin air. "Can I come too, Fordy? I love horses."

Ford glances at Cade, who smiles indulgently before nodding. "Course you can, Bug. Be a good girl for Ford."

Bella jumps up and down excitedly, grasping hold of Ford's extended hand and following along behind him, chattering nonstop.

Beau sidesteps towards Drew's barbecue as Cade and I watch while Bella and Ford leave with his parents and sisters in tow.

I spin in Cade's embrace, pressing my ear to his chest, and exhale softly in utter contentment. "Today has been wonderful."

His hum of agreement vibrates through his chest. "I could have done without Noah being here, but other than that, it's been perfect, Bam."

"You're in big trouble for manipulating me into letting Jesse go horse-riding tomorrow."

I pop a brow and shoot him an evil look. "*Big* trouble!"

He chuckles, nuzzling his face into the crook of my neck as he whispers. "I can't *wait* to experience your special brand of trouble, Bam."

I shiver when he presses a kiss against my exposed neck. "Later." That single word is a whisper of a promise across my delicate skin, and I can feel myself melting even more.

"Get a room!"

I jolt at the sound of Henry's voice as Cade mutters a quiet expletive, and we turn in synchronicity to find two smiling couples and a sleeping baby in an infant car seat.

"Are you guys leaving?" Caden's voice is high-pitched with disbelief. "Did Mum not invite you to stay?" He looks around, undoubtedly ready to berate his mother.

"No, no. She did." Mila laughs, shaking her dark head. "We're flying to New York in a couple of hours."

Henry scrunches his face up in distaste. "I have a meeting I need to sit in on with Alex in the AM."

"He wouldn't have asked you unless it's something he genuinely needs your help with, Henry!" Liv nudges her husband in the side, shooting me a playfully exasperated smile.

Henry rolls his eyes, shifting his sleeping son into his other arm. "Mila's best friend is performing in her first off-Broadway performance this week, so these guys are hitching a ride with us to catch tomorrow evening's show."

Mila slants her eldest brother a dark look. "*You* aren't getting out of it either."

"Tell your mum thanks for thinking of us." Henry continues as though his little sister's words have landed on deaf ears. "Getting to see everyone meet Jesse…"

He trails off, smiling softly. "We wouldn't have missed it."

Once we've bid farewell, the foursome, alongside a stirring baby Sebastian, make their way to the waiting SUVs in the driveway. Henry and Mila are bickering back and forth, much to their partner's blatant amusement, and Cade closes the front door with a fond smile on his handsome face.

"Your friends really are quite something!"

He sobers, tugging me against his chest to pierce me with a deep look. "*Our* friends, Bam. What's mine is yours." Pressing a kiss atop my nose, he spins me in his embrace and steers me towards the emptying patio with a swat to my bottom.

"Come on, let's try to get rid of the stragglers. Or else Dad will break out the guitar, and we'll never be free."

I chuckle quietly. "I need to use the little girl's room. Do you know where I can…"

He smiles softly. "This way."

Leading me upstairs, through a long corridor of closed doors, he finally comes to a stop and pushes one open.

"This is our room."

My eyes take in the huge bedroom with a four-poster bed and floor-to-ceiling windows looking out across acres of beautiful, wide-open space.

"Wow."

The single word is little more than an exhalation.

"It's really something, isn't it."

I nod mutely, my eyes drinking their fill as Cade presses a kiss to the back of my head.

"Freshen up. Take your time. I'll get moving on shutting this shindig down."

I spin about, blinking owlishly, wholly awed at the beauty of North Star.

"No wonder your dad loves it here. It's…it's…"

He smirks, winking theatrically before moving back down the hallway and tossing over his shoulder. "Not half as breathtaking as you, Bambi. Not even close."

Once I've drunk my fill—or as much as I can absorb at this time—I make short work of using the ensuite to freshen up.

Someone has had my suitcase brought up to the room, alongside my crossbody bag. I send a prayer of thanks up to the heavens as I take a minute to slip into a long dress that's much more suited to the Texan heat.

I'm giving myself a once-over when I remember to plug in my cell, which is surely dead at this point. Digging into my handbag, I find to my surprise, it still has ten percent battery left.

As I pull out my charger, I smile, noting several text messages.

ANNA

I'm so happy for you, love. I'll keep the memory box safe in the meantime.

I smile at her thoughtfulness before sending a reply.

ME

I'm walking on air, Anna.

My smile freezes and falls from my face when I click on a message from Vaughn from earlier today.

VAUGHN

There's no easy way to say this, sweetheart.

Griff died this morning. I'm so sorry.

My stomach churns as I read and re-read the message over and over again. My breathing is coming in short bursts, and tears prick behind my eyes as emotion threatens to overwhelm me.

He can't be dead. He was fine last night. He was *fine*.

My gentle giant. My friend.

Another text pops up beside the previous one, and my forehead puckers in befuddled hesitation when I read it.

VAUGHN

Call me immediately when you get this. From THIS cell. In private.

I don't understand.

My mind feels like it's wading through quicksand, and my hands shake dangerously as I dial Vaughn's number.

"Are you alone?"

Vaughn answers my call with a stern voice that jolts me to awareness.

"Y-yes."

"Are there any devices near you? Any devices *specifically* owned by the North family?"

I glance around the room, shaking my head, when I find nothing other than a television.

"Summer? Are there any devices?"

At Vaughn's repeated question, I realise I've not spoken aloud. "There's only a TV."

"Is there a bathroom near you?"

"Y-yes…"

"Go inside. Turn on the shower."

I do as he's instructed, hearing the barely concealed urgency in his tone and feeling a little like a fool, but having trust that I'm doing it for a valid reason.

As I twist the shower handle, water begins to stream from the showerhead, crashing loudly into the tray beneath. "Okay. What next?"

"Everything—absolutely every single thing at North Star and every other North-owned property—is tapped. *Everything*."

Chills race up my spine, and I glance around the white-tiled bathroom, half expecting to see a camera dot blinking at me from the ceiling.

"He found something. My guy found a *lot* of somethings."

I inhale sharply, sinking to the cool tiles. My stomach is all twisted and knotted as Vaughn continues.

"Remember we decided to dig into Layla? Well, it led us down a very dark road, which has wound up shining a light on a certain someone. I hope you're sitting down because this is one hell of a story. Are you ready?"

"Probably not, but you're going to need to tell me anyway."

Vaughn blows out a heavy breath. "Layla sent you a letter, citing that she'd miscarried, right?"

"Yes."

"Okay, well, two weeks after that letter was sent, there's a record of her visiting her GP. She went alone and was immediately referred to hospital, where she received treatment for uterine sepsis."

"What?" My breathing accelerates, knowing the next words out of my friend's mouth will be the game changer.

"They called her next of kin—her mother, who by all accounts was a waste of space—but she didn't come. But her *father* did."

"Her father died four years earlier, Vaughn. Her mother didn't remarry until *after* Caden and Layla were married. That makes *no* sense."

"I know, sweetheart. All further records were unobtainable, so I don't know who claimed to be Cole Gardiner, but I have a hunch."

Me too.

"I was able to get my hands on a record from Layla's admission form, where a nurse recorded that the patient was concerned that the infection was caused by an incomplete abortion."

Vaughn stops for a beat when I suck in a shocked breath.

Oh my God!

"So, my guy dug a little deeper. Money can buy pretty much anything and, this time, it bought the records of a private abortion that took place in London only two days after you left. The person who set it up and paid for it? Noah. Fucking. Spellman."

I bite my bottom lip, mulling it over and coming up with nothing.

"I don't get it, Vaughn. Why would he pay for her to abort Sutton's grandchild after going through all that hassle of taking me out of the picture?"

My stomach sinks when I come to the realisation just as Vaughn verbalises my thoughts.

"Neither of the North twins were the father of that baby."

Thirty-Six

SUMMER

Standing at the top of the staircase, I take a moment to calm my racing heart.

Breathe, Summer. Just. Breathe.

Several deep inhalations later, I stiffen my spine and slowly make my way towards the darkened back patio, which has cleared out substantially.

Glancing around the lit-up space, I spot Caden alongside Beau and Jake, deep in conversation.

Alyse and Cassidy are bickering over the last slice of Mississippi Mud Pie while Bree shoos Cade's many nieces into the kitchen, citing that its way past everyone's bedtime.

Finally, I find Jesse. He's showing Clary his newfound poker skills, while Sutton watches on with a broad grin on his kind face.

Noah, of course, is at his side.

He glances in my direction, narrowing his eyes so slightly I'd say I imagined it if I wasn't altogether fully sure of this man's unfettered animosity towards me.

I shift my gaze to Cade, forcing my legs to move until I reach his side.

"There she is!"

He beams up a smile, but I can only return a shaky version. "Would you like to bring me to the stables?"

Beau and Jake begin to cat-call and whistle, drawing the attention of the rest of the bodies on the patio, and I can feel my face heat. "To show me the horses. Get your minds out of the gutter, boys."

Jake nudges Cade, a huge grin front and centre. "Go on then, North. Show her your *horses*."

Beau snorts behind his hand as Caden stands, entwining our fingers to lead me away from his chortling bandmates.

"It's a bit dark to go to the stables, Bam. Let's go in the morning when Jesse goes riding with Ford, hmm? You'll like it—"

"No. *Now*."

I cut him off, my voice coming out agitated and much higher than I anticipated. Everyone stops their chatter, glancing at us for the second time.

Jesse drops his cards, murmurs something to Clary, and stands to move closer, only for Noah to reach out and catch him by the arm.

Every square centimetre of my body moves into high alert.

Caden links his arm through mine, beginning to move in the direction of the stable, but I stand still, rooted to the spot in abject fear.

I need to tell Caden what Vaughn has discovered, away from the house and the ever-present digital Big Brother. But hell will freeze over before I trust that man with our son.

I've known for a long time now that Noah Spellman is capable of deviousness, but Vaughn's findings have blown me away.

"Neither of the North twins were the father of that baby."

My breathing starts to falter, each inhalation isn't enough, and I frantically gasp for air. How had I not known she was sleeping with someone else?

"Breathe, sweetheart. I'm only getting started."

Oh, shit!

I sink lower onto the bathroom tiles until my forehead is flush with the pristine white, and I'm once again breathing at a normal-ish level. I inhale heavily, filling my lungs.

"Okay?"

Vaughn's voice comes down the line, and I whisper, "Okay."

I can hear his own deep breath just before he drops the next bomb.

"Layla's sponsor for rehab—the very first time at eighteen—it wasn't Caden. It was Spellman. He had access to all her records, having paid for everything. He's named as her legal guardian on the paperwork, as a matter of fact. However, *during the process of sifting through her records from another rehab stint following the birth of her child, my guy came across the goods."*

I blow out a breath when he pauses, mentally steeling myself for whatever is about to come out of his mouth.

"In her required therapy sessions, she mentions her regret for past transgressions and how the drugs and meaningless sex were her way to quiet the voices. She mentions—and this is verbatim, okay?"

I murmur my assent, entirely unsure of whether I want to know, but altogether certain that I need *to.*

"That day at the river should never have happened. But I was young,

foolish, and believed he loved me. I was willing to do anything for him, and for years, I did. It wasn't until recently that I've seen that he never cared for me. He only cared about what I could do for him. How I could manipulate people into doing what he *wanted. I want to stay clean, but every time I think I can do it, he reminds me of what I did, and the cycle starts all over again."*

I pull myself up into a sitting position, incomprehension zipping through my mind. "She can't *be talking about Archer. He was dead at that point. So, who's she talking about?"*

"I'm getting to it, sweetheart. Hold your damn horses."

"Get to it faster, Burton!"

He huffs, but continues. "That was the only entry from her many *therapy sessions that mentions anyone other than Archer. It's ambiguous, but the timeline doesn't add up. So, we dug even deeper. Did you know Spellman holds shares in a little-known electric company based out of London?"*

"Christ, don't ask questions you know *I don't know the answer to!"*

"This small electric company is owned by a massive corporation that handles security for the one percent of the one percent. World-fucking-wide, sweetheart. And wouldn't you know, that security company is—"

"Holloway Security Detail?"

"Bingo!" He confirms my suspicions.

"Caden said HSD has run his father's security for years. It runs his own now, for fuck's sake."

"Try not to have a coronary, okay, sweetheart?"

I blow out a breath. "I'll try," I deadpan.

"We found the financials. HSD is funded in full *by Spellman Sounds. There's no doubt that Noah Spellman is controlling and monitoring every single damn thing that goes on in every house HSD 'protects,' including the one you're inside. Right. Now."*

My brain whirrs, trying to catch up with what I've been told. "Can they hear me now?"

"Doubtful. The water should muffle your voice, and you're not using a device monitored by HSD, so we should, in theory, be fine."

"Vaughn, I need you to tell me what to do."

"Take a breath first. Then pull up your big girl pants and act like everything is fine. If you can get allies on the ground, then do so, but only if it's safe. I'll figure something out, sweetheart."

CADEN

Summer tugs on my arm, stopping me from showing her to the stables, despite her adamance only moments before.

I squeeze her hand to gain her attention, but she is firmly fixated on Noah, who is chatting with our boy. The sight doesn't particularly warm my heart either, but now's not the time or the place for fisticuffs.

"Come on, Bam. I thought you wanted to see the horses."

She turns back to me, indecision and something else galloping across her face. "Um…I think we should call it a night."

She pulls her hand from my hold, raising her arms in the air to yawn in such an over-the-top manner that I'm helpless to stop myself from heckling her.

"Didn't know you were an actress!" I shake my head as I grip her upper arms in concern. "What's going on?"

Her eyes go round, and she mouths the words, *"Not. Now."*

I draw my brows together in confusion, on the precipice of asking another question, when she leans up on her tippy toes and presses her mouth to mine. Her tongue demands entry, and after a moment of hesitation, I pull her closer against me to deepen the kiss.

She takes the opportunity to glide her lips across my cheekbones, urgently pressing her mouth to my ear. "Noah has tapped the house. Say nothing. End the party."

As she pulls back, smiling from ear to ear, I laugh softly, but it sounds strange even to my own ears.

Dad stands, walking closer. "You two okay?"

"We're *great*." Summer presses her lips together in an utterly false smile that every person here would notice immediately if her back wasn't to everyone other than me and Dad.

Despite that, Dad pulls her against his side. "Let's grab a drink. I've not had you to myself all day because I've been too occupied with the glorious grandson you bestowed upon me."

Summer smiles back, and it seems more genuine when Dad steers her in the direction of the bar at the edge of the patio.

Alyse and Cass glance in my direction, blatant questions in their eyes. I pull my phone from my back pocket, shooting Ford a text as I pretend to read a message that's not there.

ME

Tequila Sunrise.

"Ladies, your husbands have messaged that your children require their mothers."

Both of them narrow their eyes, and I shoot a glance at our mother. "Children will never *stop* needing their mothers, and I'm a clear example." Mum chuckles, and I shoo both sisters off the patio as they flip me the bird over their shoulders.

Summer sends me a look of gratitude from the far end of the patio, where she's in deep conversation with my father.

"Jesse, my son." I move closer to Mum, Jesse, and Noah, who's still monopolising my son's attention. "It's well past time for… PlayStation Five."

Jesse's eyes blow wide. "Seriously?"

I nod, smiling genuinely at his delight. "Yup! Wash up, and I'll be upstairs to kick your ass in…" I check my non-existent watch. "Five minutes. Move, move, move, soldier."

He grins his farewell at both Mum and Noah, slipping past me at a run, but backtracking to plant a kiss on my cheek that warms me to my very bones.

"Go on." I smile right into my son's big blue eyes. "I'll be there in a minute."

With a flash of his perfectly straight teeth, he's gone.

Spinning to my mum and Noah, I clap my hands together. "Well, it's been a blast. Thank you for such a wonderful introduction for Jesse, Mum."

She beams a bright smile at me, stepping forward to pull me into her arms just as Noah's phone rings.

He slides his hand into his pocket and checks the caller before shrugging. "I've got to take this." Then, without moving, he answers with a sharp salutation.

As he presses his ear into the receiver, I hold Mum close to my chest and meet Summer's eyes across the patio. Jake's loud guffaw peels through the tense night air, and I glance in his direction.

"Shut the fuck up, Milano!"

Noah jerks his phone from his ear and barks the order. In typical Jake fashion, he parrots Noah in a deeper-than-usual tone, earning a chuckle from Beau.

Hanging up the call, Noah turns a flushed face towards me, then shifts his gaze to Summer before his lips raise in a semblance of a smile that sends a shiver of foreboding right through me.

"I underestimated you, Caden." Noah's voice is a deep intonation meant for my ears alone.

Mum steps out of my hold when Noah addresses me. His tone is harsher than she would be used to, and she frowns uncertainly.

He curls his top lip as he levels me with an unrelenting stare. "Frankly, I didn't think you were intelligent enough to figure things out…" he trails off to lift his phone up, shaking it. "But Eduardo tells me certain records pertaining to your deceased wife were recently accessed, and, well…no one else gave enough of a shit about her to actually bother to look beyond the surface."

Eduardo? As in from HSD?

"I thought he was recuperating from an accident. In a coma or something!"

"You think what I *want* you to fucking think, Caden. Have you not realised that yet?"

My eyes blow wide when I realise what Summer meant.

The house is tapped–because it's secured by HSD. So he must have an inside man there!

"Yes…you're joining the dots. Keep going…"

The words are a whisper as they leave my mouth. "You own him."

He snorts, glancing sideways across the patio when my father and Summer move closer to Beau and Jake.

"I own *everyone*." He shrugs indifferently. "You see, there's nothing money *can't* buy, young North. I had none of it growing up. All I had was a deadbeat slut for a mother and a father who wouldn't even acknowledge my existence. I watched your father live the life that should have been *mine*, and I swore I'd never go without again."

"You have plenty now. And all the power. All I want is to live my life with the people I love." My brow creases with my plea, attempting to appeal to the man I thought he was. The man I *hope* is still somewhere inside of him. "You can keep everything. All the royalties. All the copyrights. I'll pay the fees to get out of the contract. And you'll never hear from any of us again."

"I can't trust you now, Caden. Don't you see?"

I shake my head, having no idea what he's talking about.

"Eduardo told me *precisely* what files were accessed. I know you know more than you're letting on."

"I know nothing. I swear, Noah. I admit it, I *did* look into you, but your record was clean as a whistle." I hold my hands up, glancing at my mother, who's stood listening in silent disbelief. "I found nothing. I have nothing on you. I *promise*."

He narrows his eyes in thought before turning his head across the patio.

"*You*!"

His bark echoes across the open, almost empty space, and all eyes shift towards my unravelling manager as he spears Summer with a hateful glare.

"You should have stayed a-fucking-way. I *warned* you if you ever came back, there'd be repercussions."

Summer meets his stare head-on with an impenetrable one of her own, tilting her chin in silent defiance. Refusing to be cowed.

Noah barks a harsh laugh. "You should have stayed gone, Summer. Everything was playing out perfectly. Layla left him the forged letter that broke his little heart. I removed *this* gem…"

He dips into his pocket, extracting a glinting silver necklace. It takes a second for me to register the locket Summer always wore before she left as it dangles from between Noah's thumb and index finger.

"Caden thought you'd left without a care." He throws the locket in her direction, where it lands and breaks in half on the patio paving, and still, she doesn't flinch as she stares down her aggressor.

Pride fills me from the top of my head to the tips of my toes.

"I *allowed* you to live in peace with your spawn, even though

I *knew* I should have ended you both when you were still within reach…"

He trails off, dipping his chin down and talking as though to himself.

"The moment you were taken into Burton's care, you were beyond even my *reach. That bastard will pay too."*

He jerks upright, pinning Summer with a dark look. "You should have listened to me, Summer. You should have stayed away…the repercussions *will* be harsh."

Summer exhales heavily through her nostrils. "You *don't* scare me anymore, Noah. I'm through being frightened by you. You *stole* everything from me."

Noah throws his head back, laughing to the heavens. He laughs and laughs as each bystander turns confused eyes toward one another.

The laughter stops abruptly, and the night air is pierced by a sudden ear-splitting *bang*.

There's an audible grunt, and Jake falls to the paving with a grimace, a hand pressed across his midriff. We all watch on in silent shock when he lifts his palm from his stomach to display his white t-shirt rapidly staining with blood.

Beau steps forward, catching our friend before he falls and pressing his own huge palm across the bullet wound.

I swing my incredulous eyes back to a manically grinning Noah.

"You should be scared of me, Summer." He waves a gun in his hand. "Very. Fucking. Scared."

Thirty-Seven

SUMMER

Everyone moves to rush toward a gasping Jake, whose head is resting in Beau's lap. But we all freeze when Noah's voice booms through the night surrounding us.

"*Don't* fucking move!"

I exchange glances with Clary and Cade, both of whom stand still and unmoving, telling me with their eyes to do the same.

Sutton steps forward, and I place a stilling hand on his upper arm. His brown eyes turn to me questioningly, and I shake my head.

He stops in his tracks, doing as I've silently requested, but instead of remaining silent, he addresses Noah.

"What the hell are you playing at, Noah? Put that damn gun away and stop being fucking crazy."

Noah regards his oldest friend with blank eyes.

"You really had *no* idea, did you?"

Sutton throws his hands up in exasperation. "Noah, so help me *God*. Jake needs medical attention, and fast. Call 911 right the hell now!"

Noah huffs a laugh. "Wow! You really *didn't* know. Did you never *once* question the similarities?"

Sutton exhales through his nose, glancing quickly towards a moaning Jake. "*What* similarities? What the hell are you talking about?"

"The similarities between me and your father."

My stomach drops, remembering Vaughn's discovery.

"Far enough to find that Noah was the result of an affair. His mother refused to tell anyone who his father was, so that's something I've had my guy dig further into."

"Your father. My father." Noah tilts his head, his eyes boring right into Sutton's, before he spits two jaw-dropping words. "*Our father*."

Sutton shakes his head once, then twice. "No. *No*! I don't believe that. You're full of shit. My old man—"

"*Our old man*, you waste of fucking space!"

He brandishes the gun again, waving it around as he laughs dementedly. "He wanted to leave *your* mother to be with *mine*, but she got pregnant with *you* at the same time Mum told him she was having *me*."

Sutton inhales sharply beside me. "He—he wouldn't—"

Noah cuts him off with a snarl. "He stayed with his picture-perfect wife to live a picture-perfect life, leaving me to *rot*." Spittle flies from his mouth on the last word, his face turning almost purple with sheer rage.

He narrows his eyes, smiling dangerously at all of us and none of us. It's almost as though he's talking to himself.

"But his guilty conscience is what tipped me off. He was paying

Mum to keep me—although the worthless bitch snorted most of his hush money—and he paid for my schooling. Unfortunately for him, we became friends."

His smile widens maliciously as he spears Sutton with a stare. "And wasn't that a turn-up for the books? Dear old Dad had to see me *all the time*. I never let that bastard forget it, either. It wasn't long before he was paying *me* to keep quiet."

He sniggers almost giddily, his gaze travelling over every person paying witness to his supposed glory.

"I saved every goddamn penny and then used you and Cole to help me build Spellman Sounds. I have more money than *he* ever had. But more importantly, I have more power. So much power that I can control *everyone* and *everything* without lifting a finger."

He exhales dramatically. "It's quite exhilarating, to be honest. I hold so much power that I can get away with—and *have* gotten away with…" He barks a wild laugh and then shrugs nonchalantly, chuckling almost as though to himself. "Just about *anything*."

Tapping his gun against his temple, he barks a laugh. "Archer thought he was smarter than me. Stupid fucking punk."

"*What*?" A shiver runs the length of my body as Caden whispers the question. "What does Archer have to do with you?"

He levels me with a calculating stare. "All these years, you thought *you* were the reason Archer North drowned." His lips tug upwards. "His death was *my* doing, stupid girl. He saw something he shouldn't have…" he trails off, curling his lip. "Layla knew what she needed to do to keep me safe."

Clary's horrified gasp resonates through the night. "My boy!"

My heart starts to palpitate as all the dots join together seamlessly.

"He saw you *with* Layla, didn't he? *You* were her baby's father." I flick my eyes to Caden, witnessing the moment it all comes together for him. "You tried to get her to pass it off as Caden's… but you couldn't because he wouldn't sleep with her."

Noah inclines his head, his lips turning downward in exaggerated distaste. "An abortion was the only option. She understood. She knew I'd look after her. And I did. For years. I made sure she had everything she needed. Caden's guilty conscience made him easily swayed into the role of babysitting, eventually leading to their marriage. Controlling Layla meant controlling Caden. And that gave me what I'd long desired: full control of the *entire* North family. The one with *all* the power."

His shoulders slump slightly, and his forehead creases. "Unfortunately for Layla, she wanted to get clean for the kid. But I couldn't risk it…" He glances at Cade, the picture of wide-eyed innocence. "Every time she got clean, her mouth loosened. Her guilt crept in, and…well…"

He shrugs, almost sadly. "I made sure it was quick."

Oh my God!

Then he focuses on me with laser precision. "And you'd be six feet under now, too—if you hadn't given the wrong damn sub to that dumb security guy in New York."

I suck in a breath, but it's not enough. My head feels light, the floor looks uneven under my feet, and my heart rate quickens beneath my breast. "Wh-what? Griff?"

He carries on, staring into the distance with a thoughtful look on his face. "And when that didn't work, I was *sure* a home invasion would see the back of you."

Pinning me with his stare, he hisses, "But you weren't home when you were supposed to be." Then he heaves a sigh. "And so, here we are."

I can't move past what he's said about my gentle friend, and a single tear rolls down my face when I sob quietly. "Oh, *Griff*."

"The cyanide in that sub would have been an easier way to go, Summer. Even the home invasion may not have been *too* bad." He narrows his eyes as his lips turn up in a calculating smile. "You can be guaranteed this way won't be as gentle."

CADEN

My mouth drops open when I realise what he's saying.

He had Layla kill Archer. He killed Layla. He tried to kill Summer.

I exhale on a shaky breath as I realise the one overpowering factor here.

HSD buries everything *for him.*

I turn concerned, questioning eyes towards Beau, knowing that time is of the essence for our fallen guitarist. My stomach takes a swan dive when Beau's eyes fill with fat tears that slowly fall down his cheeks as he shakes his head.

My eyes drift shut, praying he's wrong and that it's not too late for Jake. When I open them again, Beau is pressing a kiss atop our friend's forehead, having dropped his hand from the gunshot wound on Jake's stomach.

He's gone!

I break out in a cold sweat at the knowledge, allowing my watery gaze to rest on the stillness of Jake's body. My stomach churns, threatening to expel its contents with little to no care for the repercussions.

Jake is dead. My *friend* has paid the ultimate price, and it's all because of the son-of-a-bitch holding court in the middle of my parents' patio.

"Why are you telling us all this, Noah?" I snap my gaze to Noah, the question hissed through my clenched teeth. "You don't have enough power to silence all of us and get away with it."

I'm bluffing, and he knows it. He knows that he holds all the power right now. That he's held it for a long fucking time.

But I can't help hoping that help is on the way. That *somehow,* we can escape this madness before anyone else gets hurt.

Noah snorts, aiming his gun right at my chest. "That's where you're mistaken. Eduardo has been made aware of what to do in case of an emergency." He winks, then stage whispers, "Or, as you and young Holloway like to say, *Tequila Sunrise*."

My stomach dips.

Please stay away, Ford. Keep my girl safe.

"Don't look so shocked, Cade. There's *nothing* in your life that I'm not fully aware of. I told you…I own *everyone*. I control *everything*. And later tonight, while you're all sleeping, there's going to be a tragic house fire, killing every single occupant, courtesy of the cleaning crew Eduardo has dispatched from HSD." He pouts and presses his hand to the place where his heart should be in exaggerated tragedy. "Rest in peace, North family."

"What was that?"

Jesse appears at the patio door, scratching his blonde head in confusion.

"*Get inside*!" The words are yelled at the top of my lungs just as Noah aims the gun at my son.

Mum jumps toward Noah as both Summer and I sprint towards Jesse. His face is frozen in shock, and fear edges down my spine as my feet propel me forward as fast as they can.

My ears register a faint *whop-whop* sound somewhere behind me, but I can't place it. I can only focus on getting to Jesse, to Summer, and protecting them as quickly as I can.

The inimitable sound of a gun discharging resonates before I can get to either of them, and a cry pierces the air just as Summer crashes into Jesse, knocking both of them to the patio.

I turn my head almost in slow motion to find my mother lying motionless on the stone paving, blood slowly trickling from a gash on her forehead where the bullet appears to have nicked her.

Dad, having closed the distance between himself and Noah, roars a yell and launches himself at his old friend before he is able to raise the gun again.

Knowing that Jesse is safe with his mother, I run to ensure my mother is okay. Her eyelids flutter open just as I fall to my knees at her side. Big blue eyes, identical to mine and Jesse's, are brimming with unshed tears as they pierce through me.

"Is he—is he okay?"

A sob catches in my throat when I press my palm over the abrasion on her smooth forehead. "He's okay."

She exhales heavily before smiling softly. "I couldn't bear the thought of losing another—"

Her sentence is cut short when Noah stumbles closer as Dad manages to land a solid blow to his face.

I gather Mum into my arms, carrying her from the fracas as Dad swings a left hook that Noah blocks with the hand that's holding the gun. The force of the blow knocks the weapon from Noah's meaty grasp, sending it flying across the patio and into the darkness.

Suddenly, a spotlight beams down on the patio, lighting up the dimly lit space as though it's mid-afternoon. A black helicopter hovers overhead, emitting a gentle *whop-whop,* while several black-clad bodies rappel out of both open sides of the enormous machine.

My eyes shift to Beau, who has turned red-rimmed, teary eyes towards the masked newcomers, and Noah's words swim in my ears.

"There's going to be a tragic house fire, killing every single occupant, courtesy of the cleaning crew Eduardo has dispatched from HSD."

Tears fill my eyes when I realise he's won.

This is it.

We're going to die.

I choke on a sob.

And I'd only just begun to live.

A tear glides down my cheek when I set Mum by the backdoor, crouching to her level and begging her with my eyes to do as I ask.

"Press your hand to your forehead, Mum. And stay behind me."

I stand, inching slowly back towards Summer and Jesse to shield them with my body, as if that will make any difference at this point. Yet I cling to hope while sending up a silent prayer to Ford.

Please keep her safe. Keep my little girl from harm, Ford.

My father lands on his back on the patio before us with a heavy thud when Noah gets the better of his much smaller opponent and throws him to the ground.

"For crying out loud, I thought you'd never get here."

Noah's smug tone hits my ears, and my eyes follow his path towards the occupants of the chopper when Jesse's small whimper draws my attention.

Having been so fully intent on the horror unfolding before me, I was oblivious to the nightmare evolving at my back.

At my son's cry, my gaze is immediately drawn to him, hunched over a pale, still Summer. A noise somewhere between a howl and a keen is ripped from my chest as my legs cease to work, making me stumble and fall to pieces beside her motionless body.

Jesse's hands are painted in blood, covering what must be a

gunshot wound. I crawl closer, falling to the paving several times when my arms refuse to hold me up, before straddling her legs. Tearing off my t-shirt with unsteady hands, I wad it into a ball as tears threaten to blind me before jerking my chin at Jesse.

He scrambles backwards, his face streaked in tears and chest rising and falling as rapidly as my own. My gut twists painfully as panic swells inside of me, threatening to swallow me whole.

Forcing myself to take a deep, steadying breath, I try to focus on what needs to be done.

You don't get to fall apart just yet, North.

I press my t-shirt to the wound with my right hand, reaching my left out to grasp Jesse's trembling, bloody hands. Despite my own, almost crippling fears, I squeeze his red, sticky fingers reassuringly before checking Summer's pulse in her neck.

Jesse's wide eyes are full of questions when he stares at me with one concern at the top of his list.

"She's alive, kid. We just have to keep her that way and hope—"

A deep Texan drawl comes from the tallest newcomer, interrupting my sentence, and I twist my head to take in the scene before me.

"Noah Spellman?"

The man in question stops in his tracks, his eyes roving over each faceless person before him as his forehead puckers. "Those masks are not HSD regulated…" he trails off uncertainly before rallying and growling an order. "Remove them *immediately*."

The owner of the Texan accent removes his first, revealing a blonde buzzcut, a broad smirk, and a look of complete disdain. "Bull Salvatore. Elite Forces."

I frown as my brain whirrs.

Where's HSD?

Noah's face drops as Bull turns to me, taking in Summer's condition before calling behind him, "Medical assistance needed. *Now!*"

Bull finds my eyes again as my forehead scrunches up in perplexity. His lips twitch when he offers me a wink. "Mr Burton sends his regards."

Shock paints my face as the realisation hits.

Vaughn Burton, you motherfucker!

My body sags in relief as Noah pales.

"W-what? You're n-not HSD?"

Bull shakes his head slowly, a smirk growing on his face. "No, sir. The crew you're expecting got a little held up."

He begins to back away from our saviours, shaking his head in disbelief until he stumbles at the edge of the patio, falling flat on his ass. Beads of sweat pop up on his broad forehead while his gaze whips around behind him, searching for a helpmate who's clearly not there.

Another body rappels out of the open-sided chopper, landing with ease mere feet from the huge Texan.

"Gunshot wound to the left shoulder. Two o'clock."

His companion unmasks herself before following her leader's instructions to the letter.

She crosses the space, dropping down to my right before placing a hand on my upper arm. "You can let go now. I've got her."

The soft sincerity in the face of such horror is almost my undoing, but I slowly rise to stand, gathering a sobbing Jesse into my embrace as the apparent paramedic begins to triage Summer.

"It's okay, kid. She's going to be okay." I force a certainty that I'm not altogether sure of into my voice, years of covering my pain with a smile once more taking control.

Jesse's hands claw my t-shirt as a fresh wave of emotion rises in his body. I rub soothing circles on his heaving shoulders, allowing him to let it all out.

As my son sobs in my embrace, the weight of what's transpired here hits me square in the chest. The force of impact steals the breath from my body, and I gasp for air almost desperately. The movement draws Jesse's attention.

"How do you know, Dad? How do you know Mom's going to be okay?"

He turns wild eyes up to mine, pleading with me with those big blue orbs to comfort him with my words. There's only one thing I can say.

There's only one thing I *need* to believe. I need to keep hope alive, because that's what kept Summer with me all these years.

That's what kept our love burning.

And the thought stabilises my racing heart.

"Because the universe sent her back to me. And I won't allow her to be taken from me ever again."

He swallows harshly as he nods, his brows knitting as he tries to pull himself together. I tug my child back into my arms, resting my head on his to pay witness to an utterly different scenario than that of mere moments before.

It almost feels as though my eyes flit from one scene to the next in the span of a heartbeat.

A panic-stricken, hand-cuffed Noah can be heard offering any sum of money to the Elite Forces team if only they'll help him.

Two other members of the squadron are with Beau and Jake. One of them appears to be confirming what we already know while Beau is talking softly to the other beside our fallen friend.

Dad has rallied enough to cross the space to join my mum. They are holding one another tightly as tears stream down both of their faces. My father appears to have aged at least a decade in the last half an hour; his usual vivacity and lust for life dimmed beyond all recognition.

"Mr North?"

Jesse jumps out of my hold, crouching beside his mother as fast as the speed of light. My attention too instantly shifts to the paramedic who's called me, and I kneel beside my son.

"Ms St James's vitals are good. The bullet was a through and through, and the bleeding is now under control. My best guess is that she fainted, whether, from shock or pain, I don't know. But, as these things go, I've seen a lot worse."

I expel a breath I didn't realise I was holding.

"I've indicated that we'll need to have her airlifted immediately to discern how extensive her injuries are, so there is a medivac en route if you'd like to accompany her."

"I'm going. I'm staying with my mom." Jesse's voice is firm, and he grips her hand more tightly. At that movement, Summer's eyes flutter open, only for a second, shifting from Jesse to me, before fluttering closed once more.

"We can both go, right?"

At my question, the paramedic nods softly. "Absolutely—"

Her words are cut off when out of left field, Ford steps onto the patio via the back door, raising his hands when Bull and his entire team aim at least a dozen weapons in his direction.

He takes it all in his stride, dropping to the ground beside us with a nod to the team. "I'm one of the good guys."

My heart pounds painfully, and my question comes out little more than a croak. "Where's Bug?"

My friend spears me with intent. "She's safe with my baby sister. I promise. I would *never* endanger her, Cade."

I exhale a sigh of relief as the *whop-whop* of the medivac sounds once more.

"When I got your text, I secured Miss Bella and got back here as quick as I could. I heard a gunshot as I pulled up, and your sisters all made to run outside. I stopped them, and urged them back into their rooms, knowing that it was a *Tequila Sunrise* out here. I didn't get to Jesse in time—"

"You went above and beyond." My heart fills with gratitude for this man who I'm fortunate enough to call my friend. "Thank you, Ford." I put every ounce of appreciation that I can muster into my voice. "*Truly*. Thank you for everything."

The medivac lands on the wide-open space beyond the swimming pool to the left of the expansive patio, the wind from the blades slicing through the night, whipping the hot Texan evening air into our faces.

The paramedic begins to ready Summer for transportation, and we all rise to stand.

"Ford? Could you please grab my Bug and bring her to—"

I stop short, turning to the paramedic. "Excuse me? Which hospital?"

"Hemmingway Memorial in Austin."

Turning back to Ford, he nods sharply and turns to do as he's bid without a word.

"And Ford?"

He spins to me. "Yeah, Cade?"

"Could you reach out to...to..." I trail off, the name sticking in my throat. Swallowing the bitterness, I try again. "To Vaughn Burton?"

Ford presses his lips together with wide eyes, and I continue. Begrudgingly.

"Clearly, if *he* sent these guys, he knows more than we do about what happened here tonight."

Thirty-Eight

CADEN

"You want a coffee?"

Ford's voice breaks the trance I've been in as I watch Summer sleep, waiting for her to come around from her sedation.

It's been almost twenty-four hours since the events transpired at North Star. Upon our arrival at Hemmingway Memorial, we were granted access to an extensive suite while Summer was assessed.

She had roused as they were debriding the wound and had become distraught. The doctors had then sedated her, and she has yet to wake.

"Yeah, sure."

Ford nods at my affirmation before twisting about to look at Jesse. "Wanna stretch those legs? You've not moved in hours."

My boy looks up from his phone, glancing at Summer before

turning conflicted eyes to me.

"I'll call you the minute she wakes, kid. Go on." I smile genuinely. "Get some air. You look like crap."

His lip twitches as he pulls himself out of the chair beside his sleeping sister. "Maybe you should take a look in the mirror if you want to see what crap really looks like."

A chuckle rumbles in my chest, though I'm too drained to do much more than smirk as Jesse follows Ford from the room.

My eyes drift across Bella's sleeping form, marvelling at her ability to pass out anywhere and at any given moment. She smiles in her sleep before a soft laugh tumbles from her lips, breaking the silence.

"Cade?"

I freeze for an instant before jumping to life at the sound of Summer's raspy voice. Rising from my chair at the foot of the bed, I round the side to find her big doe eyes wide open and full of questions.

Grabbing her water glass, I help her sit forward, careful not to touch her bandaged bicep as I place the straw on her bottom lip. She takes a small sip while I prop her pillows higher, settling her back against their softness as lightly as I can.

Gently sliding onto the edge of her bed, I take one of her hands in mine, unable to keep a broad smile from my face.

It's not until she reaches up with her free hand to brush her thumb across my cheekbone that I realise I'm crying. Matching tears fill her own eyes when I bring her hand to my lips, peppering kisses across her knuckles.

"Oh, Bambi." I close my eyes and take a steadying breath.

Summer tugs her hand from my grasp as I open my eyes, placing her palms on either side of my face. Her chocolaty eyes hold me in their thrall as her brows draw closer together, deepening her intent.

"I'm here. I'm not going anywhere. I *promise*."

I lean closer to press a tender kiss to her soft lips. Then, resting my forehead against hers, I choke out the words that have haunted me.

"I thought I'd lost you. I—" My voice breaks, and I swallow roughly as my emotions threaten to overcome me. "I can't lose you again, Summer. I won't."

Tears crest her bottom lashes, spilling down her pale cheeks while her bottom lip trembles under the force of her emotions.

"You won't lose me, Cade. You never did." Her voice drops to a whisper. "I've always been yours. And I always will be."

The tension that has flowed through my entire body for the last twenty-four hours—or perhaps it has been there for the last fifteen years—slowly ebbs away, leaving nothing but hope and possibility in its wake.

I stare into those big brown eyes that own my soul. Eyes filled with the promise of dreams coming to life, and I smile, giving her my whole heart just as I did all those years ago.

"I think it's long past time we make that life together, Bam."

SUMMER

Having been kept under observation for the following five days and nights, I'd been beyond grateful to be discharged from Hemmingway Memorial with instructions to continue to rest before I could slowly resume my normal activities.

As gunshot wounds go, I'd been exceptionally lucky. The bullet had been a through and through, having missed all nerves and muscles in my left bicep.

It had hurt like a motherfucker, but considering the alternative, I wouldn't be complaining any time soon. And the pain was lessening by the day as I regained movement relatively quickly.

Following the unwelcome revelations about HSD, Ford was not in a good place and, having spoken to Cade outside my room door, had decided he needed time away to clear his head.

Bella had been so upset to see him leave, but he'd assured her that he would check in all the time. Even going so far as to leave her a small bracelet with her name on it, which seemed to pacify her somewhat.

Our foursome returned to North Star, courtesy of a car sent by Sutton, to find a flurry of people swooping in and out of the sprawling ranch.

Authorities of all kinds had been called in, and a complete overhaul of HSD was ongoing, much to Jasper Holloway's sheer displeasure. He was utterly adamant that he'd not known what Noah was using his company for—claiming that Noah had only been the money in the operation, despite evidence to the contrary.

Vaughn had—crazily, in my opinion—chartered a private plane to Austin. He had rocked up on the North Star property the day after the shooting while we'd been in Hemmingway Memorial with an onslaught of his tech-savvy people.

His "guy," we came to learn, is actually a girl called Addison. She had found a trail ten miles long of misdeeds, hidden agendas, and lies that pointed the finger firmly at Noah.

And Jasper.

There were years of Noah blackmailing high-profile figures whose homes and security were handled by HSD. Jasper had granted him access to everything, with Eduardo Diaz acting as the go-between.

It was no small wonder why Ford had needed to take off.

Having handed everything they'd found over to the proper authorities—and leaking *just enough* about Noah's dirty deeds to Alex DeMarco's media outlets to ensure justice was served by the relevant authorities—Vaughn had disbanded his crew upon our return and announced he was taking a sabbatical. At North Star.

Cade had been wholly thrilled at the news if the unrestrained grimace on his face was any indication.

"I'm looking forward to getting back to normal."

My boy's voice hits my ears, carrying through the recording studio where he's jamming with his father and grandfather.

"Or some kind of new normal." There's laughter in his voice, putting a smile on my lips. "My normal from before wouldn't have included *knowing* you guys, let alone getting to do this shit with you."

Initially, my stomach dips at the reminder that he's not known his father and grandfather until now, then I register his profanity. I narrow my eyes and am about to step around the corner where I'm eavesdropping to tell my son to wash his mouth out, but I'm saved from making the trip when his father does it for me.

"Mind your mouth, kid!"

I smile proudly when I can just about make out a muffled apology, only for my smile to slip and my eyes to blow wide open with Cade's follow-up.

"I mean, if it was just us guys, I'd probably be a little lenient, but considering that your mother is listening from the other side of that wall..." he trails off, then howls his signature booming laugh.

I pop my head around the corner with my eyes narrowed. "How did you do that?"

Cade gently deposits his acoustic guitar onto its stand, his eyes never leaving mine as devilment plays across his sincerely gorgeous features. Then he stands to his full height, tilting his head adorably as he makes his way closer.

"There's a special bond between soulmates, Bam. I can *feel* it when your heart is nearby. My senses come alive..."

He slides his arms around my waist, mindful of my arm, when he finally closes the distance between us, pressing a chaste kiss to my mouth. His words whisper across my lips. "Also, there was a mirror behind you."

I'm unable to stop snorting a laugh when he straightens up, smiling right into my eyes. Happiness is evident on every inch of his face.

"I've just put Bella down for the night. She was asleep before Queen Barb sent the letter to Queen Poppy."

Cade's eyes fall closed, and he shakes his head as a laugh rumbles from his chest. "*When* will the obsession with that damn movie quit?"

Answering laughter bubbles up my throat, spilling from my lips at the genuine desire for an answer held within his tone.

"She's four," I deadpan. "It's not lifting any time soon. When Jesse was four, he was Pokémon obsessed for...oh, wait. He's still obsessed!"

"Am not!" Jesse's voice calls out behind Cade, and I poke my head around the side of his arm to stick my tongue out playfully at my son.

"You are too! Last month, you asked me to get you a Pikachu plush to bring to Camp."

His neck pinkens, and his cheeks flush with embarrassment as his father spins around. "If you want to talk embarrassing obsessions, I got you beat, kid. Check this out."

Cade lifts his left hand, urging Jesse to come closer. Sutton follows, his lips pressed together while silent mirth dances in his dark eyes.

"See here?"

Cade parts his fingers, allowing Jesse to view the Bambi silhouette tattoo between his ring and middle finger.

Our son's mouth drops open. He raises disbelieving eyes to his father before curling his lip. "The Disney deer?" Incredulity colours Jesse's voice. "I *knew* you were way more cringe, Dad."

He shudders dramatically as Sutton chuckles, stepping closer to sling an arm over his only grandson's shoulders. "Come on, Jess. Sing me my favourite Johnny Cash, and make this old man happy."

Jesse's face lights up as he hugs his grandfather around the waist. "You're the least cringe, Pops. That's why *you're* my favourite."

Mine and Cade's mouths drop open wide as Sutton belly laughs. "As it should be, Jess. As it should be."

They disappear further into the studio, leaving Cade and me to turn disbelieving eyes on one another.

I roll my eyes. "Teens."

Caden snorts a laugh, pulling me closer. "You're going to need to excuse my ignorance, Bambi. I can barely parent Bella, and she's not long turned four. Fourteen is…*shit*." He slams to a stop, his big blue eyes blowing wide as the realisation strikes. "I was thinking about your boobs at four-fucking-teen!"

I shake my head slowly while taking hold of Caden's left hand with my right. Then, smirking, I lead the love of my life from his father's studio in the direction of the main house as Caden's features freeze almost hilariously.

"Oh. My. *God*. You were two years older than Jesse when… when…."

He trails off as he turns to face me with sorrow painted across his beautiful face. "Christ, Bam. You were little more than a *kid*." His brows crease as he exhales, reverence engraved on every beloved feature. "I—I'm in *awe* of you."

As we reach the expansive pool area, I stop in my tracks, tugging his hand roughly to make him look into my eyes. "It makes me so angry to think of all the time stolen from us, Cade." I step closer, angling my body, so our fronts are flush together.

"I want to be this close to you forever and a day. And even then, it won't make up for what we've lost…but…" My eyes dip down and to the side before flitting back to his extreme depths. "But I want to try."

Cade's eyes flash bright blue fire, startling me in their fervency. He glances around us before turning back to pierce me with his gaze once more. "This way."

I follow him as he ducks behind a small water feature to reveal a hidden grotto, lit up by the lights inside the small plunge pool held within. The waterfall we've passed by shields us from view, and the whole place is surreal, like something from a movie.

My eyes take in my surroundings greedily before Caden's voice centres me.

"Summer St James."

My eyes shift around…and down to find Caden on one knee, staring up at me as though I've hung the moon and all the stars in the night sky.

My breathing accelerates, and I blink rapidly to dispel the sudden dizziness that has overtaken me.

Cade clasps my hands in both of his, sending me a lazy half-smile. He chuckles deeply at whatever he sees on my face before clearing his throat.

"The light left my world with you, Bambi. I have spent so much time wandering in the dark. Unknowing. Lost and *so* fucking alone. The last fifteen years have been hellish, not only because I craved you with everything I have inside of me. But also, because every single night, I would dream of you. Of *us*. I would dream of loving you in my waking moments, not just in the depths of my wildest dreams. And every morning was like stepping into a nightmare. Life without you…."

He glances away as he huffs a dark laugh. Tears fall down my face, knowing precisely how he felt.

Except I had Jesse. I had a reason to live.

"It wasn't until Bella was born that I felt anything. She brought the sunshine back into my life, but then *you* found your way home. And you brought Jesse, too. It was as though everything was lit up from within. Life had a new purpose. New meaning. Life had *you*."

"Oh, Cade." His name escapes my lips on a sob and answering tears fill his own expressive blue eyes.

"When you came back, you unlocked my heart. You set it free because you *alone* hold the key. You have since the day we first met. And you will until my last day."

He reaches into his back pocket while I inhale sharply, my words escaping in a high-pitched exclamation wholly unlike me. "*Oh. My. God*!"

"Calm your tits, Bam."

He shoots me a shit-eating grin, entirely at odds with his tear-stained face, and I throw my head back when a yelp of almost deranged laughter erupts from my mouth.

When I look back at Cade, his heart is in his eyes as he pops open a small navy box to display a platinum band with a solitaire diamond in the centre. It's simple, elegant, and understated. And perfect.

"They say the heart knows when the search for its other half is over. Mine knew it since the day you arrived at my house with blonde pigtails and flushed cheeks. You walked into my life and stole my heart, and I've *never* wanted it to be anywhere else."

He stops and swallows roughly before his nostrils flare with emotion. "You have my whole heart for my whole life. You've had it since the start because it was made to be yours. Just like you were made to be mine."

Taking my left hand in one of his, he slides the band onto my ring finger, where it sits perfectly. "I had this made the same day I got my tattoo. I've carried it with me every day. I never lost hope, even when I had no reason to believe."

Emotion overtakes my body as a sob escapes my lips when he rises to stand, holding our hands clasped together between us.

His forehead rests on mine while we absorb one another's presence, never once breaking eye contact. My senses are on fire, my heart filled to bursting as tears flow easily down my flushed cheeks.

"Looking at you feels like I'm looking at the rest of my life, Bambi. And it's the sweetest sight I have ever seen. Say you'll marry me. Say you'll let me love you until we're grey and old. Say you'll continue to carry my heart all the way through until forever. Say yes and make the only dream I ever truly had become my reality. Be my forever—"

I cut him off when I throw my right arm around his neck, pulling his mouth to mine while carefully angling my tender left arm.

He plants his palms on my cheeks, kissing me with everything inside him. Giving me his whole self.

"*Yes,*" I breathe against his lips before moving closer again to kiss him, caressing his tongue with mine slowly, deliberately.

I break the kiss to whisper.

"I love you. I love you, Caden. I don't remember a time I haven't loved you. You're so deeply embedded in every part of my being; I could never *not* love you. I fell for you then…I'm still falling *now*."

His Adam's apple bobs when he swallows roughly before he takes my mouth with his in a searing kiss that soars straight through my body, making my heart take flight. Our kisses begin to turn desperate until a voice invades the space, breaking the spell.

"For crying out loud! Can you two *please* find an actual bed?"

We break apart to find an unimpressed Vaughn, clearly on his way to take a dip in the plunge pool beside us.

He crosses his hands over his chest and raises a dark brow. "Though chumps may not require beds, so yeah…this makes sense."

Cade's snort of laughter elicits one of my own, and before we know it, both of us are bent double as mirth overtakes us. Every time one of us begins to sober, our eyes shift to Vaughn, whose underwhelmed expression becomes more pained with each chuckle that rebounds through the grotto, and it sets us off again.

Vaughn shakes his head exaggeratedly as he slowly turns to leave. "I'm not saying I hate you, Caden North." He glances over his left shoulder, his parting words setting us both off all over again.

"But…I would unplug your life support to charge my cell."

Thirty-Nine

CADEN
EIGHT MONTHS LATER

The sound of Ray Lamontagne's "You Are The Best Thing," courtesy of Beau's deep baritone, booms across the daisy-strewn meadow beneath our feet as I spin my new bride into the safe haven of my embrace.

She throws her head back, laughing to the late spring sky above us as our friends and family members watch us annihilate our first dance.

"Beau is going to murder you, husband." She lowers mirth-filled, doe eyes and pops a devilish brow. "We're ruining his big solo debut."

I hold her body as close to mine as possible, swaying our hips in unison. As I rest my forehead against hers, I feel her whole body relax into mine.

"He'll live, Bam."

Her eyes glimmer with emotion, and her brow furrows against mine as she holds my gaze. We continue to sway, drinking one another in, wholly grateful for this hard-won moment.

The events of the last eight months have been nothing less than a rollercoaster.

Jake's funeral had been the hardest hurdle to overcome and the catalyst that the three remaining members of Misdirection needed to spur them towards their true passions.

Danny and Wolfe had announced they'd fallen in love—something Noah had known about for years but had forced them to keep under lock and key—and three weeks after Jake's send-off, they were married in a quiet ceremony in Cornwall.

Four weeks after that, I donated bone marrow to my boy. Summer and I had been beyond nervous—my entire family, both blood and found, had been up the damn walls waiting for news—but he'd come out the other side like the champion I know him to be.

It was in the interim that I'd campaigned for this wedding, which Summer had been keen to push back in favour of ensuring Jesse's health. But both Jesse and Bug had begged her—and she couldn't refuse when they joined forces so beautifully.

The ceremony had been quaint, just a handful of our nearest and dearest—and Vaughn fucking Burton.

Asshole.

I pull Summer closer, and she drops her cheek to my chest, her body relaxing against me instantly.

My eyes drift across the meadow at the back of my childhood home, landing on the faces of all the people I love most, all gathered together to celebrate the most glorious of days.

My heart is filled beyond compare, and I inhale deeply through my nostrils in an attempt to keep my emotions under control.

Beau's rendition of the Ray LaMontagne classic slowly floats to a stop, and Summer leans back to applaud alongside everyone else present with a great big smile on her make-up free face.

My father steps onto the makeshift stage while Beau steps back, handing him the microphone with a nod.

"Thank you all for coming today." Dad's face splits into a shit-eating grin, way too similar to the one I see in the damn mirror, and I'm helpless to stop my face from imitating his.

My hand finds Summer's, drawing her close against my chest as Jesse sidles up alongside me.

"I've known most of you for longer than I want to—I'm looking at you, Henry DeMarco."

Everyone laughs as Dad chuckles while shooting a wink in the direction of a bird-flipping Henry.

"All I'm saying is that introductions aren't necessary at a show like this, so I'll move right onto the good stuff. Caden Atticus North—"

He breaks off to smile broadly, his eyes glistening in total contradiction. "To say that I am proud of the man you have become would be a vast understatement. *You*, my boy, are the most loving, selfless, and kind human being I have ever known. And seeing you *here* today—living the dream you have held close to your heart even when it seemed so far out of reach—my heart is filled to bursting."

My breath catches in my throat, and I clear it with a hoarse cough as I keep eye contact with my teary-eyed father.

"I love you, son."

I rasp a response. "Love you too, Dad."

He clears his own throat and continues, smiling brightly at my beautiful wife.

"I have known my new daughter-in-law for her whole life.

Her father, Peter—Lord rest his soul—was my dearest friend, and I know he's looking down today, smiling at how our families have finally become one."

He raises his champagne flute skywards in a silent salute, and everyone present follows suit.

"I think this is the part where I'm meant to formally welcome Summer to the family, but I can't do that. Because the truth is… you've been part of this family since the day you moved into this house."

I glance down just as tears crest Summer's bottom lashes, spilling down her cheeks while she smiles fondly at my father.

"You have been blessed with two beautiful children. Our little Bug—"

"I'm here, Pops!" Bella's high-pitched shout rings out from her place in Ford's arms at the side of the stage, making everyone laugh.

"I can see that!" Dad's deep chuckle makes our little girl smile even wider.

"And, of course, my Jess." I swivel my head to find the signature North shit-eating grin plastered to my son's face. "Come on up here, and make this old man happy."

Jesse flies across the floor, racing up the steps to throw his arm around his Pops' shoulder as Dad faces our guests once more.

"But before that, I have something I need to say to these newlyweds."

His eyes slowly amble across his captivated audience. My father has long had a way with words, and today is no different.

"It's not *what* we have in our life that matters, but *who*. And time spent with those precious few is an irreplaceable gift. No one understands that as much as this beautiful couple standing before me."

His eyes hold mine before shifting to Summer's.

"Life with your soulmate won't always be sunshine and rainbows. There will be dark days where you need to share an umbrella so that you can weather the storm together. And I have *no* doubt in my mind that you two can withstand just about anything life can throw at you."

Summer wraps her arms around my waist, curling in against my chest. My heart expands as I enfold her in my embrace, pressing a tender kiss to the soft skin of her forehead.

"So let's raise a glass to the bride and groom."

Dad clamps his hands on Jesse's ears as his smile turns mischievous. He lifts a bushy, more salt than pepper brow as his next words bring down the house.

"May all your ups and downs be under the sheets."

"Bella finally settled. Serena's sleeping in with her."

My wife shoots me a quirked brow through her reflection in the mirror. She's perched in front of the dressing table in our bedroom at my parents' place.

She's changed into a black satin robe whilst I've been settling our girl, and her shoulder-length platinum curls brush off the material as she shakes her head.

"Didn't I tell you I would have happily stayed with her, Cade?"

My feet move ever closer as I huff a dry laugh. "Our wedding night is for *us*. Meaning me and *you*, Bam. Your presence is kind of a requirement, yeah?"

Her pink lips lift in a soft smile as her gaze holds mine. "True, husband. And, as such, I have a gift for you."

Her eyes darken before she swivels in her seat. Her robe falls open to reveal her alabaster skin and nothing else.

She eases her legs open and nibbles her bottom lip while stifling a smile when my jaw blatantly drops. My eyes devour every inch of the perfection before me while my feet propel me close enough to drop to my knees before her.

Her eyes never once leave mine as I slide my palms along the silky-smooth expanse of her calves, over her bent knees to slip between her thighs. I urge them wider, and she obeys my silent command. Her instant compliance sends a zing of lust straight to my already rock-hard cock.

"What an obedient wife you are, Bambi."

She draws her bottom lip between her teeth, her nostrils flaring as she nibbles furiously.

The sight almost makes me chuckle, except the uninhibited desire in her eyes impels me to give her what she needs.

"And good girls…" I trail off as I edge my index and middle fingers higher. Her legs drop open even further, allowing me to slide both fingers along her already-soaked slit.

She moans low in her throat, her head falling back to display the curve of her delicate throat. I'm helpless to stop myself from leaning closer as I run my flattened tongue from her collarbone all the way to the delicacy of her right earlobe.

"Good girls get rewarded, Mrs North." My words whisper across the shell of her ear, and she exhales sharply when I plunge two fingers roughly into her needy core. "Are you ready for your reward, Bambi? Are you ready for what I'm about to do to your body?"

I tug her earlobe into my mouth, nipping it harshly and making her cry out before I soothe the hurt with my tongue.

"Because, Bam…" I draw back, grasping her chin with my free hand and spearing her with an intensity I feel in my fucking soul.

I lazily thrust my fingers in and out of her throbbing centre, my own dick pulsing with the need to own her even as my words delay the claiming to come.

"First, I'm going to make you come apart on my fingers. Just like *this*."

I rotate my wrist, my thumb finding her throbbing clit. Her gasp of pleasure ghosts across my upturned lips when I circle my thumb before pressing harder.

Her tight channel contracts around my fingers, and she whimpers as her eyelids flicker closed. Ecstasy plays across her features, making my cock jump in the confines of my suddenly too-tight pants.

As she comes back down to earth, I claim her mouth, roughly thrusting my tongue against hers. She moans into my mouth while her arms lock around my neck to hold me closer.

I ease my drenched fingers from her slick core, flicking her clit with my thumb to make her jolt against me. Our lips are still fused when I pull her against me before standing to carry her to the bed.

I deposit her gently, breaking our kiss to find both our chests heaving.

Summer lies back against the sheets, her satin robe having slipped wide open now so I can feast my eyes on her idyllic body.

My eyes travel along her toned legs, over the curve of her gently flared hips, and onto the flat of her stomach before coasting higher. Breasts capped with dusky pink nipples rise and fall with each breath she takes, and I can't stop myself from palming my cock through my lounge pants.

Calm down, buddy.

"Like what you see?"

My eyes dart to her smirking face, and an answering one of my own tugs at my own lips.

"I *love* what I see, wife. And now..."

I lie down on my stomach between her thighs, urging her to rest her calves on my shoulders as I part her pussy lips with my thumbs.

"Now you're going to feed me, Bam. 'Cause this perfect pussy is begging for a kiss." I draw my pointed tongue along her glistening pussy, my eyelids falling shut as her sweetness sets my taste buds alight.

"Oh, *Cade*!"

I swirl my tongue around her thrumming bundle of nerves, and her back arches off the bed as a cry of pleasure is torn from her flushed chest.

"Don't move!"

I fold my arms across the tops of her thighs, pressing my mouth firmly against her wet heat. Her eyes find and hold mine when my tongue slides through her folds while she inhales a shuddering breath.

"Mmm..." My moan of pleasure fills the room. "You taste like fucking heaven."

Her nostrils flare as she reaches down to caress my head before she sinks her fingers into my hair, holding me in place.

She quirks a brow, and I grin against her wetness before diving in and fucking her mercilessly with my tongue. As she shamelessly grinds her pussy against my face, little whimpers and moans spill from her parted lips until I suck harshly on her clit.

The inimitable taste of her orgasm fills my mouth when she reaches her pinnacle, and my dick can't wait any longer.

As she comes back to earth, I stand before her. Gazing down on her writhing body, I wipe the back of my hand across my drenched chin, savouring her essence.

"And now, wife. *Now* I'm going to use this perfect cunt…"

Stripping down faster than I thought humanly possible, I grab both of her ankles and tug her to the edge of the bed with my cock resting against her pulsing slit.

"I'm going to fill up my good girl until my cum is dripping down your ass, Bam."

I notch my hardness against her core, slipping the head between her wet folds as we moan in synchronicity.

"And you're going to keep your eyes on me when I use you to get us both off. Look at me while I'm deep inside you."

I jerk my hips forward sharply, filling her in a single thrust. She cries out, her eyes flickering precariously, but she doesn't allow them to close.

"Fuck, Bambi. You take me so good."

Her jaw tics as she brings her hands down to palm my ass, holding me firmly inside her. My cock throbs at her need for more. "Move, Caden. *Now*. I need you to move."

Fuck!

"Then keep your eyes on mine, and I'll give you everything I have."

And when I move, the sound of skin slapping against skin fills the room, alongside our joint moans. Her dark brown eyes hold mine captivate, the sheer love that rolls off her body fills my every pore, and I can feel my hips falter as I begin to lose the battle.

"You feel so good, Bam. *So fucking good*! You're going to make me come."

Her pussy clamps down on my cock as my words clearly affect her. "I'm coming, Cade. *Fuck*!"

Her heels dig into my hips, holding me firmly against her, and almost without warning, I erupt inside her warmth. My vision blurs with the force of my release, and I lose sensation in my legs, falling forward onto her perspiration-soaked body with a deep groan.

"Fuck, Bam. That was…that was…"

She draws me in against her chest, stroking my hair back from my sweaty forehead before pressing a kiss to the top of my head.

"You really outdid yourself."

Despite my boneless state, my mouth splits in a shit-eating grin, and I twist my head slightly to look up into her smiling eyes.

"Do you think we might have made Bug a big sister tonight?" My fingertips trail reverently across the damp skin of her stomach, and my heart skips a beat in hope.

One side of her mouth fishhooks upwards in a half-smirk. "Unlikely."

Her eyes twinkle impishly as my brows draw together in confusion at her conviction. As she places her palm on the side of my face, she brushes her thumb across my cheek.

"I told you already, husband. *I have a gift for you.*"

Her eyes leave mine to linger pointedly on my hand that's resting on her stomach before coming back to imprison me in her chocolaty orbs.

Goosebumps break out across every inch of my body when I realise what she means.

"You're pregnant?"

Her eyes shimmer with emotion as she nods.

With that simple gesture, my heart clenches almost painfully, and my throat seizes when an onslaught of feeling overwhelms my entire body.

I ease my body away from Summer's, moving down until I'm in line with her stomach.

Taking a moment, I gaze in sheer awe, as though I can see inside to the tiny miracle our love has created.

Tears fall unheeded from my eyes, landing soundlessly on her perfect skin. I brush them away, gently guiding my fingertips along her exposed flesh in nothing less than complete worship.

Leaning closer, I close my eyes as I press my lips against my wife's stomach, kissing both her and the babe within with every ounce of love I have to give.

Summer's quiet sob lands on my ears as her hands glide across my head. I begin to softly croon "You Are My Sunshine" with tears in my eyes and happiness in my soul at this dream come to life.

Because the time is finally right.

Epilogue

SUMMER
SIX MONTHS LATER

"Where in the name of God are you taking us, Cade?"

My husband's deep chuckle beside me makes me smile despite myself.

My nose twitches beneath the soft cashmere wrap he's asked me to place over my eyes in a makeshift blindfold as he drives us to a mystery location.

His left hand lands on my burgeoning bump, gently rubbing our little one safely growing within, instantly soothing my creeping nerves.

"Do you trust me, Bam?"

His whisper eases me further as he softly pats the top of my belly.

"Always."

He chuckles. "Then have some patience and enjoy the ride."

I snort. "That's what got me into this state, or don't you recall."

My husband's booming laugh echoes through the car, and I smile as my heart swells at his easy exuberance.

"We're not too far away now." He removes his hand from my stomach to flip the indicator before turning left. "Put your head back, and try to relax."

I expel a breath, butterflies dancing in my abdomen in anticipation of my surprise, and as I relax back into the plush passenger seat of our newly purchased BMW 7-series, Cade's husky voice fills my ears.

Before he's even made it to the first chorus of "You Are My Sunshine," I'm out like a light.

I don't even realise I've fallen asleep until the passenger door opens, jarring me to alertness.

"We're here, Bambi."

Caden's hand finds mine, and he helps to ease me out of the car; no easy feat with my bump in tow. My feet touch the ground, and he gently spins me about so that his chest is pressed to my back.

I hear a car door slam, the sound of the ignition followed by the crunch of tyres on gravel.

"Did someone just take our car?"

There's unmistakable devilment in Caden's light-hearted chuckle. "Sure sounds like it. Hmm, Bam?"

"I would have thought you were done with surprises, Caden North!"

He edges us forward, careful to keep my movements slow and measured until he finds the perfect spot. "This isn't a surprise, Bambi. This is the universe in action."

I furrow my brow but hold my tongue as Cade takes a deep

breath and places his mouth by my ear.

"I want to come home to you for the rest of my days, Summer St James. I want that life—the one we dreamed about as kids who knew next to nothing about anything, but believed the love we shared was the real deal."

His voice drops to a whisper. "Because it *was*. It still *is*. And it always will be, in this lifetime and all the lifetimes to come."

He presses a kiss to the sensitive skin below my ear before gently tugging the makeshift blindfold from my eyes.

The light of the late autumn afternoon blinds me momentarily, and I blink several times until the world around me finally swims into focus.

We're standing on a gravelled driveway, outside of a red brick two-storey house. There are tall white pillars on either side of the front door, with matching white trim around each of the windows.

"The attic is a two-bedroom conversion, bringing the total room count up to seven decently sized bedrooms."

I squint my eyes, confusion taking centre stage. "What…what *is* this?"

I glance back at Cade, taking in his puffed-out chest and proud-as-punch grin. "It's where we'll raise our kids, Bam. It's where we'll grow old together."

My inhale catches on a sob when I realise where we are.

"This is it, right? This is the life we dreamed."

Tears prick my eyes as emotion rolls through me. Cade steps closer, palming my cheeks as his beautiful blue eyes hold me a willing prisoner in their depths.

"In all those years apart, I carried hope. Hope that one day I wouldn't feel so lost. And that hope became a reality when you found your way back to me. Because that day, I knew I was never really lost at all."

He drops his forehead to mine as tears crest my bottom lashes, spilling freely down my rosy cheeks. When he speaks again, his breath whispers across my lips.

"That day I remembered that I had found myself *in you*. Back when I gave you my heart at eight years of age. My heart has loved you and my soul has felt you, even when my eyes couldn't see you. You never left me. *Not ever*."

When he presses his mouth to mine, I grab his wrists, holding him in place to kiss him with everything I have inside of me.

He breaks the kiss when he steps back and grasps my hand, tugging gently until my hesitant feet move to follow.

A smile plays across his features, that devilment from before rearing its head again. "I have something for you."

I shake my head even as I smile. "You're the pits. But I love you anyway."

He huffs a laugh, coming to a halt outside the white front door. I stop beside him, a frown marring my face. "What now?"

Tossing me a devil-may-care wink, he side-eyes the door pointedly. I follow his line of vision, my breath catching in my throat when my eyes land on his surprise.

"Oh my God. Is that…is that…my *locket*?"

The lump that appears in my throat makes speech impossible, so all I can do is stare mutely at the necklace draped on the door knocker.

He steps forward, unlooping it carefully before stepping closer to me once more.

"I know you said you'd left me your heart that day Noah forced you to leave, but until you told me, I was none the wiser." He unfastens the clasp, stepping behind me to drop the locket over my head so that it rests on my chest.

As he closes the fastening, I reach a hand up to reverently

touch my much-loved, long-missed birthday gift.

"Where did you find it?"

He wraps his arms around my waist, resting his head on my shoulder as he palms my stomach.

"After you were shot, all hell broke loose. Everything was taken into evidence, including your locket. We had to wait until after Noah's sentencing before your friend—the one I can't stand—"

I snort a laugh despite myself. "You're hardly talking about Vaughn."

My husband rolls his eyes, continuing as though he hasn't heard my jibe. "—well, he pulled strings to have it retrieved from evidence, though Christ knows *how* because I had precisely zero luck."

He presses a kiss to the curve of my neck, his lips brushing against my skin as he murmurs, "I've had it repaired so that it's as perfect as it was the last time you wore it."

I click the side of the locket, my breath stalling in my lungs when my eyes land on the images of Cade and me, the ones from all those years ago. They're exactly as I'd left them, the smiling faces of two carefree teens staring back at me, oblivious to the heartache in their very near future.

As though reading my mind, Caden whispers across the shell of my ear. "We've weathered the storm, Bam. It's clear skies and calm seas ahead of us, and I'm going to love you every day as if it's our last day."

I lean back against this man with the soul of a poet, and the heart of lion, as I soak up the start of our forever.

The front door flies open, making us both startle.

"Mum. *Mum*!"

Bella flies out onto the porch, her big brother at her back, stopping her gently from ploughing into my rounded belly.

She shrugs him off impatiently. "Did you *see* our garden, Mum?"

My chest tightens at the relatively new title I've earned from Bella before I shake my head.

I hold my hand out, shooting a soft smile over my shoulder at my grinning husband. "Show me, Curly-Sue."

Our daughter grasps my hand in her much smaller one as our son reaches for my free hand. They both begin to chatter wildly, clearly having made themselves right at home in our forever house.

I twist my head towards Cade just before we round a corner. My eyes find him leaning against the door, watching us with a content smile on his handsome face.

"Love you."

I mouth the words over Bella's head, my heart filled to overflowing.

Cade's parting words follow me around the corner, accompanied by a bark of laughter that echoes through the house, making me smile so wide, it almost hurts.

"Ditto, idiot."

Extended Epilogue

CADEN
EIGHTEEN MONTHS LATER

"Did you pack Blair's diaper bag?"

I smirk as I shake my head. "How many times do I need to remind you, Bam?"

Pushing myself off the jamb of our bedroom door, I advance on my wife and press a kiss to her forehead. "We call them nappies here."

She steps out of my embrace, shaking her head as a soft laugh spills from her mouth. "Old habits die hard."

As she drops Blair's Huddles Puppy alongside Bug's Huddles Bunny into the open overnight case resting on our bed, I wrap my arms around her waist, settling my palms on her gently rounded stomach.

"Well, you'll be using *nappies* for the foreseeable, so I can see that habit taking a hike."

She relaxes against me, placing her own hands atop mine when she angles her head to the side, capturing my adoring gaze.

"Have you spoken to Beau yet?"

I nod, a shit-eating grin taking centre stage. "Yeah, I did. I called him after I put Blair down for her nap this morning."

She looks at me askance. "And…?"

"And…he loves the material for the new album. Said it's genius!"

Summer's smile is dazzling as she spins in my arms to throw her hands around my neck.

"Oh, Cade. I'm ecstatic for you!"

I fold her in against my chest, resting my head by her temple and inhaling her intoxicating scent.

Having disbanded Misdirection in the days following Jake's funeral, Beau had decided to take a stab at a solo career while the rest of us embraced normalcy.

Except, I'd never truly *had* a normal life to begin with. And after some time, I struggled to fill my days with something I was passionate about besides Summer and the kids.

It was during a visit from Beau several months earlier that he'd mentioned his distaste for the songwriters his new label had been sending his way. And inspiration struck.

I'd offered to pen one song for his next album, but that had turned into half a dozen, which had just continued to multiply.

My love for music was never in question. My distaste for the lifestyle that went along with it was the problem.

Writing the music was where my passion lay, and I could do that from the comfort of my wife's embrace.

"And he's donating my fee to Katherine's House in lieu of the charity gigs we used to perform."

"Oh, Cade. That is so thoughtful." My wife pulls back just

enough to spear me with glistening doe eyes. "You are the most wonderful man I have ever known, and that I get to call you *mine* blows my damn mind."

"I've said it before, I'll say it again, Bam." I furrow my brow, putting every piece of myself into my next words. "You're the air I need to breathe…and I could never be without you."

"You never *will* be without me, Cade. Not *ever*."

I lean forward, taking her mouth with mine in a languorous kiss. She arches her body against me shamelessly, and I deepen the kiss, making her whimper against me.

Breaking the kiss when a chuckle rumbles deep inside my chest, I press our brows together. "Christ, I'll keep you pregnant all the time if you stay this fucking horny, woman!"

Her face splits in a self-deprecating grin as she rolls her eyes good-naturedly. "You are the pits."

"So you keep telling me, Bam. But you love me anyway."

Her eyes smile up into mine, sending butterflies swarming through my stomach even after all this time, and I send a silent thank you up to the universe for gifting me this life of rainbows after so many years in the rain.

"We're going to be *late*!"

Our heads swivel simultaneously to find an irate, foot-tapping, almost seven-year-old in the doorway of our bedroom.

"Jesse just changed Blair's diaper, and—"

"It's *nappy*, Bug." Summer slips out of my arms, returning to her packing while I face our clearly annoyed daughter.

"Does it even *matter*?"

The inflections in her sentences these days grate on my last motherfucking nerve, and I glance back at Summer to find her hiding a grin behind a handful of t-shirts.

"Anyway, as I was *saying*—"

Summer snorts but manages to cover it when she pretends to clear her throat.

Fucking girls will be the death of me!

"We've put *our* bags in the car, so now we're just waiting on *you*! Enough kissing, more packing."

And with a loud harrumph, she spins on her little heel, tosses her blonde curls over her shoulder, and marches back down the hall.

Summer turns back to her packing with a smirk. "You heard her. Best move your ass, Cade. We can't be late to little Nathan's christening, or she'll lose her shit altogether."

I move to follow Bella, shaking my head slowly as Summer calls after me. "Best hope this one is a boy, husband."

Snorting a laugh, I pivot on my heel and close the gap between us. I palm my wife's soft cheeks, resting my head on hers. "Why would you say that, Bambi? Jesse and I are blessed if our lot in life is to be surrounded by beautiful women."

Her lips twitch. "You're good, I'll give you that."

I shrug. "What can I say? There's smooth…and then there's *me*."

Leaning up on her tiptoes, she brushes her lips across mine as she smiles. "And I'll be yours. Forever."

NATE

"Thanks for coming, guys."

I wave at Nola and Josie as they bicker loudly in the elevator before the doors close, leaving me to wipe the sweat from my brow.

Christ, those two are hard fucking work sometimes.

"Penny for them?"

A smile breaks out across my usually dour face at the sound of my wife's voice at my back.

"They're not even worth that, Hellcat."

I spin on my heel, finding her smiling broadly. "You're so transparent, Nathaniel. You're thinking that my friends are hard work and don't even bother trying to lie. I know you *too* well by now."

This woman.

Closing the distance between us in one smooth stride, I palm her face and hold her golden gaze intensely. "The day I gave in to our love was the day my life began. To have been fortunate enough to find the other half of my soul is something I will *never* take for granted."

I lean closer, brushing our noses together before kissing her forehead.

"I never wanted more until I met you, Hellcat. And I'll love you till the day I die."

She steps out of my embrace, her adoration-filled eyes never leaving mine. "I'm going to check on Nathan, but I want you to stay right here because when you say things like that, it speaks straight to my pussy."

I chuckle but nod as she backs away in the direction of our sleeping son's bedroom.

Once she's disappeared out of sight, I spring into action.

After having a wonderful day celebrating our boy's christening with our nearest and dearest, I've made plans to make the evening even more memorable for my soulmate.

Grabbing the box I'd packed and hidden earlier from the laundry room, my feet quickly and silently take me out onto the garden terrace. Knowing precisely what I'm doing this time around, I make short work of setting up and have just straightened to survey my handiwork when a gasp from behind me demands my attention.

I twist about to find my wife with our six-month-old son in her arms. He's in his sleepsuit, his mass of dark hair standing out in every direction as he clutches Mila's Jellycat plush, Mitzi, with a chubby fist.

My wife's eyes shine as they survey the transformation before her.

Fairy lights twinkle amid the shrubbery and along the red brick walls of our penthouse. A light peach sheet—why can I never find a white one?—is hanging from the wall while a small portable projector silently screens *Never Been Kissed.*

She steps closer as Nathan focuses on me, a smile lighting up his beautiful face.

"What's all this, Nathaniel?"

I pluck our son from her arms as he snuggles right in against my chest with Mitzi tucked under his chin. His eyes flutter closed as he settles easily in my hold, and my heart fills to bursting.

"I wanted to make another memory with you, baby." Sliding my free hand into hers, I pull her closer and kiss her softly. "I never want to stop making memories with you. And as we usually stay at the lake, I thought today was the perfect occasion to relive one of my favourites."

A smile splits her face, lighting her up from within, and my own lips answer willingly with a grin of my own.

I glance over my shoulder, finding that right on cue, Josie and Mr Coulson are having their first kiss on the pitcher's mound.

"Siri, play 'Don't Worry, Baby.'"

The Beach Boys' inimitable and much-loved hit gently sounds through the outdoor speakers. I tug Mila closer, enfolding both her and our son in my large embrace while we sway to the familiar beat.

Our eyes hold one another's as I commit yet another idyllic moment with the love of my life to memory. Except for this time around, we're holding the embodiment of our love between us, something I'd never have thought possible the first time we danced to this song.

"You told me so, you know."

My forehead puckers in puzzlement, and Mila giggles lightly.

"You told me not to worry. That everything would turn out alright."

An impish smile dances on her lips, coaxing a grin from me before my wife—my best friend, my lover—snuggles her cheek against the free side of my chest.

I close my eyes, soaking up this moment, committing it to memory alongside all of the other glorious moments we've shared as we continue swaying to the music floating through the night air surrounding us.

Sighing softly, I begin to hum along with the song, entirely happy and utterly at peace in the life I never saw myself as deserving of, but will hold on to with my dying breath.

"Thank you for being my once-in-a-lifetime. To say I love you doesn't even come close, Mila Hawthorne."

She tilts her head upwards, resting her chin on my chest, as a mischievous smile lifts her lips.

"Do you still have the Superman costume?"

One side of my mouth twitches, and I nod.

Her smile widens as she gently lifts our sleeping son from my arms.

"I'll put Nathan back down. I've heard Metropolis is in peril…"

Fuck, she's perfection.

I wink down at my beautiful wife with a single-dimpled grin as she edges backwards.

"As you wish, Hellcat."

HENRY

"Goodnight, Seb."

I press a kiss to my four-year-old's forehead, ruffling his dark locks before pulling his duvet cover higher over his slight body.

"Night, Dad. I love you."

I stiffen, as I do every time I hear those precious words spill so easily from my child's mouth. The love of my children is something I will never take for granted.

"I love you too, son."

I flick his volcano nightlight on before I hit the main light on my way out the door, making sure to leave it open a crack, just the way he likes it.

Slipping out of Sebastian's room, I duck in next door to his baby brother Theodore's room.

Our Theo has to be the strangest sleeper I've ever seen. He sleeps on his knees with his face planted to the mattress so that his little nappy-covered bottom is pointing towards the ceiling.

The sight never fails to put a smile on my face.

Having checked on both our boys, I make the quick trip to mine and Peach's bedroom, finding her already tucked up between the sheets.

She's glued to her Kindle, mouth slightly open with her eyes wide at whatever smut she's currently devouring.

I won't complain. After all, I'm the lucky bastard who benefits from her newfound kinks.

I make short work of stripping down to my boxers, and my oblivious wife finally notices me when I slip in beside her, pressing my cold feet to her warm, smooth legs.

"Henry!"

Her tone is one of irritation, but the smile in her big navy-blue eyes belies her beratement.

My laugh fills the bedroom, and she shakes her head as she rolls her eyes. "Revenge is a dish best served cold, you know."

"You and those adages, Peach. Father Thomas has a lot to answer for."

She shoves my shoulder good-naturedly before twisting about to deposit her Kindle on the nightstand.

Her movement makes her old t-shirt rise at the hem, allowing me to glimpse her usually toned stomach, now gently rounded in her third month with our third child.

When she turns back to me, I hold my arms out for her, and she immediately moves to settle against me, with her head right over my heart.

"Theo was out like a light. Did Seb settle okay for you?"

"Mmmhmm." I make a noncommittal grunt deep inside my chest while my body relaxes for what feels like the first time all fucking day.

I press a kiss to the top of her blonde head. "Did you get to speak to Alex before he left? I know you wanted to share the news with him face-to-face."

Liv shakes her head as she runs her fingers through the smattering of dark hair on my chest several times before angling her head up.

"He got a call from someone back in Manhattan. Whatever was said, he didn't hang around."

I nod slowly, equally nervous and excited for the next words to come out of my mouth.

"I've decided to scale back my involvement at DeMarco Holdings, baby."

My wife's audible gasp fills the room as she rises to sit yoga style whilst pinning me with a questioning look.

"*What*? But why, Henry? You love what you do!"

I sit up, grasping her face in my large palms. "And I love you and the boys *more,* Peach. I saw what a workaholic my father turned into, to the point that he ignored his own fucking kids."

Running the back of my knuckles along her cheekbone, I slip my hand around to the nape of her neck, pinning her with an intensity I can feel in my bones.

"A long time ago, I told you no one would come between us. And that includes me. I'm done being away from you, from the kids. I can still have a behind-the-scenes role at DeMarco, but with the new baby coming, I want to be here. With *you*. With our kids, whilst they're still kids."

Her eyes glisten with emotion, and I can feel a lump form in my throat. I continue quickly before speaking becomes an impossibility.

"From Monday, I'm scaling my involvement back and increasing Alex's. He's already the face of DeMarco in the U.S. media. He'll revel in taking a step up the corporate ladder."

I've barely finished my sentence when Liv launches herself into my arms, peppering kisses across every centimetre of my face. My chest rumbles with a deep laugh.

"Oh, Henry! This is wonderful, especially now…"

She trails off, her eyes shifting down towards her stomach.

"Umm…remember I had a check-up yesterday, but you missed it because of that conference call with the Dubai branch?"

Her eyes pin mine, and I nod in answer to her question. "Yes.

It was another reason on my list for scaling back at the company."

She nods slowly, chewing on her bottom lip for a beat. "Well… we were busy at the christening today, so I didn't want to tell you until we were alone."

Sweat breaks out across my brow, and my heart rate kicks up a notch. "Is everything okay with the baby? With you? What—"

She catches my face between her hands, quelling me with a firm look. "It's nothing like that, Henry. It's…that's to say… umm…we're not having *a* baby."

I jerk my head back, blinking in bewilderment. "What do you—"

"We're having twins!"

The End

Thank you for reading the Brotherhood *series.*
The first book in my new series, Rogues of Manhattan, *following*
Alex DeMarco, will release in summer 2023.

Also by Pamela O'Rourke

THE BROTHERHOOD SERIES

1. *Painted Truths*
2. *Unwritten Rules*
3. *Broken Strings*

Book one in the new Rogues of Manhattan *series, Alex DeMarco's story, is coming in summer 2023!*

To keep up to date with all of my releases, subscribe to my newsletter: https://bit.ly/PORourkeNews

Acknowledgments

The Brotherhood series is complete! I'm astounded to have written one book, let alone three. To say that this is a dream come true falls short.

I'd like to take this opportunity to thank some exceptional people who have been a part of this wild ride.

Adi…this one is all for you. When I think of how different my days would be if we had never met, it makes me even more thankful to have you in my life. You don't just inspire me to write better stories, you inspire me to be the best version of myself. In case it wasn't entirely clear, I adore you! Apologies to Rod and the boys for being such a time suck xxx

As I have been blessed with such amazing alpha/beta readers, I need to make sure to thank you wonderful ladies. Adi, Selena, Aimee, Joan and Katie – I am so grateful for you and the precious time you give to help shape my stories. Thank you, from the bottom of my heart, for everything you do. I value you more than you could ever know.

To my newly formed Street Team. Girls – you're all legends! The banter, the books and the laughs in our Insta-chat brighten my days. I am FLOORED by your enjoyment of my words, and I can't adequately express just how much your support means to me.

To Sara, my kickass, take no prisoners PA – giiiiiiiirl!!! You are amazing. I'm a stage five clinger, and you'll never be rid of me. Thank you for being so damn awesome. So much love xx

In 2020, I discovered T.L. Swan and her beautiful prose. I discovered how she'd begun writing—having been entirely unfamiliar with the indie world prior to that—and upon further investigation, I found she had, in her infinite wisdom, decided to pay it forward, setting up a Cygnet group for aspiring authors. Thank you, Tee, for paving the way for so many others. I'm forever in your debt.

To my beautiful friend, Lilian Harris. When I grow up, I want to be you. You are one of the best people I have met in this industry. Love you, girl!

To my writing sisters – KJ Michaels, K. Woods and ER Sloane. There's no one else I'd rather be figuring this out with! I love you guys so much xxx

To my sister, Michelle. I have been a terrible bridesmaid while writing this book. I'll be better. I promise! Bring on the 'I Do's'.

Thank you to my parents, William and Bernadette, for your support and encouragement. I know you have no idea what this is all about, but your acceptance is truly appreciated (PS: Dad, please stop recommending my books to your friends!)

To my five miracles. If there's one thing I teach you in this life, it's to march to your own beat. I'm so proud of the people you are becoming. Each of you can be whatever you want to be so long as you keep chasing those dreams. I love you, my little minions xxxxx

James O'Rourke. I love you. You are my favourite person. My rock. You pick me up when I'm feeling shit. You make me laugh every single day. And you put up with all my flaws because when you've found your person, the world feels right. Thank you for being my biggest cheerleader, my unpaid PA and my number one fan.

And *finally*, to each and every person who has read my words. Who has read my stories and *enjoyed* them. To each reader who has been transported from their life into the world I have created. To every reader who has contributed to making my dream a reality. THANK YOU SO MUCH! I see you. I appreciate you. I am so honoured that you took a chance on my book baby.

Rogues of Manhattan comes next, and I can't wait for you to find what I have planned for the players: Alex DeMarco, Vaughn Burton, Ford Holloway and Grayson Hunter.

Pamela O'Rourke

perfectly imperfect romance

Pamela O'Rourke lives in Ireland with her husband, James and their five young children. Life is hectic, but she wouldn't change a single second of it. She loves sunny days, strong coffee and daydreaming about her next book boyfriend.

Her debut novel in the *Brotherhood* series, *Painted Truths*, is currently available on Amazon, alongside *Unwritten Rules* and *Broken Strings.*

Watch out for Alex DeMarco's story, the first book in her new *Rogues of Manhattan* series, coming in the summer of 2023.

In the meanwhile, come and join my Facebook reader group for a first look at sneak peeks and teasers. Please note that this is a private group, so only other members can see posts and comments.

Follow on social media!

Newsletter: https://bit.ly/PORourkeNews
Facebook: www.facebook.com/authorpamelaorourke
Instagram/TikTok: @pamelaorourkeauthor
Amazon: https://tinyurl.com/PORourkeAmazon
Goodreads: www.goodreads.com/pamelaorourke
BookBub: www.bookbub.com/profile/pamela-o-rourke

Printed in Great Britain
by Amazon

46414198R00254